P9-CSF-968

ALSO BY FIONA BUCKLEY

To Shield the Queen

The Doublet Affair

Queen's Ransom

To Ruin a Queen

AN URSULA BLANCHARD MYSTERY AT
QUEEN ELIZABETH I'S COURT

FIONA BUCKLEY

SCRIBNER

New York London Toronto Sydney Singapore

SCRIBNER
1230 Avenue of the Americas
New York, NY 10020

This book is a work of fiction. Names, characters, places, and incidents either are products of the author's imagination or are used fictitiously. Any resemblance to actual events or locales or persons, living or dead, is entirely coincidental.

Designed by Brooke Koven
Text set in Bembo

Manufactured in the United States of America

1 3 5 7 9 10 8 6 4 2

Library of Congress Cataloging-in-Publication Data
Buckley, Fiona.
To ruin a queen: an Ursula Blanchard mystery at Queen Elizabeth I's Court/Fiona Buckley.
p. cm.
1. Blanchard, Ursula (Fictitious character)—Fiction.
2. Great Britain—History—Elizabeth, 1558–1603—Fiction.
3. Elizabeth I, Queen of England, 1533–1603—Fiction.
4. Women detectives—England—Fiction. I. Title.

PR6052.U266 T6 2000
823'.914—dc21
00–058819

ISBN 0-684-86268-9

This book is for John and Kerry,
without whom it would never have been written.

MORTIMER FAMILY TREE

Fictional characters in italics

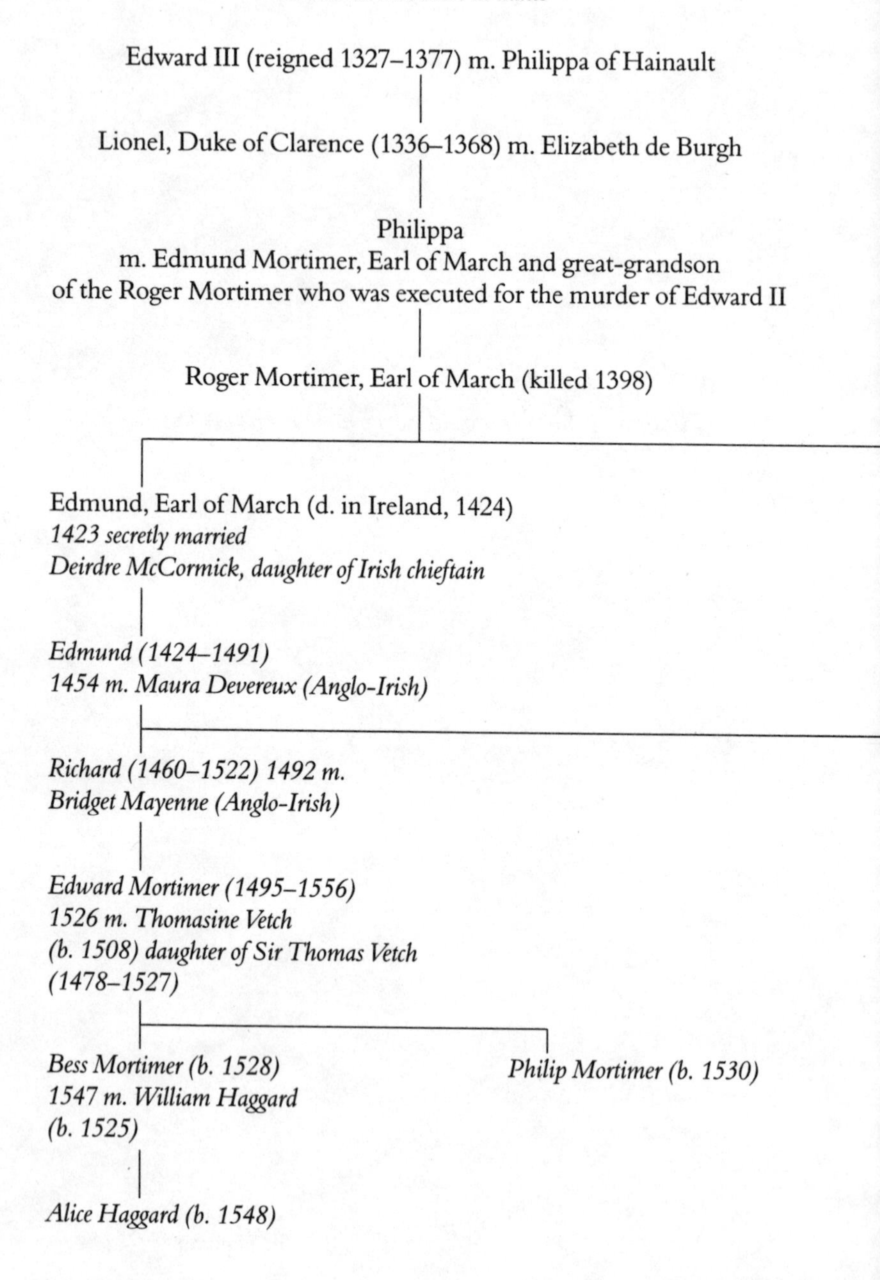

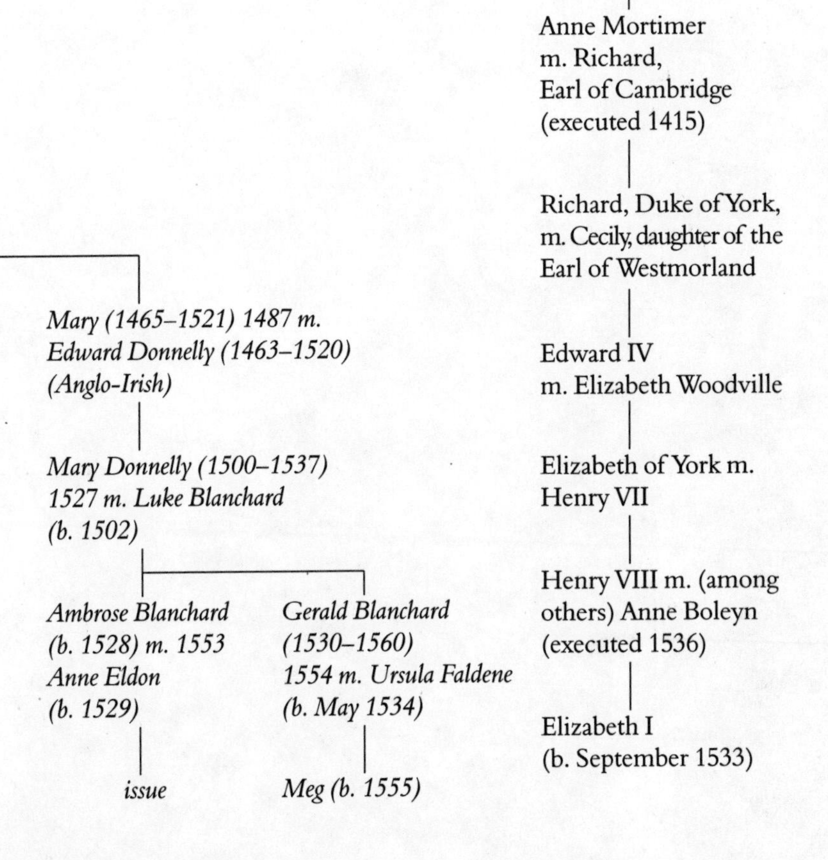
Anne Mortimer
m. Richard,
Earl of Cambridge
(executed 1415)
Richard, Duke of York,
m. Cecily, daughter of the
Earl of Westmorland
Edward IV
m. Elizabeth Woodville
Elizabeth of York m.
Henry VII
Henry VIII m. (among
others) Anne Boleyn
(executed 1536)
Elizabeth I
(b. September 1533)
Mary (1465–1521) 1487 m.
Edward Donnelly (1463–1520)
(Anglo-Irish)
Mary Donnelly (1500–1537)
1527 m. Luke Blanchard
(b. 1502)
Ambrose Blanchard
(b. 1528) m. 1553
Anne Eldon
(b. 1529)
issue
Gerald Blanchard
(1530–1560)
1554 m. Ursula Faldene
(b. May 1534)
Meg (b. 1555)

To Ruin a Queen

1

The Power of Life and Death

The journey that took me from the Château Blanchepierre, on the banks of the Loire, to Vetch Castle on the Welsh March began, I think, on April 4, 1564, when I snatched up a triple-branched silver candlestick and hurled it the length of the Blanchepierre dinner table at my husband, Matthew de la Roche.

I threw it in an outburst of fury and unhappiness, which had had its beginnings three and a half weeks before, in the fetid, overheated lying-in chamber in the west tower of the château, where our first child should have come into the world, had God or providence been kinder.

I had begged for air but no one would open the shutters for fear of letting in a cold wind. Instead, there was a fire in the hearth, piled too high and giving off a sickly perfume from the herbs which my woman, Fran Dale, had thrown onto it in an effort to please me by sweetening the atmosphere.

The lying-in chamber was pervaded too by a continual murmur of prayers from Matthew's uncle Armand, who was a priest and lived in the château as its chaplain. It was he who had married us, three and a half years ago, in England. To my fevered mind, the drone of his elderly voice sounded like a prayer for the dying. Possibly, it was. Madame Montaigle had fetched him after using pepper to make me sneeze in the hope that it would shoot the child out, and then attempting in vain to pull him out of me by hand, which had caused me to scream wildly. She told me afterward that she had despaired of my life.

Madame Montaigle was my husband's former housekeeper. She had been living in a retirement cottage but she had skill as a midwife and Matthew had fetched her back to the château to help me. I wished he hadn't for she didn't like me. To her, I was Matthew's heretic wife, the stranger from England, who had let him down in the past and would probably let him down again if given the ghost of a chance. I did not think she would care if I died. I would have felt the same in her place, but I could have done without either Madame Montaigle or Uncle Armand as I lay sweating and cursing and crying, growing more exhausted and feverish with every passing hour, fighting to bring forth Matthew's child, and failing.

During the second day, I drifted toward delirium. Matthew had gone to fetch the physician from the village below the château but I kept on forgetting this and asking for him. When at last I heard his voice at the door, telling the physician that this was the room and for the love of God, man, do what you can, it pulled me back into the real world. I cried Matthew's name and stretched out my hand.

But Madame Montaigle barred his way, exclaiming in outraged tones that he could not enter, that this was women's business except for priest and doctor, and instead of pushing past her as I wanted him to do, he merely called to me that he had brought help and that he was praying to God that all would soon be well. It was the physician, not Matthew, who came to my side.

The physician was out of breath, for he was a plump man and Matthew had no doubt propelled him up the tower steps at speed. "I agree," he puffed to Dale and Madame Montaigle, "that this is rightly women's business. It is not my custom to attend lying-in chambers. However, for you, seigneur," he added over his shoulder, addressing Matthew and changing to a note of respect, "I will do what I can." He turned back to my attendants. "What has been done already?"

Madame Montaigle explained, about the pepper and her own manual efforts. Dale spoke little French and her principal task was to lave my forehead with cool water, smooth my straggling hair back from my perspiring face, and offer me milk and broth. The shutters made the room dim and the physician asked for more lights. I heard Matthew shouting for lamps. When they were brought, the physician, without speaking to me, went to the foot of the bed and began doing something to me; I couldn't tell exactly what. I only knew that the pain I was in grew suddenly worse and I twisted, struggling. The physician drew back.

"The child is lying wrong and it is growing weak. Seigneur . . ."

Matthew must still have been hovering just outside the room, for the physician was speaking to him from the end of my bed. He moved away to the door to finish what he was saying out of my hearing, and I heard my husband answer though I could not hear the words that either of them said. I called Matthew's name again but still he wouldn't defy convention and enter. I was left forlorn, bereft of any anchor to the world. I was dying. I knew it now. Here in this shadowed, stinking room, tangled up in sweaty sheets and with Uncle Armand practically reciting the burial service over me; before I was thirty years old; I was going to slip out of the world into eternity.

"I don't want to die!" I screamed. "Matthew, I don't want to die! I want to see Meg again!"

My daughter, Meg, was in England. I hadn't seen her for two years and this summer, she would be nine. Now, a vision of her, as vivid as though she were actually there, filled my overheated mind. I saw her, playing with a ball on the grass outside Thamesbank House, where she lived with her foster parents. Her dark hair was escaping from its cap, and her little square face, so like the face of her father, Gerald, my first husband, was rosy with exercise. I could see the gracious outlines of the house, and the ripple of the Thames flowing past. For a moment, it was all so real that I called her name aloud, but the vision faded. She receded from me and was gone.

"If I die now I'll never see Meg again and I'll never see England again!" I wailed. "Somebody help me!"

"Hush." Dale was in tears. "Don't waste your strength, ma'am. Take a little warm milk."

"I don't want milk!" I flung out an arm in a frantic gesture of rejection and sent the cup flying out of Dale's hand, spilling the milk on the trampled rushes and also on Uncle Armand. "I want to give birth and get this over and I wish I'd never married again!"

Uncle Armand, brushing white spatters from his black clerical gown, said reprovingly: "Hush, madame. All things are according to the will of God. Women who die in childbirth may, I think, receive martyrs' crowns in heaven."

"I don't want to be a bloody martyr!" I shouted at him. "I want to live!"

Peering through the lamplight and the red fog of my pain and fever, I saw the physician and Matthew anxiously conferring in the doorway. The fever seemed to have sharpened my senses for although the physician's voice was still pitched low, this time I heard what he was saying.

"It is a son, seigneur, but there is little chance of saving him, I fear, and if I try, we shall almost certainly lose the mother. If we try instead to save her, the chance of success is better, but it will surely mean the child's death. I cannot hope to save them both; that much is sure. It is for you to decide."

I cried out, begging for my life. I had wanted Matthew's child but in that moment it ceased to be real to me. Nothing was real except the threat, the terrible threat of extinction. Everything became confused. As delirium finally took over, I saw the physician come back to me but after that I remember very little. The pain became a sea in which I was drowning. Then came darkness.

When I became conscious again, I was still in pain but in a new, localized way. My body was no longer struggling. Its burden was gone. Dale and Matthew, very pale, were beside me and the physician stood watchfully by. Uncle Armand and Madame Montaigle had left the room.

"You're alive," Matthew said. "But there is no child. It was one or the other and I chose you."

I smiled. I thanked him. I held his hand.

I had rarely been so angry in my life.

The anger wouldn't go away and mingled with it was a bleak misery that refused to lift and which did not even seem to have much to do with my grief for the lost baby, although I did indeed grieve. I was glad when Matthew told me that Uncle Armand had managed to baptize him, and that he had been laid in consecrated ground. He had been called Pierre, after Matthew's father. Physically, I got better, and I let Matthew think that my silences, my inability to smile, were all on account of grief. I knew I was hurting him but I could not help myself. My mind was sick and would not heal.

But by the fourth of April, Matthew was growing worried because I was so remote from him, and over that momentous dinner table, he said so.

We were not alone. Uncle Armand was dining with us as he usually did, and the butler, Doriot, was waiting on us. So was Roger Brockley, my English manservant. Fran Dale was actually married to Brockley although I still called her Dale, because she had been in my service before Brockley joined me.

They were both well into their forties, solid people, very English—Dale a little too given to complaining and slightly marked by childhood smallpox, but handsome in her way and very much attached to me; Brockley, stocky and dignified, with a high, polished forehead, a dusting of pale gold freckles, a slight country accent, a gift for expressionless jokes, and a knack of combining respect with criticism which over the years had inspired me with trust and exasperation in roughly equal proportions.

Brockley had originally been my groom, but when we came to Blanchepierre, the stables were full of grooms, and he had carved out a highly individual niche for himself, acting as my personal messenger and serving me at meals. Doriot didn't like it, though Brockley tried to be generally helpful and not usurp the butler's authority.

Brockley was at the sideboard, spooning wine sauce over my fish steaks, when Matthew said: "I have asked the physician to call tomorrow, Ursula. You are not recovering your strength or your spirits as you should. We've had a sad loss, but it's not the end of the world, you know."

I gazed down the table, past the silver dishes and the very beautiful silver salt and the matching candlesticks. The day was bright and the candles weren't lit, but they were there as decoration. We always dined in this formal fashion, with the length of the table between us. Blanchepierre was a very formal place.

There he sat, my husband, Matthew, whose dark, diamond-shaped eyes and dramatic black eyebrows, whose tall, loose-jointed frame and graceful movements, had captivated me long ago. He was good-hearted, too; essentially kind. In the end, after a long struggle, I had chosen him and Blanchpierre over a life as a lady of Queen Elizabeth's Presence Chamber and an agent in the employ of her Secretary of State, Sir William Cecil. I had been willing to live with Matthew as a Catholic, here in France, even though I remembered all too well the cruelties wrought in England by Mary Tudor in the name of that same religion.

Matthew loved me, and I had thought I loved him, but at this moment, he looked like a stranger.

"I don't like the physician," I said. "I'd rather not see him."

"That's a little ungrateful, isn't it? He saved your life, after all. I'm sure he can prescribe something for you—a tonic, perhaps."

"Dale can make a tonic up for me," I said. "She is quite skilled in such things. Even I have a little knowledge of herb lore."

"The physician surely knows more than either you or Dale. Why don't you like him?"

Doriot and Brockley brought the fish steaks to the table and began to serve them. I tried to think of a way to answer Matthew, but couldn't.

"Well?" he said. "Ursula, I'm worried about you and these silences of yours are one of the reasons. What is the matter with you? If I ask you a question, why can't you reply?"

Sometimes, I knew, it was because I was too lost in depression to hear him. But at other times, and this was one of them, it was because I knew he wouldn't like the answer. I stared at him and then, without speaking, started to eat.

"What is wrong with the physician? Ursula, I mean to have an answer. So will you say something, please?"

He had never pressed so hard before, and in any case, the answer was festering in me. I set down the piece of bread with which I was mopping up the sauce.

"Very well," I said. "The last time he came here was to my lying-in chamber. He said there was a chance of saving me or the child, but not both, and he asked you which he should try to save. He asked *you*. But I was conscious. I was crying out that I didn't want to die. Why didn't he ask me instead? He never even spoke to me. I might have been just a log of wood."

"Ursula, for the love of God! A physician would always ask the husband in such a case. Naturally."

"I've just said, I was crying out that I didn't want to die. Why didn't he just set about saving my life without further ado?"

"And leave me with no say in the matter?"

"It was *my* life! I was terrified of dying—terrified!"

"That was needless," said Uncle Armand. "You had heard Mass and been shriven only an hour or two before your pains began. You had nothing to fear."

"Yes, I had!" I snapped at him. "I wanted to live!"

"I know," said Matthew. "And I wanted you to live too. I told him to save you. You know that. The child was a son but believe me, I cared nothing for that, if only I could have you back, safe."

"But where would I be now if you had chosen otherwise?"

"Ursula, what is all this? I saved your life!" Matthew thundered. "You're completely unreasonable."

"And unwomanly, I fear." Uncle Armand shook a reproving head. "What you should have done, my child, was declare that you wished your infant to be saved. Your husband would still have chosen your life instead, of that I feel sure. The very purpose behind asking the husband is to free the woman from the burden of choosing between her child and herself. But . . ."

"I didn't ask to be freed of it!"

"The last time you saw the physician," said Matthew, "you were delirious. I think, Uncle Armand, that Ursula cannot be blamed for anything she said at that time."

"Blamed!" I shouted.

"Calm yourself. I also think," said Matthew, "that you spent too long dancing attendance on that red-haired heretic queen in England. She used to raise her voice quite often, if I remember aright, and you are talking the kind of nonsense that she might very well talk."

"It isn't nonsense." I tried to speak more quietly. "I still greatly admire Elizabeth," I added.

"But you left her service because she and Cecil between them had betrayed you."

"It felt like that at the time. But since then, I've come to understand them better. I've had time to think."

"I would have expected," said Matthew, "that now you are here in my home, you could have left the thinking to your husband, as other women do. It is not a feminine occupation. But since you have been thinking—to what conclusions have you come? Do you regret staying with me?"

"It would be most shameful if you did," said Uncle Armand, signaling Brockley for a little more fish. Doriot and Brockley were continuing to serve as imperturbably as though we were all discussing the weather. "When one considers, after all, that the Seigneur de la Roche is of an ancient, most respected French family while you, madame, although you have served at a royal court, were penniless when you were married to him, and furthermore, cannot put a name to your father."

There was a breathless silence. I felt as though I had been kicked in the stomach. Brockley froze in midfloor, the serving platter in his hands. Even Doriot looked embarrassed and became very anxious to make sure there were enough clean spoons ready for the next course.

"My wife's family history is of no importance to me," Matthew snapped, but if he was glaring at Uncle Armand, he was still glaring when he turned to me.

"I am beginning to think," he said coldly, "that perhaps, Ursula, you are once more planning to abandon me—as you have done in the past. Are you? Do you want to go back to England? If so, in God's name tell me. I'd rather know."

It was too much. It all hurt far too much. I had sat down to dine, not happily, but at least in the belief that my domestic world was secure around me. It had fallen to pieces in the space of a few minutes and I didn't know how it had happened. What I did know was that grief for my dead child and the memory of those horrible hours in the lying-in chamber had flooded over me together, reviving the fear and pain and helplessness, the sense of loss when I called for Matthew and he would not come to me. Even now, he was at the far end of a long table; I could not reach out and touch him.

I had no words, only a surge of emotion: nameless and wordless but too huge to contain. So I picked up the nearest candlestick, threw it at Matthew, and then leapt from my seat and fled headlong from the dining chamber.

I went straight to my own bedchamber, collapsed on the bed, and thereupon fell victim to one of the sick headaches which have plagued me for most of my life. When Matthew came after me, as he did before long, he found me groaning in semidarkness, and had the good sense not to try to talk to me, but to send Dale to me.

Dale did her best for me, but the chamomile potion which sometimes eased the symptoms this time had no effect. The malady ran its usual unpleasant course, and the headache did not subside until late that evening. Then I told Dale to let Matthew know I was better, and once again, he came to me. He sat down on the side of the bed and looked at me gravely, his face a blank mask. He waited for me to say something first.

There was only one thing I could possibly say. "I'm sorry I threw the candlestick," I whispered. "But I couldn't bear it—oh, Matthew, how could you believe I was plotting to leave you? Of course I'm not."

"I shouldn't have said that," Matthew told me quietly. "I too am sorry. And Uncle Armand shouldn't have made those comments about your family, either. As for the physician at your lying-in, he asked me a question and I gave him the answer I knew you wanted. I had heard you crying out for your life. It broke my heart to hear you."

"I didn't want the child to die," I said. "How could I? I was praying that somehow we could both live. But I was so afraid, Matthew, so afraid, and I felt so helpless."

"It's in the nature of women to feel helpless, but you should know that you can trust me to look after you." He paused and then said steadily: "But now you are longing for the child you already have, I think. In your delirium, you cried out for your daughter, and for England. You are missing Meg very badly, and you're homesick."

I nodded, with caution. The remains of the headache still throbbed.

"I'm sorry," I said again, miserably. Matthew and I had quarreled before, more than once. We had shouted into each other's faces and I had wept with rage and despair, and once, when we tried to settle our differences with passion, even our lovemaking had turned savage. But never before had any quarrel gone as deep as this. I wanted no more of it. In venting my rage with that candlestick, I had lanced the worst boil in my unhappy mind. Now, I longed for peace between myself and Matthew. "This is my home now," I said. "I know that. I ought not to be homesick; women aren't supposed to be. Aunt Tabitha told me that," I added. "You know—Aunt Tabitha, who brought me up."

"You must be really out of spirits if you're quoting your aunt Tabitha. I remember her well, and I didn't care for her at all. What did she say, exactly?"

"It was when my eldest cousin, Honoria, was betrothed. She was afraid of leaving home because she thought she would be homesick. Aunt Tabitha told her that a woman's home is where her husband is, even if it's Cathay or Ultima Thule."

"That sounds very like your aunt Tabitha. Poor Honoria."

"But most people would agree with my aunt, wouldn't they? The only one I know who might not is Queen Elizabeth. Her feelings for England run deep."

"So do yours, it appears. Oh, Saltspoon." We both smiled involuntarily, at the sound of the nickname he had given me, years ago, because he said I had such a salty tongue. "It seems long since I last called you that," he said now. "Dearest Saltspoon, why can't you love France in the same way as you seem to love England? Would it be easier, I wonder, if we fetched Meg over? I have always said she would be welcome. Didn't you once say that she should come after—well, after your confinement? Suppose I arrange it? You might feel more settled, then."

"I don't know," I said restlessly. "She is happy with the Hendersons. They are good people. They write quite often, and so does she. It's not that I don't have news of her."

I was choosing my words with care. I had spoken my mind at the dining table, but if I wanted peace with Matthew, I must not speak it now. I had hesitated to bring Meg to France because I did not want to separate her from England. I wanted England—the land, the language, the religion—to be hers by right.

If I said that to Matthew, he would be hurt anew, and he would begin to doubt me once again. He had been surprised to hear me quote my aunt Tabitha, but if my aunt were here now, much as I disliked her, I knew what advice she would give me and she might well be right.

She would tell me to repair my differences with Matthew by pleasing him, even if it meant hiding my own opinions. (Not that my aunt ever needed to hide hers, since they usually chimed to perfection with those of Uncle Herbert. My uncle and aunt were a pair of righteous bullies who worked together like a team of flawlessly matched coach horses.)

But Matthew and I were very different from Aunt Tabitha and Uncle Herbert, and very different too from each other. Yes. I would be wise, I thought wearily, to hide what I was thinking. I said no more, and then Matthew made up his own mind.

"You need more than news of your daughter," he said. "You need Meg herself." He stood up. "No more arguments, Ursula. I am sending Brockley over to fetch her."

"But he'll need the queen's permission and . . ."

"No, he won't. He will stay for a few days at Thamesbank—that's the name of the house, is it not?—as though to make a full report on her studies and her well-being. The Hendersons will get used to him and so will Meg herself. He can take her out, on the river, or for rides. Then, one day, he will slip away with her and take her to the south coast, where he will find a boat in which to cross the channel. I will give him the names of three skippers who will help if he carries a letter with my seal on it."

For a moment, I closed my eyes. It was still going on, then. France had been torn by civil war between Huguenots and Catholics and Matthew had been in the thick of it, but still, it seemed, he had found time to keep up his secret work in England, where he had agents constantly seeking support for Mary Stuart of Scotland, who in Catholic eyes was England's true queen, and who would bring the Catholic faith back to my country. Along with the Inquisition.

"I understand about homesickness," Matthew said. "And women are as prone to it as men. My mother was English, and she always missed her homeland. That was why I took her back when my father died. She died too, not long after, but she was glad to be in her own country and to know that she would be buried in her own soil. But I think, Ursula, that if Meg is here, you will feel better. Take some rest now. Your daughter will be with you very soon."

He kissed me and went away. I lay there, letting my headache fade, and wondering if he was right. I had lived abroad, in Antwerp, when I was married to my first husband, Gerald Blanchard, who was in the service there of the queen's financier, Sir Thomas Gresham. I had never felt homesick then. But of course, in Antwerp, I had had both Meg and Gerald.

Gerald was dead and gone and if he were to come back now, this moment, what would he find? Getting up from the bed, I went to my toilet chest and looked at my face in the little mirror which lay there. I still had the wide brow and pointed chin which Gerald had called kittenish, but there was little of the kitten about me now. The hazel eyes of that mirrored face had seen many things since Gerald last looked into them. Some of those things had been sad and some horrific. Mine were experienced eyes now.

Gazing more closely, I saw too that there were a couple of silver strands in my dark hair. My youth was passing. The Ursula that Gerald had known had changed. I was Madame de la Roche now, of Château Blanchepierre, by the river Loire.

One could not go back. But Meg was still part of the present, living and growing, and yes, I needed her, to fill the empty place which my dead child had left. How long, I wondered, would it take Brockley to bring her back to France?

2

Lost in the Mist

I sent Dale to England with Brockley. They rarely had such a chance to be alone together and I knew quite well that Dale was not happy in France. She had once been arrested and had spent several weeks in a cell under the palace of St. Germain near Paris. She had been frightened ever since. Only her affection for me, and Brockley's loyalty to me, had kept her with me through the two years of the French civil war, which we had spent in Paris, fairly safely, but always with danger prowling nearby. Now that peace had come, I hoped she would settle down, but a visit to England might help her.

Also, I thought it would be better for Meg if Dale was there, for I doubted if her nurse, Bridget, would come to Blanchepierre. Brockley himself had remarked on it. "She's a good-natured soul but I don't see her ever being at home in any foreign land." Then he made one of his expressionless jokes, "In France, madam, I reckon she'd be like a cat in a dog kennel."

After the usual fractional pause while I worked out that despite the blankness of Brockley's face he was jesting, I laughed.

"I'll give you some money for her," I said. "Then she'll be free to make a new start without anxiety. I think I can trust you not to embezzle it."

"Madam!" said Brockley, in mock reproach. "The very idea!"

After they set out, Matthew and I quarreled again.

He had found me a maid to replace Dale for the time being,

a competent enough girl, but somewhat unsmiling and, unfortunately, from my point of view, related to Madame Montaigle. When Matthew asked me how I was getting on with Marie, I was unwise enough to say—albeit mildly—that I felt as though she disapproved of me.

"Now that's nonsense. It's not her business to approve or disapprove of you and Marie knows her place."

We were in my sitting room, where I often spent the afternoons over a little embroidery, sitting by the window with a view of the Loire below, my workbasket at hand on a small walnut table with a charming inlaid pattern of ivory. I was working on a kirtle which I hoped would fit Meg, embroidering meadow flowers on pale yellow silk, and Matthew, who admired my skill, had come to see how the work was progressing. Marie's name struck a jarring note.

"She never says anything out of turn," I said. "It's just—her expression. After all, she is a Montaigle and Madame Montaigle dislikes me. You know that. She has her reasons but it's difficult to live at close quarters with them. I'll be glad when Dale comes back."

"As to that," said Matthew, sitting down, "there is something I want to say to you. When Dale and Brockley bring Meg home, I would like you to reward them well—I will be generous over this, I promise—and then send them back to England for good. It will be much the same arrangement as you expect to make with the child's nurse."

"Pay them off, you mean?"

"Yes."

"But why? They're very devoted servants and I'm as fond of them as they are of me. They've done nothing wrong."

"Why are you so quarrelsome, Saltspoon? I used to like that edge on your tongue but it can be tiring sometimes. Could you not be a little sweeter?"

"I'm sorry." Knowing that I would see Meg soon had done something to ease my unhappiness but it was still there, and could easily be reawakened. "But I'm much attached to both Dale and Brockley," I said. "I would miss them."

"I know," said Matthew. "But that's just the point. I think you are a little too attached to Brockley."

"What? Ouch!" I had been startled into pricking my finger. I sat sucking it and looking at Matthew in astonished indignation.

"Brockley's a good man," he said. "I know that. I gather that he has shown many kindnesses to the elderly people in the village, such as mending roofs and chopping firewood for them. But I have noticed that you talk to him a great deal and often share jokes with him. I've heard you."

"But there's no harm in it!" I was truly appalled by this unlooked-for criticism. "And it's true; Brockley *is* a good man," I said defensively. "The old folk down in the village would miss him. He has a liking for them. I know he did his best for his own mother when she was alive."

"And it's a virtue. I recognize that. I also realize that he was a great help to you when you were in Paris and I was away fighting. But now we are together again and you have me to lean on. You no longer need Roger Brockley."

"Brockley has never been anything other than perfectly respectful. He's like Marie; he knows his place."

"I'm well aware that he's respectful. If I thought otherwise, he would have been on his way to England long ago. Nevertheless, as I said, you have me to lean on now and you no longer need a personal manservant. We've been married for three years and a half, but we've spent much of that time apart, and we've only been settled in Blanchepierre since January. However, we are at last arranging the pattern of our real married life. And surely, Ursula, you can see that there is no place for Brockley in it? I already have enough grooms—enough to take care of more horses than I possess—and Doriot doesn't need Brockley to help him at table and doesn't like it, either. And also . . ."

"Yes?" My finger had stopped bleeding but my hands were shaking and I rested them on my lap rather than try to go on stitching. I could not imagine being permanently without Brockley and Dale. They were part of me. We were a threesome held in a precise relationship to each other by a web of shared experiences. We had worked together, been afraid together, and even saved each other's lives. Didn't Matthew understand, Matthew, who was supposed to be the other half of myself?

"You often say how fond you are of Dale," Matthew was saying, "but you seem blind to the obvious. Dale loves you, but you know very well that she longs for England, and in addition, you and Brockley often hurt her."

"What? What are you talking about?"

"I'm trying to point out to you that your intimacy with him gives her pain. Didn't you know?"

"Of all the things to say! How can you?"

"It's true."

"It's *not* true! I can't bear this. How can you? No, let me pass; I'm going to my room."

Here, once again, was something that was too much, that hurt more than I could bear. Throwing my work down on the walnut table, I sprang up, evaded Matthew's protesting hand, and fled from him. When I reached the sanctuary of my own bedchamber, Marie was there, brushing clothes. She looked at my white face and tear-filled eyes and at once, as a good personal maid should, asked if there was anything she could do for Madame.

"Yes. Just leave Madame alone," I said ungraciously. She curtsied politely and went away and I longed to have Dale fussing around me, offering me chamomile possets. I bolted the door to keep Marie from coming back and then threw myself onto the bed and burst into tears.

Matthew pursued me, of course. He tapped on the door and called to me. "Let me in, Ursula. You solve nothing by running away. Come, unbar the door."

I sat up wearily, rubbing my eyes with my palms, and knew that I must not shut him out. I got up and drew back the bolt.

"Saltspoon, I didn't mean to upset you." The pet name brought a fresh flood of tears from me. Standing in his arms, I soaked the front of his doublet with them. My cap had gone awry. He pulled it off and stroked my hair. "You are so sharp-minded," he said, "and yet sometimes you seem not to know things that anyone else can see with their eyes closed . . . oh well, never mind. There, there. You're not strong yet, I know. You have been so very ill, my dear."

Since that dreadful, useless delivery, I had not been able to face lovemaking. Matthew's masculine beauty, which had once filled me with desire so that every bone in my body seemed to lean toward him when he came near me, had ceased to move me at all. Now, however, I felt his need of me and knew I must respond. I let him take me to the bed. It was agony at first, in a way quite new to me. I had never known lovemaking to cause me pain before, not even the very first time, with Gerald. Now I gritted my teeth and kept my eyes closed and could do no more at first than endure.

Matthew sensed my distress and held his urgency in check, coaxing and caressing, until at last my body remembered what to do, and my juices began to flow, soothing away the pain and letting him move easily. Afterward, I lay curled against him and thinking that one day, soon, all would be as it used to be. We would be happy together again, and I would love Matthew as I used to do. All I needed was to grow a little stronger—and for Meg to come.

Perhaps when I had Meg, I would even be able to contemplate life without Brockley and Dale!

Matthew did not again mention the idea of paying them off, and neither did I. By tacit agreement, we left all that until they should return. Two and a half weeks after they had left for England, I saw a hired barge approaching up the river, and as I looked from my sitting room window, I recognized Brockley and Dale on the deck. But although I peered and strained my eyes, I could not see any little girl with them. I sped down to the château landing stage and their grave faces confirmed my fears even before I spoke to them. It was I who spoke first, before they had even come ashore. "Where is she? Where is Meg?"

They stepped quickly onto the jetty, Brockley giving a hand to his wife. "Madam . . ." he began, and then stopped.

"What is it? Brockley! Dale! Tell me at once!"

"Meg was there when we got to Thamesbank," Dale said earnestly. "Very lively, very healthy, and asking after you, and how she's grown, ma'am; you'd hardly credit it . . ."

"Dale!"

"We had a good journey," Brockley said. His even voice made me attend to him. "We were there in four days," he said. "We meant to spend a week at Thamesbank and then get the child away. We thought it would be easy, for the house was busy. Sir William Cecil came, the day after we did, to spend a few days there and he brought his wife, Lady Mildred, and a guest of theirs, a Lady Mortimer. There was entertaining and any amount of coming and going . . . I'm coming to the point, madam. We were laying plans. As we expected, Bridget didn't want to come to France, but she was willing to help us. Also, I'm sure she didn't talk; she's got plenty of sense. We were all careful and I'm as sure as I can be that what happened had nothing to do with our plans. But . . . well, one morning, Bridget and Meg weren't there. They'd vanished in the night. Just gone."

"Gone?" I said blankly.

"Yes, madam. No horses were missing from the stable and no one had seen or heard anything. They had slept in their beds—one could see that—but a hamper had disappeared from a cupboard in the room, and so had some of their clothes, Mistress Henderson said, although not everything—just a set of daily wear and a change of linen. Master Henderson sent riders out everywhere, to inquire if anyone had seen them, and I rode out too."

"What?" My voice was still blank. I could hardly take in what he was saying.

"We couldn't hear of a single sighting," Brockley said. "Not on any road or on the river. I helped the search for three days but there wasn't a trace, not a single trace. Mistress Henderson was frantic, shut in her room in tears most of the time. It was a foggy morning when they went; you know how the vapors rise off the river. They'd just—vanished into the mist."

3

Hawk or Donkey

"I won't be away longer than I must," I said to Matthew, as he stepped onto the barge, bringing an extra rug to protect me from the breeze. "But I have to find Meg. I must. Once I have her safe, I'll bring her home. I wish you could come too."

As I took my seat, I looked up at the château. It was very beautiful, its turrets and crenellations elegant as well as practical. It was built of pale Caen stone, which changed color according to the weather. Under cloudy skies, the walls were white, but sunlight would tint them with gold, and at sunset they flushed to the softest shade of rose, and their reflection in the Loire, wavering with the ripples, was like the outline of a faerie fortress.

"I'd gladly come, but I'm a wanted man in England," Matthew said. "Be careful, Ursula, my dear one. According to Brockley, Sir William Cecil urged him to fetch you to England to look for Meg. Be careful of Cecil."

"I will." It still saddened me to say that. Sir William Cecil and his wife, Lady Mildred, had in the past been very kind to me. They had found me my post at Elizabeth's court; they had arranged for Meg to be fostered by the Hendersons. It was Cecil, mainly, who had enhanced my income by employing me on secret tasks, watching and investigating the enemies of Queen Elizabeth.

And then Cecil and Elizabeth between them had sent me to France on a seemingly innocent errand, and I hadn't known that they were using me as bait to draw Matthew out of hiding. We had been married for some time by then, but were estranged. When I learned how I had been used, I ended the estrangement and chose to stay with Matthew. I had told him that I understood that betrayal better now, but I still could not see how I could ever really trust either Cecil or the queen again.

I said: "I only want to find Meg. That is the only reason why I am going, and the only thing that I intend to do."

"I shall pray that both of you will return to me soon," Matthew said. "I shall pray in my chapel, every day."

"And I." Uncle Armand had come to the jetty to say good-bye as well. "I shall keep a night vigil once a week, until you return, madame. It is very right that you should wish to find your daughter and bring her here." He spoke quite warmly and it occurred to me that like many priests, he was uncomfortable with women in general but got on better with those who were mothers. Screaming out my enraged rejection of martyrdom by parturition I had scandalized him; but in my present anxiety for my little girl, I was an object of sympathy.

Dale and Brockley were aboard, their bags at their feet. The boatmen were settling to their oars. It was time.

"Matthew . . ."

"Godspeed, Saltspoon."

We had a parting embrace, long and fierce. Then he stepped ashore and stood on the jetty, waving farewell as the barge slipped away downstream. I watched him grow smaller as the distance between us grew.

A divided heart, divided loves, are a terrible burden to carry.

It was a quick journey. We reached Nantes in a day and there we had good luck, for we found a ship in which Matthew had shares, about to sail for England with a cargo of wine. When the *Cygnet* left next day, we were aboard her. The winds were playful, but they drove us in the right direction. I had feared seasickness but none of us fell ill, although the tossing sea made Dale nervous. "I just wish the wind would drop a bit, ma'am," she said miserably. "I can't abide the sea. I wouldn't do it for anyone but you and Roger and that's a fact."

"You'll soon be on dry land again," I said comfortingly.

"I hope so, ma'am. The way those timbers creak; they make me think the ship's going to fall apart and drop us all in the water."

"Matthew de la Roche," I said, "doesn't buy shares in unseaworthy buckets. The *Cygnet* will get us to England; don't worry."

The *Cygnet* did. We landed safely at Southampton late on a May evening and went to an inn where a good night's sleep made Dale more cheerful and the sound of the English language was a delight to me. In the morning, Brockley found us some hired horses, and we set out for Thamesbank.

The house where Meg had been living with Cecil's friends, Rob and Mattie Henderson, was beside the Thames, near Hampton. I was in a furious hurry to get there and because posting inns couldn't always provide proper sidesaddles—only pillion saddles, but riding pillion would have slowed us down—I rode as Dale always did, astride and in breeches, though over them, I put on one of the open-fronted skirts which I usually wore on top of an embroidered kirtle. In my impatience, I also shocked Brockley with my curses when the hired horses were less than ideal.

They often are, of course, for they are ridden hard, in all weathers, by all kinds of riders. They nearly always have iron mouths and temperaments either phlegmatic or cussed. I remember that one of my mounts nearly drove me mad with its reluctance to go faster than a slow jog and with its big clumsy feet, which seemed to find every single pothole in the track. "This damned horse swerves out of the way on purpose to tread in a hole and stumble!" I raged, and thereafter named the animal Dogmeat. "Blast you, Dogmeat, pick your feet up!" "Get on with it, Dogmeat; we haven't got forever!"

Yet through it all, the beauty of England in early May reached and touched me. It was subtly different from France: the new young leaves a more delicate shade of green; the sunshine gentler. No golden orioles whistled in the woodland; thrushes and blackbirds sang unchallenged. Villages were quiet and mostly prosperous; there had been no civil war in England to take men from the land. France was now my home, but I would never cease to care for England. I was glad to see it once again.

We had to spend one night on the road, but in the morning, we found ourselves with better horses and I made good use of them, pushing us on as fast as possible, deaf to Dale's protests that it was surely dinnertime and when were we going to eat? By three in the afternoon, we were all very hungry, but the ornamental red-brick chimneys of Thamesbank House were in sight. "We're there," I said.

The lodgekeeper sent his son Tom running ahead to announce our arrival and by the time we rode into the courtyard, Rob Henderson, tall, fair-haired, and handsome, jauntily clad in green with a feather in his cap, as though he were about to go a-hunting, was out there to meet us. Brockley made to dismount and help me down, but Henderson reached me first and I was out of my saddle before Brockley was out of his.

"I knew you would come. I knew it!" Rob exclaimed. "Welcome!"

"Of course I came. Is there any news of Meg? Have you found her? I've been frantic."

"I feared you would be. I'm sorry. Yes, there's news." Rob smiled and I saw that his expression was both cheerful and tranquil. "Put your mind at rest and come indoors."

"She's safe?" Relief weakened my knees, so much so that for a moment the whole courtyard spun. I must have gone white because Rob looked at me in concern and took hold of my arm.

"Steady, now. Meg is all right. I promise. There's nothing for you to worry about."

"But where is she? Is she here? What happened?"

"She's not here but she's perfectly safe and you can go to her soon. Have you dined? No?" Dale was shaking her head. "Brockley, leave the horses to my grooms, take Dale to the kitchens, and ask for some food for the two of you. Come inside, Ursula. A meal will be brought to you and you shall eat while I talk."

"But where is Meg?" I let Rob lead me up the porch steps and steer me into a parlor, but I would not stop asking questions. "If you've found her, why isn't she here? What is all this? And where's Mattie?"

"My wife is with Meg." A maid appeared to take my cloak, and someone else arrived with a tray of wine. Rob barked some orders to a hovering butler, concerning food. Then he steered me to a settle, poured a glass of wine, and offered it to me. Impatiently, I put it aside. "Rob," I said, "I mean, Master Henderson . . ."

"We know each other well enough to be Rob and Ursula, even if we haven't met these two years past. Meg is with Mattie and with her nurse, Bridget. She is safe and well. She's growing into as bonny a wench as I ever saw and when you see her, you'll think so too. But she's not at Thamesbank," said Rob. "She's in Herefordshire. To be precise, she's near the Welsh border, at a place called Vetch Castle, a few miles west of the Malvern Hills."

"Rob, I've never heard of the Malvern Hills or of Vetch Castle. What is Meg doing there? How did she get there? Who took her and why?"

"Drink some wine, Ursula. . . . On the day they vanished, Meg and her nurse were taken quietly from Thamesbank before dawn. They stayed for a few days in a comfortable household until Brockley and Dale gave up hope of finding them, and set out for France to fetch you."

"What?"

Rob picked up my right hand and my wineglass and firmly wrapped my fingers around the stem. "Take a good long draft of that, and don't agitate yourself so. . . . As soon as Brockley and Dale had gone, Mattie set out with Lady Mortimer, who was our guest at the time, and who also happens to be the chatelaine of Vetch Castle, until such time as her son marries. They joined Bridget and Meg and then they all went, well escorted, to Herefordshire. Meg supposes herself to be on a visit. Mattie and Bridget are with her; she hasn't been frightened or upset in any way. She . . ."

"But why? What's it all about . . . ?" I saw him looking at me quizzically. "It was to get me back to England, wasn't it? Rob, how could you? How could Mattie? Brockley told me that when Meg vanished, Mattie was so distraught she shut herself in her room. Was all that a mere performance? In God's name, why? No, don't tell me. This is some scheme of Cecil's, isn't it? Bloody Cecil—I might have known!"

"He is a good man, Ursula. No queen ever had a more trustworthy Secretary of State. Which means, of course, that at times he puts his loyalty to her first—ahead of other things and other people. Are you not wise enough to understand that?"

"Yes, I am. I understood it some time ago," I said grimly. I gulped some of the wine as bidden, feeling the need of it. "But this!" I said. "Am I wanted back in England for some particular purpose? Does the queen want me, or is it just Cecil?"

"This request didn't come originally from either of them," Rob said. "As a matter of fact, it came from Lady Mortimer. But it concerns the queen; most certainly it does. And for the moment, my dear—my very dear—Ursula, that is all I can say. You will hear the rest when Cecil arrives. He is with the court at Richmond, but young Tom from the lodge has gone off by boat to tell him that you're here. Ah." A butler had come into the room and was clearing his throat. "I think, Ursula, that your meal is nearly ready. There should be hot water in your room, if you want to wash before you eat."

"Thank you," I said. "Listen, Rob. I want to be reunited with Meg as soon as possible and I then intend to take her straight home to France and I am not prepared to take no for an answer."

"I said you'd say that. But," said Rob, with a glint of disquieting laughter in his blue eyes, "you'll have to fetch her first."

He wouldn't explain further. I must wait until Sir William Cecil arrived and then I would understand everything. I ate my meal, fuming. After that, I roamed restlessly from room to room and asked questions which Rob wouldn't answer, until I realized that I was wasting my time. On Dale's sensible recommendation, I then settled in the parlor and tried to play backgammon with Rob's twelve-year-old son, Harry, a jolly lad with a marked resemblance to his merry dumpling of a mother.

In the early evening, glancing out of the window at the sweep of lawn and the river beyond, I saw a barge draw quietly alongside the Thamesbank landing stage, and tie up. Whereupon, I sat down again and remarked to Harry that we needed to light the candles if we were to play another game. I would not hurry out to greet Cecil. I had come to find Meg as a hawk comes to the lure and he had known I would. But I would take wing at his bidding no longer.

Within a few minutes, however, there were voices outside the room. Rob was speaking in quiet, respectful tones. Then the door opened and his head came around it. "I am sorry, Harry, but I must interrupt you. Ursula, will you come to the study?"

Beyond the tall leaded windows of the study, a quiet blue dusk was falling across the land but the room itself, with crimson velvet curtains and cushions and vivid rugs, was bright and welcoming. It was quite a big room, and I saw that a supper table laid for four had been placed at one side. There were lighted candles on the table and in wall sconces, and a small fire burned in the hearth, for the evenings were still cool. Sir William Cecil was there, standing beside a chair in which a cloaked woman was seated. I looked at her and as I did so, she raised a long-fingered hand, laden with rings, to push back her hood. She smiled and automatically I dropped into a curtsy.

"Good evening, Ursula," said Queen Elizabeth sweetly.

She looked older. Elizabeth was senior to me by only a few months, but had I not known this, I would have said three or four years. Her golden-brown eyes had always been watchful but now I would have called them wary, and there were tiny scars at her temples, where the light red hair was drawn back into its crimpings. She had had smallpox since I saw her last but she had been luckier than my Gerald. She had escaped not only with her life but with most of her complexion.

Her pale shield of a face was as I remembered it, though, and so were those long, jeweled fingers, and so too was the curious quality of unexpectedness, which was one of her most outstanding characteristics.

Elizabeth lived, for most of the time, just as her father, King Henry, had done, wielding her power openly, amid splendor and protocol, in ornate rooms, surrounded by a crowd of people. Yet she could at will detach herself from all of it, wrap herself in an anonymous cloak, take a journey by barge with no escort beyond Cecil, seat herself in the parlor of a private house, and look as though she had grown there. Like the ermine whose white winter fur was part of her regalia, she could change to match her surroundings, taking one by surprise.

I sometimes thought that this mercurial side of her perhaps came from her mother, Anne Boleyn, who had been described to me by my own mother, who once served Anne. Elizabeth never mentioned her mother by name but there were times, such as now, when I felt that Anne was glimpsed again in her royal daughter.

Cecil had changed a little, too. His neatly combed fair beard and intelligent blue eyes were the same, but the line between his eyes was deeper, and seemed now not so much a line of worry as of sternness. I noticed as he stepped forward to meet me that he was limping a little, and he said briefly: "Gout, I fear. The years exact their toll." His tone did not encourage further inquiry.

He had always been formidable; I thought that over the last two years I had forgotten just how formidable. Now, face-to-face with him, I saw the weight of responsibility that he carried—for England, and for the person of Elizabeth, who was England's representative. Against all that, the claims of my private life and loves seemed to shrivel. When I had kissed the hand that Elizabeth offered me, I rose and gave my hand in conventional fashion to her Secretary of State, and I did not find it possible even to burst out into questions, let alone accusations. I waited.

"Let us cast away formality," Elizabeth said. "Supper is to be served here; we will all sit down and behave as friends. I am happy to see you, Ursula. Is the supper ready, Master Henderson?"

They did not keep me waiting long for an explanation, however. Once the supper dishes had been brought in and the servants had withdrawn, Elizabeth said: "Cecil and I have a story to tell you, Ursula. It is the reason why we have lured you here. I suppose you would put it that way." I did open my mouth to speak at that point, but she raised a hand to silence me. "I will begin and Cecil shall continue." True to her wish for informality, she was not using the royal plural. "I can only hope, Ursula, that we can make you understand. As a child, did you study history at all?"

"Yes, ma'am. I shared my cousins' tutor and he was fond of the subject."

"Good. Tell me, did he ever mention a family called Mortimer?"

I had come to learn why my daughter had been whisked away to Herefordshire and what the queen had to do with it. I hadn't expected to be examined on my knowledge of English history. But the queen was conducting the examination and I could do nothing but reply.

"Yes, ma'am," I said, although I knew my puzzlement was in my voice. "At least, that was the name of a powerful family who lived on the Welsh border in bygone times. Are those the Mortimers you mean?"

"They are. Continue."

I rubbed my forehead, trying to remember. "They were barons on the Welsh Marches, very powerful indeed, with huge estates. In the fourteenth century—I think—Edward II's queen had a liaison with one of them—Roger Mortimer. In the end, he was executed for his part in the murder of the king."

"All correct," said Elizabeth. "Go on."

"It didn't extinguish the family," I said. My cousins' tutor had been a highly moral man and he had felt strongly that such behavior ought to have reduced the Mortimers to penury and obscurity. He had described their subsequent career in tones which were quite resentful. "I think they lost most of their honors and estates when Roger Mortimer was executed, but it was all given back a few generations later. In the end, they married themselves legally into the royal line. One of Roger's descendants married a granddaughter of King Edward III."

I stopped once more, and Elizabeth took up the story. "Yes. Those two had a son, another Roger, who held the title of the Earl of March. His daughter, Anne Mortimer, married the Earl of Cambridge. They were the grandparents of King Edward IV, and, therefore, are among my own forebears." Elizabeth had her family tree at her fingertips. "But Anne Mortimer," she said, "had a brother, Edmund. He fell out with King Henry VI and was banished to Ireland, where he died young. He is generally thought to have left no descendants. I have recently learned, however, that Edmund did apparently marry in Ireland the year before his death. His wife was Irish, a member of the McCormick clan. Now you can go on, Cecil. You may be interested to know though, Ursula, that by marriage you are a connection of the Mortimer family."

"Am I?"

"Yes, you are," said Cecil. "Edmund Mortimer and his Irish wife, Deirdre, had a son, born after Edmund's death. He was apparently reared as an Irishman and either didn't realize that he could have come home and challenged Anne Mortimer's descendants for the title of Earl of March; or else was discouraged from doing so. Anne married into a family quite as powerful and ambitious as the Mortimers. If they knew of her Irish nephew, they may well have taken steps to persuade him to stay in Ireland. At any rate, that is what he did. He lived and died in peaceful obscurity as did his son after him. But when his grandson, Edward Mortimer, was a young man, an Englishman called Sir Thomas Vetch . . ."

"Vetch?" I said.

"Vetch," Cecil agreed. "Of Vetch Castle in Herefordshire. Sir Thomas paid a visit to Ireland—to buy horses, I believe."

"They breed good horses in Ireland," Elizabeth said. "I have a number in my stables. Sir Thomas presumably appreciated Irish horses too. He went over there to purchase some, and he took his daughter, Lady Thomasine, with him."

"But she didn't return to England with him," Cecil said. "Edward Mortimer met her and they fell in love. They were married in Dublin and they stayed in Ireland for a year or so. Then Sir Thomas died. His daughter was his sole heiress and therefore inherited Vetch Castle. She came back to England and Edward accompanied her. He wasn't the only descendant of the Irish Mortimers, as it happened. He had an orphaned first cousin called Mary Donnelly, and they brought her along as well, as companion to Thomasine.

"It seems that Lady Thomasine was worried because more than a year after her wedding, there was still no sign of a child, and so one of the first things she did in England was to make a pilgrimage to Canterbury to pray for fruitfulness. This was in the days of the old religion, of course, when King Henry was still married to his Spanish queen, Katherine of Aragon. On the journey, they met another family who were also on pilgrimage to Canterbury. A family called Blanchard. One of them was named Luke."

"They met Luke Blanchard?" I sat up. "Gerald's father?"

Cecil smiled. "Mary Donnelly eventually became Gerald's mother. Soon after the two families returned from Canterbury, Luke Blanchard asked for her hand and they were married later that same year. You never knew Mary Donnelly, or not to remember. Your family and Gerald's are neighbors, of course, but you could only have been about three when Mary died. All the same, Mary was your mother-in-law and Meg is her granddaughter. The Blanchards keep up a correspondence with the Mortimers of Vetch Castle, and it is Mortimers in the plural, because Lady Thomasine did have children. She had a daughter the year after the pilgrimage and a son, Philip, two years after that. And, yes, it was the same Lady Thomasine who was a guest here at Thamesbank only recently. And do you know why she was here?"

"Why she was here?" I repeated bemusedly.

"She had heard of you," said Elizabeth. "Your work has always been kept secret, but these things do get out. Luke Blanchard has never been officially told about it, but he knows, all the same. He has mentioned you to Lady Thomasine in letters. She did not know you were in France, though. She came here to seek an audience with Cecil and ask if he would let you help her."

I nearly said: "Help her?" and then realized that I was constantly repeating their words, as though I were an echo. Restraining myself, I put on an expression of polite inquiry.

Cecil said quietly: "When I had heard her story, I confided in Her Majesty. We at once began to consider how we might tempt you home again. Then I heard that Brockley was over here, inquiring after Meg. I admit that it gave me an idea. In fact, it seemed providential."

I opened my mouth to say: "Providential?" but once again stopped myself, this time for fear of sounding sarcastic.

"Lady Thomasine," said Elizabeth, "is worried about her son. I know very little of Sir Philip Mortimer beyond the fact that he is now in his thirties and still unmarried. Lady Mortimer told me that. He was at court for a short time during my sister's reign. He left under some sort of cloud. I can tell you nothing of the circumstances for I have no memory of him. It seems, however, that when his father Edward came to live in Vetch Castle, on the Welsh borders, he became interested in the past of the Mortimers and took to studying it. Edward seems, sensibly enough, to have assumed that the lands and titles had long since passed out of his reach. But he was still proud of them and taught his son Philip to be proud of them too. Unfortunately." Elizabeth's tone was dry. "Because according to Lady Mortimer, Philip *does* want to restore his family's fortunes, and has wasted a great deal of money on lawyers in trying."

"The Mortimer landholdings, of course, were all split up long since and have been in the hands of others for generations," said Cecil. "There were castles in North Wales, Wigmore Castle in Herefordshire, manors scattered through a dozen counties. Sir Philip may very well be a genuine descendant of the Mortimers, but too much time has gone by for him to stand a chance of getting back the lands or even the titles. He can't, for one thing, actually prove that the Edmund Mortimer who died young, was really married to Deirdre McCormick. And that ought to be that, except . . ."

"That according to his mother," said Elizabeth, "he has boasted to her that he intends to get back the family wealth all the same, if not by acquiring the same lands and titles that his ancestors had, then by acquiring others of the same value, or at least their equivalents in money. He proposes to do this, apparently, by simply asking me. He told his mother that I would certainly say yes. He said," said Elizabeth expressionlessly, "that he had means to compel me to say yes."

"To . . . ?" I said, and then stopped. There was a silence. I was shaken. I had come back to England simply and solely to find Meg, but in spite of myself, I had grown interested in this story, and now I was shocked by the denouement. So, by their faces, were Cecil and Elizabeth.

"Lady Mortimer can't get out of him exactly how he intends to bring off this remarkable scheme," Cecil said. "But it frightens her. She seems to think that it implies some kind of threat to the queen—of pressure being brought to bear on her."

"It must do," Elizabeth said. "What he is asking is impossible, unless he has a lever."

"But what kind of lever?" I said. "What kind of pressure could he possibly have the power to apply?"

"That," said Cecil, "is what worries his mother and worries us, too. Lady Mortimer is desperately anxious, I may say, not to harm her son. What she wishes to do is to prevent him from harming himself by pursuing foolish schemes. That is why she wants someone like you, Ursula, to visit Vetch Castle and try, discreetly, to find out what his plans are. The fact that you are a family connection makes it simpler. Meg is already at Vetch on what she—and Philip Mortimer—take to be a family visit, at Lady Thomasine's invitation. Now her mother will join her. What could be more natural?"

Before I could stop myself, I had said: "Do we really know nothing at all of the scandal which made Mortimer leave the court?"

Cecil shook his head. "It was ten years ago. You are thinking that if we knew what had happened then, we might understand better how Mortimer's mind works—what he is likely to do now?"

"Something like that, yes. But I don't think I want to . . ."

Cecil cut me short. "We need to find out, quietly, what Mortimer is about. If it involves anything that might injure the queen's credit, then we can perhaps secretly frighten him into good behavior."

"I have never done anything," said Elizabeth in a cold voice, "which could harm my right to the throne. But lies can be told and much made of little. I have had some experience of that."

I knew what she meant. She had suffered much from the scandalous gossip when the wife of Robin Dudley, Master of the Queen's Horse, had died mysteriously, for most of England believed that the queen was in love with Dudley. Even now, though she had shown no sign of marrying Dudley, and I had heard that she had actually offered him as a husband for Mary Stuart (though that came to nothing), the scandal was not quite dead. But Mortimer could hardly hope to use that against the queen, not after all this time.

"When we know what Mortimer's scheme is," Cecil said, "we will know how best to evade or destroy it. But we need to begin discreetly. With you, Ursula."

* * *

I didn't want to do it. I didn't want to be a secret agent or a spy again. I wanted to find Meg and take her home to France. Surely, I protested, they could arrest Sir Philip and make him tell them his plans. (I knew perfectly well that they had their methods. A day or two in the bowels of the Tower of London, and most men would tell anybody anything.) "You don't need me," I pleaded.

I might have been talking to myself. "We don't want to arrest him until we understand what we're arresting him for. Haven't I just explained that?" said Cecil.

"But . . ."

"You have our permission," said Elizabeth graciously, "to collect your daughter, and take her home to your château. But you will have to go to Vetch Castle to get her."

"I will do so, ma'am. But I am most unwilling to . . . to search Sir Philip's study while I'm there or in any other way pry into his affairs. I never want to be involved in such work again. Surely, surely, you could find somebody else."

"Would you be so determined," inquired Elizabeth kindly, "if I offered you a valuable fee?"

"Ma'am, my husband is a man of means. I have all I need." I looked her in the eyes. "When I began to work as a secret agent, I was short of money. I needed it, to clothe and house and educate Meg. All that is changed now."

"My dearest Ursula. I know. Nevertheless, would you not like to have, shall we say, a foothold in England? Life is full of unhappy chances. You have been widowed once; what if it happened again? What if—for any reason—you wished to come home? It would be easier for you if you had a home here already. When your husband left England as a wanted man," said the queen, "the house and land he had in Sussex were sequestered. What if I gave them back?"

I stared at her and the golden-brown eyes smiled into mine. "What if I returned Withysham to you?" she said. "Or you could have some other house, if you think Withysham unsuitable. It hardly matters. The point is that here in England you would have a place to call your own. To obtain it, you need only agree to stay for a certain modest length of time at Vetch Castle—two weeks, perhaps? Surely that isn't too long?—and do your best while you are there to learn the details of Mortimer's extraordinary plans to extract a fortune from me?"

"Do you blame me for this?" Rob asked, when Cecil and the queen had taken their leave and been rowed away up the darkening Thames, leaving me to "think it over," as they put it. "I'm sorry if so. But you are needed, Ursula. You are valued."

After seeing our august visitors depart we had returned to the study. The supper had been cleared away, and the candles were burning down. I was very tired. I gazed at Rob with weary defiance. "I know how I am valued," I said. "Have you forgotten the way I was once used to bait a trap for my own husband?"

"It was for Elizabeth's safety, and that means the safety of England. You know that." He looked at me steadily, dispassionately. Rob was an attractive man but there was never any magnetism between us. He always talked to me as though I were another man, and I found this natural. "Cecil said that he brought Lady Mortimer here because he had heard that Dale and Brockley were visiting me. It was I who told Cecil about that. When you settled in France, Cecil asked me to let him know whenever you communicated with me, and what the latest news of you was. I do as Cecil says, as well you know. Well, when Brockley and Dale arrived, inquiring after Meg's welfare, I naturally informed him. He and Lady Thomasine arrived almost at once. Were Brockley and Dale intending, at the end of their visit, to take her back to France, by the way?"

"Yes."

"I thought so. So did Mattie. I let Cecil know as much."

"And when Cecil heard that I was pining for my daughter," I said, "he rubbed his hands together, thinking how convenient; getting Ursula back to England will be easy. All I would need was just a little push—or little pull." I knew I sounded bitter. "So he arranged for Meg to disappear. And now I'm here and I am to follow her to Vetch Castle. As a hawk follows the lure, or a donkey follows a carrot."

"Yes. But you are bound to follow the carrot, are you not? You want to fetch Meg. Well, Ursula, what will you do when you find her? Will you leave at once—or stay two weeks as you've been asked, and look about you—and win a home in England?" He scanned my face. "Or will you refuse both the task and the payment, because Matthew might object?"

I sighed, rubbing my forehead, hoping that my head was not going to start aching again. "I shall accept," I said. "I shall write to Matthew and tell him what I've been asked to do and what the reward will be, and say that I intend to stay at Vetch for the two weeks that will earn it. I shall also say that I will, if he so wishes, ask for a different estate, not Withysham. Withysham was taken from him because he had plotted against Elizabeth. I would be getting it back as a reward for services rendered to Elizabeth. He might well find that—well . . ."

"Tasteless," Rob agreed. "Yes. That crossed my mind, too. But you are willing in principle to accept property in England?"

"Yes," I said. To forgo Withysham was one thing. To forgo the reward altogether was quite another and from the moment Elizabeth mentioned it, I knew I could not bear to do that. "After all," I pointed out, "why should I refuse payment for services honestly rendered? I shall say to Matthew that I look on it as an increase in our wealth."

"And trust that he will see it in that light?"

"Yes. The queen spoke the truth. I do need somewhere in England to come back to—just in case. I know how fragile life can be." Gerald had gone from full health to a hideously disfigured death in a matter of days.

I also knew now, though it troubled me to realize it, how homesick I had been at Blanchepierre; how much and how deeply I had missed England. It would ease my heart to know that I could come here at will, and find a place to call my own.

"I feel sure you'll manage Matthew," Rob said with a smile. "You'll go to Vetch and earn your pay. You'll do it for pay. But not for Elizabeth?"

"Would you expect that—now?"

"She is not just a woman called Elizabeth Tudor. She is England too," said Rob.

Again, I remembered my homesickness in France and how glad I had been to hear the English tongue when I disembarked at

Southampton. I remembered the green of the woods and the sound of the birdsong, so familiar and beloved, so subtly different from their counterparts in France. Elizabeth was their representative, and the two were one and indivisible. Elizabeth the woman had once betrayed me, but Elizabeth of England could ask of me whatever she wished and I could not refuse her. I sighed again, giving in. "I know," I said.

It was really most aggravating of Rob, at this point, to add: "I'm sure you'll enjoy yourself when you get there."

4

The Castle on the Hill

Cecil, in a final briefing before I set out, told me that according to Lady Mortimer, Sir Philip intended to approach the queen later in the year. "He's heard that Her Majesty is to make a Progress to Cambridge toward the end of the summer. He studied at Cambridge University and has friends in the town with whom he proposes to stay. Then he will try to find a way of presenting himself to the queen."

"Does he really think . . . ?"

"I doubt very much," said Cecil, "if one could call it thinking. Whatever it is, it's a delusion. But Lady Thomasine thinks he is hanging his crazy ambition on some kind of solid peg." He considered me thoughtfully and made an ominous joke. "He could hang himself instead of his ambitions if he isn't careful. That's what she fears, and I use the word *fear* very deliberately. She's very frightened—brittle with it, if you understand what I mean. She will be glad to see you at Vetch, and I am glad you're going."

I left for Vetch the next morning.

It was difficult to travel swiftly. For one thing, I had baggage and for another, Dale had never really got over that dreadful experience in a French dungeon, two years before. She was in her midforties now, and feeling her years. The rough sea voyage and the fast ride from Southampton had tired her out. I had few secrets from either her or Brockley and they understood our errand and my wish for haste. But nevertheless, for Dale's sake alone, we would have to journey at a moderate pace.

At least this enabled us to take our own mounts all the way. When I went to France, I had left two horses in Rob Henderson's stables, telling him to use them until I returned. He still had them. I was glad to be back in my own familiar saddle and riding my pretty mare, Bay Star, once again. Brockley was equally glad to be again riding Speckle, the flea-bitten gray cob I kept for him. Dale traveled on his pillion, happy just to perch behind her husband on the long road to Herefordshire.

Rob provided us with packhorses and an escort, including himself. "I'm coming along to join my wife; it will seem quite normal," he said. "Besides, I think I should be at hand, just in case."

The journey in the end took five slow days, mostly in wet weather. We spent the final night of it in the cathedral town of Tewkesbury, beside the rich river meadows of the Severn, where sheep grow fat. The Hendersons had friends in Tewkesbury, a prosperous wool merchant and his wife, who lived in one of the smart new timbered houses which were being built in the town. The Woodwards would gladly accommodate us, Rob said. However, we had some trouble in actually reaching them for we had to wait half an hour on the outskirts of the town, in heavy rain, until a bleating, woolly river of sheep had finished pouring through the main street.

"What in the world is going on?" Dale asked wearily, from the depths of her soaked hood, as we crowded into such shelter as a wide oak tree could give us. "Where are they taking all those sheep to? There are thousands of them."

When, dripping and cross, we eventually reached the Woodwards' house, our host explained. "The pastures to the west of the town often flood in wet weather. The Severn runs beside them and it can overflow. The sheep are being moved as a precaution. You can see from the upstairs windows how low-lying the meadows are."

When we were shown up to our chambers, we all looked out of the windows at the flat green river meadows and understood what he meant. Already there were many silvered pools of rainwater on the grass. Beyond the pastures I could see a line of hills, which Rob, looking over my shoulder, said were the Malvern Hills. "They're maybe ten or twelve miles away and Vetch Castle is seventeen miles or so beyond, lying to the south of Hereford. We could be there by tomorrow, though, if we start early."

I looked worriedly at the pastures and wished for wings, so that I could fly across them, floods or no floods, and be with Meg. She was there, beyond the misty blue line of the Malverns. I could feel her. "If we get this far and then we're held back by a few falls of rain . . ." I said.

"They move the sheep in good time," Rob said reassuringly. "The local folk are used to the way the Severn behaves. You'll be with Meg tomorrow. And then," he added slyly, "you can begin on your real task in Vetch Castle."

"Fetching Meg is my real task."

"Of course," said Rob Henderson annoyingly, sweet and smooth as cream custard.

The following day, it stopped raining and there was wind enough to dry the tracks. The Severn was certainly flowing high; when we crossed it on a bridge, we could see its waters swirling only just below the level of its banks. However, nothing actually hindered us. By midday, we had passed through the hills at the southern end of the Malverns and reached a market town called Ledbury, where we paused at an inn for a brief meal. Then we rode on and at last, as the sun was dropping westward, we emerged from a belt of woodland that had cut off the view for some time, and there in front of us, on a solitary hill, was Vetch Castle.

It was Norman, of course, one of the string of fortresses that the Norman kings had founded all along the borders of Wales, to keep the Welsh from making incursions into England. The eastern walls, facing us across a valley, were built above a steep, rocky drop and looked as though they were growing up from it. But the evening sun lay kindly on the pale gray stone of the castle, and all around it were rolling hills, rich with woodlands and sloping pastures, where flocks of sheep were grazing.

In fact, despite its solid round towers, its stout buttressed walls, and its battlements, Vetch looked at first sight quite hospitable.

Later, it occurred to me that one could say the same of the cheese in a mousetrap.

There was a moat below part of the castle, though not where the steep drop made it unnecessary. The approach road curved around to the south, however, and crossed the moat on a drawbridge, which looked as though it still worked. At the gatehouse, a porter came out to greet us, accompanied by a big red-complexioned man who remarked in a bass Welsh accent that he'd just been having a gossip with his friend the porter here, and would show us the way inside.

The porter was neatly dressed but his friend was scruffy. His old-fashioned green jacket and hose had seen much wear, his plain linen shirt collar was frayed at the neckline, and all his garments were marked by white streaks, which looked like bird droppings. He seemed to have authority, however. As he led us in, he shouted in a commanding fashion, and at once, a couple of young fellows appeared at a run, and said that if we would dismount, they would take the horses to the stable.

We did as requested, although Brockley, who never really trusted anyone else to see to our mounts properly or unload our luggage without pilfering it, determinedly went with the horses, and Rob instructed his men to do likewise. Dale, Rob, and I, however, followed the big man on foot through a wide outer bailey, part of which was arranged as a tiltyard, and through an arch into a cobbled inner courtyard.

The courtyard had a well in the middle, a rather charming affair with a high coping and a little sheltering roof, neatly thatched and supported on three stone pillars entwined with honeysuckle. It was clear, indeed, that since the harsh medieval days when the castle was first built, efforts had been made to soften its martial air. It had battlemented towers on the outer walls and also at each corner of the courtyard but only one of the courtyard towers was plainly visible, because the lower storeys of the others were obscured by a very fine hall, surely no more than a hundred years old, and a number of other buildings, some of which were more recent still.

One, a small house in itself, built of warm red brick in the style of King Henry's times, stood to the right of the archway. Opposite this was a most extraordinary affair, which looked like the bottom level of a Norman keep, with a modern house, plastered in white and patterned with black timbers, perched on top and overhanging the stone walls beneath. I took all this in with one interested glance and then forgot it just as quickly because suddenly a door opened in the base of the keep and out ran a leggy little girl perhaps eight or nine years old.

"Meg!" After one breathless moment of uncertainty, I knew my daughter, though she was inches taller than when I last saw her and her red woolen dress was too short for her. I ran to meet her, leaving the others behind. At the same moment, Mattie Henderson hurried from the keep with Meg's nurse, Bridget Lemmon, following. Mattie was exclaiming: "Meg, mind your manners! Make your curtsy." Meg stopped and tried to do as she was bid, but I had reached her already and caught her up in my arms.

"Meg, oh, Meg! Oh, how you've grown. And how well you look. It's been too long. I'm so sorry!" I clutched her, kissed her, and then, because over the top of her head I could see Mattie smiling but also shaking her head, and Bridget looking quite put out, I set her back from me and said: "Now let me see how beautifully you curtsy."

"My lady mother." She did a most exquisite curtsy for me. I saw that she had changed a little; her face had lengthened, becoming more triangular than square, more like my face than Gerald's. But her brown eyes would always be his. She had not inherited my hazel ones, or my particular kind of dark hair, either. Mine had brown gleams in it but Meg's, now escaping from its little embroidered linen cap, was the true raven black of the Blanchards.

"We saw you approaching," Mattie said. "Meg has had her nose to the window this past half hour and when you came through the archway, there was no holding her. Meg, you are so impatient."

"Oh, it's no matter. I've been longing to see her." I held out a hand to Bridget as she came puffing up to us. Bridget had never been slim and was now decidedly fat. "How are you, Bridget? Well, you've seen a bit of England since we last met. How did you manage the journey from Thamesbank?"

"On a pillion, ma'am, and I was that jolted, I thought my spine would go through the top of my head. I'm glad to see you, and you looking so well. We've all kept pretty stout . . ."

"Especially you, Bridgie," said Meg, giggling.

"That will do, Meg. Don't be impertinent. You're overexcited," said Mattie. Mattie had always been a very merry soul who often found it quite hard to maintain the dignity proper to a well-bred lady, but now she seemed unwontedly serious. "Bridget, take her indoors. They're serving supper in the hall very soon, Ursula, and I'll bring her to you there, when she's washed her hands and face. And combed her hair and put her cap on straight. Off you go, Bridget. Oh, Rob. I am so glad to see you."

Meg reluctantly let herself be led away and Rob, who had held back while I embraced Meg, came up to greet his wife. Then our guide, who had gone on toward the hall, came hurrying back accompanied by a tall, gray-haired man wearing a formal black gown and a butler's chain of office. Mattie drew herself out of Rob's arms. "Here is Pugh, all ready to announce you. Mistress Ursula Blanchard is here, Pugh, and this is my husband, Master Robert Henderson."

"If you will accompany me to the hall," said Pugh, "Sir Philip and Lady Mortimer are waiting to receive you."

I was gazing wistfully after Meg, but guests cannot refuse to be introduced to their hosts and besides, I was here on a mission. I was about to meet the man I had come to investigate. As my daughter disappeared into the curious keep-cum-timbered-house, I obediently accompanied Rob and Pugh toward the hall. Our red-faced escort came too, bird droppings and all.

There was a gabled porch and then a massive, studded door which led straight into the hall, the heart of the castle. First impressions were of great size, gloomy grandeur, and domestic confusion, all at once. The place was forty feet long at least, hung with tapestries, most of which looked old and faded. There were numerous cushioned settles and a wide hearth with an intricately carved stone surround. A fire burned there, and for some reason, an untidy heap of fur rugs lay in front of it. Beside it, a man in russet doublet and hose, slashed with yellow, was reading.

Opposite him, a lady in blue was working at embroidery and a pale, quietly dressed woman was spinning. Servants were hurrying about, setting out trestle tables, presumably for supper, and at some distance from the hearth, an unprepossessing crone, with hanks of gray hair trailing from beneath a grubby shawl, sat on a stool with a pail of milk beside her and a small lamb on her lap. She was dipping a cloth in the milk and squeezing it into the lamb's mouth.

As we came in, the draft from the porch door set the hearth fire smoking, and the heap of furs suddenly moved and dissolved into two shaggy sheepdogs, two greyhounds, and a huge mastiff, which got onto their score of feet and began barking and baying. The lamb on the crone's lap bleated. Pugh had to raise his voice to make himself heard.

"Mistress Ursula Blanchard and Master Robert Henderson!"

Some of the servants had stopped work to look at us and someone recalled them to their task with a sharp order in a language I had already heard a few people speak in the Ledbury inn, and now recognized as Welsh. The man in russet stood up, shouting at the dogs to be quiet. The woman in blue laid down her stitchery, came gracefully to her feet, and swept toward us, hands outstretched and azure skirts rustling over the rushes, though the gracious air was slightly damaged as she shot out a daintily slippered foot in order to kick a barking greyhound out of her way.

"For the love of heaven, what a din! These are friends, you silly animals. Did you bring our guests over from the gatehouse, Evans? My thanks. I am so sorry for the noise, Pugh. We so often keep you from doing your office with proper dignity."

The bespattered Evans and the dignified Pugh both denied being inconvenienced in any way, and looked at her as though they adored her. They withdrew, bowing. The lady patted the affronted greyhound, which subsided onto the mat, presumably not much hurt, and the man in russet, who had by now quieted the other dogs, came forward to meet us. The lady, turning a smile of great charm onto us all, offered me her right hand while drawing the man to her side with the other.

"Welcome. I am Lady Thomasine and this is my son, Sir Philip Mortimer. I apologize for first speaking to Pugh and Evans but they are the most devoted of servants and I care for them as they care for me. They were born to my father's service here at Vetch."

"We are delighted to see you," said Sir Philip. "We had a courier from Sir William Cecil, who told us that you might arrive today but, in fact, we had given you up—or we would have made sure you had a quieter welcome. You must be tired. Please be seated."

We let ourselves be led to a long settle, and the pale woman, who was evidently Lady Thomasine's maid, fetched some extra cushions. "I believe," Lady Thomasine said to me, "that your present married name is really de la Roche but that in England you still use the name of Blanchard. I am rather glad. It makes you seem more of a relation, and it is always such a pleasure to meet new relatives. Your daughter, Meg, has already enchanted us all."

I made a suitable reply. The crone had now put the lamb on the floor and got it sucking from the cloth while the cloth was actually in the pail, the first step in teaching it to drink instead of suckle. She murmured to it as though reciting a spell and Lady Thomasine's lovely smile faded for a moment as she noticed what I was looking at.

"That is Gladys," she said to us. "She used to work in the castle but I sent her back to her home in the village last year. Frankly, I don't like to have such unlovely beings about the place. Gladys looks like a witch and the villagers say she is one." Gladys, overhearing, gave us all a grin, or perhaps the word *leer* describes it better, revealing that she had very few teeth and that the ones which were left were horridly like fangs.

"But she is good with orphaned lambs," Sir Philip explained, "and our shepherd always brings them first to the hall. I take a personal interest in my flock. Sheep are the gold of the Marches. That is a late-born lamb whose dam won't suckle it. I sent for Gladys to take charge of it and she thought it should have a feed at once, as it is very weak. She'll take it back to the village soon, Mother."

Lady Thomasine resumed her smile, and I smiled back and began covertly to study the woman who had brought me here very nearly by force, and her son Philip Mortimer, who thought he knew a way to extract wealth from the queen, and had left court after a brief sojourn ten years ago because of some unspecified scandal.

Lady Thomasine of the enchanting smile must be in her fifties, but she was still straight-backed, tall, and slender—almost thin—with beautiful cheekbones. Her fine dry skin had few lines and her hair was still brown. Her voice, as she continued to talk about Meg and our family relationship, sounded younger than her years.

"Meg's father, of course," said Lady Thomasine, "was my son Philip's second cousin. How sad that you and Gerald Blanchard never met, Philip. You might have been good friends."

"Indeed, yes," Sir Philip agreed. To me, he said: "But at least we now have the pleasure of entertaining Gerald Blanchard's wife and child. My mother has looked forward so much to your coming, Mistress Blanchard."

He could scarcely know quite how much she had been looking forward to it, let alone why. He must suppose I was simply a hitherto unknown kinswoman, discovered and invited by Lady Thomasine. He took after his mother, I thought. His hair was lighter than hers, but he was tall and long-boned, as she was, with the same fine dry skin; his eyes were like hers, greenish-blue and almond-shaped, with the right and left sockets set at slightly different angles.

The conversation broke off then, as maids arrived with cans of hot water. We were invited to wash our hands and faces in a room off the hall, since supper, Lady Thomasine said, was just about to be served. Our baggage had already been taken to the guest rooms and she would show us the way there after we had eaten. Rob's men had been looked after, added Sir Philip, and they and Brockley would take their meal with the castle guard, in a separate dining hall.

I was hungry, and the food was welcome. Dale ate with us, and with some anxiety, I saw that she was too tired to do more than toy with her meal. But I ate well, happy because Bridget had brought Meg to supper, and I had her beside me. My little girl was shiny-faced with washing, freshly dressed in orange damask, sparkling with the excitement of having me there, and just a little reproachful because I had been absent so long.

"I had to stay in France, darling, and because there was a civil war going on, I couldn't risk sending for you. When you're older, I'll be able to explain it all. But I can tell you that the war is over now, and when I go back to France, I shall take you with me. That is, if you want to come. I know that you have been happy at Thamesbank."

Meg considered this, her eyes going to Mattie, who said: "Your mother's home is now in France and if you would be with her, then to France you must go. Her new husband is there, and her place is with him. The queen has given her consent."

I detected reservations in Mattie's tone. She liked me, but in marrying Matthew, I had married an enemy of England. She regretted it and so did Rob.

"I think I want to be with my mother," Meg said, though in little more than a whisper, since all the attention was making her shy. Mortimer heard, however, and laughed.

"Meg, my sweeting, you can make your home with us if you choose, with our right goodwill. You've won all our hearts. Has she not, Mother?"

"Indeed," said Lady Thomasine.

Mattie, however, shook her head at them, much as she had done at me in the courtyard, and said: "Flattery is bad for children."

"Oh, come. Who's the worse for a little praise?" Mortimer nibbled the last vestige of meat off a chicken bone and then sucked the bone to make sure. "Meg won't have her head turned so easily, will you, Meg?"

Meg looked bashfully down at her platter. I put my arm around her and gave her an understanding hug. Mortimer caught my eye. "In time to come," he remarked, "Vetch Castle may well be a center for good society and noble company. If Meg were living here, she would in due course have an unrivaled chance to make a splendid marriage."

He said it in a manner so extremely matter-of-fact that I almost missed it. Then I saw the alarm in Lady Thomasine's face and understood. This was what she had meant. He was referring to his grandiose future plans, and his tone was one of absolute, calm certainty.

"Well," I said tactfully. "We'll see." Meg looked up anxiously into my face and I breathed: "Don't worry," into her ear, before taking a little more chicken and beginning to talk about our journey. It was too soon to embark on any searching questions.

"The guest rooms are here," said Lady Thomasine, leading the way into the curious keep with the timbered house on top. Mattie, who was already well acquainted with the guest rooms, was with us but our hostess was clearly determined to show us our quarters herself. "As you can see, my family built on to the old medieval keep—the last line of defense in more warlike days. It was disused for years and became ruinous in its upper portions. My husband had them removed and we kept the basement and ground floor for storage, until he had the happy thought of building new rooms on top where guests could have some privacy. My husband," Lady Thomasine explained, "did not care about privacy for himself. He grew up in an old-fashioned home in Ireland and thought it just a modern English fad. 'But if our guests want it, we'll provide it,' he said to me. 'It's part of good hospitality, these days.'"

"I've noticed that you still keep up the old tradition of hall life," I remarked.

"Yes, indeed. Philip wishes it. He holds the same views as his father did, so we dine with the household, though I usually breakfast in my chamber, and the guards always eat separately. I see no need to share our mealtimes with soldiers. We scarcely need a castle guard these days, of course; there is no danger now of attack from Wales. But once again, it is a tradition here. Our men even patrol the walls at night. Memories are long on the Marches. Pugh's first name is Harold—after King Harold who died at Hastings and before he was a king was Earl of Hereford. On the river Dore, to the west of here, there's a place called Ewyas Harold. At least, I think it was named after the prior who founded a monastery there, but he must have been called after King Harold. However, as I was going to explain, in the keep—we still call it that—you can live much as you would at home. There are two servants' bedchambers here on the ground floor—Mattie tells me that your Brockleys are a married couple, so they can share one of them. And in here"—she opened a door to show me—"there is a small kitchen. The main kitchens are only yards away and will send in anything you want so that you can eat in private whenever you like, but if you also wish your servants to cook special dishes for you, they can.

"And up here"—she picked up her skirts and skimmed up a flight of wide, shallow stairs, as nimble as a girl on her prettily slippered feet—"are the bedchambers and parlor which my husband added. I hope you will like them."

The rooms were in excellent order—the furniture waxed, the beds curtained in velvet, the floors strewn with sweet herbs, and the walls adorned with pleasing tapestries. I expressed admiration and Lady Thomasine, pleased, said that she would leave us.

"Two of our own servants are seconded to the keep when we have guests," she said. "Mattie will introduce you. They're a couple like the Brockleys and they sleep in the other servants' room. They're English—Jack and Susanna Raghorn—so you won't have them whispering to each other in Welsh. In the morning, though . . ." She paused and looked at me, with anxiety in her eyes. "In the morning, will you break your fast with me in my chamber? I will send someone at eight of the clock, if that pleases you, to bring you to me. Then we can talk."

When she had gone, I kissed Meg, told Bridget to see her into bed, promised to come soon to say good-night, bade Dale find the Raghorns and see if we could all have some mulled wine to help us sleep, and asked Rob to excuse me, as I wanted to talk to Mattie alone. Then I led Mattie into my bedchamber and shut the door after us.

"How could you?" I said. "How could you?"

Mattie sat down slowly on the edge of my bed. She did not waste time in asking me what I meant. Her round face still had that unfamiliar expression of seriousness.

"Ursula, my dear, what choice had we? We were under Cecil's orders. Meg has enjoyed it all; the journey and the stay in a castle."

"You talk as if Cecil were God."

"He is in Elizabeth's service," said Mattie.

"Elizabeth isn't God, either."

"No. She's the queen of England," said Mattie.

"I know," I said, collapsing onto a settle. "I *know*. I understand that. But all the same . . . I thought Meg had been stolen away. I was terrified. And you knew I would be, and so did Rob, and the queen, and Cecil. They gambled on it."

"Ursula, there was no help for it. I did my best to see that Meg was happy and safe. I insisted on coming with her for that very reason. And now," said Mattie, "I'm going to urge something else on you. I know that you haven't seen Meg for so long that you're parched for her company . . ."

"Yes, I am."

"But you're hoping to take her back to France, are you not?"

"Yes. You have cared for her wonderfully well and she has been happy with you, but she wants to be with me and I want that too. Will you mind very much?"

"Rob and I will both mind but we have been prepared for it for a long time. But listen. If she goes with you to France, you can look forward to spending any amount of time together. Will it matter all that much if she isn't here for the two weeks or so that you've agreed to spend in Vetch?"

"Not here? But she *is* here."

"Quite. But I don't think she ought to be," said Mattie. "I don't think this castle is a good place for her. You would do better to say that you wish me to buy her new clothes for her journey to France, and send her off with Rob and myself while you continue with your visit. Say that we are going to London. We wouldn't really, of course. We wouldn't want to leave you here without support. We might go back to the Woodwards' in Tewkesbury, and wait there for you. You could get word to us in a day if you needed us. I've already made opportunity to speak to Rob, and he agrees."

"But . . . what do you mean? What is it that's wrong here? You'd better tell me, Mattie. It might have a bearing on the mystery I've come to solve."

"I don't think so. And it's difficult to discuss. You'll see for yourself presently. Let me put it this way. Our home at Thamesbank is very orderly, as you know. There's no laxness among our servants. I may sometimes giggle like a girl," said Mattie, "but I know right from wrong and how to run a household. If I were running this one, there would be some drastic changes. Sooner or later, Meg will have to learn about the world but as yet she's too young. Now that you've come . . ."

"Now that the donkey has caught up with the carrot, yes. Mattie, what on earth are you talking about?"

"I'm simply saying," Mattie informed me, "that I want to take Meg away from here as soon as I possibly can."

5

Lady Thomasine

At eight o'clock next morning, a handsome and well-dressed youth, with smoothly combed dark hair, presented himself at the guest lodgings and inquired for me.

"Lady Thomasine asked me to show you the way to her room, Mistress Blanchard." His bow was most courtly. "The castle is confusing until you know it. You are breaking your fast with her this morning, I believe."

"Yes, that's so." I had dressed in readiness, complete with a fresh ruff and a farthingale, and had been waiting for a servant to collect me. This young man, though, did not give the impression of being a servant. His full brown eyes were too direct, his voice too frank, and his clothes too good. He wasn't Welsh, either, and most of the castle servants were, except for the Raghorns, whom I had now met (and didn't much like, as they were dour, middle-aged, and far from clean).

In the days when Wales was a likely source of attack, I wondered if the border castellans had had to forbid the Welsh language in their castles. How undignified it would be to learn, too late, that the serving men you thought were just gossiping in their own speech were blandly discussing, in your presence and in your hearing, how best to take your fortress.

"And your name is . . . ?" I said to the young man as we set off across the courtyard.

"I'm Rafe Northcote, Sir Philip's ward. Until next year, when

I shall be twenty-one, that is. My father and Sir Philip were good friends. Father died a couple of years ago and left me a manor in Shropshire, but he took the view that a young man should not have to shoulder full responsibility for an estate until he had turned twenty-one. He himself inherited at nineteen, and found it difficult. For myself," Rafe confided, "I wish things were otherwise. I am not even allowed to live there until I take over though I know Rowans is being well administered by its present steward. Sir Philip takes me there often and we look into everything."

"I didn't see you yesterday," I observed.

"No. I was out moving sheep."

"Ah, sheep. The wealth of the Marches?"

"Well, so they are," said Rafe. "And I need to learn to manage them. Yesterday, I was helping to shift the Vetch flock to higher ground in case we had more rain."

"Tewkesbury was full of sheep when we came through it," I said, interested. "They were being moved off the river meadows in case the Severn flooded."

Rafe glanced up at the sky. The sun was out, but wisps of cloud were blowing from the west. "It well may. It often does. There's more rain on the way, the shepherds say."

"Tell me about the castle," I said. "Where are Lady Thomasine's rooms—where we're going now?"

"All the family's bedchambers are in the Mortimer Tower." He pointed to where the battlements of the tower in the northeast corner of the courtyard were just visible above the red-brick building. "The servants mostly live in the northwest tower behind the kitchen, and the retainers—I mean the guard—in the gatehouse tower."

"What about that one?" Pausing, I pointed back toward the tower in the southwest corner, which he hadn't mentioned. It was the only one that didn't have another building in front of it, but it had an oddly deserted air and its door was solidly shut, with no key in its stout iron lock.

"Oh, that." Rafe was amused. He gave me a sidelong grin, which undid the impression of courtliness and made him look mischievous. "That's the haunted tower. Every castle worth its salt has a haunted tower, you know."

Hampton Court was said to be haunted, in particular by the shade of King Henry's fifth wife, Kate Howard, who was arrested there before she was taken to the tower and then beheaded at Henry's orders. Elizabeth didn't stay there often but occasionally she did and once, when I was still serving as one of her ladies, I had found myself alone, at dusk, in the gallery where Kate's screams were still said to echo. I had heard nothing, seen nothing, but I had been uneasy, as though I were being watched from the shadows. I was not as inclined as Rafe to laugh at such things.

"What kind of ghost is it?" I asked.

"There are two. They're supposed to be the phantoms of a medieval castellan's lady and the minstrel she fell in love with. The husband caught them, and he shut them in the tower and left them to die for lack of food and drink. Not a pleasant end. Imagine it," said Rafe, and to my surprise gave me another sidelong glance, as if to see if my efforts at imagining it would produce some tenderhearted feminine vapors.

"Nasty," I said coolly.

"It's said," Rafe informed me, "that sometimes you can see their faces at the window and that if you go inside, even in daylight, you may hear them moaning, or hear the sound of the minstrel's harp. The place is disused now but Sir Philip has it swept out once or twice a year and the servants who do the sweeping go in all together and look over their shoulders all the time. I went in last time it was cleaned and nothing happened, but I admit," said Rafe more seriously, "that I wouldn't care to spend a night there."

"Has anyone, ever?"

"Not that I know of. It's kept locked most of the time. It's virtually empty, except for a few bits of furniture that no one wants. If you will come this way . . ."

It was a polite reminder that Lady Thomasine was waiting. The way to her apparently led through the modern red-brick house. "This is called the Aragon Wing, or sometimes just Aragon," Rafe said. "Lady Thomasine's father, Sir Thomas Vetch, had it built. He liked modern building styles—not like the Mortimers. They prefer things to be ancient and hallowed. Lady Thomasine says that Aragon was completed on the very day when King Henry married his first wife, Katherine of Aragon. A great party was held in the wing, as a housewarming and to celebrate the royal marriage, both at once. Careful as we go in; the entrance is rather dark and there's a step."

Courteously, he offered me a hand, and steered me over the threshold with a firm grip. We passed through a shadowy little entrance lobby and then through an inner door into a pleasant parlor with windows overlooking the courtyard on one side, and the tiltyard on the other. A staircase at one side led to the floor above and an ornamental clock, with a pale blue enamel surround rimmed in turn by gilt sun-flames, hung on one wall. The wall tapestries and the cushions on the settles were all in shades of blue.

"The blue parlor, for obvious reasons," Rafe said, leading the way through to where the parlor abruptly narrowed, because a corner had been walled off to make another room. "That's Sir Philip's study. It looks out onto the courtyard, so that he can keep an eye on the life of the castle. The stairs lead up to a music room. I enjoy music. I sometimes play my lute for Lady Thomasine."

"I hope I shall hear you play during my stay," I said civilly.

Beyond the blue parlor was another room of similar size but more masculine, with a bigger hearth and a lot of antlers on the wall. Still trying to map the castle in my head, I worked out that the door to the left must lead into the great hall. But Rafe, explaining that this was called the tower parlor, because it was at the foot of the Mortimer Tower, made for a spiral stone staircase in one corner. "This leads up into Mortimer. The steps are narrow, but there's a handrail."

He offered me his hand again but I declined it. The wedge-shaped steps were not unduly steep. After two flights, we came to a door on which he tapped. Lady Thomasine called to us to enter.

"I've brought Mistress Blanchard," said Rafe, opening the door and then flattening himself against it to let me go in first. I had to turn sideways to get my farthingale past him and as I did so, I had momentarily to press against him. It occurred to me, uncomfortably, that he had placed himself against the door for that very purpose. I could still feel in my right palm the pressure of his thumb when he took my hand at the door of Aragon. I caught his eye with a reproving frown, and was answered by an amused and knowing glint. Drawing my stomach muscles in, I eased myself and my farthingale safely by and turned my back on him.

"Here I am, Lady Thomasine. Good morning."

"Good morning, Mistress Blanchard." Lady Thomasine was sitting at a toilet table, examining her face in an antique silver hand mirror while her pale-faced maid put finishing touches to her mistress's hair.

"Very well, Nan. That will do." Lady Thomasine held up the mirror, sighed, and regretfully fingered the very faint lines at the corners of her eyes. "If only I could pull these out, or dye them, as I do with gray hairs. Thank you for bringing Mistress Blanchard across, Rafe. I'll see you later. Nan, go and tell Olwen to bring breakfast." Rising, she moved over to a window seat. "Come and sit beside me, Mistress Blanchard. We have much to talk about."

I would have liked it to include Rafe's behavior but after all, what could I say? That he had given me a challenging look when talking about the haunted tower, had held my hand too closely as he helped me over a step, and that it had been difficult to squeeze past him in a doorway? I pushed Rafe out of my thoughts, and joined my hostess on the window seat.

The window, which looked down toward the courtyard, was no dismal arrow slit, but was large and handsome with diamond-leaded panes and decorative mullions. No doubt it had been put in by the up-to-date Sir Thomas Vetch. It shed rather too much light on Lady Thomasine, though. She was beautifully dressed, in a loose gown of oyster damask, with a fresh pair of slippers, high-heeled and very pretty, of tawny velvet embroidered with roses in gleaming cerise silk. But although her skin had been powdered, I could see a cobweb of lines not hitherto visible, and the amethyst and agate rings on her fingers could not quite conceal her thickening knuckles.

She wasted no time on small talk. "You know why I have asked you here," she said. "Cecil has sent you to help me, has he not?"

"Yes, Lady Thomasine." I studied her gravely, and then put into words the problem that had been worrying me since I first agreed to undertake this inquiry. "But I must say I am puzzled as to how I can help. I believe you are anxious to learn what is going on in your son's mind but if you, his mother, are not in his confidence, how may I hope to do better? I have said I will try, and I will, but all the same . . ."

"How much did Cecil tell you, Mistress Blanchard?"

"He told me that Sir Philip wishes to get back the property and honors which belonged to his Mortimer ancestors, or at least their equivalents, and that he seems to think he can persuade the queen to give them to him. Do I have it right?"

She nodded. "Yes. Quite right. And yesterday, at supper, you heard my son hinting at these plans of his. Did you understand?"

"When he talked of Vetch Castle becoming a center for good society and noble company?"

"Exactly. You heard the way he said it, too. With such *assurance*. Do you wonder that I am worried? I can't get him to tell me how he means to go about it. But Luke Blanchard told me that you have some skill at learning secrets."

I wished my former father-in-law had kept quiet. "I've uncovered secrets in the past," I said frankly, "but I wouldn't boast of my skill. As I said, I will try, but . . ." I hesitated. "There is a question I think I should ask. I hope it will not offend you. But I believe that Sir Philip was once at court and was obliged to leave for some reason. I would like to know . . ."

"What that reason was? I understand why you are asking, but I can only tell you that it has nothing to do with this. He fought in a duel and the other man was killed. Those were the days of Queen Mary. She did not approve of such things. Philip would never explain fully what the duel was about though both his father and I tried to get it out of him, but he did say once that it was to do with a woman. He said it was a commonplace affair that he wanted to forget. He never mentioned the lady's name. In the end, we ceased to press him. It hardly concerns this present matter, anyway."

She might or might not be telling the truth, but I could see no way of discovering more, at least not for the moment. I considered. "I suppose," I said, "that I could begin by talking to him in case I can get him to let out anything of interest. That would be the simplest approach. Does he—forgive me—does he drink much wine?"

"Not to excess." Lady Thomasine accepted the question as

sensible. "All the same," she said thoughtfully, "when he makes the remarks which alarm me so much, it usually is after he has drunk a little. He was taking wine at supper last night. He still didn't let out any details, but—yes, why not? Try persuading him to drink more than is good for him at dinner today and then ask a few artless questions. He likes to impress guests and with a charming young woman, perhaps he may be more forthcoming than he is with me. I spoke with Master Henderson last night and he tells me that you are willing to stay for two weeks. If this scheme fails, there is time to try others."

"I'll make every effort," I said. "Lady Thomasine, have you no idea *at all* what form these plans of his take?"

"No, my dear, I haven't." Lady Thomasine paused, as someone bumped against the door to the stairs. "Come in. Is that Olwen?" she called. The door opened to admit a sturdy, pretty girl, slightly breathless and disheveled with the effort of carrying a heavy tray up the spiral steps. Her brown, curly hair was tumbling out of her cap and her face was flushed.

"Your breakfast, my lady."

"Thank you, Olwen. Bring that table over here and leave the tray on it. And do tidy your hair. These girls!" said Lady Thomasine, as Olwen set our breakfast down, bobbed a curtsy, and withdrew. "One must watch them all the time. One of the others has a baby at nurse in the village although there's no sign of a husband and Olwen will be in no better case, one of these days."

"Indeed?" I said, wondering if this was what Mattie had meant by her mysterious hints. But why, if so, hadn't she said so straight out, and why should she take it so seriously? Flighty maidservants were hardly a rarity. But perhaps Olwen had been particularly blatant and set what Mattie thought was a bad example to Meg. At any rate, I had agreed to send Meg out of the castle, and I would keep to that.

"Lady Thomasine," I said, as we began to partake of the excellent breakfast, "I'm not entirely happy about having my little daughter here while I am . . . well, looking into things. But I do intend to take her back to France with me and I want her to have some new clothes before she travels. While I am here, Mistress Henderson has offered to take her to London and get the new gowns and so forth. You would not think me discourteous if I sent Meg off with her?"

"Oh, my dear, of course not. I hope you have found your daughter well, though? I think she has enjoyed her stay here. But it might indeed be better if you had no distraction during your two weeks. In fact, you are likely to be somewhat distracted as it is. It is most unfortunate, but—did Sir William Cecil tell you I had a daughter?"

"Yes, I believe he did. What is her name?"

"Bess. She's married and lives on a manor some miles away. It doesn't compare with Vetch," said Lady Thomasine, faintly disdainful, "but St. Catherine's Well is a respectable estate, up on the west side of the Malverns—it's a few miles north of a landmark you may have heard of, called Herefordshire Beacon . . ."

I shook my head. I knew nothing of the local geography. Lady Thomasine said: "Well, the Beacon is high and exposed, of course, you can see it for miles; but the fields of St. Catherine's are lower and more sheltered—it's quite good land. Bess and her husband are to visit us in a day or two. Philip has been helping to arrange a match for their daughter and the betrothal will be celebrated here. The castle will be very busy. I hope you won't find . . ."

There was a rush of feet on the spiral stairs. Then the door crashed unceremoniously open and there was Mattie on the threshold with Dale at her shoulder, both of them wide-eyed with alarm.

"Lady Thomasine . . . !"

"Oh, ma'am!"

"What is it?" I shot to my feet, too startled to let Lady Thomasine speak first. "Is Meg . . . ?"

"Meg is quite all right. It's Brockley!" said Mattie breathlessly. "Rob's gone off hawking with Sir Philip so they can't help, and Brockley's got himself mixed up in something to do with a witch."

6

Champion for a Witch

I was bewildered but Lady Thomasine was quite unsurprised and also undisturbed. "A witch? Oh, Gladys Morgan, I suppose. You saw her in the hall yesterday, Mistress Blanchard, tending one of our lambs. She took it home with her last night. Ah well. Trouble's been brewing there this long time."

"Well, the trouble's arrived, and Roger Brockley's in the middle of it. He's Mistress Blanchard's manservant. He's down in the village now. Lady Thomasine . . ." said Mattie appealingly.

"My dear Mattie," said Lady Thomasine, not moving from the window seat but on the contrary, continuing with her breakfast, "we rarely interfere with the villagers. They are all either half-Welsh or all-Welsh and they have their own ways of running their affairs. The village elders keep order and they do it very well. Whatever is happening, they will deal with it themselves."

"But . . ." I began.

Lady Thomasine glanced at me. "I myself never intrude. If Philip were here, I would send him, but since he isn't—well, if this man is your servant, Mistress Blanchard, you had better fetch him into the castle immediately and tell him to mind his own business in future."

"Do I need to take any men with me?" I was already at the door.

"Of course not. You are my guest and will be respected. They will know who you are. The village always knows everything. You are in no danger. Show Mistress Blanchard the way, Mattie. You know the shortcut through the stable yard gate that my father had made for bringing in fodder?"

"Quickly!" pleaded Dale.

I could scarcely believe that Lady Thomasine meant me to deal with this on my own, but she seemed to think the matter merely trivial. Dale, however, was frantic, and fairly hustled me down the tower stairs. "But what's *happened*?" I demanded.

"Roger and I just came out to walk, that's all. We went out of the gatehouse and walked round the castle," Dale gasped, as we rushed through a door at the foot of the tower and into the stable yard. "We found a village and . . . they were going to stone her! They were calling her a witch . . ."

"Over here," said Mattie urgently, tugging me across the stable yard to a small door in the outer wall. I went with her, groaning aloud. I had once told Matthew that Brockley had been a good son to his mother. What I hadn't told him was that Brockley's mother had been accused of witchcraft, and he had only just succeeded in saving her from the gallows. Since then, I had seen him rush to help another aged woman in danger of the same accusation. The combination of old age and a charge of witchcraft was guaranteed to have Brockley, figuratively speaking, leaping astride a white horse and galloping to the rescue like Sir Galahad, and with about as much regard for personal danger.

The door let us out onto a path above a steep hillside. Down below was a squat church tower and a cluster of thatched roofs, which had to be the village. A rapid scramble down a zigzag path brought us to it. Led by Dale, we ran past some outlying cottages, until we heard the sound of raised voices and then, suddenly, found ourselves at the back of a crowd. We stopped, gasping. I stood on tiptoe to see over the shoulders of the people in front of me, and saw Brockley.

There he was, my gallant manservant, arms folded, confronting the throng, which gave off hostility as green firewood gives off smoke. They were of every age and both sexes, the women with either tall black hats or shawls on their heads, most of the men bareheaded, but all united in calling abuse, in a mixture of English and Welsh. A pile of stones was nearby and many of the crowd had stones in their hands. Behind Brockley, backed against the wall of a cottage, was Gladys.

She was certainly not an attractive old woman. She had on the same grubby gown and shawl that she had been wearing yesterday, and in daylight, her gray trailing hair and fanglike teeth looked even more horrible than they had in the shadowed hall. From behind Brockley, she was glaring at the crowd and screeching ruderies back at them. But there was a red splash of blood on her forehead and she clutched her shawl across her skinny chest as though to protect herself. "Come on!" I said, and we started to shove our way to the front. As we came near enough to see her clearly, I saw that, for all her defiance, she was trembling.

Pity instantly stabbed through me. I was willing to believe in ghosts, but Gerald and Brockley between them had taught me not to believe in witches. The crowd probably thought they were attacking one of hell's minions. I saw only a woman made ugly by age, injured and afraid. So did Mattie. "Poor old thing," she muttered.

A man at the front of the crowd had stepped into my path. "You will be Mistress Blanchard?" he said. He had the Welsh intonation but his English was easy. "Your woman"—his eyes went briefly to Dale—"said she would fetch you. I am Hugh Cooper, freeholder, and senior man in this hamlet. The man is in your service, I think. He is interfering in our business. I have held the villagers back from harming him until you—or someone—came from the castle but now that you are here, will you do us the kindness to remove him?"

"What's he done?" I asked.

"I told you, mistress. He's pushing into matters that are no concern of his."

His authoritative voice was loud enough for Brockley to hear. "It's the concern of any decent person who chances to be passing!" he shouted. "This poor old soul here has been accused of putting the evil eye on someone's child. These splendid people had pulled her from her cottage and they were going to stone her to death."

"Not to death, not unless she's fool enough to defy us. We were going to drive her from the village," said Cooper calmly. "Which is more merciful, indeed, than English law would allow. In England, they would burn her for doing murder by witchcraft. We merely wish to be rid of her. At the moment," he added, jerking his head toward Brockley, "we also wish to be rid of *him*. So, once again, mistress, I ask you to take your man away."

I looked helplessly at my retainer. Roger Brockley was a down-to-earth kind of man, neither handsome nor homely, and today he was dressed as usual in workmanlike brown fustian. But his stocky, compact build was full of strength and his impassive face with its high forehead was full of dignity. Standing there, defending Gladys, he was not only behaving like one of King Arthur's knights, he even somehow looked like one. I knew quite well that I had no power to take him away; he wouldn't budge no matter how I ordered him, and I admired him for it.

But I wished with all my heart that Lady Thomasine, or Sir Philip, or someone with real authority at Vetch were with me, because since I couldn't control Brockley, I would have to try to control the villagers instead. "What exactly is the woman's crime?" I inquired. "Her name is Gladys Morgan, isn't it?"

Quite a number of people tried to tell me what Gladys had done, all at the same time. Cooper made damping-down gestures at them and the babble faded. He turned to me.

"Yes, this is Gladys. She's been trouble for a long while, selling love philters to silly wenches and making believe to tell fortunes but this time she's gone too far. She laid a curse on a child of nine years old, the son of David and Pen Howell. Come forward, David and Pen."

A couple stepped out of the crowd. They were about my age, but with the worn faces of people who have had hard lives. The woman had a baby in the crook of one arm. They looked at me with dislike. "After Gladys cursed the boy," said Cooper, "he fell sick. They begged her to reverse the curse but she would not. Last week, he died."

"And he deserved it!" Gladys screeched from behind Brockley. "Little bugger threw stones at me, called me an ugly old hag. So I put a curse on him. How'd you like it, Pen Howell—bein' called names because you're old and you've lost your looks? If you live long enough, maybe it'll happen to you! You've got a long nose and a stickin'-out chin already. Make a good nutcracker face, yours will, one day!"

Somewhere in the crowd was an unmistakable snigger.

It is annoying to find that you have taken an instinctive dislike to someone you fully realize you should pity. I knew I ought to sympathize with the bereaved and weary Howells but their sharp, hard eyes and straight, hard mouths sent my sympathy veering straight toward Gladys.

"Our son's dead," Pen snapped. "Dead of a fever that no one can explain. What else is that but witchcraft? Answer me that!"

"But people are always dying of fevers," I protested.

"Quite right, they are," Brockley declared. "Young and old. It happens. It's the will of God. If this woman Gladys had the power to curse, why doesn't she curse *you* and be done with it?" He jabbed a finger at the Howells. "Seeing what you've brought on her today, why doesn't she bring you out in a rash or turn you into toads? In her place I'd do it this minute!"

"Yes, I would!" shouted Gladys.

"But you both look healthy enough to me," Brockley said relentlessly.

"True enough. My husband says there are no such things as witches," Mattie declared, backing us up, head high and plump hands clasped at her waist; the lady of the manor reproving ill-behaved servants.

"I've just lost a child," I said to Pen. "My son was born dead and I nearly died myself. But it was misfortune, not witchcraft. My first husband died of smallpox, before he was thirty. That wasn't witchcraft, either."

"That's as may be, but this *was*!" Pen shouted at me. "She cursed him. She cursed him! I heard her!"

"Your bloody brat stoned me for being ugly. I'm glad he's dead!" shrieked Gladys, hardly helping her own cause.

"And we're going to stone you out of Vetch Village!" shouted David Howell, and with that, he picked up a stone from the nearest pile and threw it.

A shower of other stones followed. Brockley ducked, putting

up his hands to protect his head. Dale screamed and threw herself in front of him, and without stopping to think, Mattie and I ran to join her. "Stop this, or you'll have Lady Thomasine and Sir Philip to deal with!" Mattie shouted.

The stones stopped momentarily, but then someone called out something in Welsh. The name of Lady Thomasine was embedded in it somewhere and I thought I heard the word Mortimer as well.

"What are they saying?" Mattie demanded of Gladys.

"That Sir Philip and Lady Thomasine won't care for the likes of me," said Gladys sullenly, and after a suspicious pause, as though she had belatedly decided on discretion. What had really been said had been more disparaging than that. I wondered what it was. Then another stone came through the air and I lost interest in the matter. I ducked just in time, and a frighteningly big stone followed, barely missing Mattie. "Master Cooper!" I screamed. "Do something!"

"Then take yourselves off, all of you!" Cooper retorted. He made more damping-down gestures, however, and those who were lifting stones ready to throw paused in the act. "Leave Gladys to us. Or else take her with you; we won't object. We want her gone. Take her to the castle if you want, but don't let her come back."

I moved to Gladys's side and caught her arm. It was so thin that my fingers went right around it.

"All right," I said. "Come on."

"I got a lamb to rear," said Gladys exasperatingly.

"Master Cooper," Brockley barked, "a lamb belonging to the castle was in Gladys's care. See that someone attends to it."

"There you are, Gladys," I said. "Now come along."

After all, it was as easy as that. Well, almost. There was an element in the crowd which still wanted to hunt Gladys into the wilderness on all fours in front of a hail of stones, but Cooper held them back, while we all edged past them in a tight group with Gladys in the middle and hurried her back past the outlying cottages, making for the zigzag path. It was steep for her and she complained that her knees hurt, but we pushed and pulled her up it somehow.

In fact, the most difficult part of the rescue came when we arrived back in the stable yard, to be at once accosted by a crowd of Vetch servants and retainers, including the girl Olwen and led by the red-faced Evans, who announced that they'd heard what was afoot because Dale and Mattie had let it out when they rushed back to the castle and started asking where I was. "And we don't want that Gladys here and Lady Thomasine won't have her here either. She's sent her away once already."

"Well, let's ask her," I said. To my relief, Lady Thomasine herself had just appeared from the door to the Mortimer Tower and was crossing the courtyard toward us. "Here she is."

"Now what's all this to-do?" Lady Thomasine had exchanged her elegant slippers for clogs, but walked awkwardly in them. "You've brought Gladys in? But why?"

"The villagers were about to stone her from the village for being a witch," I said shortly. "But I don't believe in witches. Nor does Brockley here."

"No, Lady Thomasine. I don't. And I won't stand to see an old soul stoned and mistreated." Brockley spoke up strongly.

"I intend to find somewhere for Gladys to go," I said. "Perhaps she could go with Mattie—if you'll take her with you when you leave, Mattie?"

Mattie had supported me loyally so far and she shared my skepticism about witchcraft but she didn't look overjoyed about this suggestion. At this point, however, Gladys joined in. "I got kinsfolk in the Black Mountains. They'll take me in, once I get there. Came from there as a girl, I did; and don't I wish now I'd stayed and not fallen for Morgan's bright eyes, God rest his soul. There's been nothing right with me since he went, and there were lads would have wedded me if I'd stayed in Wales where I belong."

"There you are," said Mattie, with relief. "Rob will surely lend you a man to take you on his pillion, Gladys. Maybe Lady Thomasine will provide a guide."

I looked Lady Thomasine in the eyes. "While I am your guest, I would rather be a help to you than a hindrance. I mean to do my best in every way. But if you could help us over the matter of the guide, we would be so very grateful."

She took the point. "A guide into Wales I can certainly provide. Most of my men know the Black Mountains. I wish Gladys to leave by tomorrow, at latest."

"I'll not trespass in your household for long, my lady; never fear," said Gladys acidly. "Nor put a curse on you. Or your lamb. They'll have handed it to my neighbor. Someone 'ud better go and make sure she's treatin' it right. And what about my things? Clothes I got, and an old ornament or two that Morgan gave me when I weren't ugly and brats didn't jeer at me."

"Gladys, be quiet," I said, although I was beginning to admire her. Old, powerless, and hated, she still had the guts to stand up for herself.

"We'll look after her and send for her things," Mattie said to Lady Thomasine, who shrugged gracefully and said that as long as she herself need have nothing to do with Gladys, we could see to her as we chose.

Mattie took charge of our rescued witch. Once she was out of hearing, I had a few sharp words for Brockley, about involving himself in local affairs without proper knowledge of them, but he merely replied: "With respect, madam, in the same circumstances I'd do the same again, and what's more, I think you'd be ashamed of me if I didn't." Which was true.

He went off to the stable, saying that our horses needed attention, and I returned to the guest rooms with Dale. Mattie was there, supervising while her own maid, Joan, attended to Gladys's cut forehead. I let them get on with it and asked Dale to make me a chamomile draft. My temples ached but I couldn't possibly have a sick headache just now.

A few moments ago, face-to-face with Lady Thomasine, I had, obliquely, hinted that if she would not cooperate over Gladys, I might not cooperate over Sir Philip. But she had agreed to help and now I must do my part. Rob and Mortimer had ridden back into the stable yard just as I was leaving it. They would be at dinner. It was my duty, and I knew it, to be there too; to be full of sprightliness and flowing conversation, and to get Sir Philip Mortimer drunk.

7

Overdoing the Canary

Supper the previous evening had been quite ordinary but I now discovered that the Mortimers liked to dine in state, although their notions of state were somewhat odd. It was as though Sir Philip desired to live splendidly but had an imperfect grasp of how to go about it.

I was no stranger to ritual, heaven knows. Mealtimes were ceremonious at Blanchepierre, and at Elizabeth's court I had attended many an official banquet. But these occasions had never been other than dignified. At Vetch, alas . . .

To begin with, the hall at Vetch was depressing; too shadowy and subject to stealthy drafts which made the aged tapestries stir disconcertingly, as though shaken by unseen hands. It was pervaded, too, by a doggy smell from the sheepdogs, greyhounds, and mastiff, which once again were dozing by the fire.

Rob, Mattie, Meg, and myself were, however, ceremoniously led by the butler Pugh to our places at the top table, which was draped in white damask and set with silver. We were required to remain standing while Mortimer and his mother, both of them dressed as if to receive royalty, came in to seat themselves in high-backed chairs. Then the food was borne into the hall by a dozen servants in procession, singing in Welsh and preceded by an elderly and gray-bearded harper dressed in an archaic tabard of pale green, with a vetch plant, purple flowers, and darker green leaves, embroidered on it.

Rafe, arriving late, after the food was on the table, apologized gracefully to his guardian and then hurried to kneel beside Lady Thomasine and apologize a second time, not so much gracefully, as abjectly. He might have turned up late for her coronation instead of merely for a meal.

"Think nothing of it," she said, but laid her hand on his head as forgivingly as though he really were being excused for a serious offense. For a moment they stayed motionless, Lady Thomasine gazing kindly down on Rafe, and his profile outlined against her plum-hued gown.

In profile he was a little less handsome than he was full face, for his nose was too sharp and his chin just too long for perfection, but he and Lady Thomasine made a charming tableau and I wondered if the pose was deliberately meant to echo the figures in the threadbare tapestry just behind Lady Thomasine. It showed a woman resting her hand on the horn of a unicorn, as if bestowing a regal blessing. Except that the woman in the tapestry was much younger than Lady Thomasine, and the horn of a unicorn, I knew, was a symbol which was hardly appropriate in this case.

When Gerald and I were in Antwerp and Gerald was employed by the financier Sir Thomas Gresham, we had often dined in Gresham's splendid house and there I had seen some fine tapestries featuring unicorns. Gerald, gleefully, had explained the symbolism to me. I hoped that both Lady Thomasine and Rafe were unaware of it.

The mastiff chose that moment to get up from its place in front of the hearth, jump onto the dais, sit down on the other side of Lady Thomasine and gaze at her, dribbling hopefully in expectation of tidbits. Beside me, Mattie let out a little snort of amusement, and I repressed a chuckle Meanwhile, Lady Thomasine, ignoring the dog, withdrew her hand from Rafe's hair. He rose and took his own seat. Mortimer smiled at his mother, apparently finding nothing strange or laughable in the little playlet with Rafe, and began to recite a lengthy grace.

At the end of it, as we sat down and the servants crowded around us, offering dishes and pouring wine, Evans strode into the hall. I had the impression that he had been waiting just out of sight until Mortimer had said *amen*. Once more, he was dressed in green, but this time it was clean. He had a hooded falcon on one arm, and from the other hand dangled a brace of hares. He came up the hall, onto the dais, and around the table to Lady Thomasine, where he went down on one knee and gravely presented the hares to her, as a gift from her loyal falconer.

"Is that what he is?" I whispered to Mattie. "The falconer?" That explained the streaks of bird droppings.

"Simon Evans? Yes, he's the head falconer. Mortimer has three of them," Mattie whispered back.

"I have asked," said Evans, in booming tones that could be heard all over the hall and were meant to be, "that these shall be served to my lady tomorrow, cooked in wine."

Thanking him, Lady Thomasine formed another tableau by resting her hand, this time, on the falconer's rough dark head. Once more, Mattie emitted a small, disrespectful gurgle. After posing for a count of about three, Evans stood up, bowed, and withdrew, taking his hares with him. The mastiff leaped down from the dais and went with him and the other dogs also got up and followed him out. I heard him in the courtyard, shouting at someone to for God's sake feed these animals, before they stole his catch. On the dais, the serving of food and wine resumed. Our goblets were filled and our silver platters loaded. Pugh made it his personal task to look after Lady Thomasine. In my ear, Mattie whispered: "I think she thinks she's Eleanor of Aquitaine."

"Who?" I whispered back.

"Eleanor of Aquitaine. You know. Henry II's queen. She invented courtly love. Noble ladies had pretend lovers who swooned over them and sang songs and wrote poems to their beautiful eyes and their hard hearts and presented them with dead hares as well, I expect."

I dredged my memory for more recollections of the history lessons I had shared with my cousins. I could dimly recall hearing about Eleanor of Aquitaine, although not about courtly love. Our tutor had probably regarded that as either too frivolous for his pupils or else improper. But it was obvious enough what Mattie meant. In this castle, which was run like an imitation palace,

Lady Thomasine was queen of an inner court and her son took it all as normal.

Conversation had begun, and was promisingly political. Mortimer had started to talk about Mary Stuart of Scotland and the current speculation over her marriage plans. An English noblewoman called Lady Lennox, who was descended from a sister of Henry VIII and was, thus, a cousin to both Mary and Elizabeth (Elizabeth detested her), was reportedly interested in promoting her son, Henry Darnley, as a bridegroom for Mary. It would be a powerful alliance in the eyes of those who considered Elizabeth to be illegitimate and, therefore, not entitled to the throne.

"The sooner our good queen is married and with a son, the better," Sir Philip remarked. "A secure succession would steady people's minds. She must herself be aware of that." Rob observed that the future peace and happiness of England depended on Elizabeth's choosing the right husband and over that, she would have to exercise care. Lady Thomasine said that everyone hoped the queen wouldn't marry Robin Dudley, her Master of Horse, but that it looked less likely now, since the rumors had been circulating for years and nothing had come of it.

"I believe it has even been said that last year she offered his hand to Mary Stuart of Scotland," she added.

I agreed that this rumor had reached me in France, but evidently nothing had come of that, either. I agreed too that it had probably never been seriously meant and was no doubt nothing but a political ploy, perhaps to distract Mary Stuart from thoughts of Henry Darnley. I sipped my wine but found it uncomfortably strong. There was water on the table as well and I would do best, I thought, to drink that instead. Such strong wine might well have the desired effect on Philip, though, if only I could get him to overindulge in it.

I then discovered what I ought to have realized before, which is that a host at his own table is in control of it and drinks or doesn't drink whatever he pleases. You can't very well say such things as: "Do try this wine, Sir Philip. It's a great favorite of ours. It comes from such and such a vineyard in such and such a province of France," because it's his wine in the first place and he presumably knows where it comes from and what it tastes like. You can admire the wine and hope that he will take extra to keep you company; you can perhaps push a flagon invitingly toward him; but that's as far as you can go.

I did my best but Mortimer drank very little. In fact, he remarked as the meal progressed that he would have estate business to deal with later on and needed a clear head.

"Two of my tenants are behind with their rent and I've summoned them to explain why. They'd best be convincing," he added with an ominous grin, "or I'll have them hung in chains, in the middle of the courtyard." He actually leaned forward to point through the window at the courtyard. "So no more wine, thank you, mistress." He set aside the flagon of canary which I had edged encouragingly within his reach.

Well, if I couldn't get him fuddled, I could still carry out his mother's suggestion about asking artless questions. "You sound," I said, "as though you almost wish you really could hang them in chains for not paying the rent. A little drastic, surely? Do you really want such power?"

The answer was illuminating. "There was a time," said Sir Philip, "when the Mortimer family truly had power to that extent. I am a justice of the peace now, of course. It goes with the lordship of Vetch Castle. But the Mortimers once were much much more." Twisting in his seat, he pointed to a coat of arms on the wall nearby. It showed the vetch plant, proper, as on the servers' tabards, its reddish-purple flowers and rounded green leaves, on a field vert.

"Those are the arms of the Vetch family. The Mortimers had a coat of arms too although my branch has never claimed it. But I intend to do so before long. One of my forebears—Roger Mortimer, his name was—was the lover of Edward II's queen and for a while he was king in all but name." He let out a nostalgic sigh. "In those times," he said, "the Mortimers were mighty Marcher barons and had the power of life and death over their serfs. Those were our great days. I have read of the deeds and the eminence of my forebears and sometimes I think that as a Mortimer, it should be my duty and pleasure to rebuild the greatness of our family. I long so to do and I believe that one day I shall."

I saw my chance. "But how?"

He gave me a challenging glance from those oddly set greenish-blue eyes. "Ah. Well, that remains to be seen." He smiled knowingly. "But one day, you will see."

Here it was again, the theme that had come up at yesterday's supper, although once more he had stopped short of detail. I felt extremely disturbed and I knew that Rob, Mattie, and Lady Thomasine all felt the same. I could feel their unease. I would have pressed on in the hope that even sober, he might be coaxed into indiscretion, but Rob and Mattie were so very disconcerted that they inadvertently spoiled my plans by beginning at once to talk of something else. Lady Thomasine then turned to Rafe, and asked if he would play his lute for us after dinner. The conversation dissolved into commonplaces and escaped from me.

But I was quite certain now that Lady Thomasine's worries were not misplaced. Beneath the surface of this pretentious household, beneath the outdated rituals and the absurdity, was a serious and alarming undercurrent. I wondered if Philip Mortimer were quite normal. At the very least, I thought, he was living in a world of daydreams in which he had begun to believe.

One way and another, that dinner was an odd, uncomfortable business. The culminating discomfort came at the end, when Rafe duly played and sang for us and managed to embarrass me yet again, more publicly than when he had shown me over to Lady Thomasine's room.

"Rafe must sing us something he has written himself," Lady Thomasine said. "My son is no musician," she added regretfully. "Are you, Philip? But Rafe has the gift, and we have had him well taught by Gareth, our musician." The gray-bearded harper, who was now seated just below the dais, bowed at the sound of his name. "Gareth shall play for us tomorrow," said Lady Thomasine. "But now, Rafe, if you please . . . ?"

Rafe obliged without any modest disclaimers and proved to be skilled. He sang a ballad about a noble knight who ventured into a dark cave full of sharp rocks and patches of mud, and there found a splendid sword with a scabbard of gold and a jeweled hilt, which shone through the darkness and the dirt.

> The ruby shone amidst the mire
> With pure and undiminished fire;
> The gold all damascened remained
> Amid the murk, unharmed, unstained . . .

Which was all quite harmless and charming, but that was before he reached the last verse, where, unfortunately, there was a risqué twist that likened the sword to a woman whose charms were improved after nightfall.

"Whose shining eyes, whose pearly limbs," sang Rafe, "are beauty darkness never dims, but all the more enchant, invite, when encircled by the night . . ." And as he sang, he smiled boldly at his audience, and winked naughtily at me. I turned pink and saw Sir Philip eyeing me thoughtfully. Silently, I cursed Rafe. This was a complication I could do without.

For the moment, I tried to seem oblivious. Indeed, just then a new idea came to me. When at last the song was over and we had all applauded suitably and Mortimer had announced that he must be off to terrify his defaulting tenants, I cleared my throat and issued an invitation.

"Sir Philip! One moment. You are offering us such good hospitality. Please let us return it in a small way. Our guest rooms have a kitchen. If we may ask for what we need from your own stores, will you sup with us tonight? Become a guest, as it were, within your own walls? We should be so happy if you—and you too, Lady Thomasine—would honor us. I am sure we can prepare something to your taste."

I managed to catch Lady Thomasine's eye as I spoke. "How kind," she said. "We should like that very much. Should we not, Philip?"

Mortimer himself looked slightly bemused but with me gazing at him pleadingly and his mother watching him expectantly, he could do little but reply: "I shall of course be delighted. At what hour?"

* * *

"You understand?" I said, as I stood with my friends in the parlor at the keep. "After we've supped, you must all withdraw. Meg is to be in bed before our guests arrive. Bridget, you will stay with her."

"And we'll take ourselves off, yawning, when we've finished eating," Mattie said. "We can say that after all, we're rising early tomorrow, to set out for Tewkesbury—to London as far as Lady Thomasine and Sir Philip are concerned."

"I don't like going, but you may be right to want Meg away from here," Rob said. "I can't make a display of the fact that you're being guarded but I'll leave a man—Geoffrey Barker—at Ledbury, with a fast horse at his disposal. If you need me, send to him. He'll be at the Sign of the Feathers."

"Thank you. I wish you were staying, but after all, Lady Thomasine invited me here. I am under her protection, if such a thing should be needed," I said. I turned to Brockley and Dale. "After supper, you must keep out of sight as well. I want to talk to Sir Philip alone. I have had a word aside with Lady Thomasine and she understands that too. By the way, where's Gladys?"

"Downstairs, with Joan," said Mattie. "I sent Joan to fetch Gladys's belongings and she brought them but her two spare gowns were so disgustingly dirty that we've thrown them on the midden. Joan is altering a couple of her old kirtles to fit Gladys. She's to be off first thing in the morning too. One of our men is going with her, and one of Mortimer's Welsh retainers, who knows the way to her home in the mountains."

"Good," I said. "Now, what are we to serve for supper?"

"Madam," said Brockley.

"Yes, Brockley?"

"I shall be within earshot. On duty, as it were. I too think that it is right to send your little daughter away from here. There are things in this castle that I don't care for."

"What sort of things, Brockley?"

"As Fran and I were going out for our walk this morning, madam, we saw something we haven't mentioned to you yet. Well, maybe you'd better tell it, Fran. With your leave, madam, I'll go and ask Pugh for a good wine for this evening."

He left the room. "Dale?" I said.

"Well, ma'am," said Dale, flushing slightly, "what we saw was

Sir Philip, ma'am, down by the big kitchen. He was dressed to go hawking, but he didn't have falcons on his mind just then. He was with that girl Olwen, that waits on Lady Thomasine. He'd backed her up against the wall and well—you can guess."

"Guests shouldn't speak slightingly of their hosts," said Mattie. "But do you begin to see what I was hinting at, Ursula?"

"I'd already gathered that Olwen was flighty," I said. "Lady Thomasine said as much. These things do happen. Mattie, if it was only a matter of a servant girl and the master of the house, I think you would have said so. Is there something more? Why *do* you keep hinting instead of saying outright what you mean?"

"There is more," Mattie said. "But I'm not sure of some things. I only guess at them. Rob thinks I may be wrong." Mattie glanced at her husband, who nodded. "You do jump to conclusions sometimes, my love," he said.

"Perhaps. Well, Ursula will come to her own conclusions. But I'm very glad you've agreed that we should take Meg away," said Mattie. "And I agree with Brockley. Be careful, Ursula."

I had never thought of myself as seductive, and indeed, seducing Mortimer wasn't at all what I had in mind. But I did need, as it were, to soften him. As though, I said to myself, he were a piece of clay. I gave serious thought to the preparations for supper.

There was a sideboard in the guest parlor, which I had already discovered contained silver-plated cups and dishes and some rather handsome wineglasses. The parlor candlesticks were only pewter, but there were plenty of fresh candles, and I had also found a well-stocked linen cupboard.

Under my supervision, the dour Susanna (a puddingy woman with eyes like black raisins, who wheezed ostentatiously when asked for the slightest exertion) made the table fine with polished glass and silver and clean white napery and candles, lit in readiness. After some anxious consideration, I put on a gown of tawny velvet over a kirtle and undersleeves of cream satin, with a fresh ruff, and Dale tidied my hair into a white cap with cream embroidery. It was a pleasing ensemble but not too striking. It said *courteous hostess* but not *come hither*.

I chose simple supper food; here too I had to find the fine line between offering too much or not enough. Sir Philip's second cook, when asked for advice, entered into the spirit of the thing. He was a plump and cheery young redhead, who was apparently called just Higg. We learned that, like Susanna and Jack, he was English but in other respects he was a delightful contrast to the Raghorns, whom neither Matthew nor I would ever have let over the Blanchepierre threshold.

At Higg's suggestion, I settled for fricasseed chicken, rolls, a salad of radishes, primroses, and borage flowers, and a sweet cheese flan. He brought the food to the guest kitchen, and prepared it there. The all-important wine, supplied by Pugh, was the same strong canary that had been served at dinner.

I could think of nothing more that I could do, but I wondered if my efforts would work. I was trying hard, but was this the right approach? Did it have any chance of succeeding? And if it didn't, then what would? What could I try next? I was barren of ideas.

I was also very nervous.

"I know that we are really drinking your own canary, Sir Philip," I said, in my sweetest voice. "But this evening you are my guest—so let me pretend that the wine is mine. I think it an excellent vintage and I hope you are enjoying it. Let me refill your glass."

"You are an admirable hostess," said Mortimer. I filled his glass, leaving mine as it was, nearly empty. I had drunk sparingly during supper, but I could feel the effects nonetheless, and I had to make sure that my own head survived the evening.

Mortimer raised his brimming glass to me before he drank. "If you had not a husband already," he said, "I might be offering my heart and hand to you myself. Though it is true that I would be foolish to consider marriage until I have rebuilt my family fortunes. I would wish, when I wed, to offer my bride a choice of fine houses to enjoy—better than this ancient castle. I have a dream of one day entertaining the queen. Tell me, Mistress Blanchard, you have been at court. What does the queen require in the way of hospitality when she visits her subjects?"

So far, so good. Sir Philip and I were alone together. His mother, having shared the supper, had taken her leave, saying that she was tired. My own people had withdrawn too. Now, as Sir Philip and I sat over the last of the supper dishes, the subject of his future hopes had come up of its own accord. If only I could play my fish with sufficient skill.

"I don't believe," I said, "that the queen would think the house of any loving subject unfit for her. She would enter the humblest cottage without hesitation."

"A tactful answer, mistress." He took a long drink of his wine and then picked up the flagon, and to my annoyance, topped up both our glasses. I sipped at mine with caution.

"I was serious," he said. "To be a Mortimer, truly a Mortimer, one must be informed of many things. What are the queen's tastes? What kind of food does she eat? Would a host need to provide scented candles for her bedchamber?"

"The queen has a most sensitive nose," I said. "She dislikes strong smells of any kind. She likes her candles unscented. Sir Philip . . ."

"Yes, Mistress Blanchard? I agree," he added gravely, "that this wine is of a most superior vintage. From which merchant did you buy it?"

"He keeps a cellar in a place called Vetch Castle, on the Welsh border," I said, equally grave. "Do you know it? Sir Philip, there's something I don't understand."

"Indeed? And what might that be? Mistress Blanchard, it is a pleasure to sit opposite you and look into your fair face, which is worth any man's study, but it would be pleasanter still if you came round here and shared my settle with me. Come. Then tell me what it is you don't understand."

"It will mean turning my head to look at you, Sir Philip. It's easier to talk across the table." I said it mildly, but as a frown began to appear between his eyebrows, I made haste to soften the refusal by giving him the most delightful smile I could conjure up.

It was a mistake. I had taken care to dress with propriety but I was quite old enough to know that a lovely smile can outweigh sackcloth and ashes; never mind tawny velvet and cream satin. Mortimer put down his wineglass, leaned across the table, and seized one of my hands in both of his "You know how to lead a man on, by God you do. You're a lovely thing, Mistress Blanchard."

I thought wryly that since the castle had a tiltyard, it was a fair assumption that Sir Philip liked tilting and anyone who made a habit of controlling a charger with one hand while leveling a lance in the other acquired a powerful clutch. Mortimer had a handclasp like steel ivy.

I hadn't really expected this. After all, I was a guest and a lady of standing, and as Mortimer himself had observed, I was married. He amused himself with maidservants but I hadn't thought he would get dangerously amorous with me. Slightly flirtatious and very very fuddled—that was the effect I wanted. I didn't quite seem to be achieving it. Unwisely, I used my spare hand to pick up my glass and provide myself with a heartening draft of canary. My head began to swim alarmingly, almost at once. I dragged my scattered thoughts together and tried to keep to the point.

"Sir Philip," I said, "you often speak of restoring your family fortunes. But how *do* you intend to do it? Isn't it a rather daunting task?"

"Maybe it is and maybe it isn't." Releasing my hand, he turned sideways on his settle, presenting his profile to me, and gave me a gleaming sidelong glance. And then fell irritatingly silent.

I persisted. "You seem so sure of yourself, Sir Philip. And that's what I don't understand. I think you have a secret!" I tried not to stumble over my words and attempted to sound sweetly roguish, but realized to my annoyance that I had overdone it. The wine had got me after all. I was more fuddled than he was. "You're hiding something from me." I started to wag an arch finger but stopped myself hastily. "Do tell me how you intend to achieve your ambition. Have you found a hidden treasure?"

My host-cum-guest put a knowing forefinger alongside his nose, and grinned at me. "Ah," said Sir Philip Mortimer slyly. "Now, wouldn't you like to know that, my pretty one? And why would you want to know? I've heard that you could get your marriage set aside if you wished. Would you like to be chatelaine of the Mortimer castles yourself?"

It would have been rude to tell him that I wouldn't want to be chatelaine of any castle at all if I had to marry him to do it, and that

Vetch Castle in particular was drafty and out-of-date. I began on a modest assurance that I would never think of such a thing but I never got to the end of the sentence. With startling suddenness, he reached once more across the table, shoving our two glasses aside so that they slopped, and this time seized both my hands. He pulled me toward him, changed his grip to clasp the back of my head, turned me so that he could get at my mouth, and planted his own over it.

I had a horrible vision of Gerald watching this scene, and then an even more horrible one of Matthew bursting in on it. With my upper half stretched awkwardly across the table and my reeling head being almost dragged off, it was difficult to put up an effective resistance. Since my mouth was stopped up, I couldn't even ask him to desist, let alone shout for help. I strove to get my left ear out of the remains of the sweet cheese flan and clutched at the edge of the table, trying to anchor myself against being pulled any farther. My fingers touched a heavy silver platter. I caught it up and walloped it down on the top of Mortimer's head.

He jerked his mouth away from mine but it was no respite. "You bitch! What are you doing? You lead me on and then you . . . I'll show you!" said Mortimer savagely, and getting to his feet, he hauled me roughly around the table, right into his arms. I still had hold of the dish but it was useless at such close quarters. I tried to use my knee but he was ready for that and avoided it, shoving me down on my back on the settle.

"Don't!" I gasped. "Please, Sir Philip, don't do this. I didn't intend . . ."

"Didn't you? Well, I do!" His intentions were all too obvious and most alarming. I then tried to sink my teeth in his wrist, but he grabbed my unoccupied hand and smashed the knuckles against the table so viciously that I let go. Still struggling, I saw beyond Sir Philip's shoulder that the door was opening. Brockley's head came around it. His expression at once became scandalized. Mortimer's mouth was down on mine again. Desperately, I signaled for help with my eyes but to my bewilderment, Brockley merely disappeared again.

Mortimer was too strong, and I was too drunk. The worst was going to happen. Now what do I do? I asked myself wildly. I tried, and failed, to free my mouth in order to scream (where in hell's name had Brockley got to?). Should I give in, in the cause of duty, in the hope that a sated Sir Philip might yet yield up his secret? No, absolutely not. Even if I hadn't been a wife, I wouldn't want to give in to this. I didn't want Mortimer and didn't intend to let him force himself on me. He lifted his mouth at last, presumably in order to breathe, and I drew a lungful of air, ready to shriek for aid. Then I realized that someone else was ahead of me. Somewhere, close at hand, a child was screaming for her mother.

"That's Meg! Let go! Let me up!"

"Oh, in God's name! What a time for a child to have a nightmare!"

"Get off me! Get off, I say!" Meg needed me, and with her need came instant sobriety and a strength which surprised me much as it did Mortimer. I heaved and kicked with such violence that he toppled off me. Hurling myself off the settle, I rushed out and was in Meg's room in moments. And there was Meg, sitting up in bed and screaming at the top of her lungs, while Bridget, Brockley, Dale, and the Hendersons all stood around smiling with approval. She stopped as soon as she saw me, jumped out of bed and ran to me, laughing.

"Did I do it well? Did I, Mother? Mr. Brockley said you needed help and this was how to do it. He said Sir Philip was drunk and being rude."

"Shhh. Pretend to be crying," I whispered, and held her close as Mortimer lurched into the doorway behind me.

"Oh, the poor child, sir!" cried Bridget, wiping her eyes with her apron. "She has bad dreams sometimes and cries for her mother's arms. When her mother's been away, I've had such times with her. This time she says she dreamed of a face looking out from that haunted tower. That Susanna told us today that the southwest tower is haunted. I said she should be ashamed, repeating such a tale to a child, and now see what's come of it."

Bridget was nearly illiterate, not always clean, and decidedly overweight, but she was no fool. This superb flight of imagination proved it. I had always known that Meg could have no better nurse.

"Sir Philip," I said, savagely polite, as I cradled my daughter and surreptitiously massaged the knuckles my affectionate supper guest had bruised against the table, "I must cut our evening short, I fear. I think I must stay with Meg."

His face was thunderous but he knew he must accept defeat and as he had not seen Brockley look around the door, he also assumed I was shielding him. "Quite," he said. "Quite." To my relief, he turned away and we heard him stumping off down the stairs.

"I've heard the story of the haunted tower," I said. "They're supposed to be the ghosts of a lady and a minstrel. Did Susanna really tell Meg about them?"

"Yes, ma'am, she did. And that girl Olwen, that's no better than she ought to be, she came in for a gossip and she joined in and she and Susanna both swore that they'd heard a ghostly harp played in the tower once or twice and Susanna said she once saw a face looking out. Then when Lady Thomasine came to say good-night to Meg this evening after supper, before she went away, Meg asked her if it was true that there were ghosts in the southwest tower, and she said there were."

"I wasn't frightened," said Meg proudly, drawing herself out of my arms. "Susanna said the ghosts sometimes come out of the tower. She said the harp's been heard in other places in the castle, always when something terrible is going to happen. But Lady Thomasine said I wasn't to be afraid because the ghosts wouldn't hurt me, even if I did hear them, or see anything."

"Of course they wouldn't, my love. None of us would let ghosts or anything else do you any harm." Bridget picked her up and lifted her back into her bed.

I looked at Brockley. "Thank you. It was an inspiration, getting Meg to scream. I wondered why you'd disappeared."

"I hoped it would give you a chance to get away without me interfering directly and giving extra offense," said Brockley. "I'd have interfered if I'd had to."

"I take it," said Rob, "that the scheme failed."

"And you put yourself in peril, Ursula," Mattie said reprovingly. "I did try to warn you, you know."

"I had to try something. I'm afraid it did fail, yes. I'll have to think of a new ploy now."

"Please, madam, try not to take such risks again," said Brockley in a harassed voice. "The things you do!"

8

Haggard Falcons

I had started my inquiries by making a complete mess of them. I did not know what to do next. The following morning, though, the first thing I had to do, as soon as breakfast was over, was to say good-bye to Meg as she set off with the Hendersons, ostensibly for London, in reality for Tewkesbury.

Gladys left as well, perched behind one of Rob's men, and accompanied by a Welshman who would guide them to the Black Mountains and bring Rob's man back so that he could go on to rejoin his master. Some of the servants turned out to stare and mutter at Gladys. One or two of them made the sign against the evil eye, and from her pillion saddle, Gladys sneered back, but the presence of the Hendersons made sure that there was nothing really unseemly.

Meg and I both cried at parting, even though it was for only two weeks. Whether I succeeded or failed in my task, I had no intention of staying longer. Once the fortnight was over, she and I would be off to France together and I was as impatient for that day as though I were a child myself. I wanted to be with her *now*. I wanted to hear everything that had happened during our two years apart; I wanted to read poetry with her, to play music and sing songs with her; to dance and embroider with her and talk to her, talk to her, making up for all the time we had lost. Two weeks felt like eternity.

I watched her go, and then went up to the top of one of the

watchtowers on the outer walls. From there, looking over the battlements, I saw Gladys and her escort part from the others and turn west, and watched the rest of them, with Meg sitting very upright on her little pony, dwindle slowly out of sight on the eastward road.

When I returned to the guest quarters, I called Dale and Brockley to me and said briskly: "I've agreed to stay here for a fortnight but I want to cut it short and there's only one way to do it and that's to make a quick job of finding out what Sir Philip is up to."

Brockley's answer was unexpected. "Madam, I was shocked when you told us how Sir William Cecil had used your daughter to fetch you to England. But there is one thing. Before we left France, you were very low in spirits. You seem very different now."

"I've seen Meg and soon I'll be with her all the time. Can you wonder?"

Brockley smiled, rather grimly. "Madam, we know you so well. No doubt seeing Meg again has helped. But I don't think that's the whole story, by any means. Is it, Fran?"

I glared at them. "What are you talking about?"

Not in the least impressed by my frowning brows, Dale sighed audibly, and Brockley shook his head at me. "You're going hunting again. That's what's made the difference."

I told him not to talk nonsense, but secretly, and to my dismay, I realized that there was much in what he said. From that moment in Rob Henderson's study, when I involuntarily asked whether it was true that nothing was known of the scandal which had made Philip Mortimer leave the court ten years before, something had woken in me which had been asleep too long. From that moment on, my depression had begun to lift. Rob Henderson had sensed it too. I would enjoy myself when I got to Vetch, he had told me. It worried me. It was a poor augury for the future and besides, I didn't want it to be true. I didn't want to be a huntress. It was merely something that had been forced on me.

"Never mind all that," I said. "I have to think of a new ploy. I must talk to Lady Thomasine again."

When I once more went out into the courtyard I found it full of bustle. Servants were hurrying about with bedding and fuel, buckets and mops and armfuls of fresh rushes. I made my way through the confusion and in by way of Aragon and the blue parlor. A fire had been lit there, and mattresses and linen were spread in front of it. I met the girl Olwen and asked her if Lady Thomasine were in her chamber. "Yes, ma'am," she said, and I hastened on to the Mortimer Tower.

The sound of a lute drifted down the spiral staircase to meet me. I found Lady Thomasine, her tawny and cerise slippers poking out from under an elaborate brocade skirt, elegantly disposed in her window seat while Rafe Northcote played a romantic ballad for her. I curtsied to my hostess but waited in the doorway while he finished the melody. He bowed to us both, and I patted my palms together in applause.

"You really do play well, Rafe," I said politely.

"My own Mark Smeaton," Lady Thomasine said with a smile. "I was always sorry for him, you know. Smeaton, I mean. You know who he was, Mistress Blanchard?"

"The musician who was one of the men executed for committing adultery with Anne Boleyn," I said. "My mother served Queen Anne for a time. She knew Smeaton. She said that he was a fine minstrel and a handsome fellow but that there was nothing wrong between him and the queen."

"And I'm sure that was true," said Lady Thomasine. "You can go, Rafe. I know you have other tasks. But I hope to hear that melody again later. It is charming."

She smiled after him as he bowed again, and I moved quickly forward into the room so that he wouldn't have to squeeze past me as he left. "A delightful young man," Lady Thomasine said, "and nearly as good a musician as Gareth. I shall miss him when he goes home to take up his inheritance."

"Does Gareth not mind it when Rafe sings after dinner?"

"Not he. Gareth's old and wants to go to sleep after he's eaten. He's already asking for a young minstrel to take over when Rafe leaves us. He taught Rafe, you know, and he's proud of him. Well, Mistress Blanchard? Have you any news?"

"Alas, no. After supper yesterday, I tried my best to get Sir Philip to talk freely but he wouldn't." I didn't enlarge on what he had done, or tried to do instead. "He hinted again at his plans to become wealthy," I said, "but he kept the details to himself. Lady Thomasine . . ."

"Yes? Speak as freely as you wish, Mistress Blanchard. I would be a fool to call you here to help me and then not be willing to listen to you. What is it?"

"Well, I was wondering—does he really have a scheme at all? Or is it all just—talk? An obsession—a fantasy."

"You think he may be ill in his mind?" Lady Thomasine was not offended. Her eyes were serious. "No. I think his scheme exists. He certainly intends to go to Cambridge at the same time as the queen. He has exchanged letters with his friends there and made arrangements to stay with them."

"I see. I wonder if they know anything?" I hoped my quest wasn't going to lead me to East Anglia. Lady Thomasine, however, was shaking her head.

"Philip doesn't know them all that well; they're acquaintances rather than close friends. I've met them, though, and they struck me as the stolid kind. I think they would laugh at any grandiose schemes and Philip doesn't like being laughed at. I doubt if he'd confide in them."

She passed a thin hand across her brow. "Let me think . . . if I can. Oh, dear. I called Rafe to play for me because I wished to be soothed. My daughter and her husband, William Haggard, and their girl Alice are arriving today, for Alice's betrothal. I mentioned that to you, didn't I? Philip arranged it while I was away at court, trying to find you. I do hope the presence of guests won't hamper you. If I had been here, I would have urged him to hold the affair at Alice's home. She is such a difficult girl. When they stayed with us at Christmas . . ." She broke off, apparently contemplating some unpleasant memory of Alice at Christmas. I wondered what the girl had done and waited with interest, hoping that Lady Thomasine would tell me, but she shrugged her slender shoulders and dismissed the matter.

"Oh well. Let that be. Philip has brokered the match and he wants to host the betrothal at Vetch. The bridegroom-to-be arrives tomorrow—Owen Lewis, his name is. He comes from Brecon, in South Wales. It's a good match. He's older than Alice, but in my opinion that is just what she needs. He owns a fair amount of land but he wants to acquire property in England and Alice's dowry includes a farm of some size in the Malverns. He is also paying Philip a commission for promoting the marriage; everyone will gain. But . . ." She passed a hand over her forehead once more. "You want to know how else you can approach this mystery. Well, all I can think of is that Philip just may have committed something to writing. When he makes plans, he makes notes. In that case, his study is the place to look." She clicked an irritated tongue. "And my daughter and her family will be sleeping in Aragon, just above the blue parlor and the study. Oh, what a nuisance."

"I thought the stairs in Aragon led up to a music room."

"They do, but there are some extra guest rooms, too." Her worried eyes sought mine. "Well, never mind. You had better search the study, and your best chance is at night, only you will have to take extra care, as now there will be people sleeping overhead. Aragon is locked at night but I can give you a key."

"But, Lady Thomasine, have you never looked in the study yourself?"

"Yes, of course. Several times. But my son keeps all documents that he regards as confidential locked in a strongbox and carries the key with him." She sighed. "I hoped I wouldn't have to ask you to open his strongbox. It isn't a nice thing to ask. I must say, I hoped you would be clever enough to find out what we want to know without that. That was why I didn't mention it yesterday. But according to Luke Blanchard, you know how to force locks. Is that true?"

I cursed inwardly. Luke Blanchard wasn't supposed to know about my lock picks but I knew of someone who could have told him, someone who had actually watched me use them. I had brought them with me, just in case. Searching other people's studies, however, and forcing the locks of their document cases was not my favorite occupation. I was always afraid of being caught.

I could also see that it was now the only logical move. "Let me have a key to Aragon," I said with resignation. "I'll search the study and tackle the strongbox. I may be able to open it, yes."

* * *

The Haggard family arrived in time for dinner. Lady Thomasine invited me to join Sir Philip and herself in the hall to greet them. When they were seen approaching, I made my way there with Dale.

We found that Rafe was there too, complete with lute, practicing a serenade of welcome. Dale withdrew tactfully to the background, sat down beside Lady Thomasine's maid Nan, who was stitching up the hem of a gown, and began to help her with it. Between us, we all created an air of cultured domesticity, a pleasing reception for the guests.

The guests themselves came as a shock.

Lady Thomasine was one of the most elegant women I had ever seen, to the point of vanity, and Sir Philip, however deplorable his manners in some respects, at least had a suave veneer. I had supposed that his sister and her husband would be similar.

But their arrival in the hall was heralded by masculine curses and placating female voices and when the door opened to admit the butler, Harold Pugh, he was pushed aside before he could announce the guests. The pushing was done by a thickset, sandy-haired man unremarkably dressed in brown, with a matching hat, which he could not remove as courtesy dictated, because his left arm was weighed down by an unhooded and angry goshawk, which was beating her wings furiously and plunging a ferocious set of talons into her master's beard. His spare hand was damaged already. He was shaking it about and drops of blood were flying in all directions from a jagged tear on his thumb.

"Damn this bird! Get your claws out of my beard! All right, Pugh; they all know who I am, anyhow. Good day to you, Lady Thomasine . . . Good to see you, Philip. I'd hoped for some sport on the way but I didn't bargain on being the quarry . . . bugger it, she'll have it out by the roots in a minute!"

". . . and Mistress Bess Haggard and their daughter Alice!" declared the butler stoutly, getting through his introduction anyway, and putting extra distance between himself and the goshawk's impressive wingspan, as two ladies and a patient-looking maid came warily through the door, keeping their distance, like Pugh, from the indignant hawk.

"Allow me," said Mortimer. He stepped forward, found the

hawk's hood stuck in her owner's belt, and put it over her head. The hawk became quiet and Sir Philip, removing her from his brother-in-law's arm, deposited her on the back of a settle and shouted for someone to fetch Evans from the mews and someone else to bring salves and hot water.

"She wanted to go after a puppy in the outer bailey," said Haggard. "I wouldn't let her. Typical female. Always wanting what they can't have."

"What the devil did you unhood her for?" demanded Sir Philip.

"There were rabbits about as we came up to the castle. I was hoping to bring you something for a stew. Make your curtsy, Alice."

Bess had already greeted her mother in a properly respectful fashion. Bess Haggard didn't look as though she would ever dare to want anything without first being granted permission by someone. She had a vague resemblance to her mother and brother but none of their elegance. She was simply dressed and she was as meek and faded a woman as I had ever seen.

The difficult daughter, who had misbehaved in some unspecified way last Christmas, was about sixteen. She was good-looking in a strong-boned way, and probably had character. She had a clear skin, with none of the spots which so often afflict girls of that age, and her brown hair was thick and glossy. She was better dressed than either of her parents, in a moss-green brocade, with a feathered green hat and gauntlets tasseled in green and gold. She sank gracefully into her curtsy before rising to kiss her grandmother and her uncle.

"Well, Uncle Philip, and my lady grandmother." She had a clear, carrying voice. "Here I am, all ready for Owen Lewis, dressed in fine clothes as a gift is put in pretty wrappings."

There was a tense silence. Over the head of the servant who had come running to attend to Master Haggard's thumb and the further bloodstained tear on the chin which the hawk had given him, I saw Haggard's prominent pale blue eyes harden in annoyance. Bess looked miserable. I supposed that Alice objected to the plans her elders had made for her. Very likely, she didn't want to marry an older man whom she hardly knew—perhaps didn't know at all. Was this, I wondered, what Lady Thomasine meant by misbehavior and being difficult? If so, I was inclined to be on Alice's side.

No one answered her. Lady Thomasine presented her to me, and Alice expressed well-mannered pleasure at meeting a new kinswoman. Face-to-face with her, I saw that she had greenish-blue eyes, oddly set, like Philip's and Thomasine's, and I saw too that they were full of unhappiness which her polite social smile did not touch. She had an aquiline profile, like that of the goshawk. A haggard falcon, I thought, making a private pun. It would not be easy, bending this wild bird to the will of others.

"Rafe here has a song prepared for you," said Sir Philip. "Got your lute ready, Rafe?"

Rafe came forward. He smiled at the new arrivals, strummed a few introductory notes and began his song—a simple, harmless greeting, expressing joy in their arrival and the hope that their stay would be happy. But while he was singing, I saw that this time he was not interested in me. He could scarcely take his eyes from Alice and she could scarcely take her eyes from him.

So that was it.

"Give over yawning, Dale," I said. "You had a rest after dinner and you can go to bed as soon as I've finished in the study. I don't intend to take long." I peered from the parlor window. "We'll go in a few minutes. The candles in those upstairs rooms have been out for half an hour. They should all be asleep by now."

"I feared they'd sit up late for a family quarrel," Brockley remarked. "There'll be trouble among them before long, mark my words. All through dinner, young Northcote and that girl never stopped ogling each other."

"I think they're trying to marry her off to a doddering old man because he's a landowner, and Sir Philip can have a cut off the joint," I said. "My sympathies are with Alice. Even Rafe might be an improvement on that."

"Even Rafe?" queried Brockley sharply.

"He's not a particularly pleasant young man," I said. "Never you mind how I know. In my opinion," I added, "the Mortimers and the Haggards don't add up to a particularly pleasant family."

I wished I didn't have to search Mortimer's office. At dinner, which had been festooned with what I now knew was the usual Vetch formality, I had nursed a faint hope that he might show off to his new guests and come out with some interesting revelations. Accordingly, I had said very little but listened earnestly to all the conversation. Unfortunately, it could hardly have been more mundane. Mortimer and Haggard talked hounds and horses solidly, while Lady Thomasine told Bess that she looked tired and lectured her on the art of fending off wrinkles. The technicalities of repairing a hawk's tail feathers and treating cracked hooves mingled with advice on tonics of red clover and nettles, face packs of olive oil and rice flour, and the use of crushed eggshells as a powder. Schemes for extracting land and wealth from Queen Elizabeth were not mentioned.

Supper was no better, although Mortimer did refer to the queen just once, when he broke off in the middle of a story about a peregrine falcon which had escaped from the mews and decimated the population of a neighbor's dovecot, to ask me if Elizabeth liked hawking. I rather think he did so because he had been distant with me all day, but had eventually realized that this looked pointed. Yesterday evening had no doubt embarrassed him. In jovial tones, he explained to the Haggards that I had been at court.

I told him that Her Majesty enjoyed both hunting and hawking, whenever her numerous duties of state allowed her the time and tried to give the impression that I was eager to go on talking about the queen. But Mortimer, instead of taking the bait, merely nodded and then, presumably deciding that the exchange of a few casual words with me was enough, turned to his mother and asked her if she could suggest an ointment to soothe Haggard's thumb where the goshawk had torn it. Haggard at once leaned across the table to display the jagged, weeping wound to Lady Thomasine and me. "Bess has tried her comfrey and elder flower ointment, but it's still shockingly sore."

Lady Thomasine and I suggested, between us, various alternatives. He kept on showing us his wretched thumb and it nearly put me off my food. Mortimer went on talking about hawks. I was glad when supper was finished and I could go back to my quarters and set about planning the night's excursion.

It was midnight when, reluctantly, and in a mood of let's get this over, I left the shelter of the guest rooms in the keep, accompanied by Dale and Brockley. As we stepped into the courtyard, Brockley whispered that it was quite like old times and I whispered back that I thought so too, and sincerely wished it wasn't. I looked up at the sky. There had been heavy rain earlier in the evening, but now the clouds were broken, giving glimpses of a waxing moon and patches of starry sky. I wondered if Matthew was looking out at the same moon and stars, and wished fiercely that I were free of this place and this task; that I could simply collect Meg and go home to Blanchepierre. I did *not* want to be a huntress.

The courtyard was silent and empty, but not wholly dark. I was carrying a candle-lantern, and the occasional moonlight helped. As we moved quietly across the cobbles, I was very much aware of the age of the castle; of the myriad lives which had been lived here and the violent acts which must have taken place within these walls. That was not a pleasant story, that tale of the lovers who had been shut in the southwest tower and left to perish of hunger and thirst. The castellan must have been a cruel man; it was little wonder that his wife had turned to someone who perhaps was kinder.

I wondered if at the end she and her minstrel had still loved each other, or if they had blamed each other for their misery; if love had turned to hate before they died. Involuntarily, I looked at the tower, and for one nerve-wrenching moment, as the moon came out from behind a cloud, I thought I saw a pale ghost face at one of the windows. Dale saw it too, and squeaked in fright. Then I glimpsed it again, against the sky at the corner of the tower and at the same moment heard a faint *tu-whoo*.

"Don't be silly, Dale. It's a barn owl. I expect they've got into the tower and I daresay that's the truth behind those stories of ghostly faces peering out."

"Even in daylight, ma'am? Olwen was telling me she once saw someone peering out at noonday."

"Barn owls sometimes hunt by day," Brockley whispered. "Keep your voices down. Have you got the key, madam?"

Lady Thomasine had supplied me with one, as I asked. I unlocked the outer door of Aragon, and we crept in. We left the door ajar and Brockley placed himself just inside it, ready to warn me if anyone approached from the courtyard. Dale and I tiptoed through the porch and into the blue parlor. The fire had died down but it still cast light enough for us to see our way to the door of the study.

This might be locked too, Lady Thomasine had said, but the key would be on the lintel over the door. I reached up and found it at once, but before using it, I gently pushed the door and it yielded. Putting the key back, I nodded to Dale, who moved to the stairs and positioned herself there to listen for any sound of movement in the rooms above.

Wary of making any accidental creak, very conscious of the people sleeping overhead, I inched the study door carefully open and stepped inside.

Then I stopped short. Sir Philip must have used his study earlier, for here too, a fire had been lit. The day had been chilly and he would have needed warmth. The glow of the embers and the lantern between them showed me the room quite clearly. There was a big desk with an inkpot and sander, both of brass; a tall candlestick to match; a small dagger with an ornate golden hilt, for opening sealed documents. There was another little knife for sharpening quills, and a supply of quills in a carved ivory holder.

The room also held a chair and a polished settle, and the wooden floor was strewn with rugs and not with rushes. There were shelves of books and boxes and the strongbox which I had come to inspect was on the floor by the window. I saw it at once. But there was no question of searching it tonight, for the study was occupied.

The firelight and the lantern revealed more than just the furniture. They also showed me the two people who lay fast asleep in each other's arms in front of the fire, on a pile of cushions borrowed perhaps from the settle.

Whether this was or was not the sleep that follows love, I couldn't tell. They were both fully dressed. They looked endearing, he with one arm cast protectively over his companion; she with her head resting trustfully in the hollow of his shoulder.

Rafe and Alice.

I edged out backward, closing the door with infinite care behind me.

I would have to try again tomorrow.

9

The Fearless Suitor

In contrast to dinner, breakfast at Vetch was positively haphazard. Food was set out in the hall for the household in general to take, but those who wished could breakfast in their own rooms. Lady Thomasine nearly always did. The morning after my failed attempt on Sir Philip's strongbox, the Brockleys and I breakfasted in the guest rooms and, over the food, we discussed the previous night's adventure.

"It's always like this," I said, dredging up exasperating memories. "Whenever I want to search a room, I find ridiculous obstacles in the way. A servant appears to light a fire, or someone decides to work in his study at three in the morning or comes in to fetch something, and I end up hiding in a cupboard." All these things had happened to me in the past. "Now it's a pair of lovers asleep right in my path. I feel sometimes that I'm being watched over by the opposite of a guardian angel."

"You've never been caught, madam," said Brockley blandly. "Perhaps your guardian angel was working harder than you thought."

I tried to look annoyed but found myself regarding him with affection—spruce in his brown working doublet and hose, his high forehead gleaming from the recent application of soap and water, his wiry hair, brown except for the silver at the temples, neatly combed. Breaking bread with his shapely horseman's hands, he was a thoroughly wholesome and reassuring sight. His face was as usual quite expressionless, but there was a smile in the depths of his blue-gray eyes.

"You'll manage it in the end, madam," he said, and his pleasant voice, with its slightly rustic accent, was calmly confident. "You always do."

"Thank you, Brockley. I hope you're right."

Dale said: "Ma'am, will Lady Thomasine not want to know how you got on? What will you tell her?"

"That I had to give up the attempt last night, because someone was moving about upstairs and I feared I might be discovered. I shall tell her I mean to try again tonight. I shan't mention Rafe or Alice. Their love affair is none of my business."

From where Dale was sitting, she could see out of the window and across the courtyard to the great hall. "Lady Thomasine is in the hall now, ma'am," she remarked. "She has just passed across a window."

"I'll go across, then. I've finished eating." I drank down the last of the ale in my beaker and stood up. "Let us hope," I said, "for better luck tonight."

"Best put a shawl over your head, ma'am," said Dale. "It's raining again."

The previous night, Brockley had prophesied a family quarrel among the Mortimers and the Haggards. The moment I set foot in the hall, I realized that the quarrel was in full and acrimonious flower. Lady Thomasine was certainly there, but so also were Sir Philip, the three Haggards, and Rafe Northcote, who stood side by side and hand in hand with Alice, at bay against a tapestried wall. Their elders seemed all to be shouting at them at once. I came a few steps into the hall, pulling off my damp shawl, and then halted. My report on the previous night's excursion was the last thing on Lady Thomasine's mind just now.

". . . such ingratitude!" William Haggard was purple with fury. "Nothing but a serpent's tooth. Your uncle and I have worked for you, given thought and time and effort to making the best possible plans for your future . . ."

"And for your happiness!" cried Bess, her eyes brimming.

"I have never been so offended." That was Sir Philip. "Owen Lewis is my friend—a very good friend. Ten years ago, at the court of Queen Mary, I was caught up in a scandal through no fault of my own, and obliged to leave the court and come home. Owen wouldn't let his father forbid him to visit me. He stood up to his father and stood by me. He will be here this very day, expecting to find a smiling bride-to-be and you choose this very morning to announce . . ."

"We could leave it no later, sir." Rafe's chin was up. "Alice cannot go through with the betrothal . . ."

"Alice will most certainly go through with the betrothal. A pretty return for Owen's loyalty if he comes here to find her trying to avoid it." If fury had turned Haggard purple, it had turned Sir Philip Mortimer white. "He will be here before noon and . . ."

"If only you had listened to us at Christmas!" wailed Alice.

"Listen to the babblings of a silly girl and boy who have exchanged a kiss under the mistletoe and think they've plighted their troth for life?" Lady Thomasine was shrill with indignation. Abruptly, she turned on Bess. "I believe you have taken great pains with your daughter's education, my girl, and had her instructed in Latin and Greek but she doesn't seem to have learned anything of importance. I have never approved of intellectual education for girls. It seems to addle their common sense."

"The queen studies Latin and Greek, or so I've heard." Bess, staggered by this attack, tried feebly to defend herself, and catching sight of me, turned to me for support. "Mistress Blanchard knows her. Mistress Blanchard, isn't it true that the queen loves her studies?"

"I daresay she does!" snapped Lady Thomasine, before I could frame an answer. "And look at her! Unmarried still at thirty. And here is Alice, with a head full of education and no sense of any kind, or filial obedience either. In love with Rafe? What nonsense!"

"It isn't nonsense! Rafe loves me. He's written a song for me!" Alice cried. "He has told me the words. It's about a beautiful sword that was found in a dark cave, and he likened me to the sword . . ."

"You silly girl. Rafe wrote that song more than a year ago and it is not a proper song to dedicate to a young girl in any case. If you were older and wiser, you would know that. Young men will be young men, but oh, Rafe, how could you mislead poor Alice so? Listen to me!" My hostess was exquisitely dressed and shod as usual but outrage had put new lines on her face. She looked as though she had been eating a plum and bitten a wasp. "There is no question of a marriage between you and Alice, no question whatsoever. You are my son's ward and cannot marry without his consent, which you most certainly will not get. How could you behave so deceitfully? After all we have done for you . . ."

"But why can't I marry Rafe?" Alice demanded. She moved nearer to him, holding his hand more tightly. "We love each other. Why is it wrong? He's suitable. He has an estate. He's told me all about it—there's a flock of a hundred sheep and deposits of copper . . ."

It was a pathetic plea, a sop to what she saw as adult obsessions, far removed from the all-engrossing matter of mutual desire. From the sound of it, she and Rafe had not been caught last night, but had whistled up this morning's storm themselves, by defiantly announcing their intentions.

"It's wrong because we have made other and better plans for you!" shouted Haggard. "Lewis is wealthy, far wealthier than this young puppy. You will have . . ."

"I don't want to marry an old man! Not even if he owns every single one of the Brecon hills!"

"Oh, Alice, how can you, how can you?" The tears were now pouring down Bess Haggard's face.

"You'll do as you're told, my girl, and one day you'll thank me," bellowed Haggard, and striding forward, he seized his daughter's arm and wrenched her forcibly away from Rafe. "If he's had you, God help him—and we'll get the truth out of her, don't you doubt it!" he added, rounding on Rafe. "You take heed, boy. You may not be my son or my ward, but you'd best get out of my sight before I knock you flat. How dare you trifle with my daughter?"

"You can knock him flat if you like, brother-in-law, but I'd rather do it myself. Oh, what is the point of all this talk? There's nothing to talk about. Rafe, get yourself to your chamber and stay there until I come." Mortimer's voice was grim.

"What about Alice?" I considered Rafe to be oversexed and

unreliable but to his credit he now displayed a decent anxiety for his beloved's welfare.

"Alice is none of your business. I am utterly ashamed of you. Your father," said Mortimer furiously, "was also my friend, as good a friend as Owen Lewis. It is a shocking thing, to see my two best friends betrayed at the same moment. I still miss John Northcote, as much as if he died yesterday and not two years ago. We met when I was sent as a boy to learn courtesy in your grandfather's household. I was eleven years old then, and John was sixteen, and I looked up to him."

For a moment, Mortimer seemed almost overcome by his memories. Then he said: "Your family has a tendency to weak lungs, as well you know. You are fortunate, for your chest seems sound, but your grandfather and your father both died young. Your father was married early, at your grandfather's wish, for the sake of ensuring an heir, and your mother, poor lass, was little more than a child herself, still only fifteen when you were born, and she died bearing you. Later, when your father became ill, he asked me to be your guardian if he died. He had no other living relatives except you yourself, and although I was only a friend and not a relation, he trusted me.

"He inherited Rowans," Mortimer said, "before he was twenty and he didn't find it easy. The first thing he had to deal with was a dishonest steward who was falsifying the proceeds from the wool sales, and pocketing the difference. I was fourteen then, but bright enough at figures to help John with his accounts, and I was the one who found the discrepancies in the records—and the places where the steward had altered them. He threw the man out and got someone more reliable and he was grateful to me for my help. By then, he was almost looking up to *me*.

"And so he chose me to watch over you, and in return for his trust, I have tried to do as much for you as he could have done. And how have you repaid me? I ask myself: what would John say if he could see you now?"

"I hope he would have been on my side," Rafe said bleakly. He looked vulnerable now. "He wouldn't have scorned me like this."

"I advise you," said Haggard, still gripping his daughter's

arm, "to do as your guardian has bidden you, and go before I beat you to jelly here and now."

"Quite right. I've said enough for the moment," Mortimer snapped. "Away to your chamber, Rafe, and wait for me there."

"No!" screamed Alice. "Don't hurt Rafe!"

"To your chamber!" thundered Sir Philip, and advanced on his ward with clenched fists.

"I'll go, I'll go. But don't hurt Alice! Please don't hurt Alice!"

"Leave Alice to us!" Haggard shouted.

"On the whole," said a quite new voice from the porch door, "it might be wiser to leave her to me. I may succeed better than any of you, if I have a fair chance."

We all spun around. The man in the doorway had been brought in by Pugh, but as so often at Vetch, the unfortunate butler hadn't been able to perform his office. The uproar must have drowned his first effort, and finally, the new arrival had got in ahead of him.

The newcomer removed a dashing blue velvet cap, darkened by rain but brightly adorned with a golden brooch, and made us all a most courteous bow. "I am Owen Lewis of Nant-y-gwyn in the Brecons. Nant-y-gwyn means the White Stream," he added to Alice, speaking directly to her as though they were alone together, and the scene into which he had walked had no existence. "There is a waterfall near my house, which pours down the hillside in a streak of white foam. But it's not the only cascade in my valley. There are four more. Beautiful, the place is, as you will one day see for yourself."

"Owen! You're here already! We expected you today, but you are so early!" said Mortimer in confusion.

"I could get no farther last night than Ewyas Harold, on the Dore, but I pressed on this morning, anxious to make my bride's acquaintance. My man is unsaddling my horse. Will someone be kind enough, perhaps, to welcome me in?" said Owen Lewis mildly. "It's raining and I'm wet, and your butler and I have been standing here unheeded for several minutes."

There was a moment in which we all gazed at him in silence. I was still close to the door and he was quite near me. I remember very well the powerful impression he made on me. It was so powerful that I stepped back, reminding myself that he had come to meet Alice; that I was merely a guest, and a married woman at that. In truth, if I had met him before I met Matthew, and if he had shown the slightest interest in me, I think Matthew would have been lost in his shadow.

Owen Lewis was by no means an old man. He was certainly older than Alice, but at most he was in his thirties. He was dark, which I suppose is my preference, for Gerald had been dark, and so was Matthew. Owen was shorter than Matthew and a little more heavily built than Gerald, and as he now removed his damp cloak and resigned it to Pugh, who looked relieved to have something useful to do, I saw that his costly blue doublet was cut to accentuate a broad chest and shoulders. His square, symmetrical features were not only strong but staggeringly handsome, and his deep-set dark eyes were vividly alive. His voice was deep and steady. But most impressive of all was his air of assurance. It emanated from him like a vigorous wind or the scent of the sea. We could all sense it.

The pause lasted for an appreciable time. Then Rafe, not looking at anyone, walked to the far door of the hall, which led to the tower parlor, and went out.

Alice was gazing at Lewis in silence. I looked at her and I actually saw it, the moment when her cosmos changed and the foundations of her world shifted under her feet. Then her father pushed her forward and because she had been well brought up, she automatically did the proper thing—which was to curtsy to Master Lewis. He lifted her to her feet and gave her a kiss, but a very restrained one, before handing her back, not to her father, but to her mother, apparently not noticing Bess's tearstained face.

Alice turned to her mother and hid her face against her. "Come," said Bess. "Your hair's coming down, my girl. You must have it put right and we must get you into prettier clothes." She led her daughter away.

"I am so sorry," Haggard burst into speech. "I suppose you heard most of that . . . what must you think? You . . ."

"There is no cause for concern," said Lewis calmly. "Your daughter, Master Haggard, has never seen me before and she is at an age when a personable lad can easily sway her heart. Give me a little time with her, and I hope to change her mind. We can delay the betrothal ceremony for a few days, can we not? It might be best not to force the pace." His smile was so attractive that my head swam. I actually took hold of a nearby table to steady myself. "I am not afraid of a callow youth," he said, and although the words sounded conceited, they were not. They were a simple statement of fact, born of a knowledge of personal worth.

He held out his hat, with the gold ornament in it. "I was in the doorway listening when I heard the wench say that that young man has an estate with copper on it. I have gold on mine. Not much—but this brooch is made of my gold, and I will give her a wedding ring of my own gold, as well. There's romance for her. Be kind to her, and a bit forgiving to the lad too—no need to make her too sorry for him—and let me do my own courting. Now, I have ridden a good few miles today already and I took little breakfast. I wonder if . . . ?"

Bemusedly, Sir Philip went to the door of the kitchen quarters and bellowed a demand for service and food. Lady Thomasine, turning at last in my direction, caught sight of me and raised inquiring eyebrows.

I moved to her and she drew me away to the corner of the hall, where I gave her my somewhat censored report of my unsuccessful foray the previous evening. A kind of normality had returned, if anything in this extraordinary household could ever be described as normal.

10

Dagger and Roses

It wasn't really normality. The whole day was strange.

Rafe did not reappear. Lady Thomasine went about her duties as a hostess but in a harried fashion, giving household orders in sepulchral tones, as though there had been a death in the family. Bess Haggard, having seen Alice arrayed in a fetching gown of orange tawny, with her hair folded glossily into a gold net, brought her back to the hall, where the men were talking horses and hawks. Alice came in with a wary face, but the moment she saw Lewis again, I saw the foundations of her world shake for the second time.

"I know," he said, holding out his hand to her. "You were expecting some wrinkled old horror of a Welsh savage. Believe me, some of us are civilized gentlemen and this particular gentleman is a fine capable fellow too. Come along with me now to the blue parlor. Lady Thomasine's had a fire lit there to brighten this wet old day and you and I can talk in comfort. And in private," he added in a voice guaranteed to warn off intruders.

With that, away he went, Alice tripping obediently and bemusedly at his side. Mortimer and Haggard, tacitly withdrawing from the situation, demanded their cloaks and went off to the mews to see how Haggard's ill-tempered goshawk was settling down. Feeling in need of a restful occupation, I went back to the keep and did embroidery with Dale.

At dinner, I saw that Sir Philip had changed into doublet and hose of black velvet, which looked fashionable but did nothing to offset the funereal atmosphere which still unaccountably surrounded Lady Thomasine. I say unaccountably, for Lewis's courtship seemed to be progressing rather well. He was sitting beside Alice and they were talking quite freely. Several times, he made her laugh. Rafe was still absent, and Bess asked Mortimer if he had told the boy to keep to his room..

"No. Owen himself asked me to forgive the lad and I have, therefore, told him that provided he behaves himself henceforth, I would say no more about all this. He has stayed away of his own free will."

"Ashamed to show his face, I suppose," said Bess. "Well, it's not surprising."

"No, indeed," said Mortimer in a heartfelt voice. "I still feel I must apologize to you, Owen. He has acted very wrongly."

"He is a good boy at heart," said Lady Thomasine sadly. "And he plays the lute so well. He is my devoted minstrel. I was telling Mistress Blanchard that sometimes I call him my Mark Smeaton."

Lewis broke off from wooing Alice to remark that Smeaton's fate had been discouraging and that he hoped Rafe would have a happier future. "I wish him no harm," he said. "I can hardly blame him for falling in love with Alice."

"I am not fickle," said Alice suddenly, in a high, nervous voice.

I saw Mortimer and her parents stiffen, but Owen just smiled at her. "There is no question of fickleness and I would never say such a thing. Listen." Leaning toward her, he lowered his voice and spoke to her earnestly. He also meant to speak privately, but I was on Alice's other side and although no one else could have heard what he said, I could make it out.

"It is a matter of wisdom and making a right choice," he told her softly. "I do not ask your blind obedience, to me or even to your parents. I only ask to place before you what I have to offer. Then you will think and no one will hurry you; and you shall choose, and you will be wise, and choose aright. You are young, but you are not foolish, and you know well enough that all of the life that lies ahead of you is now in hazard, like a sovereign on a gaming table."

As well as admiring his more obvious attractions, I began to have considerable respect for Owen Lewis's intelligence.

The weird day wore on. Rain continued to fall. Gareth played for us after dinner instead of Rafe. He played well but there was a wrong note or two, and looking at him from close quarters, I saw that the gray-haired Gareth was very elderly indeed and had swollen finger joints. Sir Philip apologized for keeping him from his afternoon rest and released him after just one tune.

Dinner over, the not-quite-betrothed pair went back to the blue parlor. I made friends in a mild way with Bess Haggard, and in the afternoon, I went on embroidering but this time with Bess, in the tower parlor. She confided to me that Alice was their only surviving child, the others having succumbed to illness as young children so often do.

"Alice is dear to us. So far, she has kept in good health, but she is an anxiety to us in other ways, alas. Haggard by name and haggard by nature." Bess heaved a sigh. "She is as wild as any untamed falcon. She rides horses too strong for her; she studies attentively, but she does not just accept what she reads or what she is told, but must needs ask questions. It is not fitting in a young girl. And now this! Well, we must leave it all to Master Lewis. I wonder he didn't walk out in disgust. We warned him that she was headstrong, but he can hardly have expected . . . haggard by name and haggard by nature . . ." The sad litany started again.

Suppertime came. Rafe remained invisible; Lady Thomasine remained sepulchral; Bess remained fretful. Lewis and Alice sat side by side again but talked less. Alice was thoughtful and Lewis seemed willing to let her think undisturbed. Night descended. Lewis had been accommodated in the Mortimer Tower, but the Haggards were still in the rooms over the blue parlor. I could only hope that after all this emotional upheaval, exhaustion would make them sleep deeply, and that this time Alice had no midnight assignation with Rafe.

"Because," I said to Dale and Brockley, "tonight we're going to try again."

"Then, ma'am, you'd best lie down for a while," Dale said. "You were up beyond midnight last night. You've not had enough sleep."

She was yawning herself and I studied her with concern. Poor Dale needed her rest. I understood how she felt, for I too had been feeling tired as the day wore on. Once, I had been able to survive several bad nights in succession without too much difficulty (which was just as well, for like Elizabeth herself, I had a tendency to sleeplessness). But I was no longer the young girl I had been and these days, I felt my bad nights more.

Well, I had got to stay awake, but Dale did not. "You needn't come tonight," I said gently. "You get your sleep. I'm sure I can manage with just Brockley to stand guard."

At midnight, Brockley and I were ready to start. I was as usual wearing an open-fronted overskirt which, like all my overskirts, had a hidden pouch sewn inside it. In this I had put my lock picks and the keys to Aragon. Both Brockley and I had hooded cloaks to protect us from the rain. We had a candle-lantern, as before, and Brockley handed me a tinderbox. "Put that in your pouch, madam. It's windy out there. The lantern might go out."

Then, of course, there was a delay. I looked out of the parlor window to make sure that all was quiet and that the castle was asleep, and found that it wasn't. I wasn't anxious about the faint glow in the window of the blue parlor, since I knew that a fire had been lit there during the day; while the fitful glint from the window of the study was only the reflection from a torch which had been left burning in a niche over the hall porch and was flickering in the wind. Nor did the occasional lantern carried by one of Mortimer's traditional night patrols worry me. They were on the outer walls, beyond the bailey, and to them, the courtyard would be a distant pit of darkness. But up in the Mortimer Tower, one room was brightly lit. I watched it for a moment, and a dark figure moved across it. My eyesight was good and I recognized Philip Mortimer easily. He seemed to have a book in his hands and to be wandering restlessly about while reading it. He was still wide-awake, anyway, and I didn't want him to glance up from his reading and catch sight of two cloaked figures carrying a lantern across the courtyard.

"We can't start yet," I said irritably.

Half an hour later, the room was still lit. However, after watching for a while without seeing Mortimer, I concluded that by now he was reading in bed. I was tired of waiting.

"We must just be very quiet and very careful," I said, "and we'd best not use the lantern. We'll light it when we get there. Come along, Brockley."

As warily as stalking cats, we tiptoed downstairs, passing from the wide staircase which was part of the modern upper storey to the gloomy, stone-built entrance of the old Norman keep. We stole past the door of the Raghorns' room and slipped out into the courtyard.

"Now," I whispered, "keep in the shadows. We'd be wise to go round rather than across. We don't want to bump into the wellhead."

We reached Aragon without mishap and I let us in. All was quiet. As I had surmised, the fire in the blue parlor was still alight. I knelt to light the lantern candle from it, and Brockley breathed that he would remain in the parlor. "I can hear if anyone moves upstairs, and see from the window if anyone comes across the courtyard."

"Good. I'll be as quick as I can." Once again, I was about to reach up for the study key on the lintel, but as I did so I saw that as before, the door was slightly ajar. Warily, I pushed it wider and looked in.

This time, the study was dark, but I knew at once that someone had been there recently. The flickering gleam which I had seen from the guest parlor had not been the reflection of the flambeau over the hall porch. It had been a candle, and the smell of it still hung in the air.

I raised my lantern and played the light over the room. A partly used candle stood in the candlestick on the desk, and around the wick, the wax was still liquid. I moved the light again. There was no fire in the hearth this time, no pile of cushions. But on the floor, halfway across the room, I caught the gleam of gold. I lowered the lantern to look.

Once more, the study was occupied, but not, this time, by a pair of lovers. Only one person lay there on the floor, a rug pushed awry under his twisted body. He was half on his side, and half on his stomach. His head was turned sideways and I could see his face. And the glaze in his blank and open eyes.

I knelt down beside him and felt for the pulse in his wrist but although he was still warm, there was no throb there and I was not surprised. I knew already that he was dead.

It was also clear how he had died. The gleam of gold was the golden hilt of the dagger from the desk, the slim-bladed gadget for opening sealed letters. It was sticking out of his back. He wore no doublet, only shirt and hose, and there was a scarlet patch on the shirt, from which a red rivulet had run down to make a small stain on the floor. There wasn't much blood, though. He must have died quickly. The point of the dagger must have gone straight into Rafe Northcote's heart.

I said: "Brockley," in what I thought was a low, calm voice but he came into the study so quickly that something in my tone must have warned him. He looked down at Rafe. Brockley never swore except under desperate circumstances but these undoubtedly qualified. In a heartfelt whisper, he said: "Ch . . . rrr . . . ist."

"What do we do?" I said.

"Call for help, madam. We can say we saw a light down here."

"But who . . . why?"

"Never mind that now, madam. The first thing is . . ."

"What's happening here? My God, it's true! Someone *is* creeping about in my study in the middle of the night. Mistress Blanchard? Brockley?"

Light flooded across the room as Mortimer, on silent, slippered feet, stepped into the study with a branched candlestick in his hand. He saw Rafe and froze.

I realized then that he was not alone. Lady Thomasine was just behind him. She came into the study on his heels, her oyster pink wrapper huddled around her, her eyes enormous in the candlelight. She too caught sight of Rafe and her mouth opened. She clapped a palm across it as if to hold back a scream. Then she pushed Sir Philip aside and ran forward. At the sight of the blood, she halted for an instant and gasped with revulsion, but with a movement both fastidious and swift, she avoided it, threw herself on her knees beside Rafe, and shook him as though he were asleep. Her son pulled her back.

"Don't, Mother! He's dead. Look at his eyes . . . no, perhaps you'd better not. Sit down on the settle."

"Rafe, oh, Rafe!" Lady Thomasine let Mortimer guide her to the settle. She huddled there, her knuckles at her mouth. She stared at us and her eyes narrowed. "Did you do this? You must have done! You wicked creatures! Why? Why?"

"Us?" I was bewildered. "We found him, that's all. I saw a light and we . . ."

"You were found beside him. What happened?" She stared at me fixedly in the candlelight. "Was it you, mistress? Did you lead him on and then say no, and make him angry so that he frightened you and you killed him out of fear? I suppose you'll pretend you were defending yourself. But my son," said Lady Thomasine unbelievably, "has told me how you led him on when you asked him to supper. I know all about it."

I gaped at her, unable to credit my own ears. Brockley said coolly: "I think, Lady Thomasine, that you must know better than that."

"Do I? I suppose she fetched you when she saw what she had done. You were going to help her throw him into the moat or some such thing, I imagine."

My head was whirling as though I had drunk a gallon of canary. "Lady Thomasine, you can't believe that I stabbed Rafe . . . you can't . . . !" Clutching at my sanity, I reminded myself that Lady Thomasine had sent me to search the study but that Mortimer mustn't know it. This performance was probably for his benefit. "We saw a light down here in the study," I repeated, "and we came to find out what it was, that's all. We . . ."

"Oh, did you indeed?" There was no sign that Lady Thomasine was acting, not so much as a conspiratorial glance at me, or a flicker of an eyelid. "Do guests commonly take so much upon themselves? Does my son not have the right to work at his desk at any hour, day or night? You killed Rafe; I know you did. Philip, what are we to do with them?"

"For the time being," said Mortimer, "lock them in here and fetch Evans and Pugh. We can trust them."

He drew his mother to her feet and then, stepping up to me, he jerked my lantern out of my hand. "You can stay in the dark with what you've done," he said. Then he took his mother's arm and they went out. We heard the key turn in the lock. I turned instinctively to the window but this too was locked. We were, as Mortimer had said, imprisoned in the dark with Rafe's dead body.

Brockley was close to me, a steadying hand on my shoulder. "Don't be too frightened, madam. Lady Thomasine knows all this is nonsense. She knows why we're here, and she knew why you asked Mortimer to supper. She's pretending, to keep all that from him. But she'll find a way to put it right."

"But why did she accuse us of killing Rafe? She had no need to do that and she can't possibly believe it. It's mad. I feel as if I'm going mad myself. Why should anyone want to murder Rafe anyway?"

"God knows, madam. I suppose," said Brockley, "that Alice could be the cause. We know that Mortimer was angry and Owen Lewis may be more resentful than he seems."

"This angry? This resentful?"

"I know. It doesn't seem likely," Brockley agreed. He was speaking very calmly, probably in an attempt to make me calm as well. "Unless . . . it could have been Mortimer himself, madam, but not on Alice's account. Suppose he caught Rafe in here, searching his papers—looking for the same thing that you were? Maybe Lady Thomasine asked both of you to look. Now, of course, Mortimer is acting as though he were innocent."

"Deceiving his mother as well as us, and meanwhile, she's deceiving him?" I said shakily. "But I still can't understand why she accused me—or us. And what's going to happen to us now?"

I sank onto the settle, where Lady Thomasine had been. My foot slipped a little on the floor and touched something soft and heavy. I jerked it back with a gasp, knowing that I had kicked Rafe's body. "How long will they leave us here?" I whispered. "With that?"

"He can't hurt us, madam." Brockley sat down at my side and

again put a comforting hand on my shoulder. "The dead can't hurt anyone."

"So people say," I whispered back. I kept whispering because I had an unreasonable fear of waking the thing on the floor. In the darkness, the body was no longer Rafe, the boy who had stood defiantly hand in hand with Alice only that morning. And if it were to stir, to wake, then the life in it would not belong to Rafe but to some demonic trespasser. Mortimer, I thought, had understood very well the horror he was inflicting on us, or at least on me.

At least Brockley was there, his warmth and common sense a blessing beyond price. We sat together, not moving, and did not talk any more, until the lock clicked again, and into the room, candlestick in hand, came Mortimer, followed by the tall figure of the butler Pugh, and the hefty bulk of the falconer Evans, both dressed in dark breeches and doublets.

"There's a useful dungeon under the keep," Mortimer said to us. "That's where you're going to spend the rest of the night. On your feet!"

"This is ridiculous," I said. "We're guests here. I'm one of Lady Thomasine's kinswomen. All we did was see a light and come to see what it was. You can't seriously suppose . . ."

"Mistress Blanchard is perfectly right. If she is mistreated in any way, you'll answer for it!" Brockley backed me up. No one, however, deigned to answer us. In silence, Mortimer closed steely fingers around my upper arm and pulled me off the settle while Pugh and Evans seized Brockley's elbows and hustled him backward to the door. Once, Pugh and Evans had been slightly comic figures: Evans the falconer, who presented hares to his lady at dinner; Pugh the luckless butler, who was forever failing to introduce arrivals properly. But now, as they hauled us into the courtyard, they were impersonal and frightening. As we were dragged into the open, we stopped either resisting or shouting, out of a sense of dignity, for it was obvious that we could not escape and none of Mortimer's servants were likely to come to our aid.

Mortimer put the candlestick down in the parlor, but in the entrance lobby, we found Lady Thomasine waiting with a lit torch. The rain had stopped and the torch burned steadily, lighting our way as we were haled across the courtyard.

We were taken back to the keep, but not to our rooms. Just inside the entrance of the keep was an inner door which I had noticed only vaguely before, supposing that it led to a food store or wine cellar. Through this we were thrust. It opened onto a flight of dank stone steps leading down to a heavy oak door, which Mortimer unlocked. Beyond that was a short stone corridor with another stout door on each side and a third one at the far end. This was open and we were shoved through it, so roughly that I fell on all fours, landing amid a scattering of fresh straw. Turning as I picked myself up, I found my nose an inch from Lady Thomasine's pretty slippers with the cerise roses and I saw with satisfaction that the dirt and wet from the rain-swept cobbles had done them no good. In desperate circumstances, one takes pleasure in sadly petty triumphs.

"You're a lady of standing, Mistress Blanchard," Mortimer said, none too accurately, considering that I was on my hands and knees at the time. I got up quickly, in order to look him in the eye. "And by marriage," he said coldly, "you are a member of my family. I have not forgotten. I have, therefore, ordered that you be treated accordingly, and your companion may share in this. You will spend the rest of the night here, but we've put straw down for you. You can pile it into bedding and sleep, if you *can* sleep. In the morning, you'll be fed. But you will then be handed over to the authorities. I shall send to Hereford for the sheriff tomorrow. As a justice of the peace, I do of course have full authority to incarcerate you, and I can have you brought to trial for murder at the Midsummer Sessions in Hereford. Good night."

11

Precipice in the Dark

They went out, taking the torchlight with them. The door shut with a hollow echo and the bolts were shot. I stood in the rustling straw and said: "Dale will be anxious by now."

"She was probably watching from a window. I told her to sleep but she said she couldn't, not until we got back. She saw us being brought across the courtyard, as likely as not," Brockley said. "But we can rely on Fran. She'll get word to Tewkesbury."

"If they let her," I said pessimistically.

"If they don't, we'll get word ourselves, through the sheriff. You're a lady of standing, madam; even Mortimer said so. Don't worry."

The darkness had seemed absolute at first but as my eyes adapted, I saw a faint gray patch in one corner, above our heads. There must be a grating in the courtyard, to let in air. I moved toward it and immediately stepped into a puddle, which splashed my ankles. The grating had let the rain in as well.

"It seems to be dry over here," said Brockley, moving in a different direction. "We can pile the straw up just here and make a bed of sorts. We may as well rest if we can."

Fumbling in the gloom, we gathered up the straw and put it in a corner that, as far as we could tell, was free of water. Then we sat down, side by side. "What o'clock is it by now?" I wondered.

"Not one in the morning yet, I fancy," Brockley said. "Things have happened fast. There's time to sleep."

"I've never been farther from sleep," I told him. In the study, with Rafe's body lying invisibly but horridly at our feet, we had wondered feverishly who had killed him. Now the question seemed to ask itself again. "Brockley, who *can* have done it?"

Brockley rustled the straw as he settled himself more comfortably. "If you ask me, I reckon it's between Mortimer and Lewis, like we said back there in the study. Unless it's Alice."

"Alice?"

"She and Rafe were lovers," Brockley pointed out. "They could have had another secret meeting and quarreled. She seems to be turning toward Owen Lewis now. Maybe she told Rafe so and it made him angry. Maybe he grew violent and she stabbed him to defend herself. Or perhaps she's pretending, with Lewis, to please her family and it was Rafe who wanted to end their affair, and she attacked him in a temper. It's possible."

"I can't believe any of it," I said flatly. "I can't imagine a well-brought-up young girl like Alice stabbing anyone for any reason, even if she is a trifle headstrong by nature. And I can't really believe that other suggestion, that Rafe was caught searching the study. Why should he be searching it? If he can open a locked strongbox, Lady Thomasine would have told him to do it long ago. As for Mortimer killing the boy in a fury merely because he'd been trifling with Alice . . . it's just not reasonable."

"I think I agree with you, madam. That leaves Lewis, but . . ."

"Lewis *is* getting somewhere with Alice. I'd swear that's genuine. He can't have thought that murdering Rafe would further his courtship. Unless he caught them together and he and Rafe started fighting, but in that case . . . It had only just happened," I said slowly. "I could smell the candle and Rafe's body was warm. If there had been a fight, it would have made a noise. We would have heard something as we crossed the courtyard. And what about the Haggards? They were sleeping upstairs. If there had been a noisy quarrel, or a fight, they'd have got up to investigate. And if Alice had been there, they'd have found her. We'd have found her! No. It wasn't a quarrel between Rafe and Lewis at an interrupted lovers' meeting. It can't have been."

"It *is* possible to quarrel quietly," Brockley said. "Especially at a clandestine meeting, with people sleeping nearby. If Lewis somehow came to suspect that they had an assignation and went to interrupt it, he might not have wished to compromise Alice. He might have told her to get out of sight—scared her into it, maybe. Except . . . no, it still won't do. Rafe was stabbed in the back. That doesn't fit with Lewis, not if I'm any judge of men. Mortimer's more likely, whatever his reason and however it came about. It would explain why Lady Thomasine turned on us, you know."

"To protect him? Yes. That does make sense. But what do either of them think will happen when we tell our side of the tale? Oh, I can't work it out!" It was cold and I was shivering. All this talk seemed pointless. Who were we to speculate? We weren't in charge of an inquest on Rafe. Far from it. However unreasonably, we had been accused of murdering him.

Brockley perhaps felt the same. With a sigh, he changed the subject. "We can talk it all over when we see the sheriff of Hereford tomorrow. I'm sure he'll listen. Meanwhile, we've got to wait the night out. We really should sleep if we can. I know it's cold, but if we keep close together and pull the straw round us and use our cloaks as a double coverlet, we should be able to keep the chill out."

He was talking sense. We made ourselves as comfortable as we could, lying close so that we might give heat to each other, our two cloaks spread over us. Once more, Brockley's nearness was reassuring. Despite my fear and discomfort, I began to drift. I edged closer to him, snuggled my nose into his fustian doublet, and slept.

I don't know how long I was asleep. I recall dreaming of the wet courtyard, and the dirt on Lady Thomasine's pretty shoes. Then I woke and thought for a moment that I was at home with Matthew, and surfacing from sleep to the gentle pressure of my husband's desire. Half drowsing, I moved to let my mouth meet his.

Then I was fully awake and aware, knowing where I was and with whom, but my mouth was still pressed hard against the lips of the man at my side, and his need was still thrusting gently against me.

We stayed like that for . . . was it a few seconds? Or an hour? Or a century? It was like a moment withdrawn altogether from time. But it ended when at the same instant, we jerked ourselves apart and sat up.

"Madam!" Brockley gasped. "I'm sorry! I was . . . I think I was dreaming . . ."

"So was I."

"I apologize. What must you think of me? I would never in my right senses . . . you're perfectly safe . . ."

"It's all right, Brockley. I'm not angry, or frightened. Please. It's all right."

Gingerly, we settled back into the straw but this time well apart. We lay still. But my eyes stayed open and in the tiny trace of light from the grating, I caught a glint from Brockley's eyes as well. He was wide-awake too.

I was shaken. It was as though imprisonment and fear and the horror of Rafe's dead body had stripped away an old pretense. For years now, through many dangers, I had trusted Roger Brockley, exchanged private jests with him, relied on him. How long had we secretly desired each other? Matthew had known. Dale had sensed it. Only the two most concerned had remained ignorant until now; until this moment when we had only each other for comfort in the dark.

And I wanted that comfort. At that moment, in that terrifying cell, I wanted it so badly that even though I did not forget Matthew, but tried on the contrary to visualize him, he wasn't real to me. He was not there, and Brockley was. In the darkness, I said, "Brockley?" out loud, with a question in my voice.

The straw rustled. I reached out toward the rustle and his fingers closed over my hand. "I'm here, madam."

"This is an awful place. We're in a dreadful situation."

"It'll all be put right in the morning. Go to sleep."

"Brockley . . ."

"I know. But it wouldn't be . . . right. We wouldn't be able to go back. It would be like falling off a precipice."

"You mean," I said, "that we would turn from madam and Brockley, to Ursula and Roger, and we wouldn't be able to forget it?"

"That's right. It would do harm," he said. "Break us on the rocks, as it were."

I turned on my side. I left my hand in his, letting that small intimacy represent the greater one to which we had no right. Presently, he said: "Don't think I didn't want to. And don't think that when I wanted to, it was just . . . a thing of the body, madam. I value you more highly than that."

"Thank you. I value you more highly than that, as well."

There was another silence. Then I said: "In the morning, we will forget this. We need never mention it again. But I would like to say, just once—good night, Roger."

"Good night, Ursula," he said. Quietly, with one accord, our hands let go of each other. Before long, we were asleep.

We were roused before dawn, by the grinding of the bolts. We sat up blearily. In the faint gray light from the grating, we saw each other's grimy face. For one moment, my eyes and Brockley's met, in mingled affection and embarrassment. Then we got to our feet, shaking straw from our clothing, as the door swung back and in came Lady Thomasine. She was drawn and pale, as though she hadn't slept at all, and looked at least seventy.

"You must come," she said in a low voice. "Come with me now, at once. Quickly. There is no time to be lost."

We tried to ask questions as we picked up our cloaks but she shook her head at us impatiently. "Just come. I know you did not kill Rafe—and neither did my son, by the way. I daresay that's what you think, but you're wrong. He really believes it was you, Mistress Blanchard. He thinks you summoned your man here to help you hide the body. He is very angry. You do not know my son; what he's capable of. I must get you away at once."

"But who *did* kill Rafe? If we can get to the sheriff in Hereford ourselves, of our own free will . . ." I began, but Lady Thomasine, already marshaling us out of the cell, brushed all this aside.

"You must get away from here, but you mustn't go toward Hereford. You wouldn't reach it. Philip would expect you to go that way. He would catch you and deliver you in chains, and tell such a lurid tale of your supposed crimes that you might find it hard to make the sheriff believe you. Philip might even not deliver you at all! He might decide to dispense his own justice. He was talking of it last night and it would take only a little provocation to make him do it. I tell you—you don't know him. He not only wants to be a border baron with power of life and death, there are times when he thinks he really is one. Mistress Blanchard, you once hinted to me that he might not be right in the head. I think it may be true. Your only chance of escaping him is by going off in a direction he won't expect and hiding till all this is settled. I have thought of a way to settle it. No one will be accused of murder for there will be no murder, as far as the world knows."

"But Rafe *was* murdered," I said in bewilderment. "I saw his body myself."

"Leave all that to me." Impatiently, Lady Thomasine unbolted one of the other doors off the underground passage, revealing that it led not into another cell but into a farther passage, low-roofed and damp. "Along here, quickly. After a little time has passed, it will be safe for you to come out of hiding, but then you must go straight home, keeping well away from Vetch, and forget I ever called you here. This way. Hurry."

"What about Dale?" I asked as we followed her through the passage, and at the same moment Brockley said, "What about my wife?" But this time she didn't answer at all. She merely quickened her steps and we scurried after her perforce, heads bent, following the gleam of her lamp. At the end of the passage was a narrow spiral staircase of stone leading upward. Lady Thomasine climbed it and opened another door, with a key this time. Mounting the stairs behind her, we followed her into a dusty, empty chamber, with narrow windows which let in a wet, gray dawn and just enough light to reveal the quantity of cobwebs and dirt in the place.

"Where is this?" I asked.

"This is the ground floor of Isabel's Tower. Over here. Hurry!"

"Isabel's . . . ?"

"The haunted tower. You've heard the story, haven't you? Your daughter Meg has—she asked me about it."

"Yes," I said. "Rafe told it to me."

"Then you know that a castellan in days gone by shut his wife up here to die with her minstrel lover. The wife's name was

Isabel. She was my ancestress, poor soul. The minstrel's name was Rhodri. It's said their bones moldered here for twenty years before her husband would let them be taken out and buried."

In the time it took to give us these gruesome details, Lady Thomasine had locked the staircase door behind us, crossed the floor, pushed open a door into a further chamber, and led us across that too. At the far side was yet another door, small and low. Here we paused while she nervously wrestled with her key ring, searching for the right key, which at first she couldn't find. When at last, hands shaking, she managed to open the door, its rusty hinges groaned noisily and resisted her. Brockley stepped forward and added his weight to hers. The door gave way and a moment later, we were outside on the grassy slope above the moat, under a sky of low, racing clouds, threatening more rain.

Brockley shoved the door shut again and Lady Thomasine, once more, locked up behind us. Then she hurried us to the right along a narrow path between the western wall of the castle and the water below. Once more, Brockley asked about Dale and this time got a reply, albeit a terse one.

"The woman Dale is going with you. I did not forget her. Don't waste time. We go down here."

We had reached the point where the moat turned away from the castle and became simply a stream flowing in from the west. Beyond that, the fall of the ground was so steep that in the days of siege and foray, no ditch had been necessary. But there had been changes since medieval times. A winding path had been made, leading down. As we descended it, still hurrying, I realized how tired I still was, and also how cold and hungry.

Below the castle mound, the path joined a sunken lane. To the right, it evidently led to the village. I could see the church tower in the distance. To the left, it crossed the stream by means of a ford and led westward and away from Vetch altogether. Waiting for us at the junction of path and lane were the butler Harold Pugh and the falconer Simon Evans, on horseback. With them, mounted astride and peering out at us from the hood of a woolen cloak, was Dale, and Evans had two more saddled horses on leading reins.

I exclaimed: "Dale!" and Brockley said: "Fran!" at the same moment, both on a note of thankfulness. I looked at Dale's dear, trustworthy face and was grateful beyond belief that last night Brockley and I had not betrayed her. Brockley assuredly felt the same. On her side, Dale burst out, "Oh, ma'am! Oh, Roger! I'm that glad to see you both safe!"

If Dale were to come with us, she couldn't warn the Hendersons, but just for the moment, we were all too relieved to be together again to worry about it. We had no time to talk to each other, however. Lady Thomasine was pushing us toward the horses.

I say horses, but they were really ponies—sturdy, but no more than fourteen and a half hands tall, shaggy of coat, with thick manes and tails and strong legs. Their riders wore stout hooded cloaks like Dale's. Evans glanced at us and said: "Good, your cloaks have hoods. You'll need them. Get mounted. We've a long way to go."

"Just go with Pugh and Evans," said Lady Thomasine. "Trust them. You can eat as you ride. They have food in their saddlebags. It's a long way, but it's for your safety."

We did as we were told for there seemed to be no alternative. I regretted that we were not to ride our own horses and could only hope that we would get them back eventually, somehow.

Rain had begun to spatter. "Go back to the castle, my lady," Pugh said. "Leave the rest to us."

"Godspeed," said Lady Thomasine.

"Look," Brockley said, "why can't we just make for Ledbury? We've—er—got friends there."

"You've got to be out of Sir Philip's reach," Pugh said shortly. "Lady Thomasine knows what she's doing. Hereford way and Ledbury way; he'll be after you in both directions. We've our orders; just don't make difficulties."

I think we wanted very badly to make difficulties and we weren't convinced by Pugh's arguments. I would have said—and Brockley presently muttered to me—that it would have been well worthwhile to ride hard for Ledbury and why hadn't we been given our own comparatively long-legged horses to do it on? What stopped us from saying so or simply putting spurs to our mounts and making a dash for it, was the overpowering presence of Pugh and Evans, and the fact that although once mounted, Brockley and I were free of leading reins, Evans had kept Dale on one. Possibly this was because he had noticed she was a poor rider, but it also had the effect of making her into a hostage. We could not break away without abandoning her.

We did ask where we were going, of course, but Pugh, who seemed to be in charge, merely answered: "To safety in the mountains," and then exhorted us to get a move on.

So we rode westward, wondering where in the world we were bound but knowing that all the time we were putting more and more distance between ourselves and any help Rob Henderson might have given. A drizzling rain set in. Our cloaks and hoods kept us fairly dry, but the rain still blew into our faces, borne on a west wind. Its sweeping, misty curtains often obscured the view but when they parted, we saw that we were riding through a rolling, hilly land of pastures, heath, and woodland, but journeying all the time toward a rumor of higher and wilder land in the distance.

We soon noticed that our escort was avoiding habitations and taking little-used tracks. When we were forced to approach dwellings, because bridges tend to be put where there are towns or villages and we often had to cross rivers, Pugh took precautions.

Pugh was now very different from the put-upon butler we had known at Vetch and he was visibly in authority over Evans. At his orders, the party would be divided into two. Pugh would ride ahead with me, and then Evans would follow with Brockley and Dale. I supposed that the idea was to make sure that no one would report seeing a party of one man and two women, traveling together. Lady Thomasine must have given some very precise orders.

Once, as we were riding over a bridge, I said: "If you won't tell us where we're going, would you tell us where we are? What place is this?"

"This is Ewyas Harold, and we're crossing the river Dore. There used to be a priory here," said Evans, and that was about the longest speech that either he or Pugh made throughout the whole journey. They were supposed to be rescuing us from pursuit by Mortimer, but their stony reluctance to talk to us was unnerving.

"We have done nothing wrong, you know," I said to Pugh once. "Lady Thomasine knows that. Surely she explained?"

But all he said was: "Indeed she did, madam," and then closed his mouth as though it were a trap.

Brockley, Dale, and I did at length manage a little conversation among ourselves. I told Dale that we had spent the night sitting up on straw, and Dale, who knew from experience what the inside of a dungeon was like, was full of commiseration. She had seen us being taken to the dungeon, she said, and then Lady Thomasine had come and said we would all be going away in the morning. "But she locked me in and there I stayed till Pugh came to fetch me. I didn't sleep, I was so worried for you." Once she added: "And I'm worn-out now, I don't mind saying. I can't abide missing my sleep."

I saw with anxiety how pale she was, and I knew that Brockley was also stealing worried glances at her. I could only hope that this ride wouldn't go on too long.

We paused a few times to eat and drink and rest the horses. Pugh and Evans always chose lonely places. They had bread, cheese, and cold meat in their saddlebags, and also carried water bottles and ready-filled nosebags for our mounts. My hopes of a short journey were not fulfilled for it showed no sign of ending. The day wore on. Toward evening, the rain at last ceased and we could see clearly that mountains were ahead of us, towering so high that their heads showed above the drifts of cloud, as though they were floating in the sky.

I was now exhausted and Dale was drooping miserably. If ever we got out of this, I thought—if ever I returned safely to Meg, to Matthew, to Château Blanchepierre—it would be for good. There should be an end to all adventures. Once Meg was with me in France, she could no longer be used as bait to drag me back to danger and discomfort.

I also thought, silently, that Matthew had been right to warn me that I was too close to Brockley. When I returned to France, Brockley and Dale must not come with me. I must send them away, for all our sakes, no matter what it cost me, or them.

I came out of my reverie to observe that the descending sun had sunk below the cloud and was casting a red sunset over the land. The track was now winding upward into the mountains, amid lonely slopes of grass and heather, hunted by kite and kestrel. Sheep and small, shaggy cattle grazed here and there but some of the hillsides plunged so dizzily that only a goat could have kept a foothold on them. It was wilder land than I had ever seen before.

As dusk drew near, we turned onto a path which was little more than a sheep trail. We followed this up a heathery slope onto a shoulder of hill, and then altered course to ride along the crest of the shoulder, still climbing, nearing the cloud which hung about the higher ground.

I was by now not only tired out but in pain. I had tried to protect my legs from the stirrup leathers by wrapping my skirts around them, but the skirts often slipped out of place and after so many hours, I had acquired raw patches on both calves.

My pony, tough little beast though he was, was also showing signs of exasperation. Twice he balked and had to be dragged onward by Pugh, and when, as if from nowhere, a straggle of sheep scampered across our path, and a frisky lamb kicked up its heels right under my mount's nose, he showed his resentment by bucking. My saddle had a high pommel and cantle and I should have been secure enough, but my tiredness and my sore calves made gripping difficult. I fell off.

Brockley was out of his own saddle and down beside me at once. "Madam! Mistress Blanchard! Are you hurt?"

"No, I don't think so. It's all right, Brockley." With his help, I got to my feet, partly winded and slightly bruised but not seriously damaged, and found myself face-to-face with a round-eyed shepherd boy, no more than ten years old, and a hairy black-and-white dog.

Evans, redder in the face than ever with anger, rode up and poured a stream of angry Welsh over the boy's head, presumably recommending that he get himself and his flock of sheep out of our way. The lad tried to say something, also in Welsh, but dodged away with a cry as Evans struck out with his whip.

"Don't!" I protested. "He was only moving his sheep! I

expect he didn't see us in time." I gave the boy a smile, to assure him that I wasn't much hurt. I doubted if he understood English.

"Not deaf or blind, is he?" Evans was still furious. "He should have heard the hooves, seen us moving; not dark yet, is it? Be off!" He made another swipe at the unfortunate shepherd boy, who sprang away from us in fear, calling and whistling to his animals. Together with his dog and sheep, he disappeared down the mountainside. Pugh had caught my pony and brought him to me. Brockley got me into the saddle. For a moment, as I felt the warmth and strength of his hands, I remembered our shared warmth during the night. But I must forget last night, and so must he.

"Is it much farther?" I asked. "We're all so tired."

"Another hour, maybe," Pugh said briefly. "You are all right? You can keep in your saddle now?"

"I trust so," I said coldly, folding my skirts around my rasped legs once again. "I'd still like to know where we're going."

"To shelter," said Pugh. "And we should hurry."

The cloud came rolling down to meet us as we rode on, cutting off the sunset. Like phantoms we moved through a sharp-smelling mist, which blew past us on a cold wind but did not lift. Behind me, I heard Pugh say to Evans: "Are you sure we're not lost?"

"My mam came from the Black Mountains. We used to visit her kinfolk here. I know my way. There's a big old rock coming up in a minute. We turn right just after that."

The rock, a huge boulder lying beside the path, emerged from the mist a moment later. Beyond it the track forked, and Evans duly led us to the right. The darkness was falling rapidly now. Then Pugh said: "Ah! We're there," and pushing his pony past me, rode ahead. As we followed, the blowing vapors parted a little and the very last of the light showed us a stone cottage, small but solid-looking, the kind of place that shepherds use in the hills.

"Get down," said Pugh.

It was an order. We all dismounted, stiff and cold. Dale's knees gave way and Brockley reached out quickly to support her. Evans and Pugh took the ponies' bridles. "The place isn't locked," Pugh said. "Go on in. There's a shack for the animals at the back.

We'll see to them and join you. We'll all have to camp in the cottage together tonight. You should find fuel in there—get a fire lit."

The cottage door had a couple of bolts, but the main fastening was a huge oaken bar, as thick as a pony's neck, which went through staples on the door and the wall. Brockley pulled it out, propping it against the wall, and then the three of us went inside. The interior was very dark, but one tiny window let in a trace of light and we could just make out a fireplace on the opposite wall.

"But where's the fuel?" Brockley said. "That hearth's empty."

We advanced to investigate further and behind us, the door slammed. As we spun around, the bolts were shot and we heard the grinding sound of the timber bar being thrust into place. We all rushed to the door and pounded on it, shouting, but no one answered. We heard hooves receding.

Dale said shakily: "There's no fuel, not as much as a twig. And there's nothing to sleep on, not even straw."

The hoofbeats faded. We stood listening to the silence. It was cold. We had no firewood, no bedding, and nothing to eat or drink. Our last stop had been several hours before and the rations given to us none too generous even then. We were damp, for our woolen cloaks had absorbed the rain and let some wetness through.

"Isabel and Rhodri," I said.

"What, madam?" Brockley for once sounded completely overset.

"Isabel and Rhodri," I said bleakly. "They were shut in the haunted tower to die. Except that this is a cottage instead of a tower, I think Lady Thomasine's done exactly the same thing to us."

12

One Forlorn Candle

I was too tired and shaken to watch my words. I just blurted it out and Dale promptly panicked. She rushed shrieking to the door and pounded on it again. "It can't be true! They wouldn't do that! Let us out! Come back! Let us out!"

Brockley got hold of her and pulled her away. "That's no use, Fran. Easy, now. I'm here." His voice was kind and comforting and I longed so much for the same kind of comfort that I had to turn my back and appear to be interested in standing on tiptoe to peer through the window. Dale meanwhile, refused to be calmed.

"It's a mistake, a muddle! They've got to come back! I want something to eat. I want to sleep! Oh, my God, what are we to do? Can't we get out through the window?"

Brockley sat down on the floor, drawing her down with him, and cradled her, murmuring to her as though he were soothing a child. I made myself concentrate on the window. It was nothing but a little square hole in the stonework, only a foot high and less than that across. No one could possibly have got out of it. Outside, darkness had almost fallen, but I could make out that the fog seemed to be lifting. Vaguely, I could see the vapors dissolving, and after a moment I made out a dim skyline. I could hear the hissing of the wind, too, and when I pushed a hand through, I found that once again, it was raining. "I'm afraid the window's too small," I said. "Besides, we don't know where we are."

"In the Black Mountains," Brockley said. "I heard Pugh say so. But it doesn't help much, that's true enough."

I had been the one who had cried out that we had been treated like Isabel and her lover, but until now I hadn't quite understood what that meant. After all, we were indoors, in shelter of a sort, and it was the month of May. But it was still as cold as winter, up in this high and lonely place. Without food, warmth, or a way out, our shelter was a lethal prison. As I stood there peering through the window, listening to the wind, I realized that Dale was right to be terrified. But before I could give way to terror myself, Brockley said calmly: "We must break the door down if we can. It's true that we can't go anywhere now. I've an idea it's raining again—I think I can hear it . . ."

"You can. It is," I said shakily.

"Then we'd do better to stay here than go out wandering the mountains at night. But we've got to make sure that we can get out when we're ready. We need food and sleep even now, but we'll be that much weaker in the morning. Once it's daylight and we can see where we're going, then we'll try our luck outside—only we must force a way out *now,* while we still have some strength."

If the weather didn't clear properly, we might in the morning find ourselves lost in cloud again; day might be as bad as night. But I didn't say so. "What can we use as a battering ram?" I said.

In the darkness, we groped around the walls of the single room which was all the cottage contained. Dale helped, pulling herself together as best she could. On a ledge by the hearth, she found a long-handled frying pan and a half-used candle. They were hardly suitable implements for breaking down a door, and there was nothing else, nothing whatsoever.

"All right," said Brockley. "Shoulders and feet it will have to be. A thousand pities it isn't fastened with a lock, madam. You could get that open with your lock picks."

"I know. But they're no use here. Well, we must try what strength will do."

Tired though we were, one can summon up a lot of strength when the situation is desperate. But it wasn't enough. We ran at the door, throwing our shoulders against it; we took running kicks at it. It shook but it wouldn't give. The bar outside was heavy and the hinges were on the other side of a massive doorpost. In fact, when we came in, I had noticed vaguely that whole door looked as though it had originally belonged to some quite different building. There wasn't much wood up here, after all. An old door from, say, a ruined castle might well have been pressed into use, brought up here on a donkey and fixed into place.

Doors originally made for Norman castles tended to be sturdy. My cousins' tutor might have given us only limited information on Eleanor of Aquitaine, but he really had known his history, and one of the interesting details he had told us concerned the way to construct a door for defensive purposes. It was done by using two layers of oak planks, one layer set upright and the other one set crossways. Such a door wouldn't split even under ax blows. It was meant to withstand even the battering ram we hadn't got. Mere kicking and shouldering would get us nowhere. We gave up at last, gasping and bruised.

"I'm not even carrying a dagger," Brockley said. He produced a small belt knife, however, and made an attempt to lever the doorpost loose, but this too repelled his efforts. It had been bolted to the stone, and the bolts were in good condition.

Dale said miserably: "Haven't you got your tinderbox? Couldn't we light the candle? Just for a bit of light?"

"Light!" I said. "Someone might see it! Here's Brockley's tinderbox—I've been carrying it all this time." I brought it out. "Let's try signaling for help by putting a light in that window!"

"Why should it bring anyone?" Brockley clearly didn't want us to raise our hopes too much. "They would just think that someone was using the hut. That's what it's for, after all."

"Someone might come and find us anyway. Tomorrow if not today," pleaded Dale. "If people use the place, then they *come* here—they must! What about that boy we saw? Perhaps he'll come up here."

"Perhaps," said Brockley kindly. From his tone, I knew what he was thinking. The boy had been taking his charges downhill. We had not seen any sheep farther up. The local flocks were not yet being grazed on the high pastures.

"All the same," I said, "the night's clearer now. A light would be seen for some way. I did say *signal*. It might attract attention if we did something to make it unusual—kept on moving it in and out of the window, for instance."

"We could try," said Brockley. "Give me the tinderbox."

The candle made us feel better. We were cold and exhausted and hunger and thirst were making themselves felt, but we looked as greedily at that single flame as though it could end all our misery. Brockley held it up to look at the ceiling, in case there were any hope of escape that way. It wasn't thatch, but was made of planks, nailed to rafters. We might have broken through it if we could have reached it, and if, again, we had had anything to use as a ram. But as things were, the ceiling offered no more hope than the door. Brockley also attempted to get up the chimney, but it was too narrow and there were no holds for hands or feet. The thin chance offered by signaling with the candle was all that remained.

We tried, for some time. We showed it in the window three times, for a count of five each time, and then took it out of the window for a long pause, before repeating the sequence. But outside, the mountain night remained empty of all but the wind. The rain had stopped again and once there was even a gleam of moonlight, but it showed us nothing except heather and rock.

The candle began to burn down. There was no point in hoarding it. We stood it in the window, as our last hope, and then, huddling together under our cloaks, which we folded so that the dampest parts were outermost, we lay down on the dirty floor and tried to sleep.

We didn't sleep, of course, although I think we all drowsed after a fashion. We woke up all together and came to our feet in a scramble. The candle was still alight, though guttering by now, and it was still deep night, but there was at last a sound which was nothing to do with the weather.

"That's a dog barking," Brockley said, getting up. "Oh, I'm as stiff as a dotard." He blundered to the window, cursing quite outspokenly for once. Dale put her face against me and said: "I'm not brave enough. If we have to die here . . ."

"We're not going to die here. If there's a dog out there, there's probably someone with it. Shout, Brockley, shout!"

"Come over here and we'll all shout," said Brockley, clinging to the window and peering out.

My mouth and throat were dry and I didn't know how I would get any kind of shout from them but I did my best. Dale and Brockley did their best too. We clustered at the window and screamed for help in a chorus. There was an answering cry from somewhere; a high voice like a child's. Then, wondrously, below the window, the final effort of the candle showed us the face of the shepherd boy who had frightened my pony on the way up. His black-and-white dog was beside him, eyes glinting red.

"Let us out!" Dale shrieked. "Oh, dear God, don't go away! Let us out!"

The boy said something in Welsh.

"The door, the door! Oh no! He doesn't know any English!" wailed Dale.

I rushed to the door and hammered on it. A moment later I heard the boy outside, struggling with the heavy bar. The bolts were pulled back and the door opened. Brockley had already caught up our cloaks. We crowded through to freedom, oblivious of the cold wind. I bridged the language barrier by giving the boy a hug.

"Now what?" said Brockley. "How do we speak to him?"

It turned out that the boy did have a few words of English. He said them, and more blessed, more joyous words I had never heard.

"Come. Food. Get warm."

He started away, glancing back to see if we were following. The dog nosed at our legs, urging us forward. We complied, clutching our cloaks about us. Dale was swaying with relief and weakness both at once and Brockley and I had to help her, one on each side. On the heels of the boy, with his black-and-white dog prancing around us as though we were sheep to be herded, we started down the mountain.

I don't know how far we went. It seemed to take a long time and we often stumbled in the darkness. Then there was another stone cottage and an open door, and beyond it, candlelight and warmth and an unbelievable smell of food. We staggered through. We realized later that the place was actually cramped, dirty, and smelly, but that night it looked like Paradise. Grime and cobwebs meant nothing. We saw only the candle, which burned so brightly in its cracked earthenware candlestick; the bed with the red and green blankets and the white fleeces on it and a second pile of fleeces heaped in a corner; the leaping hearthfire and the encouragingly full woodbasket; and hanging over the flames, a cauldron, which a shawled figure was industriously stirring.

The boy called out something in Welsh and she turned, spoon in hand, to look at us.

"So Griff was right. It is you, then. But how did you come to be shut in that hut up there? There's no one goes there in weather like this. Not till July do they ever use those pastures up on the Mynydd Llyr, the long mountain."

"Gladys Morgan!" I gasped.

Gladys gave us her terrible fanged grin and gestured with the spoon. "Rabbit stew?" she inquired.

13

Jewels amid Squalor

"I got back to my home village all right. *But* . . ." Gladys said grumblingly, as we sat on the floor by her fire, eating rabbit stew out of a single bowl. Dale and I had a spoon each; Brockley made do with a wooden ladle. It didn't matter. The food was a marvel. It was brown, bubbling life. It even gave me the energy to ask Gladys why she was living in a lonely cottage like this and not with the kinsfolk with whom, I vaguely recalled, she had intended to seek shelter.

"My kin were there all right, but they don't want me," Gladys told us, "and there aren't so many of them left now, indeed. My cousin the smith would have taken me in but his silly bitch of a wife had heard I was a witch and said I'd put the evil eye on her brats. Hah!"

Gladys and the shepherd boy, Griff, were squatting beside us, Gladys keeping an eye on our cloaks, which were steaming in front of the fire, draped over a roughly made clotheshorse. She and the boy had already eaten, she said, but now and then she nipped bits of rabbit out of the pot with her fingers, sharing them impartially with Griff and the sheepdog.

"My cousin's brats are four demons out of hell," Gladys informed us roundly. "More likely to put the evil eye on me, I'd have said. No more manners than a pack of weasels, they haven't. They're dirty; they fight . . ."

"Is your cousin your only relative?" I asked, more to stop the monologue about her cousin's children than because I really wanted to know.

"What? Oh no. I've a sister, but she's heard the tales about me too and she and her man didn't want me either, though her children are grown and gone long since. My daughter's married and gone north into Powys, and my son's dead and his widow's another one who's scared of me—same reason as all the others. But Griff here is her boy and my grandson and he's not scared. Are you, Griff?"

She added something to him in Welsh, and he laughed, shaking his head. She fished out another bit of rabbit, and popped it into his mouth.

"In the end," Gladys said, "they settled that I'd come here and they'd let me have food and that, and Griff 'ud bring it. He's always about the mountain. Gets his living herdin' sheep. Wants a flock of his own one day. By good luck, this place was empty. A hermitage, that's what it used to be." Grunting, she got to her feet and turned the cloaks around. "Fellow called Bruno used to live here," she said. "He came from the priory at Ewyas Harold, back in the days when it was still a monastery—Priory of St. James and St. Bartholomew, that was its name. Bruno said he had a call to live on his own and be an anchorage, though I wouldn't know what he meant. We're nowhere near the sea, or even a river you can bring boats up."

"Anchorite," said Brockley. "It's another word for hermit. But hermits were sent back into the world along with the monks when the monasteries were shut. This place must have been empty a good long time. I wonder it didn't fall down."

"Good long time nothing," said Gladys, squatting down again. "Bruno only died last year. The priory at Ewyas was closed down right enough and not before time. Dissolving the monasteries, that's what everyone called it." She let out what I can only call a cackle. "Dissolved it was for being dissolute, if you want to know. Story going round was that they had as many kitchen maids as they had monks, and all of 'em pretty. Maybe that was why Bruno wanted to go off and live as a hermit. No one ever said *he* was dissolute. Whatever happened to the monastery, no one came over to the Black Mountains to dissolve Bruno. He just stayed here and went on being an anchor whatever it is and the villagers fed him like they always had. He's buried out there."

She nodded toward the window. "When he died, his place was just left. It was no good for a shepherd's hut because this is no place for sheep. There's a precipice up above and a wood down below. But it weren't empty long enough to do it much harm. So I took it over. My daughter-in-law gave me a few bits and pieces and my cousin gave me some chickens and the man Griff works for, that owns the flock—he's charitable and let me have some fleeces to keep my old bones warm. So here I am, and not ill-pleased to be away from the village and all the clacking tongues. Now, what about you? How did you get shut in up there? You've not told me yet. I'd like to know—if you can stop awake long enough."

Warmth and food were making our eyelids droop and she had noticed. "It's a long tale," I said. I wasn't sure how much to tell her and couldn't, in my weary state, work it out. Gladys gazed at me with disconcertingly sharp eyes and said: "All right. Let it wait till day. We'll have to spread these fleeces around the lot of you, but you'll be warm enough if we make up the fire. Your cloaks are dry now."

"How did you know we were up in the hut?" I asked sleepily. "Did you see our signal with the candle? You said Griff was right. How did he know who was up there?"

"Met you when you were on the way up there, didn't he? His sheep frightened your pony and off you came." Gladys cackled again. She seemed to enjoy the misfortunes of others. "Well, he heard you and Brockley speak to each other by name. He hasn't the English, or not much, but his ear is quick enough. I'd told your names to him and he recognized 'em. Talked about you, I have. You rescued me back there at Vetch and we Welsh don't forget a good turn any more than we forget an ill one. He came up the mountain again later, with a couple of rabbits he'd caught in a trap—they're what's in the pot. I put the stew on and told him: stop and share it. While it was cookin', he told me he thought a Mistress Blanchard and a man called Brockley had ridden up the path toward the shepherd's hut, with some others, who seemed to be taking 'em there, and it was queer, because what would anyone want up there this soon in the year?

"There's funny, I thought, but at the time there was nothing to be done. We had our bit of stew and we were going to bank the fire and settle in for the night. Too late it was for Griff to get home but his mam knew he'd come up here to me. But before we went to sleep, he stepped outside for a moment and saw your light and called me. We watched it awhile. It was just a spark in the night, and it kept comin' and goin', regular like, and then there'd be nothing, and then we'd see it comin' and goin' again."

Griff, hearing his name mentioned, asked something in Welsh. Gladys answered and he nodded energetically and said something more. Gladys turned to us.

"He says he told me the light looked like a signal and so he did, and right he was. I thought the same. That's why I sent him up with his dog to see what was going on. Just as well I did, from what he told me when he brought you back. Locked in, weren't you?"

"Gladys," I said. "We're grateful."

"I was so frightened," Dale said. "I thought we were going to die up there."

But her voice was drowsy. Gladys grinned her terrible grin. "A fleece under you and your cloak and a blanket on top and you'll sleep like a babe new-born."

Gladys and Griff slept on the bed; we slept on the floor, wrapped in assorted fleeces, blankets, and cloaks. I didn't care, anyway. We were safe and fed and I could have slept anywhere. When I woke, light was showing through the chinks in the shuttered windows. Taking my cloak, I slipped outside to find that the sun was well up and shining out now and then between blowing drifts of cloud.

Gladys's hermitage was halfway up a mountain. The wood that she had mentioned grew thick and dark below, and above us was an all but perpendicular hillside of grass and heather. A waterfall splashed straight down it in a line of white, and sped on to the wood as a rapid, noisy stream. But to my right, the slope of the cliff was less extreme. A few bushes clung to it and I could see the path down which we must have come, winding to and fro.

Raising my eyes, I made out the tiny shape of the shepherd's hut, last night's prison, high up on a ridge. As I looked, a rainstorm swallowed it from sight. It was a wonder that our candle had been seen, so far away.

I stood a moment, breathing the cold, refreshing air, conscious that my gown was filthy and my hair in a bird's nest and that I probably smelled. Then the rain swept in my direction and I turned quickly back into the hermitage, scenting food, to find that Dale and Brockley were up and toasting bread at the fire while our hostess beat eggs in a bowl. "There's milk too," Gladys informed us. "I was up afore any of you, milking the goat. My sister gave me that. Thought she'd ward my curses off that way."

We broke our fast with beaten eggs cooked in goat's butter and piled onto toasted bread, washed down with fresh goat's milk. I never knew a meal taste better. At the end of it, Gladys took the platters and mugs outside and put them in the stream to be washed clean by the forces of nature. Then she scurried back into the hermitage, shut the door behind her, and scanned our faces, her head on one side. "Well?" she said.

I hesitated, but she said: "I'd have been stoned out into the wild but for you people," and it struck me that although she was one of the most unprepossessing women I had ever set eyes on, she was honest in her fashion. I told her some of the truth.

"I work for the queen," I said simply. "I was asked to read Sir Philip's private papers if I could, in case he is involved in some kind of plot against Her Majesty."

The humblest peasant in the land understood what plots against the throne meant. We had had so many of them in the last two reigns that they were the currency of gossip in every alehouse. Gladys didn't even seem surprised. She just nodded knowingly.

She wasn't surprised either when I told her about Alice and Rafe. Most of Vetch, castle and village alike, had apparently heard all about that, the previous Christmas. She looked much more astonished when I explained how Brockley and I had found Rafe's body. Then I told her how we had been caught, accused, and imprisoned, and brought up here on Lady Thomasine's orders, to be locked into the cottage. Here, Gladys nodded vigorously and I stopped.

"Like Isabel and Rhodri," she said.

"The lady and the minstrel who were left to die in Isabel's Tower," I said, as a statement rather than a question. "Yes. That's what we thought, too."

Gladys nodded again. We had all by now settled down on piled-up fleeces by the fire, since the hermitage contained only one stool and Gladys had taken that. She gave the fire a poke and said: "I know the story. Everyone round Vetch knows it. You want to hear about it?"

It was plain enough to me that Gladys was lonely and eager to talk. Well, we were in her debt. I said yes.

"Lady Thomasine's descended from Isabel," she said. "And from her husband, Geoffrey de Vetch—that's what the family were called then, Frenchified like. Three sons, Isabel gave him, and all he gave her was coldness like winter and jealous cruelties, big and little. She was a beauty, but Geoffrey couldn't bear her to be admired. They say she once wore a new gown that made her look so lovely that the garrison all turned their heads to look when she walked by. So Geoffrey took the gown off her and cut it up and left her shut in her chamber all night, naked, with no fire, and took away her bedding. December it was, with snow on the ground. She was ill afterward and it was a wonder she didn't die.

"All that's in one of the songs that Rhodri made. That wasn't the only nasty thing Geoffrey did, not by any means. When Rhodri first came to the castle, to be the bard for the household, he wrote a ballad in praise of Lady Isabel's beautiful hair. So Geoffrey cut all his wife's hair off, and forbade Rhodri ever to mention her in a song again.

"Only there's no stoppin' a Welsh minstrel when the magic of words and melody is on him, so he made his songs anyway, and taught them in secret to a young minstrel, a pupil of his, who'd come to Vetch with him, and they've lived on, those songs. We're still singin' them hereabouts."

Gladys, gazing into the fire as she talked, had herself acquired a singsong-tone storyteller's way of speech, oddly compelling. When she paused, it was Brockley who said: "Go on."

"Ah well, you know what happened in the end. She was faithful for years, and Geoffrey made her life a hell. Drove her into

Rhodri's arms, he did. Then he killed them both but did he have the decency to do it outright? Not he. They say he told them he was givin' them a whole set of rooms to make love in, all nice and private; and then he shut them in the tower and locked and barred every door, even the door to the roof, so they couldn't even put an end to their misery by jumping. He had bars put at every window they might have got out of. Never took the bars away till long after they were dead," Gladys said, baring her fangs in another of her awful grins, "and then only because he had to go to war. The king of England was fighting the north Welsh in those days . . ."

"Edward I?" I asked. "I remember my tutor saying that he had a war with Llewellyn of North Wales."

"Maybe, maybe." The interruption irritated her. "The songs don't say, and all I know, I got from songs—Rhodri's and the ones his pupil made when he was dead. When he was gone, the young minstrel made ballads in his memory and taught them to others, but he only made them in Welsh. Clever, he was; Geoffrey never realized. But the ballads didn't mention King Edward. They say that Geoffrey wanted iron in a hurry, for crossbow bolts, so he used the bars. But he didn't unlock the doors and he gave orders that no one was to do so while he was away. . . . Anyhow, he went to war, but he came back safe, and no one had opened the tower. He left the bones in the tower for twenty years all told. Even Isabel's sons didn't say anything. They were all born before Rhodri came to the castle, so they were Geoffrey's, right enough. They knew all about it, but they were just like their da and thought everything Geoffrey did was right."

"Was it Geoffrey who let the bones be removed in the end?" I said. "Did he soften in his old age?"

"His kind don't soften," said Gladys with a snort. "But the old castle chaplain, who was scared out of his wits of Geoffrey, died and a new man came who was bolder and threatened him with hellfire if he didn't give Isabel and Rhodri Christian burial. So Geoffrey let the bones be brought out, though they say he had a door made, leadin' out of the castle, to take them out through because he wouldn't have his wife or her lover come back inside his castle ever again, even just as bones."

"That must have been the door we came out by," I said. "I wondered why it was there."

"Yes, so did I. Every door into a castle makes it more vulnerable," Brockley agreed. "Though that one's right above the moat, I grant you. An enemy who got that far would be halfway in already. But all the same, it wasn't a likely thing to do while the castle was still meant to hold out against sieges."

"No, it wasn't." I thought about it. "That gate into the stable yard," I said, "where Mistress Henderson and I brought you and Gladys back into the castle; that was made by Lady Thomasine's father, for bringing in fodder. Lady Thomasine said so. It's quite a recent addition. In Geoffrey's time Vetch Castle was still very much a fortress. He really must have hated Rhodri and Isabel. He put the castle at risk out of sheer vindictiveness."

"Maybe." Gladys wasn't interested in such military matters. "Well, there it is. It's said that people sometimes see the faces of Isabel and Rhodri in the windows of the tower and that Rhodri's ghost plays the harp there. They even say the ghosts sometimes come out of their tower into the rest of the castle, and that Rhodri's harp has been heard in the courtyard and the hall, now and then, and that something terrible always happens afterward."

"What a hideous tale . . . I wonder," said Dale in a horrified whisper, "how long they'd have left our bodies in that hut?"

"Not long," said Gladys, in comforting tones. "They'd have had to shift you out quite soon. The shepherds use the place in high summer."

"What I can't make out," I said, hurriedly changing the subject, "is what the point of it all was. After all, we'd been arrested. Why take this sort of revenge on us?"

"And how did Lady Thomasine get Evans and Pugh to help?" said Brockley.

"Yes. Such wickedness. And they just did as they were told!" Dale said, appalled and bewildered.

"Oh, that's nothing. Pugh's from Vetch stock himself," Gladys said. "He's her first cousin—a by-blow, of course. Her father's younger brother made love to all the castle women under forty and a few who were over it. To him, she's both liege lady and kinswoman. As for Evans, his family have been at the castle since they first built the mound. She's his liege lady too. And more."

She gave her ghastly cackle again and Dale, looking shocked, said, "Surely you don't mean . . . ?"

"Course I do. She's slept with them both in her time, and others, like as not. She likes to be worshiped, that one. Reckon she's past taking lovers now, but she's always got a page boy or a minstrel—Rafe Northcote it's been lately—trotting after her like a little dog. There was talk about her when she was young, before she went to Ireland and married, and after she came back, too—well, Bess is her husband's child, I daresay, but I wouldn't put money on Sir Philip being a real Mortimer. He takes after her, so who's to guess who his father was?"

I remembered the laughter among the Vetch villagers when Brockley and I were rescuing Gladys from them. To them, no doubt, Lady Thomasine was a figure of fun.

"Sir Philip thinks he's a Mortimer," I said, "but possibly isn't?"

"I daresay. It's a great name. He'd rather be a Mortimer than a mistake. Who wouldn't?"

"Well," Brockley said at length. "You've told us a tale, Gladys, and we've told you ours. But"—he turned to me—"what now? I think, madam, that we'd better get back to Tewkesbury. You should tell Master Henderson what has happened. He will speak for you to the sheriff of Hereford. The sheriff must take control of the search for Rafe's killer. He can search Mortimer's document chest as well while he's about it."

I looked into the fire. "Madam?" said Brockley.

It had been Lady Thomasine who first wanted me to look into her son's affairs, wanting discretion, for his sake. I no longer cared about her wishes, or his neck. But the desire for discretion had not been Lady Thomasine's alone.

"The queen and Cecil wanted secrecy," I said. "At least until they knew what Mortimer was really up to. We can put Rafe's death in the hands of the authorities—with Rob Henderson to back me, I'd risk that—but not Mortimer's schemes against the queen, if he really has any. If we do that, the secrecy is gone. I wish I could have just one more try at Sir Philip's study."

"But you can't go back to the castle now, ma'am!" cried Dale. "It's a mercy that you got your daughter out of it."

"Yes, it is. But I hate to leave a task unfinished."

"I can't see what choice you have, madam," Brockley said.

"No, indeed," declared Dale with vigor.

Brockley's inexpressive features were very misleading, and he knew it too. He really did enjoy making jokes with a perfectly blank face. He saw that I was still hesitating, and chose this moment to indulge his little quirk.

"Madam, you can hardly hide in the castle and creep out at night to search the study. Not unless you skulk in Isabel's Tower like one of the ghosts."

The scheme I wanted came into my head then, all complete. Brockley, watching my face, said with sudden misgiving: "No, madam! No, Mistress Blanchard, it isn't to be thought of."

"We can get into the castle and into that study by night, quite easily," I said. "Through Isabel's Tower. Why not? As you say, Brockley; every door into a castle makes it more vulnerable. We go in by the entrance that Geoffrey de Vetch so obligingly made—the way Lady Thomasine brought us out. Then we walk through the tower and out by the door into the courtyard. Both those doors have ordinary locks. I expect I can open them. We can go straight across to Aragon, carry out our task, and then leave again. If we need to rest, we can shelter in the tower itself until daybreak, and be away before it's fully light."

"Sleep in a haunted tower?" said Dale in a hushed voice.

"Well, yes." I was thinking while I talked. "There wouldn't be anywhere else. We can't sleep in the open; it isn't warm enough. There isn't any other shelter nearby except maybe for barns belonging to the village and we might be caught if we went near the village. But we need only stay in the tower for a few hours. No one goes there; it should be quite safe."

"Madam, *no*!" Brockley was horrified. But I refused to heed him.

"Tell me, Brockley, are you carrying any money? You usually have your purse on you. Was it on your belt when we started from the keep last night?"

"Well, yes, madam, it was, but . . ."

"Is there enough to buy a couple of horses? We'll need horses, to get back to the castle on."

"Ponies," said Gladys. "Good strong hill ponies. The man Griff works for, a landowner he is, he keeps a few pony mares as well as his sheep. He's generally got something for sale, and with sweet tempers and good mouths. He breaks them in himself and makes a good job of it." She looked at us wickedly, head on one side. "I've a fancy to come back to Vetch with you."

"There's no need for that," I said, but Gladys overrode me as I had just overridden Brockley.

"Like to see Mortimer and his lady mother get their comeuppance, I would. Yes, both of them. I'd wager it wasn't all her. You think he doesn't know you were brought up here? Probably it was all his idea. I wouldn't know why he killed Rafe, but I'd wager he did, and he's scared out of his wits that you'll say so to the sheriff if you ever get to see him. Hah! I want to know what happens, and who's to bring me word if I ain't there with you? And it ain't just curiosity. You stopped me being stoned and then Mortimer and Lady Thomasine tried to kill you. I'll not forgive them for that. Maybe I might even help in some way. I know Vetch well. I ought to. Forty-six years I spent there. I won't be a trouble to you. I'll get back here on my own. When you're on your way again, Hugh Cooper'll help me. He's reasonable enough when he hasn't got a pack of villagers all round him. I'll tell him I came back because I was homesick but I've seen it was a mistake and decided I'll settle for the hermitage after all."

She looked around at us and something in the air of the hermitage changed.

On the face of it, we were four most unimpressive people. Gladys was an aging and unlovely crone. I had once been a lady-in-waiting to a queen and wife of a well-to-do Frenchman, but just then, with my dirty gown and tangled hair, I more closely resembled a beggar woman. Dale and Brockley were no better, and as for the hermitage, our refuge, it was a grubby, squalid cell.

Yet something came into it then which was not grubby, not squalid, not commonplace. Rafe, only a day or two ago, had sung a ballad about a knight who, in a dark and filthy cave, saw the gleam of gold and gems and found a beautiful sword with a golden scabbard and a jeweled hilt. I had a good memory—that tutor had set store by training our memories—and I could recall some of the words. Rafe had used that last, risqué verse to embarrass me, but it was an earlier verse which I now remembered. *The ruby shone amid the mire, with pure and undiminished fire; the gold all damascened remained amid the murk, unharmed, unstained.*

My fealty to Elizabeth remained too, unstained either by our grimy condition now, or by the way Elizabeth had once used me. She might have betrayed me, but she had done it for love of her realm. As I had realized, back in Thamesbank, she and it were facets of the same thing and anyone who loved England must perforce keep faith with her queen. Which meant that I must keep faith with her. I would make my future home in France but nothing would ever change my feeling for the land where I was born.

Within my mind, all these things welded themselves together into a single shining shape like a sword. Almost, I could see the golden scabbard; I could draw the blade and behold the blue-white edge of the steel—feel the hard, cool jewels of the hilt against my palm.

And the others sensed the change. I saw it in their eyes, that they too had glimpsed the gold and ruby gleaming through the dirt.

"Brockley," I said, "and Dale, and Gladys. It may be that Mortimer is laying a scheme which in some way threatens Elizabeth. I hope it is not so, but it is my duty to find out if I can. I think I should try again. It could be done."

Brockley made a last-ditch objection. "I've explored the castle, maybe more than you have, madam. There are doors from the upper floors of that tower out onto the west wall and the south wall. Those doors have bolts on the outside. Now, are you sure the door into the courtyard has an ordinary lock and not a bolt? You can't pick a bolt."

"I'm quite sure," I said, once more blessing my tutor's training. He had taught us not only to memorize poetry, but to look at things when we were out walking and remember what we had seen. "And," I added triumphantly, "I still have the key to Aragon that Lady Thomasine gave me. What with finding Rafe dead, and bundling us into that dungeon and then sending us off to die on the—Mynydd Llyr, you call it, don't you, Gladys?—she never took it back." I felt in my hidden pocket, found the key and brought it out. I held it up. "Here it is. We can walk straight in."

Brockley met my eyes and then nodded slowly. Dale bit her lip and put her hand on his arm, but he took her hand and held it firmly and she too met my eyes and gave me, if unwillingly, her nod.

"And God be with us all," said Gladys.

14

Isabel's Tower

"That Lady Thomasine must be out of her mind," Dale said. "And if that son of hers *did* know all about it, and I wouldn't be surprised, then he's out of his mind too! Shutting us up in that hut like that! Didn't they think anyone would come asking after us? Master Henderson would."

"I know," I said thoughtfully. "It's very strange. Lady Thomasine implied that they were somehow going to hide the fact that Rafe was murdered. He'll have disappeared, though—that's for sure—and I think we were meant to disappear as well. But—four people, just vanishing into thin air? Yes, I do wonder how the Mortimers meant to explain it."

We were in the hermitage, pounding dough to make a supply of rye bread to take with us. We meant to carry a fair amount of food. "You don't know what might go wrong," Gladys had said in sibylline tones. "You might not find what you want straightaway like, and need to hide in the tower for a day and try again the next night. Best be ready."

"We are not going to spend a day in Isabel's Tower," I protested. "We'll search the study for . . . the evidence I've orders to find . . . and be away as fast as we can."

"I'd say we should be off without even stopping to rest," said Brockley, "except that we'll all very likely be frazzled and in need of some sleep. I don't want Fran getting ill. She's been through enough as it is. And the mistress is right; the tower's the only shelter."

"No harm in being ready," Gladys insisted, and set about making rye bread regardless. Dale and I were now helping her. We could hardly start out that day, after all. We needed to get hold of some ponies first.

Brockley, who had turned out to be carrying a fair amount of money on him, had set out to find mounts for us. Griff had taken him to the village which lay at the foot of the mountain, below the woods. I thumped the dough irritably, due to impatience at the delay, and Dale said again that the Mortimers must be crazed.

Gladys snorted. "They're neither of them quite right in the head if you ask me. But they're crafty enough in some ways. They wouldn't have wanted your bodies anywhere near the castle, in case anyone *did* ask questions. They asked Evans's advice, I expect, about somewhere to put you. Evans's ma came from the same village that I do and he'd know about that hut. It's empty most of the year because the sheep only go up to the Mynydd Llyr for July and August. They'd all reckon you wouldn't be found in time to save your lives."

"Why on earth didn't they kill us outright, I wonder, and take us away in sacks?"

"Maybe Mortimer didn't much like killing Rafe," said Gladys shrewdly. "Killing's easy to say and nasty to do. Likely enough, he found that out. Evans and Pugh felt the same, I daresay. Three of you, as well! Be like a massacre. Shutting you up like Isabel and Rhodri were, that'ud be easier. They'd have had your bodies out of the hut afore anyone could find them, I expect. As for explaining it all away, clever folk can always invent a story. You could invent one yourself if you tried. In their place, what would you do?"

"I can't imagine what story they're going to tell about Rafe," I said. "As for us—well, they could pretend that we'd left the castle in the normal way and claim that they'd no idea what had happened to us after that. They'd have to get rid of our horses but I suppose they could turn them loose somewhere well away from the castle. Mortimer could have done that at daybreak."

"See?" The hermitage had a bread oven, at one side of its hearth. Gladys pushed the first of the shaped loaves into it. "You're thinking up ideas already."

"They could just pretend that Rafe had been sent away." Dale straightened up from tending the fire, a thoughtful frown on her forehead. As always when she was upset or anxious, her pock-marks stood out more than usual. "They could say he'd been sent abroad because he behaved so badly with that girl Alice. Packed off to Venice or the Netherlands or somewhere. Later, they could say they'd heard news that he was dead of some fever or other. That would smooth everything over, at Vetch and at his home, too, the place he was going to inherit. And they could say that we'd just left, gone back toward Tewkesbury and if we hadn't got there, we must have been robbed and murdered on the road. At Vetch Castle, they'd be all shocked and horrified."

"There you are," said Gladys, with one of her diabolical cackles. "Oh, they'd think they could get away with it, all right. Your bodies would have gone down a ravine somewhere. Plenty of those hereabouts."

She cackled again. Repelled, I left off thumping dough and went to the door. Looking down the hill I saw two riders just emerging from the woods. Even from this distance, I recognized Brockley. The other one must be Griff, and they were bringing us a couple of ponies.

I was disconcertingly glad to see Brockley. This wouldn't do, I thought. It was only because I was deprived of Matthew. I needed Matthew. I needed his companionship and his physical presence. Come to think of it, I had been much too impressed by Owen Lewis. Without my husband, I was becoming susceptible to male charms in general. Well, it must stop.

Once back at Blanchepierre with Meg, I said to myself, I would adapt to the formality of Blanchepierre; I would stop pining for England. The longer Elizabeth held her throne, the more secure she would become. Perhaps Matthew would eventually desist from conspiring against her. I would settle down to domestic life and maybe, I thought optimistically, once my mind was at ease, my body would become cooperative enough to bear another child in safety.

I would waste no time at Vetch Castle, I decided. If I could not examine the strongbox at once or found nothing in it, then I would give up. I would rejoin Meg as quickly as I could, and go back to report failure to Cecil. At least I would be able to say that I had tried.

There. I had come to a sensible decision. Meanwhile, I would stop worrying at the mystery of what was going on at Vetch. I then found that my mind refused to do any such thing but on the contrary continued, obstinately, to gnaw at the puzzle. *Who* had killed Rafe and why? And if Mortimer's plans really did include some kind of threat to the queen, what manner of threat might it be?

I could think of no new theories about Rafe's murder. Brockley and I, in our dungeon, had thought of every possibility and found proof of none. The possible threat to Elizabeth offered more chances for speculation. Elizabeth was vulnerable to scandal, as she had already learned, when the wife of her favorite, Dudley, had died in mysterious circumstances. Could there be another scandal concerning her, going back ten years? Could Mortimer's abrupt departure from court a decade ago have something to do with it after all? Lady Mortimer had said he was involved in a duel over a woman, and had claimed not to know any details. But what if Elizabeth had been the woman? Perhaps Mortimer had fought a duel against someone who was spreading scandal about her, or had evidence of scandal . . .

I pulled myself up sharply. I didn't like that train of thought and didn't propose to mention it aloud. I wished I knew the truth about that duel. It was possible that Mortimer might have fought on Elizabeth's behalf ten years ago, but kept in mind what he had learned and was now proposing to use his knowledge for purposes of blackmail. One thing was certain: if scandal against Elizabeth was involved in any way, then she and Cecil certainly ought to be warned and the investigation, equally certainly, should be discreet. We must be very, very careful not to get caught.

Brockley and Griff were almost here. I went to meet them. "You've got some ponies, then. They look sturdy."

"They'll do," said Brockley. "They'd better. The lies I've had to tell! Griff here introduced me to the landlord he works for, and I told him I was buying on behalf of a wool merchant who wants pack animals that can be ridden as well. I said I was on foot just now because my mare went lame a few miles back and I had to leave her."

I had decided to adopt a tone of casual cheerfulness with Brockley. "You're a plausible rogue, once you set your mind to it," I said.

"I suppose I'm to blame for this insane scheme," he said. "It's on my conscience, madam, and I wish you'd give the idea up. But if you won't, I must do my best for you."

He had bought some secondhand saddlery as well—a couple of well-worn saddles with saddlebags, and basic bridles with snaffle bits and no nosebands. "We could set out at once," I said.

"Got to let the bread bake first," said Gladys, who had come out to look at the ponies. "First light tomorrow, when we're fresh; that's best. I got a ham we can take along and some goat's cheese. Griff'll have to milk the goat and feed the chickens while I'm gone."

"I bought some flasks for water, too," Brockley said. "We can carry them in the saddlebags. We may want some during the night in the tower. And Griff's found a bit of rope for bundling stuff up so as we can carry it. It looks like his mother's washing line but as I can't speak Welsh and he's hardly got any English, I couldn't ask, though we've managed well on the whole, with sign language." He grinned and I saw in him the adventurous gleam which had in the past made him such a blessing. He always counseled caution and urged more ladylike behavior on me, but when it came to the point, he was the best comrade in the world.

We started out at dawn the next morning, Brockley on one pony with Dale perched uncomfortably behind him; me on the other with Gladys as my pillion rider. Gladys had supplied a salve and some linen wrappings for my sore calves, and I was grateful, but I wished she wasn't riding with me, for she smelled terrible. Brockley said she would be a nuisance and shouldn't come at all, but she was determined and we dared not leave her behind in case she somehow told on us after all. Despite the debt she owed us, I think we were all rather afraid of her.

We carried blankets by using them as saddlecloths, which

was more comfortable for the pillion riders, who had to do without saddles and would otherwise have been jolting about on the ponies' spines. Each of us had a bag of food rolled up in a fleece and tied to our backs with lengths of what Gladys had confirmed was Griff's mother's washing line. "Well, her spare. Careful, Bronwen is. Always keeps spares of everything."

With the ponies carrying double, our journey was slow, but our tough little mounts served us well. I did not think my mare Bay Star could have coped with the double weight. I was very fond of Bay Star though, and wondered what had happened to her and to Speckle, and whether I would ever get them back.

It took two days to get back to the castle. The weather was overcast but fortunately dry. We lodged overnight in a farmstead near Ewyas Harold and made a few extra purchases in the little town, including some stouter footwear (we had left our riding boots in the keep guest quarters and my shoes were now letting in water), candles, a couple of lanterns, and a lute. The lute was Gladys's idea and neither Brockley nor I approved of it. "We're not really going to pretend to be ghosts," I complained. "We're just going to be as invisible as ghosts, that's all."

"A few twang-twangs in the night might keep nosey folk away," said Gladys. "You thought of that?"

"No," I said. "Besides, Rhodri's shade is supposed to play a harp. We can't afford a harp and anyone with an ear for music would know the difference. The minstrel, Gareth, for instance! It might just fetch people out to see who was playing games. The castle can't be entirely populated by timid mice! I don't see Pugh or Evans being frightened of a few twanging noises."

"Quite right, madam." Like me, Brockley had adopted a brisk tone when we talked together. "We could draw trouble on us rather than keep it away."

"You have the lute now, all the same," said Gladys. "There's useful it might be, after all. Or can't any of you play it?"

"I can," I said. "But I'm not going to."

"I can't," said Dale sadly. "It's a skill I never learned. But Roger plays."

"Just about," Brockley said. "Not that I'm in practice but I could manage a tune or two if need be, though I don't see the need of it now. Oh, very well. We'll take the lute, but in my opinion we'd be fools to use it."

The farmstead had been comfortable, and while there, I managed to have a thorough wash. But a long ride and a night in Isabel's Tower now lay ahead, a prospect so depressing that before we got there, I was regretting the whole enterprise. We could have reached the castle well before the end of the second day, but we did not want to enter the tower until darkness had fallen, so we waited in a small wood, moving off the track and out of sight of it. We had a piece of luck in that we found a spring, so that we could drink freely from the flasks we had filled at the farm, and then fill the flasks up again.

While we waited, we talked our plans over once more. Gladys was disappointed that we only intended to search Mortimer's study. "What about Rafe?" she said. "You fall over him lying dead on the floor and don't want to know for sure who killed him? Aren't you goin' to try and find out?"

"We can't," I said. "Of course we'd like to know who did it, but . . ."

"I'd reckon it was Mortimer," Brockley said. "It could have been Owen Lewis, but Mortimer's most likely, judging by the lengths his mother went to, to hide the fact that there'd been a murder at all."

"I agree," I said. "We don't know why but I can think of reasons. Perhaps Rafe and Lady Thomasine *were* lovers and Mortimer resented it."

"He never resented Pugh or Evans," snorted Gladys. "Why Rafe?"

"Maybe it was the other way about," said Dale unexpectedly. We looked at her questioningly. "I mean," said Dale, "that perhaps that's why he was so very angry with Rafe for making advances to Alice. Maybe he felt that Rafe was betraying Lady Thomasine!"

"It all sounds quite unreasonable to me," I said irritably, "but then, the Mortimers seem to be unreasonable altogether. I can't unravel them! But of course we shall report Rafe's death to Master Henderson, and he can decide what to do. One thing's certain—we can't go round the castle waking people up and questioning them. We're ghosts—remember?"

"So's Rafe. They say murdered men walk," said Gladys horribly.

"That'll do, Gladys," said Brockley. "Mistress Blanchard is right. No doubt we'd all like to go into this business of who killed Rafe. It could even be mixed up somehow with Mortimer's plans for getting his hands on a fortune. I can't see how, but when you've got two mysteries close together, it seems natural to wonder if they're parts of just one mystery. But we can't do it ourselves. We have to leave it to Master Henderson. And trying to scare us with talk of Rafe walking won't help."

"He won't walk," I said. "If everyone who died by violence walked afterward, the world would be full of wandering spirits."

"And who's to say it ain't?" said Gladys. "Maybe we can't all see the spirits, but they might be there."

"Gladys," I said. "Just be quiet!"

Secretly, I was becoming afraid of lurking in a haunted tower, and creeping back in the dark to the room where I had all but trodden on Rafe's body. I was thankful that I need not do it alone.

When night fell, we emerged stealthily from the wood. We couldn't simply ride to the foot of Isabel's Tower because the moat was in the way: we had to find the place where we had met our escort when we were brought out of our dungeon. We had to go slowly, for the night was very dark indeed. The cloudy sky had grown very heavy as evening fell and it looked as though more rain was on the way.

When we had forded the stream which fed the moat and found the foot of the path up to the castle walls, we dismounted. The hardy ponies could be left out, but Brockley, who had paid more attention to the castle's surroundings than I had, took them to a stretch of pasture with an elm copse in it, which would give them some shelter if the rain grew heavy. He hobbled their front feet, so that they could wander slowly and graze, but would be easy to catch in the morning. With luck, he said, we would be away at dawn and no one would ever know they'd been there.

I hoped so. I also hoped very much that Bay Star was not shivering out of doors in this unseasonably chilly weather. She had Arab blood and she felt the cold.

While turning the ponies loose, Brockley discovered that one of the elms was hollow. We bundled the saddles and bridles inside, where they were out of the weather and well hidden, too. Then burdened with our fleeces and blankets, food bags and water flasks, we set off to climb the path on foot.

A watchtower loomed above us and halfway up I brought us all sharply to a halt because I had glimpsed, between the battlements, the lantern carried by one of Mortimer's unnecessary traditional sentries. We remained quite still, waiting, and were glad now of the darkness. We were not likely to be detected while we stayed silent and motionless.

Presently, the lantern went away and we could move on again. Gladys and Dale both puffed and panted on the slope and I muttered at them to be quiet. To save their breath, we slowed down, which stretched my nerves to breaking point. It felt as though we were to spend forever creeping up toward that wretched tower.

Once we were up, we turned right and stole along the narrow way between the west wall and the moat, leaving the tower behind. Here we got along much more quickly, which was just as well, for the threatened rain had begun, in big, cold drops. As we reached Isabel's Tower, we heard a distant rumble of thunder and I had no difficulty in putting my lock picks into the keyhole, for a flash of lightning obligingly showed it to me. I was glad the lightning had held off until now. Earlier, it might have revealed us to the sentry on the watchtower.

Opening the lock proved absurdly easy. I did it in less than a minute. We took our loads inside. Brockley lit a candle and with its help we found our way through to the room on the courtyard side of the tower. Brockley set it down in a corner well away from the windows. Its small circle of light showed us a patch of bare stone wall and a stretch of dusty floor. There was nothing alarming to be seen but Dale at once said, uneasily: "There's such a feeling about this place, ma'am. I don't like it."

I agreed with her. When I came through the tower with Brockley and Lady Thomasine, there had been no time to notice it, but in the dead of night, it was there and inescapable. Darkness is always frightening, but here it seemed tangible. Beyond the circle of the candlelight, it hung like a heavy curtain, which seemed to stir whenever a draft moved, as though disturbed by unseen presences. The gooseflesh rose on my skin and I found myself straining my ears for stealthy sounds beyond the light.

Brockley's voice, however, steadied me. "There's nothing to fear. We're all here together. Are we leaving our bedding here, or going up a floor, madam? Going up might be safer, though we'll have to be careful that candle doesn't show. We'll have to find the stairway and . . ."

Another flash of lightning came and obligingly if briefly displayed the entire room around us: the courtyard door, the door to the dungeon steps, and a round archway beyond which I glimpsed a steep spiral stair leading upward. The arch was like a dark mouth. I had been on the point of agreeing with Brockley that we should go up one storey, but I changed my mind. A massive crash of thunder followed the flash. As it died away, I said as brightly as I could: "We got into shelter just in time, I think. With luck the storm will be over by daylight. I think it will be all right to rest here, when we get back from Aragon, Brockley. Let's get straight on to search that study. The courtyard door is over there. I saw it just now. I'm sure that's the one. If we . . ."

Lightning came again, showing me the faces of my companions. Dale's was tired and strained, Gladys's was witchlike, and Brockley's appeared to be listening. "Brockley?" I said. "What is it?"

Another growl of thunder came and went. Then Brockley said: "It's raining."

"I know. It was raining when we got here. It usually rains during a thunderstorm."

"Listen!" said Brockley.

I listened. But I still didn't take it in. I had laid such careful plans. It was not possible that a mere rainstorm could overset them. Brockley, however, took up the candle again and led the way back to the outer room and the door by which we had entered. It was still unlocked and he pushed it open. "Madam—come and see."

I went to his side. "Just try to step out into that," Brockley whispered.

I had no need to step out. The lightning flickered again and showed me all too clearly what he meant: the glittering rods of the most torrential downpour I had ever seen. It barred our way out as effectively as any bolts or bars.

"That would soak even our thick cloaks through in a moment," said Brockley. "We should be wet to the skin before we'd gone two yards and we have no change of clothes." He looked down at his feet. "These shoes that we got in Ewyas Harold are a lot better than the ones we had before, but I wish we could have found some real boots there. These would never keep out rain like this! We'll have to wait until it stops. If it does stop," he added ominously.

I understood what he meant. That rain was not only heavy but relentlessly steady. It wasn't going to slacken for a long time yet. We were not going to spend a day in Isabel's Tower, I had said. But I had not taken mountain weather into account.

"Even if we did brave it," Brockley said, closing the door, "we can't leave the castle until it stops. Fran can't ride through such weather and neither can you, madam. I'd as soon not venture it myself. So why risk getting drenched now?"

"But if we can't move from here until it stops and we can't move in daylight either—and we can't—then we might be here all through tomorrow!"

"Quite," said Brockley.

"It may stop at any moment," I said hopefully.

"Not it. All my bones are aching and they don't lie. Set in, that is, till dawn," said Gladys, almost smugly. "Told you we ought to be ready," she added. "Now do you see why I said bring plenty of food? I knew something 'ud go wrong. I knew that in my bones, as well. I said, they don't lie."

I had a repulsive vision of Gladys consulting her own skeleton, muttering spells and conjuring up a vision of the thing. I shuddered and tried to pull myself together. "Oh, this is ridiculous! The study's in Aragon, only just across the courtyard. Just because it's raining . . ."

"You've seen for yourself what kind of rain," said Brockley.

We made our way back to the inner room, where our bedding lay on the floor where we had dumped it. Dale sank onto it. "Oh, ma'am, I'm so tired."

I was deathly tired too, but I kept on protesting. "I didn't bargain for having to hide here for two nights. It's too risky."

"We've no choice," said Brockley. "Just listen to it!"

We did wait a little while longer, hoping that the rain would ease and give us a chance to cross the courtyard, but its steady sound did not change and when I went back to peer once more from the outer door, the wind sent it splashing in on me like a sea breaker. Grumblingly, disbelievingly, I gave in. We were all exhausted by that time. We must sleep as best we could and hope for a better opportunity tomorrow night instead. We settled down to rest, absurdly, within yards of an objective which I knew we dared not try to reach. We might well become ill, and it had occurred to me also that we might leave dangerous traces of our dripping persons. We would not want a hue and cry after us.

We made ourselves as comfortable as possible. We each had a fleece, a blanket, and a cloak, and we made pillows by stuffing most of the food into one bag and rolling up the others. We lay pressed together for warmth. Dale slept in the curve of Brockley's chest; I lay against his back and Gladys lay against me.

Brockley's nearness was a blessing. Gladys stank.

Outside, the rain went on and on.

15

Faces at the Window

I didn't expect to sleep much, but unexpectedly, I fell into a heavy slumber almost at once, and once again, I dreamed of lying on the dungeon floor and staring at Lady Thomasine's pretty rose-embroidered slippers. She began to kick me with them and I woke. I knew at once, from the absence of the smell, that Gladys had gone. The windows were brilliant streaks of light and the storm had passed. Gladys's fleece and blanket lay empty and I could see no sign of her anywhere.

"Brockley." I shook him. "Wake up. Gladys has disappeared."

"What?" Brockley sat up, tousled and sleepy. He stared around him. "She'll have gone up to the next floor to look round, I dare-say, or to find a privy. I suppose they had privies in the days when they built this place? Wouldn't be a bad idea if we all went and had a look. But we've got to make sure no one sees us from outside. We're trapped here for the day, remember."

"I could hardly forget," I said grimly.

We woke Dale up and got her onto her feet. Then we rolled up our bedding and put it in a shadowy corner, and set off to climb through the several floors of the tower, in search of Gladys and a privy.

It was a hard climb, for the spiral stair was not only steep but narrow, with uneven steps. It wound through the thick walls of the tower, with a door at each level, leading into the rooms. We were afraid to call Gladys's name in case someone heard us, so we searched every floor as we went. They were all much alike, each with two adjoining chambers, largely empty, although we did come across a few bits of abandoned furniture: a couple of old settles; one bedstead with moldering curtains still in place; a bench or two.

Dust lay everywhere and the stone walls were patched with green mold. The courtyard windows were glazed, though some of them were broken, but the arrow slits looking outward had neither glass nor shutters. On the second floor an indignant pair of jackdaws flew out of a nest hole just inside an arrow slit, and we saw a barn owl looking down at us from a ceiling beam, eyes round and unblinking.

On the next floor, Dale, who had been very startled by the jackdaws, suddenly announced that she could see footprints in the dust. "And they're not Gladys's prints. Some look smallish, but not as small as her feet are."

I couldn't see any footprints at all, of any size, and neither could Brockley, even though Dale pointed insistently and got us to come and stand close beside her so that we could all look from the same angle.

"There's nothing there. Do control your imagination, Dale," I said.

"The mistress is right. I can't even see a rat's paw marks," Brockley said. "You're seeing things, Fran."

"I'm not."

"You are," I said. "Forget it. Come on. We must find Gladys."

"I expect the ghosts have got her," said Dale sullenly.

"Nonsense! And," I added, "I think that little arch over there might lead into a privy."

It did. The privy, which was hollowed from the outer wall of the tower, showed no sign of having been used by Gladys, but we used it ourselves before continuing upward. At the very top, the stairs led onto the roof but we didn't venture out, for fear of being seen. We stood on the stairs and risked calling Gladys's name, just loudly enough, we hoped, to reach her if she was nearby. There was no answer, and in any case I felt that so much climbing was probably beyond her. Feeling uneasy, we made our way down again.

"When we came in," I said, "I didn't try to lock that outer door after us. I was so tired—I didn't think of it. She could have gone outside. The rain must have stopped some time ago. Perhaps she needed a privy but didn't want to climb stairs."

"But she's been gone so long!" Dale's voice rose and I hushed her with a frown. "Suppose," said Dale, more quietly but with big round eyes, "she's gone to tell someone we're here?"

"I shouldn't think so," I said. "Lady Thomasine doesn't like her, and the villagers hate her."

"It might be a way of getting back into favor," said Dale dismally. "Do a good turn to the Mortimers in the hope of being allowed back to live in the castle, maybe. She can't want to live in that lonely hermitage place."

"If she's gone to tell the Mortimers we're here," I said reasonably, "then why haven't they come hotfoot to fetch us? Where are they?"

"All we can do is wait and keep a lookout," Brockley said. "We'd better eat something. We can't go hunting for that strongbox until tonight, anyway."

We decided that we could stay on the ground floor for the day, as long as we were cautious. None of us could remember seeing anyone, ever, go near enough to Isabel's Tower to see inside, and no one wanted to drag bundles up those steep stairs. So we settled down, taking an unexciting breakfast of water, rye bread, and some goat's cheese, which I disliked. It was a far cry, I thought, from the delicate dishes at court or at Blanchepierre, where Matthew and I had prided ourselves on the excellent Gallic cuisine.

I wanted to try relocking the outer door but couldn't in case Gladys came back. We would have been wise to shift to the outer room to keep an eye on the door and keep away from the courtyard windows, but the courtyard attracted us, because there was a puzzling amount of activity there and we kept wondering why. There were voices and footsteps and people shouting orders, and when a mysterious rumbling noise began, our curiosity became too much for us and we all got up to peer out.

The sight of people with brooms sweeping the pools from last night's prolonged cloudburst into a drain was no surprise.

More intriguing was an oxcart laden with casks, which was being unloaded by the kitchen door. Then we saw Pugh escorting a party of well-dressed strangers to the hall, and noticed a number of castle servants carrying things, including candles and rolls of what looked like dark cloth, into a nearby doorway. "That's the retainers' hall, isn't it?" I whispered. "What's going on?"

"That's the castle chapel," Brockley whispered back. "It's tacked on to the end of the retainers' hall. It's only used on Sundays—I found that out chatting in the stables. You might not know. We were never here on a Sunday. We got to Vetch on a Tuesday and by Sunday, we were in Gladys's hermitage."

"But what are all those people doing?" I said.

Dale said fearfully: "There's someone at that outer door. It might be Gladys, but . . ."

It was Gladys. Her familiar shawled figure came to meet us as we hurried to the other room. "Where in God's name have you been?" demanded Brockley.

"Bein' useful," said Gladys. "Findin' things out, and now I'm famished. I'll talk when I've eaten."

Now that Gladys was back, I decided to tackle the lock of the outer door. It turned out to be of a type which my lock picks would turn either way. While I made us secure, Gladys started her breakfast. I came back to find the others waiting in revolted silence while she slurped at her water flask and mumbled the food with her gums and her few discolored teeth. Watching Gladys eat—which also entailed listening to it—was a horrid business.

After a few mouthfuls, however, she condescended to talk to us. "I wanted to ask what really happened to that lad Rafe, if you didn't," she said with an air of satisfaction. "Can't say I've found out *that* but learned other things, I have, things you'd best know. You'll need to be careful tonight. Castle may not be as fast asleep as it ought to be."

"What do you mean? Gladys, what have you been doing? Have you been talking to people?" I asked in alarm.

"Now, don't you worry yourself. I lived for years in Vetch Village. I told you, I know all about it. There's a young wench, Blod, takes geese out to the common on the north side most days, early. I met her there. Stepped out from behind a gorse bush, I did."

Gladys cackled through a mouthful of rye bread and goat's cheese, causing us all to recoil in distaste.

"She nearly passed out, poor baby," Gladys said. "Twelve years old, she is, and sweet as a rose for the time being, until some man comes along to pull her petals off. 'Now, you don't need to be frightened of me, pretty one,' says I, 'I'm only old Gladys. You just do what I tell you, and I'll put a blessing on you. I want to talk to Olwen, what works in the castle. I'll watch your geese and you go and get her. But she'd better come on her own, except for you, Blod, and no nonsense. If she tells anyone I'm here, or there's anyone with her, she won't find me, but her hair'll all fall out and her teeth as well, and what's more, her father'll hear what she gets up to with Mortimer.'"

"Her father?" said Brockley in a choked voice, between laughter and outrage.

"You've met him. He's Hugh Cooper. Very moral, indeed, is Hugh Cooper. Mortimer's been using Olwen since she first came into the castle, a year ago or so now. He don't take her to his bed; he'd reckon a maidservant's beneath that, but he uses her just the same. Up against walls; quick ones in the wine cellar; once it was even a fast in-and-out on a table in the hall. Olwen told me that herself."

"Told you?" I said.

Gladys leered. "She's a fine healthy girl and he's a healthy man. Carryin' on like that, what's likely to happen? She came to me for help and I gave her something that got her out of trouble and she's not got into it again since then. Maybe she'll never breed now; that's the way it is, sometimes, when a girl takes a draft to kill a baby. But she talked to me then; cryin' she was and scared out of her wits on account of her father. If Hugh knew about it, he'd knock Mortimer's brains out, for all Mortimer's his landlord, and beat Olwen into pulp."

Gladys paused for a few more mouthfuls. We waited impatiently. "Well," she said at last, "Blod came back, and brought Olwen with her. Looked terrified, Olwen did. 'No need to be frightened,' I said. 'Just tell me what's going on in the castle these days.' 'Going on?' she says to me. 'What do you mean? There aplenty going on. Why, young Rafe Northcote, the master's ward, threw himself off the Mortimer Tower the other night. He was found at the foot of it, in the outer bailey, all broken—flat on his back, and staring at the sky. There's been an inquest, and my da was the foreman, and they brought it in suicide, along of he wasn't let to marry Mistress Alice.'

"And that weren't all." Gladys was enjoying herself. "Olwen had a bit more to say than that, and Blod knew some of it, too. Seems there's talk about you three as well. You disappeared all of a sudden, Mistress Blanchard, and there's been whispers about it. No one's got a reason why you might have pushed Rafe off the tower, but somehow or other there's a feeling about it. There's funny, it is, someone throws himself over the battlements one night and someone else disappears the morning after. And there's some have been saying that there wasn't enough blood—that Rafe ought to have bled more when he was smashed against the ground, and why didn't he? It's all whispers, but the castle's full of them, and so's the village."

"We'd better be *very* careful to keep well out of sight," I said anxiously.

"I'm not through; there's more yet," Gladys said. "Rafe's going into his grave tomorrow—outside the wall of the churchyard, poor little sod, seein' that the verdict was suicide and there's no room in God's own soil for anyone that desperate. We've all got to be happy and thankful for what he doles out to us, even if it's poverty or bein' ugly, or accused of what you haven't done. But they're letting him lie in the castle chapel tonight—he's bein' allowed that much. And he's to have a decent funeral, no matter where the grave's been dug. A whole lot of folk are here for it—Northcote cousins, and the steward and the chaplain from the place he should have inherited, and them that are married have brought their wives. They're going to hold a wake for him."

"What's a wake?" Dale asked.

"The household and the guests'll sit up with the body for its last night above the ground," said Gladys simply. "That's what they do in Ireland and Sir Philip's father came from Ireland. These Mortimers keep Irish customs. Well, not just Irish. Some of us Welsh do the same. The chaplain's keepin' a vigil by his coffin and his cousins'll take turns there during the night, and Mortimer'll be with them for part of the time. All the rest'll sit up in the hall—Lady Thomasine'll be there, and so will Owen Lewis. He's still here. The Haggards took Alice home, of course. The night'll start off with prayers and talkin' about how they remember young Northcote, and Gareth the minstrel, he'll have made a song for him . . ."

"I wonder if it was Gareth that killed him?" Dale said suddenly. "Everyone says he's old and wants to give up, but suppose he was really very jealous and hated it when Rafe was asked to play in the hall instead of himself?"

"Well, if he did, he's got away with it," Gladys said. "He'll sing a lament for Rafe tonight and everyone'll admire it. There'll also be wine and ale for everyone, and it'll quite likely turn into a party." She snorted. "Wakes often do. When Sir Philip's da died, the funeral was late because half the folk who were to go to it had headaches and the other half were throwin' up in buckets and they were all nearly too tired to stand up straight."

I looked at Brockley. "That explains the oxcart full of casks, and all the black cloth going into the chapel. They're going to drape it, I suppose."

"That and the main hall," Gladys said. "But the point is, the castle won't sleep tonight. There'll be people all over the place."

"So we can't do the search tonight," I said wearily. "We'll have to wait yet another day, until tomorrow night, again. But have we food enough for four, to last that long?"

We looked at our supplies. We had been rather too generous with our breakfast. If we had to wait yet another day, we would be hungry.

"We might do better to try for the study tonight," Brockley said, "but not until very late. Let's get it clear, Gladys. There'll be folk in the big hall and in the chapel and crossing the courtyard. But will they have much business in the Aragon wing?"

"Not much, I shouldn't think," Gladys said. "And not Sir Philip or his mother. *They* know where Rafe was really killed. In the study there. I doubt they'll want to go there at night or want anyone else to, either. Like I said, he might walk."

Brockley looked at me. "What do you say, madam?"

"I say that we wait until well on in the night and then, if it looks safe enough, we try. We won't know for sure till the time comes. You learned some useful things from Olwen, Gladys, but I still wish she hadn't seen you. Are you sure she doesn't realize you're actually hiding in the castle?"

"Not she. Told her I was going home, I did."

"Well, that's something." I sighed. "I wish all this could be over."

By noon it was raining again. Wrapped in our fleeces and blankets, we passed the time as best we could. Brockley told us tales of his soldiering days, and I recited some of the poetry I had learned as a child. I remember wondering what had happened to the belongings which we had left behind when we were taken to the Black Mountains. Among my things was a volume of verses including some favorites of mine by Sir Thomas Wyatt. I was fond of that book and hated to think that it might have been flung into the moat.

The day dragged, despite all our efforts to entertain one another. In the afternoon, we tried to sleep again, but no one could do more than doze. We dined on ham, rye bread, and a ration of water each, all of us longing for a fireside and some hot broth.

At about five of the clock, the rain died out and the western sky turned lemon-colored. A streak of yellow light from a window lay across the floor like a splash of paint. We heard slow footsteps and sad music and looked warily out once more, to see a somber procession carrying a coffin toward the chapel. Gareth led the way, playing a lament on a small harp. The procession did not go straight across the courtyard, but paced around it, and passed quite close to us. Gareth came near enough for me to see that as he walked, he was crying. Since his hands were occupied, he could not brush the tears away and they streamed unchecked down his seamed old face. This was grief, candid and heartfelt, for a young life lost and for the gifted pupil he had trained, whose fingers would never caress lute or harp again. Dale's theory was wrong. Whoever had driven that dagger into Rafe Northcote's back had not been Gareth.

As the procession passed into the chapel, Brockley became agitated. "They came too near," he said. "And there are strangers about. They might be inquisitive about the haunted tower and want to peep inside. It was a mistake to stay down here. We should move to an upper floor now, at once, and take our food and bedding with us."

We did so, though it was a struggle and we had to help Gladys up, for the steep stairs were indeed hard on her, spry though she was in other ways. We needed to get to the second floor at least for the first floor was on a level with the windows of our old guest quarters in the keep and someone there might be able to see in.

Once on the second floor, we prepared once more to settle down and wait. But before half an hour had passed, there was another disturbance outside. We heard the door of the great hall bang; someone whistled, and then there was a volley of barks and yelps. Brockley, peering with difficulty through the dirty glass of an unbroken leaded window, said that the dogs had been let loose.

"Poor brutes. No one's taken much thought for them. They've just been turned out to do their business and stretch their legs. They've been shut in the hall all day, I'll take my oath. With all the to-do, I hope someone's remembered to feed them. Oh yes, there's Susanna. I think she's going to feed them outside."

I pushed off my fleece and blanket and joined him, in time to see Susanna walking across the cobbles with two large feeding bowls. Then I drew back quickly, because she was coming straight toward Isabel's Tower.

"It's all right," Brockley whispered. "I've seen her feed them outside before. She always puts the bowls down in this corner of the courtyard, I suppose because it's out of the way. She never pays any heed to the tower. Yes, she's setting them down now. No need to be alarmed."

But I had already moved hastily away from the window, and in my hurry, I caught my foot on a corner of a blanket. I slipped, lurched back toward the window, put out a hand to save myself, and fended myself off from the window with a thud.

"Shh!" said Brockley urgently, and too late. I hadn't really made much noise, but dogs have acute ears as well as acute noses. From outside, the mastiff suddenly set up a furious baying.

Brockley swore under his breath. "I'm sorry!" I whispered. Keeping to one side of the window, I risked another glance outside. The wretched hound was standing up foursquare and barking at the tower as though it had challenged him. Susanna was shouting at him to be quiet and demanding to know what was the matter with him, and her husband, Jack, had run into the courtyard to see what was happening. The rotund second cook Higg came out too, hurrying from the kitchen to investigate the din.

The hound's nose was pointing upward, straight at our windows. The Raghorns and Higg were staring at them as well. Once more, I stepped back. Brockley shook his head despairingly. "Sir Philip'll be out there in a minute, in person; I'd put a bet on it. Madam, really!"

"Jackdaws make as much noise as I did," I muttered, aggrievedly.

"Dogs are sharp. They'd know the difference," Brockley informed me.

"Are they coming in? Will they find us?" Dale had stayed where she was, clutching her fleece around her, her blue eyes distended in fright. Gladys, however, clambered to her feet and came to see for herself what was happening.

"It's only them Raghorns. They're as scared of Isabel's Tower as they well can be, and that Higg not much better. Soon see them off," said Gladys. She rubbed her palm across the dirt-caked sill and then across her face, and before we realized what she was about, she leaned over the deep sill and pressed what was now a sickly gray countenance to the panes.

Susanna let out a shriek of pure terror. Brockley cursed and yanked Gladys away. Cautiously, I approached another window, slightly less dirty than the first, once more positioned myself to one side, and peered. Lady Thomasine's maid Nan was just stepping out of the hall porch. She saw Susanna clutching her husband's arm and pointing upward, and Higg anxiously questioning her, and started across the courtyard toward them.

With surprising strength, Gladys shook Brockley off and pressed her dusty features to the leaded panes again, whereupon Nan shrieked, even more loudly than Susanna; Higg trumped her with a howl of panic; and Jack Raghorn, reverting instinctively to the Catholic customs of his childhood, crossed himself. All four then turned and fled. Susanna fell over the mastiff in her hurry and all but went sprawling, but Jack grabbed her hand and dragged her up again. Gladys drew back and said: "There's the last of them, don't you worry."

"It'll bring the whole damned garrison here in a crowd, you silly old woman!" Brockley almost snarled.

"No, it won't," said Gladys calmly.

Nor did it. Dale remained shivering in her coverings but the rest of us, watching fearfully from the very edges of the windows, saw Mortimer and Lady Thomasine and various other people appear from different doorways and saw the Raghorns and Higg gesturing wildly toward the tower. Jack crossed himself compulsively half a dozen times more. But the dogs' feeding bowls had been left where Susanna had put them down, and the mastiff, which had dodged away with a yelp when Susanna nearly fell on him, noticed that his friends were eating and might well eat his share too. Losing interest in the tower, he shoved his way into the pack to get at his dinner. Mortimer strode across the courtyard, followed by several others, most of them people I didn't recognize, except for Owen Lewis, who was hard behind Mortimer. They stopped, looking upward. "Don't move," Brockley muttered. "They just might see a movement. If we don't stir, they'll see nothing."

We froze. Mortimer spoke to Lewis; Lewis laughed and shrugged. They came right up to the tower and tried the locked courtyard door. Mortimer shouted up to someone on the walls, and a moment later we heard someone trying the doors which led out onto the walls from the floor above us.

"Thank heaven I locked the door out to the grass," I whispered. "They may try that, too."

Whether or not they did, we couldn't tell. It was far away below and we couldn't have heard. The excitement in the courtyard, however, seemed to be over. Mortimer was spreading his arms to herd the crowd away and Lewis making gestures which clearly said: "It's nothing. Just nonsense. Forget it."

"Dear God!" said Brockley faintly, leaning against the wall and then sliding down to a sitting position. "I thought we were two steps away from that damned dungeon again. Gladys, how could you?"

"How could I? Told you I'd see them off," said Gladys smugly. "I knew you'd need me along with you, Master Brockley. I found out what was goin' on in the castle and now I've scared those pests away. I'm more than a sweetly pretty face, I am." She favored us with one of her dreadful leers, her fangs more ghastly than ever in the midst of her smeared features. "They wouldn't have come in," she said. "No fear of that. I know the Vetch folk. They come into the tower once in a while to sweep the place and that's all. But now and again, someone'll make out they've seen a face at the window. Then a crowd collects down below and goes hysterical, and Sir Philip comes out and tries the door down there and has the other doors tried as well, and finds them all fast, and shoos everyone away again. Just a ritual, that's what it is. Happens over and over, and it's all that ever happens. It's nothing new."

"Here, Gladys," said Dale, pushing off her fleece and blanket. She produced a handkerchief, spared a few drops of water from her bottle to wet it, and came to wipe Gladys's face. Brockley, rolling his eyes in exasperation, pushed the tumbled coverings out of the way before anyone else could trip over them.

"I'm sorry," I whispered. "It was an accident."

"No doubt, madam," said Brockley primly. "But we can't afford accidents."

"There. You look better now," Dale said to Gladys. "You were enough to frighten anyone, with your face all gray like that."

"You could have left it gray, for my part," said Gladys. "Fun, it is, frightening people, when you get to my age."

"You surely don't mean that," I said. We sat down again. Brockley portioned out a bread and cheese supper and we pulled our wrappings around us again, for warmth. "You can't really like frightening people," I said reprovingly. "Look at the trouble you made for yourself in Vetch Village."

I didn't expect the answer that I got. Suddenly Gladys's old eyes, which had probably once been a deep and sparkling brown but were now faded and rheumy with a faint pink web of blood vessels in their whites, blazed at me with such a fury that I drew back in alarm.

"Trouble? Bah! In the end, frightening people's all that's left. What do you know about it? Can't really like it? It's what keeps me warm at night, better than a blanket. Laugh myself to sleep over it, I do."

"But . . ." I was too taken aback to say any more.

"Young you are, yet awhile," said Gladys contemptuously. "And pretty. People are mostly kind to you. Wait till you've lost your teeth and your looks; then you won't be quite so easy to shock, my lady. It's not so bad when your young ones are with you. But they grow up and leave you and then it's different. Ho, yes! How different, you've yet to learn. That's when other folks' children start pointin' and laughin', or runnin' away from you. Ugly old Gladys! That's what they used to yell after me. What'll you do if, when you're old, the brats run after you callin' you ugly?"

Dale said sincerely: "But that's dreadful. Dreadful."

"Yes, it is," said Gladys pugnaciously. "But that ain't all. You can't do things the way you did. Your back hurts; your knees hurt. But the peas and onions still got to be weeded, ain't they? You don't notice it at your age, but I tell you, when you pull hard, weedin', the effort goes down into your knees. When your knees start to ache, the effort's got to go somewhere else, so you make faces. Then the children and the silly girls—there's silly that most girls are, it's their nature and the men seem to like it, which makes them sillier—then they don't just call you ugly. They call you the ugly old woman that makes faces."

The yellow evening was fading toward dusk, but I could still see her face quite clearly. Suddenly, I knew her leers and her cackles for what they were—a gallant defense against a harsh world. Her next words brought still more illumination.

"You need help and you can't get it," Gladys said. "I'll have some more of that bread and cheese, Brockley, if you don't mind. My knees might hurt but my guts still work. Well, I couldn't get enough help. I'm from the mountains. I'm not a Vetch woman. Still a stranger, I am, to them, or maybe they'd have told their nasty children to behave. So I got angry. They'd shout after me and I'd turn and I'd show them what makin' faces really means." She demonstrated, so horribly that we all shied back, even Brockley. Gladys, when she really tried, could make the worst gargoyle you ever saw on a church tower look angelic by comparison.

"I did that a time or two and they ran off screaming," said Gladys with satisfaction. "And I heard 'em screeching: 'The evil eye! The evil eye!' Good, I thought. That'll keep 'em off. Then one of the nasty little creatures climbed a tree and fell out and broke his arm and I told his mother he'd jeered at me, and this was what came to them as did that. Next thing I knew, the silly girls took to slinking to my cottage after dark, wanting love potions."

"What . . . what did you do?" asked Dale breathlessly.

Gladys chuckled wickedly. "I know a bit about potions. Never could do my knees much good but I cured my children's coughs with my own horehound brew. So for these daft girls, I'd mix up something that wouldn't do much harm, beyond a touch of the trots, maybe, and they'd go and slip it in some lad's ale, and sometimes it worked, because," said Gladys, becoming instructive, "the girl 'ud start believin' he'd be hers and that 'ud give her some confidence. Half the battle, that is, for a girl—makin' the man notice she's there. Maybe she's just the daughter of his da's best friend and he's too used to seein' her about, to realize she's eyein' him till she starts givin' him knowin' looks and little smiles. Anyhow, sometimes it works, and then she'll tell her friends, and soon an old biddy like me might have quite a business. And not just love potions."

"Gladys!" said Dale. "You never . . . ?"

"I never poisoned anyone that I know of, no. Not even when I was asked, and asked I have been," Gladys said. "But I helped Olwen out of trouble, like I told you, and others like her. People pay. In kind mostly. A jar of honey, a bag of flour, a basket of eggs, some peas, some onions, to make up for what I lose when I can't weed properly. Got to live somehow and got to find a way to put one over on them as jeer at me for my lost teeth and my lost youth. Ho! It'll be their turn one day if they live long enough. It'll be your turn one day, if *you* live long enough." She stared at me, and I saw the resentment in those faded eyes. "Your future, I am," she said. "So look well."

I shuddered. I wanted to cry for her and I wanted to scream: "No, no!" It was unbearable to think I might one day resemble

Gladys. It was still more unbearable to think that Meg might. So as not to hurt her by turning my head away, I said: "How old are you, Gladys?" and made myself sound interested.

"Two year short of my three score and ten. Not many live to be that old."

"Well, it's true you saved us just now," Brockley said. "Though I swear I thought you'd bring the roof in on us." He reached out and put his hand over hers. I knew I should have done the same but I couldn't bring myself to touch her. I noticed, though, that I had to peer to see what he was about; that the faces of my companions were fading in the dusk.

"It's nearly night," I said.

"We've a while to wait yet," Brockley said. "But we mustn't go to sleep. It won't be safe to move till a couple of hours after midnight, at least. But we'd better be ready when the right time comes."

16

Poison in the Pen

As darkness fell, we crept downstairs again and I set about picking the lock of the courtyard door. It was stiff and difficult and I became panicky, thinking that I wouldn't be able to do it. The light was fading with every moment and soon I could hardly see the lock, which made things worse. "Brockley," I whispered, "can you light a lantern?"

We had brought one of our candle-lanterns downstairs with us. Taking great care to ensure that it couldn't be glimpsed from outside, Brockley lit it. The little light was comforting, for we were all unpleasantly conscious of the dark and empty tower around and above us. At the least creak, at the slightest sigh of a night wind through an arrow slit, we would stiffen and startle like coneys when they hear a fox bark, and Dale's wide blue eyes would turn affrightedly this way and that.

Once, while I was still struggling with the lock, she said: "I *did* see footprints in that dust," but I told her to stop saying that. If something not canny was abroad in the tower and stirring the dust with ghostly feet, I didn't want to know about it.

The lock yielded at last, just as I was at the point of despair. Relieved, I said, "Well, we'll have no delay when it's time to go."

The castle settled slowly to its vigil. Candlelight shone from the chapel and the hall; people with torches and lanterns crossed the courtyard from time to time. After a while, we heard a murmur of voices from the hall, which grew louder and once or twice burst into singing. The wake, lubricated with good wine, was turning into a party, just as Gladys had foretold. Brockley clicked a disapproving tongue and growled that it was shockingly disrespectful.

After about three interminable hours, however, the traffic in the courtyard grew less and then ceased, and Gladys said surely we could risk it now.

"Are you coming?" I asked her, slightly surprised.

"Not to the study I'm not but there's something I want to look at out in the courtyard. Then I'll come back here. You got the key for Aragon? And them wire things you were using just now on the door? Brockley, you got your lute? Might frighten someone off if they come near the study while you're there."

Brockley muttered under his breath, but brought the lute all the same. "Just to keep Gladys quiet," he whispered to me. I felt in my hidden pocket to make sure that the lock picks and the key to Aragon really were there. Dale took the lantern. Gingerly, I opened the door, just enough to let one person at a time sidle out. The hinges creaked, but not very much. Lights still showed in the hall and chapel, and in the hall someone was singing a Welsh lament, but the courtyard itself was empty. We crept forth. Gladys at once hobbled ahead, making straight for the well, where she disappeared into the shadow of its thatched roof. She emerged again almost at once, beckoning and grinning.

"They usually leave a full bucket of water out when there's a feast. It's there. We can all have a drink and no risk of clankin' bucket chains."

"Well done," I breathed. Our water was getting low and Gladys's ham, though good, was salty. Gratefully, we scooped water up in our palms and drank. Gladys grunted with relief.

"Good, that is. I wanted a drop of water. Now I'll go back to the tower. I'll wait there, just inside the door."

She shuffled off. The rest of us, in single file, moved on across the courtyard. We went like shadows, with the lantern shrouded under Dale's cloak, because we could see without it. The stars were out, amid broken cloud, and a few lit torches had been set here and there, in niches over various doors. There was one over the door of Aragon, but as I had the key, I did not have to linger in the light while I fiddled with lock picks.

"They say," Brockley whispered to me as we stole into the blue parlor, "that the third attempt is lucky. Well, this is the third time you've tried to reach that strongbox."

"I hope you're right. Brockley, as before, you stay by the outer door, and listen. Dale, go to the foot of the stairs. I'll have to take the lantern."

This time, the study door really was locked but the key was in place on its ledge overhead. As I entered the study, I realized that, whatever his feelings about it, Sir Philip had once again used the place during the day for it was warm and, as before, a dying fire glowed in the hearth. The strongbox was still on the floor near the window. I put the lantern down beside it. The box was fastened with a simple padlock. It was ridiculously easy to open. Within moments I was throwing back the lid.

The box wasn't especially big, but it still held a good many documents. I worked my way through them as briskly as I could, laying each one in turn on the floor beside the lantern and peering at it to see what it was. Most were dull affairs: letters about buying sheep and selling fleeces, a wad of documents concerning a lawsuit over a land boundary; some correspondence from William Haggard and Owen Lewis about Alice Haggard and her dowry, and the nice little commissions which both Haggard and Lewis were going to pay to Mortimer for his efforts as a matchmaker. Sir Philip had had good reason to be outraged by Rafe's romantic intrusion.

Though whether he could actually have been outraged to the point of murder . . . I shook my head in puzzlement over that, but went on working as quickly as I could, though with care, making sure I knew what each document was before I put it aside.

Below the letters was a sheet of parchment, of very good quality. I lifted it out and saw the words LAST WILL AND TESTAMENT penned across the heading. Then I saw the name of Northcote, and quickly moved the parchment into the light in order to read it thoroughly.

It was the will of a man called John Northcote. I frowned for a moment and then remembered Mortimer, during the quarrel with Rafe and Alice, declaring that he still missed his friend John Northcote . . . who was, of course, Rafe's father. Rapidly, I read the will through.

As far as learning how Mortimer proposed to extract land and honor from the queen, the will gave me no help. It did give me something else, however. Here at last was a clear reason why Mortimer might have wanted Rafe out of the way. John Northcote, it seemed, was a man with a sentimental attachment to his friend Philip Mortimer, and a touching degree of trust in him.

"Since Philip Mortimer once helped me to uncover a steward who had falsified his accounts for personal gain, for which reason I look on him with trust and gratitude; and there being no relatives left to take care of my son Rafe if I should perish before he reaches the age of twenty-one years, I therefore name Sir Philip Mortimer of Vetch Castle in Herefordshire as his guardian. Should Rafe in turn be taken to God before the age of twenty-one (for the chances of this world are many and all life hangs by a thread), in recognition of my past gratitude, I further name Sir Philip Mortimer as my heir after Rafe . . ."

The will then went on to describe John Northcote's estate in detail. The manor of Rowans lay a few miles to the west of Shrewsbury and consisted of two sublet farms and a home farm, the latter chiefly concerned with sheep and including around six square miles of hill pasture. So far, Rowans was not remarkable. It would represent wealth to a poor man, but to Sir Philip Mortimer of Vetch Castle it was hardly a temptation.

Then I read the last paragraph.

Alice, trying to convince her elders that Rafe was an eligible husband, had said that his manor had copper deposits. It certainly had. According to the will, John Northcote had had the hill pastures prospected, and the copper deposits found there had a value, at the most conservative estimate, eight times that of all the land and stock put together and could well be worth much more.

If Mortimer were out to make his fortune, he could do worse than start by getting his hands on Rowans. Only Rafe's life stood between him and those copper deposits. I crouched there, frowning, over the will. Perhaps he had intended at first to be an honest steward, but had been so angry when Rafe made approaches to Alice that rage had pushed him over the edge. I tried to imagine what had gone on in his mind. Not only was Rafe going to get Rowans and all its wealth instead of Mortimer, but the ungrateful youth was apparently hell-bent on swindling his guardian out of the commission Owen Lewis and William Haggard were to pay him for brokering the match, and probably wrecking Mortimer's friendship with Lewis into the bargain! Rafe didn't deserve Rowans . . . and with that, Mortimer, perhaps tempted already, perhaps teetering already on a perilous edge, might step over it.

Yes, it made sense. If a man were desperate enough for money, then here was his motive for doing away with Rafe. It was far more convincing than anger over Rafe's advances to Alice on its own, or any convoluted notions of protecting his mother's honor from an amorous young man.

I sat back on my heels, thinking of Rafe's body, lying in this very room; of Mortimer trying to put the blame on me and Brockley; and with his mother's help, getting both of us out of the way and hiding the fact that there had been a murder at all. For a moment, my mind checked. Lady Thomasine had been very attached to Rafe. But blood ties are strong. She might be fond of her admiring minstrel boy, her personal Mark Smeaton, yes; but Philip was her own son.

I put the will aside and worked on, wondering if Mortimer was in debt and whether I might find any clue to that in the box. It would account for his desire for money. I could still hear faint noises of revelry from the direction of the hall, but nothing nearer at hand. I was glad that Dale and Brockley were keeping watch, though. The memory of Rafe's body was suddenly very vivid. I wondered how his meeting with Mortimer in the study had come about. Perhaps Mortimer had enticed him to the study with a message purporting to come from Alice. And been waiting for him, dagger in hand. It was not a pleasant thought.

This was an unpleasant task altogether. I wanted to be done with it, and anyway, the candle in the lantern was burning down. I discovered that Mortimer did indeed have debts, big ones. He had spent huge sums on lawsuits, in trying to regain possession of Mortimer lands, and then needed to borrow money for repairs to the fabric of the castle, and to replace sheep lost in bad weather last winter. I also came across a couple of estimates for new tapestries and furniture, pinned together with a note which said *not under present circumstances*. Rowans would have cleared his debts and left him money to spare. Had Rafe known the full value of Rowans? I wondered. And had he seen the face of the man who killed him? Had he understood why he was to die?

I had nearly reached the bottom of the pile. So far, nothing had had a bearing on any schemes Mortimer might have for coaxing wealth out of the queen. Perhaps it was just a figment of his imagination, after all; a grandiose daydream. He amused himself with boasting about it; half believed in it, perhaps. He had planned to be in Cambridge when the queen was there . . . but what had he meant to do there? How on earth did one frame a blatant request for a string of castles and their accompanying lands and incomes? I could find no trace of any lever or threat. Daydreams, I thought: wild imaginings . . .

The last two items were letters. Like the will, they were written on parchment, but this parchment was old. Even by candlelight, I could see that it was mottled with age and that the ink was faded. The handwriting, the same on both sheets, was difficult and I moved the light to see better. I looked at the dates. I read the first one through. And then, with trembling hands, I put the second letter on top and read that as well.

I looked at the dates again.

My stomach contracted. I felt the crimson run up into my face, as though I had been caught out in some nasty, indecent sin.

This couldn't be true. Oh no, please, God, don't let it be true. If this were so, then . . . I thought about it and it was as though the whole world had turned upside down, and everything that I had thought fixed and certain had tumbled out to lie in a pattern not only alien but ugly; so ugly that every drop of blood in my body surged with horror and fury. No, no, *no*! It was not to be endured. No claims to honesty or legality could make me willing to endure it. I would not see England, or Elizabeth either, so wounded, not for anyone or anything.

It was borne in on me then that whatever might have happened in the past, I loved Elizabeth. I loved the vulnerable girl behind the royal robes; I loved the strong-minded, valiant queen who lived inside that girl and sometimes strode out into the light to startle and intimidate her council of statesmen who were all male and mostly much older than she was, and yet were often afraid of her. She was all Tudor then; her father's daughter in every way.

Of course she was. Of course she was. I made myself read the two letters again. My burning flush faded and my hands steadied. The letters might look convincing, but they lied. Not that it mattered. I felt my jaw set with determination. Whether they lied or not, for Elizabeth's sake and for England's sake, I would connive at any deception necessary to keep these letters from doing damage.

Mortimer, of course, was insane. These, presumably, were the lever by which he had hoped to wring land and money out of Elizabeth. I wondered again if the duel he was said to have fought, long ago, was somehow involved. I had a feeling, like an itch in the mind, that that duel was part, somehow, of all these machinations. Perhaps he had fought the duel and killed his man in order to suppress these letters! But if so, why had he not destroyed them? Had he, even then, thought that one day he might have another use for them? He was a fool if so. If he really hoped to gain a fortune by threatening to publish them, then he was living in cloud-cuckoo-land. Any such ploy would have put him in the Tower of London on a charge of treason faster than a shooting star can cross the sky. But even so, he might do terrible harm. If anyone not well disposed to Elizabeth should see these documents—if anyone at all who was not discreet should see them—if there were any more such documents, hidden somewhere else . . .

Something caught my eye. I picked one of the letters up for a closer look. One of the marks on the parchment was surely recent. It was a dirty thumbprint and after one appalled glance, I knew whose thumbprint it was. There was no mistaking it. This thumb had had a jagged, weeping zigzag cut across it. I had had a disagreeably close view of that cut, across the dinner table, the day before I made my first attempt to investigate this study.

These letters had been handled by William Haggard. In which case, presumably, he had read them.

They could not be left here. If Mortimer had shown them to even one other person—and he obviously had—then he might do the same thing again. Already, this deadly knowledge might be spreading. I must take the letters at once and Cecil must know what was afoot. Henderson could see them, I supposed, but no one else. I must reach him as fast as possible and we must go straight back to court.

Quickly, I put the other documents back in the strongbox, locked it again, stowed the letters in my hidden pocket, and left the study. Brockley, inappropriately armed with his lute, came toward me as I turned the key in the door.

"Madam? Did you find anything?"

"We've got to get away," I said in an urgent undertone. "Please don't as much as breathe on that lute; we've got to get out at once and we mustn't—*mustn't*—get caught. Find anything? Oh my God, yes. It's worse than I could ever have imagined. Where's Dale? Dale, come quickly! We've no time to lose."

It was raining again as we slipped back across the courtyard, but we hurried and didn't get seriously wet and I didn't think it mattered. I was wrong.

17

Deep Water

When I said we must get out at once, I meant it literally. The moment we were back in Isabel's Tower and could talk properly, I told the others that I couldn't explain to them what I'd found, but I'd rather go about with a pocket full of gunpowder or a handkerchief soaked in pus from a plague victim, and we must be off now, without delay, in the dark.

"I tell you," I said, "that Mortimer is a thoroughly evil man. I don't want to stay another hour within these walls."

But Brockley wouldn't have it. Brockley, in fact, put down his foot with such a thud that it was a marvel the tower didn't shake.

"It's raining again out there, it's the middle of the night, and Fran's still exhausted, if you're not. No matter what you're carrying in your pocket, madam, no matter if the master of this castle is the devil himself, we sleep until cockcrow. Then we'll go as quickly as we can, I promise."

"You address me as madam, but you talk to me like a tutor," I snapped at him.

"No, madam. I talk to you as a loyal companion with your best interests at heart. We'll all be ill if we go out in that weather without sleep or food first."

Again, I didn't expect to sleep but I was more tired than I knew and I slid into the depths quite easily. I woke, however, at the first tentative notes of a blackbird outside, and as I sat up, I heard the letters crackle in my hidden pocket. The noise brought me instantly out of my coverings to shake the others awake. "It's time we went. Come on."

Brockley, of course, forced us to gulp bread and cheese down first. There wasn't much left when we'd finished, and on top of everything else, I grew anxious about Gladys. "Why don't you come with us?" I asked her. "You can rest in the inn at Ledbury where Master Henderson's man is waiting. It's not so very far."

"I don't want to go to Ledbury. It's farther from home and my old bones are aching that bad. I wanted to know what 'ud happen to Mortimer, but if you're goin' away, then it's different. I want to get home. I'll get that goose girl Blod to fetch Hugh Cooper to meet me. I told you, Cooper's not a bad fellow when he's not trying to keep a mob in order. Two donkeys, he's got, and three young sons. He can lend me a donkey and send a lad with me to see me safe home. I'll be all right. A silly old woman, that's what he'll think I am, comin' back to Vetch for nothing and then goin' all the way back, all over again, but what of it? I found out what lies they've been telling about Rafe, anyhow. I've been some use, ain't I?"

"Yes, Gladys, you have. But . . ."

"You'll send me word what comes of it all?"

"Of course we will, but . . ."

She wouldn't be moved, however, so we left the last of the food with her, and all the bedding, and then I kissed her in farewell. She had earned it.

We finally left the tower in a drizzling daybreak. Everything underfoot was soaking wet. We slithered down the path from the castle and I was afraid all the time that someone would hear us, that at any moment a head would peer over the watchtower above and shout a challenge at us but nothing happened. We found our saddlery safe and dry in its hollow tree and found the hobbled ponies too. The daylight was still pale and young when we started for Ledbury.

It took nearly all day to get there. It was a good twelve miles and the storm had turned the tracks to quagmires. Again and again we had to ride out of our way to avoid patches of floodwater like small lakes, and because we didn't know the district, we were repeatedly hindered by hidden rivers, or found tracks doubling back on themselves. The drizzle persisted. As the day wore on, we saw that to the east, the sky was night-black with a flicker of lightning now and then. We could only hope that the storm wouldn't come in our direction. Shelter would be hard to come by. There were cottages and farms here and there, but they were widely scattered.

We did find one farmstead along our route, where a hospitable farmer's wife was willing to provide three damp travelers with food and ale, but by the time we reached Ledbury, in the late afternoon, we were all hungry again, not to mention tired and wet. We hadn't been caught in the storm, but the fine rain was bad enough. Mercifully, when we inquired for the Sign of the Feathers, we were directed to it at once. Then I found that, for once, my good memory had failed me and I couldn't remember the name of the man Rob said he had left there as our contact. Fortunately, although she was sagging with weariness and was complaining of a sore throat, Dale's memory was better.

"Geoffrey Barker, ma'am," she said wanly, from her perch behind Brockley.

"Whether he's here or not, we're staying the night," Brockley said grimly, as he helped Dale down in the stable yard. "You're all in, Fran, I can see it."

For once, concerned about Dale, he left our mounts to the care of the grooms while he hurried her inside and asked for bedchambers. Entering behind him, I looked through a doorway into a public room, where there were benches and a fire and a pleasant smell of ale, and there, with an ale mug in his hand and his feet stretched out toward the warmth, was a lanky man whom I recognized at once as one of Rob Henderson's retainers. "Barker?" I said.

"Mistress Blanchard!" He came to his feet at once, and then looked at me sharply. "Is something the matter? Your pardon, mistress, but you look distressed."

"I have to join Master Henderson and get back to the court as fast as possible. It's a matter of the greatest urgency . . . what is it?"

The moment I spoke of joining Henderson, Barker had begun to shake his head. His expression had become grave. "Mistress, urgency or no urgency, it'll be days before we can get across the Severn pastures to Tewkesbury."

"Days? It's only half a day's ride!"

"Didn't you know?" said Barker. "With all these storms and heavy rain, the Severn's overflowed. Remember, people were thinking it might, when we were on our way to Vetch? They were moving the sheep to safety. We heard the news yesterday. The river burst its banks the night before last, in all that downpour. The pastures are deep in water for half a mile, on this side of Tewkesbury."

Then we'd get hold of a boat and row, I said. There must be boats! Not that we could use, said Geoffrey Barker and the landlord of the Feathers, backing each other up. Boats, yes, but they were all out rescuing stock and people.

"There's a good many folk have ended up sitting on their roofs," the landlord said. "Got chicken coops up there with them, some of them have, and pigs and calves sticking their noses out of top floor windows, and those folk are calling themselves lucky. Some have been drowned. Whole houses went that night when the river first burst out. I rode over there yesterday—a lot of Ledbury folk have gone to help relatives and I've a cousin lives by the pastures. My cousin is all right but he and I saw six bodies brought out of the water. Cattle and sheep are gone that the farmers thought were on safe ground. And it'll be worse by now! I came home through another storm this morning. Everyone'll be out rescuing what they can. No one's interested in running ferry services just now."

We could go no farther that night, anyway. We all needed warmth and hot food and to sleep in decent beds. Fortunately, Barker had money. Mine had been left behind with my belongings in Vetch and we had spent most of Brockley's. But Barker said he could cover the bill so we took a good supper and retired. I slept soundly, although I dreamed yet again of the dungeon at Vetch, and of lying on the dirty floor with my nose almost on Lady Thomasine's wretched slippers. When I woke, I decided that when all this was over, I would make Meg a pair of slippers with roses on, although they wouldn't be cerise roses on tawny. That was a color scheme I never wanted to see again. Meg should have fat golden roses on emerald green or azure. What bliss it would be, I thought, to have a life quiet enough for embroidery!

Dale, when she woke, was obviously unwell—another worry. I left Brockley with her while I rode out through the hills with Barker to see for myself the floods that lay between us and Tewkesbury. It was a long ride and a desolate spectacle awaited us at the end of it. The water, gray like the sky it reflected, was full of mud and debris, with trees and posts and the tops of dwellings sticking up here and there. On the current of some swallowed-up stream, I saw four dead cattle slowly floating along, bellies distended and feet jutting upward. There were boats, but all a long way off, on the far side of the water.

"But surely we can find a way round!" I said. I wasn't surprised when Barker shook his head yet again. He was the kind of man, I concluded, who rather enjoyed saying that things couldn't be done. It would be a long, long ride, he told me, northward, to get around the floods. "I don't know the area well, mistress, but I thought you might say that, so last night I spoke to the landlord. It'll be twenty miles at least with the roads hock-deep in mud and no guarantee that the way won't still be barred when we do come in sight of Tewkesbury. There's no knowing how far the water extends. We'd do better to wait till it goes down."

"And when will that be?" I said tartly.

It wasn't raining just then but a rumble of thunder informed us that another storm might break at any moment. Barker shrugged and smiled. "A little patience, mistress. That's all you need."

"Patience! You don't understand, Barker, and I can't explain exactly what the urgency is because there's such a thing as discretion. I trust you; it isn't that. The news I'm carrying, I haven't even shared with my own servants, whom I would trust with my life. I shall have to share it with Master Henderson but apart from him, it is for the queen and Sir William Cecil only. As it is, there are too many people already who know about it."

"As serious as that?" said Barker, looking at me quizzically. I ground my teeth. I could read his mind. This sort of thing was always happening to me. In the eyes of men like Barker, I was a pretty young woman, a dear little thing, to be protected and guided, but it was of course quite impossible that I could be the carrier of any kind of news that actually mattered. I was sweet but trivial and any knowledge in my possession must therefore be trivial too. Rob knew better; Cecil knew better; but they weren't here and Barker was. I felt like hitting him.

Restraining myself, I turned my pony's head. "We must get back to the Feathers," I said.

At the inn, I found Dale up and dressed, though pale and rather hoarse. She was taking some food with Brockley. I went up to my room alone, locked myself in, and took out the letters to look at them by daylight for the first time. I had hoped, I think, that if I read them calmly in a good light, they wouldn't seem so lethal.

I had been too optimistic. They seemed deadlier than ever.

The most horrific things about them were the dates. One was dated the eleventh day of November 1532, and the other the tenth day of January 1533.

The November one began: *My dearest love, once again, I cannot help but put my passion down on paper, for though we often meet and even speak one to the other, we can so rarely say the words we wish or even let our eyes speak for us. When can we hope once more to be lovers? I was so touched by your poem . . .*

The January one began: *My heart's joy, I know that to write to you thus is perilous, but I am so full of love, I cannot always keep it within me. Oh, to relive our Christmas revels. How I wish that moments such as that, when we can be wholly together, could come more often. Yet, my sweeting, what does the future hold for us? I cannot turn back now from the course on which I am set. It gives me pain to tell you that my letters, my unwise letters which I know I should not write but which come unbidden to my pen, must be destroyed when you have read them but . . .*

January 1533. Christmas 1532. November 1532. God Almighty. Elizabeth was born early in September 1533.

If by any dreadful chance these odious epistles were real, then it was clear that others like them had existed and might still exist. And if so, where were they now?

I had likened these letters to a handkerchief dipped in pus from a bubo and that instinctive, horrified response had been right. Whether they were real or not, knowledge of their contents, if it were to travel, would be a terrible infection which might ruin the queen. Elizabeth could be destroyed and with her would go all who loved her and believed in the England that she wanted, the England she was trying to make solvent after the expenditures of her predecessors; the England in which heretics were not hunted to their death.

And the knowledge had spread at least to one other person besides Mortimer himself. One other person had certainly read these loathsome things, and that was William Haggard.

He lived at a place called St. Catherine's Well. I wondered how far away it was.

I stared out of the window at the gray sky and came to a decision. I had no certainty that what I now planned to do was the right thing, but I had to do something. Impatience and fear were a fever in my veins. The landlord seemed to know his local geography. I put the letters safely back in my hidden pocket and went downstairs to find him.

18

Without Authority

We set off for St. Catherine's Well the following morning.

This track was not flooded, for it wound uphill onto the flanks of the Malverns, that long range of hills which stands proud of the lower lands to east and west of it, like a huge, petrified roller in a sea otherwise calm. There was a gale blowing, with fierce rain squalls, but they were not like the savage cloudburst which had imprisoned us in Isabel's Tower and the thick mantles with which Lady Thomasine had so obligingly presented Brockley and myself were an adequate protection. The previous afternoon, Brockley and I seized the chance to buy things in Ledbury and we had at last acquired some genuinely sturdy boots. I had also bought some leggings to protect myself from the stirrup leathers while riding astride. Barker was already well equipped. We kept our heads lowered, and rode resolutely on.

I might have forgotten Barker's name when we first got to Ledbury, but I could recall what Lady Thomasine had said about St. Catherine's Well. It was on the Malverns, a few miles north of a landmark called Herefordshire Beacon. The landlord of the Feathers had heard of St. Catherine's and gave us further directions, though he was a loquacious man and his instructions were inclined to ramble.

"My cousin's wife worked there when she were a young wench. There's a track goes off north, just at the foot of the beacon. That'll take you straight to St. Catherine's. Used to be a shrine, in the days afore we all changed our ways. Folk still come there to drink the water. My old dad tried it when his bones started giving him trouble but it didn't help him. The water tasted funny, he said, and his aches just went on aching."

The directions themselves were accurate and we found the place without difficulty. But despite my seething impatience, which had overcome all the protests that Brockley and Barker could make, I had realized that we must spend one night away from Ledbury and I knew that when Master Haggard heard what I intended to say to him, he wasn't likely to offer us any hospitality. In fact, I didn't want either Brockley or Barker to enter his house at all.

According to our landlord there was an inn—its name, rather charmingly, was Kate's Well—which catered to people wanting to take the waters. We could sleep there and I could arrive at St. Catherine's early next day, rested, fed, washed, and capable—I hoped—of making a dignified impression.

All going well, we could be back at Ledbury by the evening of that day. It would be a Sunday, when people mostly didn't travel, but I was in no mood to worry about that.

By "we," I mean myself, Barker, and Brockley. Dale's malady had now turned into a bad cold and we had left her in bed at the Feathers, being cared for by the landlord's wife, who was an amiable soul. We had also hired a messenger and sent him off on the long and muddy circuitous route to Tewkesbury, with orders to find Henderson and bring him to Ledbury as fast as possible.

We found Kate's Well, and were given beds. The place was adequate if not luxurious. In the morning, we were relieved to find that the stormy weather had given way to a brisk breeze, with patches of sunlight between the clouds. We set out early to cover the last half mile to St. Catherine's. We rode past a little chapel, probably attached to the medicinal well, and then came suddenly upon the house itself, a beautiful place, thatched and gabled, built of mellow amber-colored brick and facing westward across a bowl-shaped valley on the knees of the Malverns. There was a gatehouse, set in a low wall which stretched away left and right. Here we halted.

After a pause while I studied the place, I gave my instructions. "If you two ride round to the left," I said to Brockley and Barker, "I think you can position yourselves where you can be seen from those gable windows. If I'm not back, in good health and my right mind, by midday, then ride for Ledbury and as soon as Master Henderson comes, ask for his help. Allow no one else from St. Catherine's to approach you. You understand?"

"I hope you know what you're doing, madam," said Brockley.

So did I. I had slept badly, dreading what I had set out to do. The things I was proposing to say to William Haggard were outrageous, and I would have to face him alone. During the night, I had almost decided to turn back. But if I did that, and in the meantime he shared the horrible implications of those letters with his wife, or a friend, or anyone at all and harm resulted, I would be ashamed for the rest of my life. He might have done so already, of course, and if he had, that would not be my fault. But if there was still time to stop the leak, then stopped it must be. I must go on.

I had dressed with care. Before the cold took its feverish grip on Dale, she had brushed and sponged my gown clean of the dust from Isabel's Tower and the mud of the road, and in Ledbury, as well as boots and leggings, I had also bought some linen, which she and I had hurriedly stitched to provide us both with fresh undergarments. I looked respectable and at least I didn't smell.

There was a porter at the gatehouse, a civil young man, who asked my name and then called a groom to take my pony and a manservant to show me into the house. I was led across an unpaved courtyard, where chickens cackled, and a blackbird was taking a bath in a puddle, in through a porch, and then through a door on the left into a pleasant parlor. Bess Haggard and her daughter Alice were sitting together, Bess sewing something while Alice sat at a table, reading.

Bess rose at once, putting her work aside. "Mistress Blanchard? But what brings you here—and on a Sunday! Is no one with you? Alice, look who it is."

"Good morning, Mistress Blanchard." Alice stood up as well and curtsied. She looked pale and unhappy. Both she and her mother were dressed in black velvet, which didn't suit either of them. Bess had no doubt put it on out of respect for the Sabbath but I wondered if Alice had chosen it as mourning for Rafe.

"I have two men with me," I said. "They are waiting outside. I really need to speak to your husband, Mistress Haggard. It's a private matter and it's of great importance, or indeed I would not have broken in on you on a Sunday. Is Master Haggard at home?"

"Yes, but he is out on the farm. This weather . . . that wind yesterday . . . the thatch of the cow byre was half ripped off . . ."

Bess at home was as colorless as she had been at Vetch. She could hardly have been less like her fashionable mother. She was only in her thirties but she was graying already. Her voice trailed away.

"Could you send someone to find him?" I asked. "It really is important."

"Oh . . . yes, I suppose so. Well, he'll be coming back soon so that we can set out for church, but . . . oh well, if it's really so necessary . . . Alice, Sims has been hanging round the kitchen again; send him to find your father. Tell them to bring some wine and pastries while you're about it. And take Mistress Blanchard's cloak."

"Poor Sims," Alice remarked, as I relinquished my cloak to her. "He's one of our outside men," she added to me as she crossed the room to the door. "He's courting one of the maidservants. He finds excuses to be near her."

"He's forever wasting his time dangling after her instead of doing his work," said Bess, quite sharply.

"No one ever wants to help young lovers," said Alice, and left the room before her mother could answer.

"Oh dear," I said.

"She's wearing black for Rafe," said Bess. "Her father is angry but I told him, let her have her way for a little while. We must get her into prettier colors soon, though. Owen Lewis has sent word that he's coming to see her. The betrothal never took place, you know. Master Lewis said it would be in bad taste, after Rafe had died like that. But when he comes here, we do hope . . . oh well." She sighed and then brightened as a maid arrived with a tray. "You'll have some refreshment?"

I sipped wine, nibbled a chicken pasty, and listened to Bess talking hopefully about brideclothes for Alice, and wondered how long it would take the lovelorn Sims to fetch his master from the byre. But in less than half an hour, William Haggard arrived, in dun-colored working clothes, smelling of the cattle shed and with a flush of irritation on his weathered face.

"It's not that I'm not happy to see you, Mistress Blanchard, and on a Sunday one ought to be able to welcome visitors, but the weather takes no account of the days of the week and if the wind rips the roof off a cowshed on a Saturday night, then the farmer has to put it back on the Sunday if he cares a straw for his stock. I doubt I'll see the inside of a church today. You must make my excuses, Bess. Well, Mistress Blanchard. Sims came running to say that you're here, on your own apparently, with an urgent message for me. What's all this about? If something's wrong at Vetch, how is it that you're the messenger? If I sound rude, I'm sorry for it, but . . ."

"I need to speak to you alone, Master Haggard. If you would be so kind."

"Very well." He pulled his cap off his thinning sandy hair. "I've got a study. Come with me."

The study was cold and untidy, with ledgers and papers and a document box all anyhow on the table, and the only seating consisted of a couple of stools, one of them at the table, the other against the wall. Haggard deposited himself at the table and said: "If you want to sit down, bring the other stool forward. Then tell me what all this is about."

I moved the stool as bidden, sat down, and then paused. I was actually thinking about Geoffrey Barker. Barker was taking my orders because Rob Henderson would expect it and Brockley was insisting, but privately, because I was female and quite young at that, Barker thought me trivial. Haggard might well hold similar views. How on earth, without credentials or natural authority, was I ever to make him listen to me?

I wished I had brought Brockley in with me but if things turned nasty, then Brockley could have been used in some way as a hostage. No doubt Haggard had men at call. No, I had been right to come alone. If I failed, I failed, but at least I would have tried. The pause was making him impatient; I could see it. Before he could burst into irritable speech, I took a deep breath, and seized the bull by the horns.

"Master Haggard, because I am a woman, you may find it hard to take me seriously but I must implore you to do so for your own sake. The queen is also a woman, and I am at this moment acting on her behalf. You are aware that I am married and have a home in France?"

"Yes, yes. Lady Thomasine told Bess all about that. What of it?"

"I just wish to explain my position clearly. My home is abroad, but I remain Elizabeth's loyal subject. Before I went to France, I was one of her ladies and in those days I sometimes undertook—let us call them private tasks—for her. During my present visit to England, I have undertaken yet another. I am here now as her representative, and a man called Master Robert Henderson, who is in the employ of Sir William Cecil, the Secretary of State, would be with me now, except that the Severn meadows have flooded and kept him from joining me. I came without waiting for him, because the matter seems so urgent that I dared not delay. Will you look at these, please. I think you've seen them before."

Haggard was so busy staring at me in astonishment that at first he scarcely heeded the two letters as I took them from my hidden pouch and spread them on the table in front of him, the right way up for him to read them. I had to draw his attention to them a second time. "Please examine them, Master Haggard."

He gave the letters a puzzled glance. I saw his weather-beaten face become very still. Then it crimsoned.

"What the devil's all this? Where'd you get these?"

"From Sir Philip Mortimer's strongbox, Master Haggard."

"What? What? You've been a-meddling in his private papers? Is that what you're telling me?" The crimson deepened to a furious magenta and he half rose to his feet, gripping the edge of his desk. "Poking about, piddling your fingers in other folks' business . . ."

"By no means." I gripped my hands together in my lap. It was difficult to remain calm and dignified. He had an intimidating presence and he was years older than I was as well. But I kept my eyes steadily on his and kept my voice level too, as I said: "From any of the gable windows which look toward the gatehouse, you will be able to see, beyond the wall, two men waiting on horseback. They are in my service. If I do not return to them by midday, they will go for help."

"What?"

"Far from poking about," I said, "I was on a serious mission. I have been officially asked to discover what is going on at Vetch, in Sir Philip Mortimer's mind. There are suspicions connected with treason. Even his mother is worried. From the look of these, no wonder! I want to know why Sir Philip Mortimer showed them to you, and where he got them, and what he intends to do with them."

"You say you're here on behalf of the queen? That one of Sir William Cecil's men is helping you?"

"Yes, Master Haggard, just that."

"D'you expect me to believe such rubbish?"

"You think I'm talking rubbish? Would you like to place a wager on it? You do realize, I hope, that possession of these letters—even knowledge of their existence—could be held to be treason?"

The flush subsided and he sank down again onto his stool but his fingers went on gripping the desk and his bulging pale blue eyes were stubborn. "Whatever these things are, they're naught to do with me." He peered at the papers, tracing a line or two with his forefinger. "I'm no hand at reading. Love letters of some sort, ain't they? What makes you think I know anything about them?"

"You recognized them."

"Wrong, my lady. I've never seen 'em before."

"Can I see your right thumb, Master Haggard?"

"My . . . ?"

"Your right thumb. Please."

He looked at his thumb as though wondering what it was. I reached out and before he could stop me, I took hold of it and turned it over. The zigzag scar was still there, scarcely healed even now. I let go and pointed to the bloodstained letter.

"You've handled that. There is the evidence."

"Nonsense. Anyone could have a jagged cut like that."

"On your thumb," I said, "about half an inch from one end of the big scar, there are signs of a smaller puncture. It's just a pale pink dot now but when you touched the letter, it was still oozing." I pointed to the letter, to the single dark spot a little away from the larger mark.

"Even to have seen these letters," I said, as his dogged stare met mine once more, "is so dangerous that it could bring a man to the block, or worse."

"But I know nothing about them!" he said obstinately.

"Oh, I think you do. Master Haggard, for God's sake—or for your own sake, and the sake of Bess and Alice—tell me what you can."

Without answering, he picked one of the letters up. Then he put it down again, quickly, but not before I had seen his hands trembling.

"What am I to do? I can't let you question me, a young lass like you. And in my own study too."

"Would you prefer a dungeon with no windows, torches on the wall to give the only light, thick walls to muffle the screams, and a man with a mask and a rack?"

Something in my voice or my eyes must have got past his fixed ideas at last. This time his face did not flush. Instead, it paled to the color of Gladys's goat cheese. His mouth slackened.

"Please believe me. I really do represent Her Majesty. Cecil's man really will join me soon. And you could be in the gravest possible trouble. Your best chance of helping yourself is to tell me the truth now."

He let out a sigh which was almost a groan and the dogged expression turned to a dismal kind of frankness. "You're in no danger from me, Mistress Blanchard. Your men waiting out there to guard you need not have bothered. I wouldn't harm a woman, least of all a young woman like you. Men ought to look after women, protect them. But you talk as if you're offering to protect me."

"I will if it proves possible. But I need to know what I'm dealing with. Telling me won't make anything worse, Master Haggard. If you talk to me then perhaps, *perhaps,* you won't be made to talk under more ruthless circumstances."

Master Haggard passed a hand over his scanty hair. And then

startled me by his next words. In tones of desperation, he said: "I'd sell my soul to be got out of this."

I felt the surge of excitement that the huntsman feels when the quarry is brought to bay. "Perhaps there is a way out," I said. "I can't tell until I know just how you came to see these letters and in what way you are involved."

"My brother-in-law don't mean any harm," Haggard said defensively. "He's not a wicked man."

I had most decidedly concluded that he was. I waited.

"Sir Philip," said Haggard, "is a most loyal servant of the queen. But he's half a Mortimer and half a Vetch. He's got all the great Mortimer barons of bygone times on one side, and on the other . . . the Vetches were never great like the Mortimers, but you'd think they were, the way they feel about their ancestors. They damn near worship them. They're proud of that castle, too. Lady Thomasine's father modernized it for comfort's sake, but all the same, he kept the legends about it alive. He never opened up the southwest tower. There are supposed to be ghosts in it. You knew that?"

"Yes. Lady Isabel and the minstrel Rhodri."

He nodded. "Philip's got long family histories on both sides, and he's a dreamer. He wants to be like his great Mortimer ancestors. Oh, how do I explain? He's all full of yearnings and visions; nothing to do with the real world. Philip imagines things that can't happen and makes himself believe they can. He's not wicked and he's not a madman; but . . ."

"He makes a new world in his mind and tells himself that it's the true one?" I was beginning to understand.

Haggard was nodding. "Yes, that's how it is. Well, somehow or other, he got hold of these. I don't know what they really are." He flicked at the letters with a disdainful forefinger. "There're names mentioned here. Well, Anne's a common name and so is Mark. People used to call their children after the names of the saints. Those are both saints' names . . ."

I picked up one of the letters. It was the one dated the tenth day of January 1533. I read aloud.

"'My heart's joy, I know that to write to you thus is perilous, but I am so full of love, I cannot always keep it within me. Oh, to relive our Christ-

mas revels. How I wish that moments such as that, when we can be wholly together, could come more often. Yet, my sweeting, what does the future hold for us? I cannot turn back now from the course on which I am set. It gives me pain to tell you that my letters, my unwise letters which I know I should not write but which come unbidden to my pen, must be destroyed when you have read them but . . .'"

I did not stop there but read on: "'. . . *but so it is. Yet truly, when I whispered to you in the dark that although I am queen of the realm, the only realm I truly desire to rule is that encompassed by your heart and your bed, I meant what I said. And then you said it was as though the whole world had turned into a song, and mine the voice that sang it. We are both minstrels now, you said, singing in duet. That moved me so much, dearest minstrel Mark . . .'*

"There's more, but that is enough," I said. "The signature is just an initial, *A.* Now let us look at the other."

I picked up the earlier letter, the one dated the eleventh day of November 1532. From this too I read aloud.

"'My dearest love, once again, I cannot help but put my passion down on paper, for though we often meet and even speak one to the other, we can so rarely say the words we wish or even let our eyes speak for us. When can we hope once more to be lovers? I was so touched by your poem. It was rash of you, dangerous, to call it To Anne . . . but perhaps you could not help yourself . . .'"

"Doesn't necessarily mean anything," said Haggard defiantly. "I said, anyone might be called Anne, or Mark . . ."

"'When I whispered to you in the dark,'" I quoted relentlessly, *"'that although I am queen of the realm . . .'"*

"Could be just a fancy, just a conceit. She could have meant 'even if I were queen of the realm.' Everyone doesn't write good grammar. I don't even speak it. It needn't mean that she was really the queen."

"I know," I said. "But even if the words weren't meant literally, they could easily be—well—misunderstood. If Sir Philip came by them accidentally, he should have destroyed them at once. As a loyal subject of Queen Elizabeth, it was his duty. Have you observed the dates? Or did he perhaps point them out to you?"

Master Haggard said nothing. He seemed to shrink.

"These letters may be forgeries," I said. "They look old, but a clever forger could no doubt make them seem so. He could write on old parchment and let the ink dry out in the sun, which would bleach and age it. Or they may be genuine but written between two ordinary people called Anne and Mark. What they appear to imply, however, is that there were romantic dealings between the queen of England and someone called Mark, between November 1532 and January 1533." I found I had lowered my voice, as though I feared enemies might overhear. "The queen of England then," I said, "was Anne Boleyn and one of the men executed for adultery with her was her minstrel, Mark Smeaton. And Queen Elizabeth was born on the seventh of September 1533."

"Was she?" The quarry was backed against a rockface, and putting up a last defense. "I don't recall when the queen was born. Who's there to remind me? We don't move in those circles."

"Perhaps not, but I fancy Sir Philip knew, if you didn't. I also suspect that he told you. Why else would he show you the letters? I think you understand the implications very well, Master Haggard." I lowered my voice still further, hardly able to bear the words that I must say. "These letters amount to a hint that Mark Smeaton was the father of Queen Elizabeth, instead of King Henry. You said that Sir Philip meant no harm, but if so, why did he keep them in his strongbox? And why did he show them to you?"

"He only meant," said Haggard wretchedly, "to show them to the queen and promise to destroy them if she would grant him—at least some of the castles and lands that belonged to his ancestors, or their equivalent in money or other property."

It was obvious, of course. I had been assuming it for some time. But it still came as a shock when I heard it said out loud. I stared at him without speaking.

"He thought," said Haggard, "that she'd want the letters hushed up at all costs."

"He would have been the one who was hushed up," I said, recovering myself. "And the costs would have been his. He would have paid dear, in the dungeons under the Tower, and then on the gallows. He's insane."

"No. It's as you put it. He makes a new world in his mind and tells himself it's real. Then he thinks they must be real to others."

"Why did he confide in you?"

"Well," said Haggard roughly, "if he is mad, he's still not too far gone to know he was doing something risky. He scared himself with his own scheme, if you want to know. Here." He picked up his own document box and clicked it open. From it, he took four more letters and handed them to me. "Take them. Take them away. I don't want ever to see them again."

"These are more of them?" I said in horror. "He gave you these? Handed them over to you? But why?"

"To protect himself. He thought that if things went wrong, he could bargain; he could say that there were more letters, that someone else had charge of them and would send them to what he called interested parties if he were arrested. He thought that the threat of these letters getting known would save him."

"He was wrong," I said. I looked at the four letters. I won't quote from them. They were all much the same as the others; except that some of the wording was even more indiscreet. The idea of such things being published abroad made me shudder.

"Can't think Queen Anne really wrote them," Haggard said. "But I suppose some folk might believe it. Whoever is supposed to have written them was a woman, and women can be foolish."

"If Queen Anne wrote them, then *foolishness* is a mild word! But it makes no sense." I was thinking hard. "My mother told me that Queen Anne and King Henry were married in January 1533—the twenty-fifth, I think. Elizabeth must have been conceived in December 1532. Smeaton was just a junior minstrel, then, in the king's suite. If she ever did play the fool with him and my mother always swore that that was a lie . . ."

"Your mother?"

"She was one of Queen Anne's ladies. She said that the accusations against Anne were lies. She herself was gone from the court long before Anne's downfall, but she said she knew the queen and she didn't believe a word of the things charged against her. But even if there was truth in them, it's hard to believe she'd have played King Henry false then! In the months when they became lovers, and the heir to the throne was conceived—and King Henry married her! After angling for the crown for years on end! . . . Why did you agree to take these and keep them?"

"I hoped no harm would come of it. Didn't think he'd ever

have the nerve to show them to the queen, to tell you the truth. He locked us into his study to show them to me and he was all of a dither—shaking, he was, with excitement and fright. Like a boy taking a dare and half-wishing he needn't," said Haggard.

"But you agreed to help him," I persisted. "Why?"

"I'm in debt!" It burst angrily out of him. "Bad debt. I heard there was copper on young Rafe Northcote's land and I thought maybe there's some on mine. So I borrowed money to have my land prospected for copper and I was told there was some, so I borrowed more money to start workings, and the seam ran out. And then there was Alice—got to get her wed. Philip offered to arrange this marriage for her—only he wanted a commission, and there's Alice's dowry too. It's in both money and land. If I'd keep the letters for him, he said he'd pay my debts, waive the commission, pay for the wedding, and help with the dowry as well."

Mortimer was in debt; Haggard was in debt. Rafe's death would solve Mortimer's problems and then he had hoped to blackmail the queen into giving him more, enlarging mere solvency into riches. Meanwhile, he would safeguard himself by kindly offering to solve Haggard's difficulties as well as his own. At one and the same time, it was all quite mad, and perfectly logical.

"He's not a traitor!" said Haggard frantically. "It was just a threat, don't you see? He wouldn't really have published these letters and he didn't really expect that I would. They're a bluff . . . a lever . . . he knew that I'd never send them to . . ."

"Mary Stuart?" I said. My skin crawled. Mary of Scotland already maintained that King Henry's marriage to Anne Boleyn was invalid and that Elizabeth was only his illegitimate daughter. If she once got hold of the idea that Elizabeth wasn't his daughter at all, lawful or otherwise . . .

"And then," said Haggard bitterly, "Alice has to go falling in love with that stupid boy Rafe. And you say women aren't foolish."

"She probably thought Owen Lewis was old enough to be her grandfather," I said. "If she'd been told more, it might have made a difference."

"She should do as she's bid. I'm her father, aren't I? What are you going to do with those letters?"

"Cecil must see them," I said. "That is unavoidable. But I may—only may—be able to convince him that you intended to do nothing harmful with them. Which brings me at last to the main reason why I came here in such desperate haste, without waiting for his representatives to join me. Have you or Sir Philip shown these letters to anyone else, anyone at all? Have you shown them to your wife?"

"Good God, no! Philip said he hadn't shown them to anyone but me and I most certainly haven't. Least of all to Bess! Involve my wife in a thing like this? Never!"

Relief made me feel weak. "If that's so, then you may escape more lightly." I looked at him very seriously. There were beads of sweat on his forehead. "You may think women are foolish, Master Haggard, but I recommend you, all the same, to listen to me now, and forget that I am someone you hold in low esteem."

"I don't hold women in low esteem." He wiped his wet brow with the back of his hand. "But they shouldn't mix themselves up in men's business."

"A moment ago, you told me that you'd sell your soul to be out of this business yourself. I am trying to help you out of it. Your best chance is to decide now that on the subject of these letters you will be utterly silent, forever. Forget they ever existed. Tell no one about them, not even your wife. You will have to invent a tale to explain my visit . . ."

"No, I shan't. If I don't choose to tell her anything, Bess won't ask. Bess concerns herself with domestic matters and never questions me about anything. She is an admirable woman and I wish all women were like her."

I refrained from saying that if all women resembled Bess Haggard, the world would be full of very bored men.

"It will undoubtedly make things simpler if you need not lie to your wife," I said. I hesitated. A thought had crossed my mind. Philip Mortimer's abrupt departure from Queen Mary's court, and the duel which occasioned it, were still nagging at my mind. "Master Haggard, do you happen to know why it was that Sir Philip left court ten years ago? He fought in a duel, I believe, but do you know exactly what was behind it?"

"No, mistress, I don't. I've heard of the duel, yes. It was supposed to be something to do with a woman, though once . . ." He hesitated. Then he said: "If you want to know, once, after we'd taken a fair amount of wine together, Philip let out that he'd told his mother it was about a woman, but it was really to do with what he called a financial misunderstanding. Then he checked himself and didn't say any more so I never found out what he really meant. Not that I tried very hard. I'm the sort to mind my own business."

"Thank you!" I said. Two ideas, hitherto unrelated, suddenly slid together at the back of my mind. "There's one other thing," I said. "Owen Lewis struck me as being smitten with Alice. If you're short of money, he might take her with less dowry. My husband, Gerald Blanchard, married me when I had no dowry at all. Men in love do surprising things. Good day, Master Haggard."

19

Inspiring Terror

I went back through the parlor and took my leave of Bess as quickly as courtesy allowed. My cloak was fetched, and Bess said she would see me to my pony. As we went into the courtyard, there was a stir at the gatehouse and in rode Owen Lewis, his manservant with him. From his tall felt hat to his polished boots, he was dressed to impress, and as he swung down from his horse and tossed his reins to his man, I saw that his beard was freshly trimmed. As he came toward us, the scent of aromatic soap preceded him. Owen Lewis had come courting.

"Mistress Haggard! I am here before you expect me, but keep away, I could not. And Mistress Blanchard! There's a surprise, now. What brings you here, mistress?"

It was an unlooked-for opportunity. I was as sure as I could be that the hateful letters lied, but they might well convince others. I needed to know, for certain, who had really written them. William Haggard obviously did not know. He knew only that somehow or other, Philip Mortimer had got hold of them. But when I asked him about that long-ago duel, he had unwittingly said something which had started a new chain of thought in my mind. From the beginning, I had had a persistent feeling that the events of a decade ago were somehow part of this present mystery. Was the right lock pick in my grasp at last?

A moment ago, I had been thinking that the only way to learn more would be to go back to court and talk to whomever I could find who had also been a courtier in the days of Queen Mary. But now, here was Owen Lewis, who had been a close friend of Mortimer's for a long time. People sometimes told friends more than they told their own families. Presented with a chance, even an outside chance, of confirming that the letters were forged, and encouraged by my success with Haggard, I seized my opportunity with both hands.

"I'm here," I said to Lewis, "on a matter very private and serious. But you could help, if you would answer one question. Mistress Haggard, will you excuse me for one moment while I speak to Master Lewis aside?"

"What a lot of mysteries. But of course, if you wish," said Bess, looking bemused. She walked away, calling to a groom to saddle my pony. With an air of puzzled courtesy, Lewis removed his hat and bowed to me.

"I am at your service, naturally, mistress. But I can hardly imagine how I can assist in any private business of yours."

"It isn't mine," I said. But I smiled at him because I couldn't help it. He was one of the most attractive men I had ever seen in my life and if Alice refused him out of devotion to Rafe's memory, then Alice must have a soft brain and a stone for a heart. "If it were," I said, "I could be more candid. As it is, I have to keep my counsel and hope to heaven that you will be more talkative than I can be."

"Try me," said Owen Lewis, and made it sound like an invitation.

I asked my question. As a way of abolishing flirtatiousness, it could hardly have been bettered. It produced a frown so intense that his strong black eyebrows nearly met above his nose.

"That is a most impertinent thing to ask."

"I am not being frivolous. My reason is far from frivolous, believe me."

"Nevertheless, I cannot answer you, and I bid you good day, mistress. I . . ."

I moved into his path as he was about to step past me. "Then I must answer the question for you," I said, and did so.

"Most unfair that is, mistress," he said, searching my eyes. "If you knew, why did you ask me?"

"I didn't know the details," I said. "Only the broad fact. Do you know the whole story?"

"Does it matter?"

I supposed not. I had guessed at the broad fact, and gambled on it, and won. Unintentionally, he had confirmed it. I smiled at him again, with most genuine gratitude. "Thank you, Master Lewis. Please don't think hardly of me. I am in the service of the queen. It is her counsel that I keep."

"How did you learn of it?" demanded Lewis, and then, realizing from my lack of response that I wasn't going to answer, he said: "Sir Philip left court after killing a man in a duel. Queen Mary did not care for such things. Many people know that much but few know more. Mortimer let it be supposed that what lay behind it was rivalry in love. Even his mother believes that. But . . . you say you are in the service of Queen Elizabeth? Is that really so?"

"Yes."

"I see. Or rather, I don't see. I would prefer to say no more, whatever. I have kept Philip's counsel all this time, after all."

I hesitated. I thought I had gleaned enough for my purposes, but the more I could learn, the better, and he obviously knew more, if he could be persuaded to part with it. I had gambled successfully when I pretended that I knew that crucial broad fact for sure when I did not. An extension of this stratagem now occurred to me.

"Master Lewis," I said earnestly, "I wish you would tell me the rest. The matter is still talked of sometimes at court. When I was last there, I heard it said that the reason behind the duel was not a rivalry in love. That much seems to be quite widely known. I also heard it said that . . ."

I produced the most scandalous suggestion I could think of, and as I had hoped, Lewis was appalled. "What? But that's outrageous!"

"I know," I said. "But it's been *said*." Well, so it had. Just now, by me. "Master Lewis, what really happened? I will not spread anything about, but if I should hear the same thing whispered again, I can at least say that I know that the story is not true."

He studied me intently. I bore the scrutiny, looking back at him, not smiling now. "He is my friend," he said at last. "Which does not mean I am blind or stupid concerning his failings. If we all chose only virtuous friends, many folk would be lonely. He is proud, and needed money to keep up appearances at court, and was foolish in pursuing it. I knew, and did not judge. Nor did I talk about his business. But since you already know some of it, and since it appears that other and worse slanders have been spoken—is that truly so?"

"I fear so," I said sadly.

He shrugged, looking at me now with dislike. "Well, then, Mistress Blanchard in the service of the queen, if I tell you the little you don't know, you can with a clear conscience deny this other slander whensoever you hear it—though I trust you *will* still keep the truth to yourself."

"I will not gossip," I said gravely.

He stared at me, as if suspecting that this was a qualified reply. Since I might well have to repeat what he told me to Cecil and the queen, his suspicions were justified. But I waited silently and at last, briefly, he told me what I wanted to know. This had to be the answer. Had to be. For a moment, the sheer strength of the relief turned me giddy. Earnestly thanking him, I moved aside. "I wish you all good fortune with Alice Haggard," I said. "I hope, most sincerely, that your courtship will prosper."

"I suppose I should be glad of your good wishes. But at the moment, frankly, Mistress Blanchard, I could do without them, and you."

"I did say I served the queen," I said. "Sometimes, I have to choose between her good opinion—and that of others."

That gave him pause. I left him frowning and doubtful. My pony was ready by this time, and after saying a final farewell to Bess, I mounted and rode out to join Brockley and Barker, in a daze of thankfulness.

Everything in the world seemed more cheerful now, but the weather really was improving. Warm sunshine attended our journey back to Dale and the Feathers, and when we got there, we learned that the floods were subsiding. Dale, too, was better, although she was still in bed. But her cold had broken, and although she was nasal and blowing her nose every few minutes amid resounding sneezes, she was in good spirits and said that she would soon be herself again.

It turned out that the messenger we had sent off had made remarkably good time, despite the distance he had had to travel. He reappeared that same evening, and not alone, for with him came Rob Henderson and the rest of Rob's men.

"The water's down enough to let people on horseback get across the pastures in one or two places, and the Severn ferries are plying again," Rob said. "So here we are. Now, my dear Ursula, what is this urgent matter? What have you discovered?"

The inn had no private parlor to offer and was also rather full, but Rob and his companions had wedged themselves into Barker's chamber. Since Rob's men were seeing to the horses in the stable and Barker had joined them for an exchange of news, Rob and I could have the room to ourselves. We sat down on its window seat, and I told him everything that had happened since he left me at Vetch Castle, up to the point where I had at last got access to Mortimer's documents. Then I took out the letters.

"These I found in the strongbox," I said, handing him the first two. "These others I got from William Haggard, Mortimer's brother-in-law. He took his family back to St. Catherine's Well after Rafe's death, but I was at St. Catherine's today. I saw Haggard there."

"But what has he to do with all this?"

I pointed to the bloodstain. "When he came to Vetch Castle, he brought his hawk with him. The bird injured his thumb and made a zigzag tear. I had a good look at it because he showed it to me, asking for advice on healing ointments. I knew the moment I saw the mark on this letter that it must be from his thumb. There was a separate talon puncture at one end—see, there. That meant he'd seen the letters. That's what sent me to St. Catherine's. I'll explain all that in a moment, but I think you'd better read these first. Please notice the dates."

I watched Rob's face as he read. He looked at the dates first and then again when he had finished with the text. I saw him stiffen, understanding what I meant.

"These are dangerous," he said. "If their mere existence were ever bruited abroad . . . and if the damned things got into the hands of Mary of Scotland, or even into the hands of some families here in England . . . have you ever come across the Countess of Lennox?"

"Yes, once or twice, when I was at court. There was some talk about her at Vetch once, at dinner. She's cousin to both Elizabeth and Mary Stuart. Isn't she supposed to be interested in marrying her son to Mary?"

"She is, and the queen doesn't care for the idea. Margaret Lennox—and therefore her children too—are descended from the Tudor line." Rob's face was grave. "Do you know the details? King Henry's sister Margaret—Elizabeth's aunt, that is—married James IV of Scotland, and Mary Stuart is their granddaughter. However, Margaret Tudor married twice. After James had tried to invade England and got himself killed on the battlefield of Flodden, Margaret married again, a Scottish lord, the Earl of Angus, and had a daughter—our Lady Lennox, whose husband is the Earl of Lennox, another Scotsman. Their son Henry Darnley is a personable young man and Lady Lennox has never made any secret of her ambitions for him. It would be a marriage between two Tudor descendants. A powerful alliance."

I nodded. "I knew most of it, yes. The queen has never trusted Lady Lennox. All the queen's ladies know that."

"Did you also know that, two years ago, Lady Lennox got the Spanish ambassador to make covert inquiries among Catholic exiles in the Low Countries, to see how many of them would come home and take up arms if necessary to back a bid for the throne by Mary Stuart with Henry Darnley as her husband?"

"*Did* she? No, I didn't know that."

"It's true, I'm afraid. The Lennoxes are in love with power; it's their nature. If they—or Mary Stuart—as much as knew these . . . these horrors existed . . ."

"I can tell you one thing," I said. "The horrors aren't genuine."

Rob looked at me sharply. "I take that for granted. But you sound as though you have evidence. May I know what it is?"

"This is where I tell you all about my visit to St. Catherine's. I saw Owen Lewis there as well as William Haggard. Listen."

When I was through, his shoulders sagged with relief but

grew tense again almost at once. "But when did truth ever overtake a good scandal? This has got to be stopped, Ursula, stopped forthwith."

"I think I've stopped it as far as Haggard is concerned," I said. "I think he was telling the truth when he told me he never meant to let anyone else see them. But what do we do about Sir Philip?"

"We ride for Vetch," said Rob grimly. "And we put the fear of God into that demented would-be mighty Mortimer. And while we're about it, we will ask him a question or two concerning the murder of young Rafe Northcote."

I sometimes felt as though I had spent my whole life trying to get things done without having the authority to do them. At Blanchepierre, I hadn't even had the authority to tell the physician to save my life; Matthew had done it for me. As for my work, it was in the nature of my peculiar career that I generally had to stay in the shadows, pretending to be a harmless guest or bystander, devoid of power and largely without protection. If I had companions, I usually felt responsible for their safety rather than the other way about.

Just once before, I had ridden into the fray with Rob Henderson and his men at my side, but that time, I was dazed with exhaustion after two wakeful and dangerous nights, and sick, too, with dread for people whom I loved. I hadn't appreciated the sheer pleasure of carrying the war into the enemy's camp, with all the advantage on my side for a change.

Now, I discovered that pleasure. The morning after my discussion with Rob, when we set out together for Vetch Castle, with Brockley and myself on good horses hired from the inn, I rode in triumph, an angel of vengeance, with swordsmen at my side, and my mood was one of pure enjoyment.

With me this time I had Rob, five of his men, including Barker, and Roger Brockley as well. Dale was not yet well enough to leave the inn, though she would not let Brockley stay there with her. I offered and he would have agreed but Dale almost shooed him away.

"Your place is with the mistress, Roger. I know you want to

see the end of this. I wouldn't keep him from his duty for a silly cold in the head, ma'am; how could you think it? I'll be up and about and ready to welcome you back. Only, I haven't been able to brush your gown again. If only you find the rest of your things safe at Vetch."

I doubted if I would, but the message that fetched Rob from Tewkesbury had included a request to Mattie to send me a change of clothes. A fresh gown and sleeves had arrived in Rob's saddlebag. I was fit to be seen. I was more anxious about Dale herself, but the innkeeper's wife, broad of face and hearty of temperament, promised to take care of her and to make sure she did, Rob handed her a sweetener of gold sovereigns—"for yourself, goodwife; put them in your own store." Brockley kissed his wife good-bye, and off we went.

On the way, I said to Rob: "We have to keep Mortimer's scheme quiet, I know, even if it means that he gets off with a warning and is never actually arrested for it. Rafe, though, is a very different matter."

"Yes, he is," Rob said. "You say that he is supposed to have thrown himself off a tower but was actually stabbed. It would seem, though, that quite a number of people know what really happened. You, Brockley, Dale, Mortimer, and Lady Thomasine and some of their servants."

"Yes, Harold Pugh and Simon Evans. Questioning them could produce results," I said.

"I shall start by questioning Mortimer and Lady Thomasine," Rob said. "I prefer to begin with the principal actors. From what you tell me, Rafe very likely was killed by his guardian, but we can hardly arrest him for it before we're sure. The servants may not know who did it—only that it was done."

"Mortimer needs money and Rafe's inheritance comes to him now," I said.

"In other words, he had a reason for killing his ward. But to have a reason for committing murder is one thing; actually doing so, is another. If everyone who had a reason for killing someone else just went and did it, the earth would soon be short of humankind," said Rob, who for all his insouciant airs was very levelheaded. "We must be careful. We have a busy day before us."

When we arrived at Vetch Castle, the porter looked at us with obvious surprise but he didn't seem to have orders to exclude us, although this was perhaps natural. If you tell your doorkeeper to deny entry to somebody, it is usually because you think the somebody in question is likely to call. Brockley and I were supposed to be dead or dying of starvation in the Black Mountains and Rob was supposed to be in London. The Mortimers certainly weren't expecting any of us.

The porter had a lad with him who fetched someone to take our horses. When we went through to the courtyard we found that the boy must also have passed word to Pugh that visitors had arrived, because the butler was just coming to meet us. I doubt if the lad had told him our names, though. When his eyes lit on me and Brockley, I saw his whole body go rigid.

Rob had dressed for this encounter with considerable care, halfway between the soldier and the dandy. His hat had a kite's rufous tail feather in it, his practical russet wool doublet was slashed to show a lining of gold satin, and the turndown collar he wore instead of a ruff was of a gleaming damasked silk. His boots could easily have been used as mirrors. I was arrayed in Mattie's contribution to my wardrobe, sunny yellow for my overskirt and sleeves, pale green for kirtle and bodice, all of it amply embroidered. The clothes were a trifle loose on me, but the general effect was striking. I walked confidently as we advanced upon Pugh.

"Mistress Blanchard! I thought you'd . . . gone back home."

"You mean," I said pleasantly, "that you thought Brockley and I were still shut in that shepherd's hut up in the Welsh hills."

"I haven't the least idea what you're talking about, Mistress Blanchard." He was keeping his head, but from the way Pugh looked at Rob's five soldierly men with their helmets and swords, we had inspired his soul with a satisfying amount of terror.

"We are here to see Sir Philip Mortimer," Rob declared. "Where is he?"

"He . . . he is occupied at the moment," Pugh stammered slightly. "He is in the hall, presiding over an inquiry. As a justice of the peace . . ."

"I really don't care what he's presiding over," said Rob

bluntly, "and peace is the last thing I intend to let him enjoy. We are going straight into the hall to interrupt him. Is Lady Thomasine there?"

"No, sir, but . . ."

"Fetch her," said Rob brusquely. "She is to come to the hall at once. We have business which won't wait."

Pugh did his best to hold on to his dignity. "Master Henderson, I really can't allow . . ."

"You've no choice," said Rob shortly, and strode on toward the porch.

It was a thankless task, being butler at Vetch Castle. Pugh was forever being brushed aside as unnecessary. He did his best now, and actually broke into a run, black formal gown flapping and gold chain of office bouncing, in order to plunge through the porch ahead of us and gasp out our names just as we marched in on his heels. Silence fell as we did so.

The hall was set out for an official hearing. Mortimer was seated in his thronelike chair, up on the dais. People from both the castle and the village stood on either side of the long room. Two armed retainers were positioned near the foot of the dais, and in front of it stood a small woman with a gray shawl over her head and shoulders. She turned as we entered, and at once the silence broke as she let out a cry of recognition and came toward us at a hobbling run. She seized my arms in a clutch like an eagle's talons.

"Oh, mistress! Oh, Mistress Blanchard! Help me! Help me!"

It was Gladys.

20

Countercharge

Mortimer's expression when he saw me and Brockley told us at once that he knew all about our expedition to the Black Mountains. His sheer disbelief was comical. He looked as if the mastiff had just addressed him in classical Latin. But he kept his nerve. "What is the meaning of this?" he demanded, and struck the right peremptory note so well that one had to admire him for it. "A judicial inquiry is in progress here. How dare you interrupt in this fashion? Guard!" He addressed the two retainers near the dais. "Fetch the accused back. We were about to hear another witness . . ."

"Don't let them! Don't let them get ahold of me!" Gladys clung to me. I put my arms around her. Within her small, wiry body, her bones were as fragile as a bird's, and she was shaking with fear. Gladys—rude, outspoken, and deplorably smelly Gladys—was once more terrified, as she had been when Brockley had rescued her in the village.

"It's all right," I said. "It's all right. Rob, this is Gladys Morgan, who saved our lives on the Mynydd Llyr."

"She's a witch!" yelled someone in the crowd. "She bewitched young Rafe and made him jump off the tower!"

"Oho!" I said loudly. "So that's the ploy, is it? There was talk that maybe he was murdered and first of all we were supposed to have done it. But now you've fixed on Gladys as the scapegoat, have you, Sir Philip? Don't worry, Gladys. I've got you."

"And I'm here," said Brockley. He drew Gladys out of the crook of my arm into his own. He wrinkled his nose slightly, but went on holding her, all the same. "You're safe now," he said to her.

Two guards had started toward Gladys at Mortimer's order, but three of Rob's men stepped forward to block their way. There was a silent confrontation. From the dais, Mortimer said: "The charge is that Gladys Morgan did by divers bewitchments, induce my ward, Rafe Northcote, to throw himself from a tower to his death. It is already established that she crept back to Vetch and sought speech with a maidservant by the name of Olwen, and slyly asked after Master Northcote . . ."

"I knew it was dangerous, you talking to Blod and Olwen," Brockley muttered to Gladys.

"If," said Mortimer, "at the end of this inquiry, I find there is cause, the woman Gladys will be sent for trial at Hereford, and if the accusation of procuring a death by witchcraft stands, she will burn. This is a serious matter. I must ask you to wait while I complete it. Be good enough, Mistress Blanchard, to tell your man to hand the prisoner over and . . ."

"This inquiry is rubbish," I said, "and you know it, Sir Philip. It's all right, Gladys."

"And our business will not wait," said Rob, "for it is also the queen's business. Sir Philip, we require to see you privately, at once. The matter concerns the Mortimer family as a whole and your mother has been asked to join us. Ah. Here she is."

Lady Thomasine had come into the hall. She too reacted in gratifying fashion when she saw me for she stopped short, her eyes widening. I favored her with an ironical smile. "I suggest," said Rob, "that we adjourn to the tower parlor forthwith."

"We shall do nothing of the sort. This behavior is insufferable!" Mortimer exclaimed angrily.

"You find the queen's command insufferable? Must I repeat myself?" Rob's voice was commanding. "We are here on the queen's confidential business and I advise you to cooperate. The tower parlor, *if* you please. Now."

For a moment, I thought Mortimer would defy us, but Rob's unwavering stare and resolute stance finally prevailed. With an air of one who yields gracefully to a superior authority, Mortimer observed that a private inquiry must naturally give way to royal business, and within minutes, the gathering had been dismissed and we were in the approximate privacy of the tower parlor.

I say approximate, for although Rob left his men outside, I had to tell Brockley to bring Gladys in, for her own protection, and so there were six of us in there: Mortimer, Lady Thomasine, Gladys and Brockley, Rob and myself. Brockley, however, took Gladys tactfully to the far side of the room. The rest of us sat down together beside the empty hearth.

"There's no point in roaming all round the forest," Rob said. He glanced at me, and from his doublet, he drew out the letters and handed them to me. "You did the hard work, Ursula. Show him the fruits of it."

Rising from my seat, I went to Sir Philip and handed him the two missives I had found in his strongbox. "Do you recognize these, Sir Philip?"

For a moment I thought he was going to push my hand away but then he realized what I was offering him. He snatched them from me, his face darkening. "Where did you get these?"

"From your strongbox, Sir Philip. I confiscated them. You should be grateful to me."

"Grateful . . . !"

"To use them as you intended would be treason," I told him quietly. "The gallows, Sir Philip. The knife."

I knew then that the theory which William Haggard and I had discussed, that his brother-in-law had been dreaming a dream and making himself believe it could be real, was right. The scheme he'd laid had substance; the letters proved that. Yet I doubted, watching him, that he would ever have used them.

I think he might have gone to Cambridge and tried to meet the queen. I think that until then, he could well have gone on imagining a wonderful future as Baron Mortimer of the Welsh March. But face-to-face with the reality of Elizabeth and the mighty, relentless machine which was her court, it is my belief that his dreams would have withered and died unspoken. He had tried to use Haggard to safeguard himself from arrest, but still, I think, he had only half-understood his danger. Now, one reference out loud, to gallows and knife, was enough. I saw the dream break; I saw him waken from it. I saw fear take hold of him. He turned green. I do mean green—the sickly kind, like mold.

It was a most agreeable moment. It almost repaid me for coming upon Rafe's body in the dark, for being shut in a dungeon, and then left to die—and Dale and Brockley with me—in a hut on a lonely mountain called the Mynydd Llyr.

"These are not all, Sir Philip," I said quietly. "We also have in our possession the letters which you gave to your brother-in-law, William Haggard."

"And we know," said Rob, "that you plotted to extract wealth from the queen as payment for not publishing them. Master Haggard has confirmed it. You are a fool. You would have been charged with treason, as Mistress Blanchard has pointed out. It is treason to suggest that Her Majesty is anything other than the lawful progeny of King Henry, eighth of that name."

"I'd never have published them . . . I'd never have done it . . . I only thought . . . I only thought . . ."

"I don't understand." Lady Thomasine spoke for the first time. She was sitting with clasped hands, her eyes fixed on me, the living ghost, visibly trying to work out how I had managed to come bouncing in at the door with Henderson, dressed in sunshine yellow and sparkling with health, when I should have been lying dead and emaciated on the floor of that hut in the mountains. "What letters are these?" she asked.

"The letters," I said to her sweetly, "which you brought me here to find. Your son's scheme for acquiring land and money. They are forgeries, of course. They convey a very damaging lie, concerning Her Majesty . . ."

"They're not forgeries!" burst out Mortimer in a high-pitched voice. "They were left me by my father. He found them in a piece of furniture he bought, when he was living here—at the end of 1536, I think! It was a desk with a little locked compartment in it. He broke the lock open and there were the letters! And it was said that it once belonged to Mark Smeaton."

Lady Thomasine gasped and even Rob looked shaken. I laughed. "So you say! I think I know better. I did wonder if perhaps they were innocent letters between another Mark, not Smeaton, and another Anne, not Boleyn. But forgery was so much more likely. Tell me, Sir Philip, when you left court under a cloud, ten years ago, did that have nothing to do with forgery?"

"No, my Lady Cleverness, it did not! I fought a duel and killed my man. But such things are not well seen at court, not now, not in the days of Queen Mary, either. Women are so tender of heart."

"The reason why you were called out," I said pitilessly, "was because you owed a gambling debt to the man concerned. You could not pay. You had spent too much on good clothes and fine horses. Some of your debtor's friends came to ask you for it, on his behalf. You showed them a receipt. They told him and he demanded to see it for himself—and then he called you out, because he had never written it. Somebody, presumably you, had forged his signature."

"Who told you that?" shouted Mortimer.

"Owen Lewis," I said. "I've seen him. I took the opportunity to ask him why you had to leave the court, Sir Philip. I thought he might be able to tell me."

"He wouldn't have told you. He's my friend. He keeps my secrets."

"Yes, he tried," I agreed. "But I had already learned from your brother-in-law, William Haggard, that a financial misunderstanding—your words, apparently—lay behind it and when I was wondering just what that could mean, I was reminded of the time when you helped your friend John Northcote uncover a swindle carried out by his steward, who had falsified the figures of wool sales. The two ideas: that of financial—er—misunderstanding, and that of falsified documents, suddenly came together. Perhaps these letters were not your first attempt at forgery! Perhaps you had some previous experience!"

"How dare you?" demanded Mortimer.

"Quite easily, in the circumstances," I said. "I gambled on my idea, in fact. I told Master Lewis that I already knew it was a matter of forgery and that took him by surprise. He couldn't deny it. He didn't want to give any details, so I invented a rumor that shocked him so much that he felt he had to tell me the truth, for your sake, Sir Philip. I said I'd heard that you had forged a love letter from a woman who had refused to become your mistress, out of revenge, to spoil her reputation. Master Lewis was so horrified that he told me the truth."

They were all gaping at me now. "You didn't mention that!" Rob said.

"It didn't seem important," I said. "I just repeated to you what Lewis had told me. How I got him to do it didn't really matter."

"Possibly not—but where on earth," said Rob, "did you learn that particular trick?"

"There's more to Mistress Blanchard than most people ever guess," Brockley remarked, from across the room. Although he had taken Gladys aside, the tower parlor wasn't big enough for them to be properly out of earshot.

I was digging in my memory. "I've an idea," I said, "that my first husband, Gerald, told me once that it was how he got a particular man to admit something to him. He suggested to him that he had done something so outrageous that the fellow blurted out the truth in self-defense. He'd really committed some lesser misdemeanor. Gerald wanted him to admit it because even the lesser offense was good enough for Gerald's purposes. He used it later to—put pressure on the man."

Part of Gerald's work for Sir Thomas Gresham in Antwerp had been to persuade various reluctant persons to hand over keys and, indeed, to commit forgery, so that treasure which was the rightful property of the Spanish administration in the Netherlands could be spirited away to swell Elizabeth's treasury in the Tower of London. Gerald never had any conscience about it. He was one of Elizabeth's most loyal servants.

"You seem to have had a very strange past, Mistress Blanchard," said Mortimer coldly. "You are a strange kind of woman altogether." He turned to his mother. "And you, it seems, brought her here to nose into my affairs."

"I did," said Lady Thomasine strongly. "I needed to find out just how you proposed to make the queen restore the Mortimer fortune. I was sure that any such scheme must be dangerous. I kept telling you but you wouldn't listen. I asked for help. Ursula has worked in secret for the queen, before now. I asked that she should come here and find out what you were about."

"You betrayed me? Your own son?"

"No," said Rob. "She may well have saved you from a horrible death. You should be down on your knees in gratitude to her."

Rising, Rob crossed the hearth and took back the letters that Mortimer and I were holding. He held them up. "Sir William Cecil will have to see these but then they will certainly be destroyed. Forgeries or not, their contents are still so scandalous that I doubt if either Cecil or the queen will wish their existence to come into public knowledge. That simple fact may—only may—save you from a charge of treason and save your brother-in-law too. We know how you pressed him into becoming your accessory. You will have to base any plea for mercy on your willingness, and Master Haggard's willingness, to observe lifelong secrecy. We shall see. I make no promises. Meanwhile, I recommend you to keep silence from this moment on."

It was I who broke the shattered silence which followed by clearing my throat and saying: "This conference is not over. There is still the matter of Rafe Northcote, who did not fall from a tower, with or without the assistance of witchcraft. He was stabbed in the back."

There was a further shattered silence. Mortimer, who had walked into the study and seen the stabbed Rafe with his own eyes, now stared at me as though I had taken leave of my senses and demanded truculently: "What nonsense is this?"

"Nonsense?" I said. "You were there, you found Brockley and myself beside the body, and you and your mother together accused us of killing him. You had us shut in your dungeon. Then you, Lady Thomasine, took us out and sent us, in the care of Pugh and Evans, to an isolated hut in the hills and left us there to die—like the poor things who were shut in Isabel's Tower and are said to haunt it still. Fortunately, we escaped. And then we arrived here to find Gladys being accused of bewitching Rafe into killing himself, although you both know that that is a lie."

"Oh, my dear." Lady Thomasine gazed at me sadly. "My dear Ursula. How very unwise of you to raise this subject. I don't know what you mean about being shut in a hut. What can you hope to gain from such a tale, my dear? It is true that I released you and your servants early that morning. You are a kinswoman of mine and family honor is important to the Vetch family. That is partly why I sought your help in discovering my son's unwise plans. I wished to protect him—but also, I did not want scandal in our midst. I wished to keep the whole matter within the confines of the family circle. Alas, Rafe's murder would have been a scandal just as bad! Ursula, I know that my son wanted you and your manservant to be taken to the sheriff but I thought it best just to let you go and put out the story that Rafe had killed himself."

"What?" I said.

Lady Thomasine shook her head at me. "Somehow or other, despite all our efforts, the rumor still got round that his death wasn't all it seemed. And then, to my great distress, a whisper started that you had been concerned, and had run away the following morning. It was all most embarrassing. For this reason, we decided to sacrifice that reeking old hag over there." She pointed at Gladys, who shuddered back toward Brockley, but glared from her safe vantage point, like a wildcat from the depths of a den.

"The fact is, Master Henderson," Lady Thomasine said confidingly to Rob, "that there is indeed more to Mistress Blanchard than most people suspect. She is attractive, and I am sorry to say that at times, she leads men on. She did it to my son. He will tell you. She has no intention of yielding to them, but she enjoys—shall we say—disturbing them. My son, naturally, took it for an invitation and then she turned very nasty."

"She attacked me most savagely," said Mortimer, nodding, and looking at Rob in a manner so grave that for one dreadful, dumbfounded moment, I thought Rob might actually believe him.

"You claim I . . . !" Indignation came to my aid. "You were trying to force yourself on me! Yes, I hit you with a silver dish and bit your wrist! And I had every reason!"

But if Lady Thomasine had been a man she would have been a magnificent jouster; nearly impossible to unseat. "I fear," she said to Rob, "that my son is telling the truth, and I fear that Mistress Blanchard may also have tried her wiles on Rafe. With Rafe, she perhaps aroused more desire than she could well cope with. Yes, I and my son did find her standing beside his body, and I have no doubt at all that it was she who killed him."

21

Music in the Night

"Of course I believe you!" said Rob. "Why should either you or Brockley want to stick a dagger in Rafe's back? And if you had, you'd hardly drag the matter up now, when Rafe is safely buried, not even for Gladys."

We were in the keep guest rooms. We had not intended to spend the night in the castle but with so much unfinished business on our hands, we couldn't help it. At Lady Thomasine's outrageous accusation, Rob had decided to end the meeting so that we could confer together. Brushing the accusation aside with a cool lift of his eyebrows and a request that Lady Thomasine should stop talking nonsense, he had demanded that Gladys be handed officially over to our care, and added that we expected to be accommodated and fed.

Mortimer tried to bluster but Rob more or less stated that failing proper hospitality, we would simply requisition guest rooms and supplies from the kitchen. As Sir Philip's only alternative was to order his men to attack ours, thereby turning the castle into a battlefield, he gave in. Susanna and Jack Raghorn were bidden to prepare our rooms; and a supper of cheese omelets and fried bacon, accompanied by a jug of ale, was (at our own request) served in our quarters. We didn't feel we would be welcome at supper in the hall.

I supped at the parlor table with Rob and Brockley. Gladys, with unusual delicacy, had taken her food into the next room, despite my objections that we had all eaten together in Isabel's Tower.

"Master Henderson wasn't there then. He's a gentleman. He don't want a dirty old woman champing her food at his table," said Gladys, and retired to champ it out of our hearing. I must admit we were all rather relieved. Even my protests had been largely a matter of form. I didn't persist with them.

"Well," I said now. "All right. We're all agreed that neither I nor Brockley killed Rafe, but somebody did. He was found at the foot of a tower as though he'd fallen, but when we were hiding in Isabel's Tower, Gladys found out that there were whispers saying I might have done it. Someone noticed that he—that Rafe—should have bled more if he'd been alive when he fell."

"The whispers obviously worried Lady Thomasine and her son," Rob said. "They wanted to hide the fact that there'd been a murder at all. Think it out. The Mortimers wanted to make Rafe's death look like suicide, and to pretend that you had simply left the castle in the normal way, if rather early in the morning. When the rumors started up, saying that you had murdered him, that can't have suited them in the least! They wouldn't want a hue and cry after you. You were on their consciences. So when they found that Gladys was within their reach, they decided to lance the gossip, like a boil. They would put the blame on Gladys and her witchcraft, and make a nice satisfying end of the business! Clever of them, really. They could put the lack of blood down to another of her magic spells. Silly, pointless spells if you stop to think about them but if you once get people worked up enough about witchcraft, they never do stop to think. They don't ask sensible questions. They'll believe anything."

"You don't believe in witches either?" I asked.

"I believe in very little, as a matter of fact," said Rob. "I go to church because it's the law. Still, there may be a God. Someone or something created the world and put people in it. But no, I can't believe in witches. They seem quite absurd to me. The things they're supposed to do are so ridiculous. Why in the world should Gladys decide to make Rafe jump off a tower? But, as I said, no one was likely to ask that. For the Mortimers, she was the perfect scapegoat."

"It's strange that people saw the lack of blood but not the stab wound," I said.

"Not really." Rob shook his head. "When you gave me that detailed report at the Feathers, didn't you say that according to what Olwen told Gladys, he was found lying on his back?"

"Yes," I said.

"If he landed on his back, the damage might easily hide the mark. Now then. *We* know he was stabbed, and when and where. We are not perfectly sure by whom, but the chances are it was Mortimer. From what you told me in the Feathers, he had reasons, of more than one kind. Still, before I set about questioning him further, are there any other candidates?"

Reluctantly, I said: "It could have been Lewis. The Mortimers might want to protect him, I suppose. He's Sir Philip's friend, after all, and Sir Philip wants the marriage with Alice to go ahead. There's money in it for him. Lewis was getting round Alice very nicely, and her father and her uncle were both backing him up, but I suppose a quarrel could still have blown up between him and Rafe."

"Were Rafe and Alice actually lovers?" Rob asked.

"I think so," I said. "The first time I tried to get into the study, I found them asleep in each other's arms, in front of the hearth. I don't want to think it was Lewis," I added. "Mortimer seems a much more likely killer to me, and he was up late that night. There was still a light in his window when we set out to get into the study."

Gladys, grumbling to herself, came back into the room. "Got any of that ale, still? They didn't treat me proper, while they had me locked up. They gave me food and water but never enough." Her glance fell on the dish of bacon in the middle of the table. "You goin' to eat all that or could I have a bit more?"

"When were you arrested?" I asked. "I thought you were going back to the mountains."

"So I was, but Blod let me down. I tried to see her again, to get a message to Hugh Cooper, but the silly girl took it into her daft head to get scared of meetin' a witch in the woods. She ran off when I stepped out in front of her, and went and told Cooper I was creepin' round the place. I never had time to give her a proper message from me to him, or talk to him myself, because he went to the castle and told Lady Thomasine. I think he didn't want another scene with the villagers, so he decided to put it in the hands of the castle people. I was still in the woods, hopin' to find someone else to take word to Hugh, and the next thing I know, there are great big men with swords all over the place, and I was found and haled off to the castle hall. Well, you heard Lady Thomasine. Whole castle was full of rumors and talk about Rafe, and did he fall or did someone shove him? Mortimer took one look at me and decided I was a gift from heaven. The perfect explanation, I was. Better than you, 'cause he'd *got* me there to throw to the sheriff. So he had me locked up till he could put on a formal inquiry as he called it."

I filled her beaker and handed her some bread and bacon. Brockley remarked that Rafe had not been dead long when we found him. "Mistress Blanchard pointed that out to me when we were talking it over in the dungeon. You said, madam, that a quarrel was unlikely because the Haggards were sleeping above the study. That makes Lewis less probable. I said at the time that it's possible to quarrel quietly, and so it is, but it's difficult. And if Lewis did it, I should think it would have been in anger. I don't see Lewis lying in wait."

"So we're back to Mortimer," I said. "And he really is the likely one. He was heir to the manor of Rowans after Rafe, he needed money, and he had several reasons to be angry with Rafe—over Alice, and even, perhaps, because he felt that Rafe was too close to Lady Thomasine or else unfaithful to her. Either might be possible, with a man like Mortimer. His brother-in-law says he's not a wicked man but I'd say there's a good streak of sheer badness in him." Mindful of Gladys's presence, I watched my words, but I added: "His plans for getting money out of the queen prove *that*."

Gladys, in the act of leaving the room, stopped and turned back. "I bin thinkin'. It maybe wasn't Mortimer as did for Rafe."

Rob looked affronted. Gladys had been right to eat apart from us. He was willing to champion her in the cause of justice, and to please his friend Ursula Blanchard, but to well-bred Rob Henderson, who wore velvet caps on his carefully barbered fair head and spent a small fortune on his shirts and doublets, Gladys was a lower form of life. Unlike Lady Thomasine, he wouldn't actually call her a reeking old hag, but he probably thought it.

Brockley, however, said: "Who else could it have been—assuming that it wasn't Lewis?"

"I said, I bin thinkin'," Gladys repeated. "Not much else to do, locked up in a dungeon. How about this for an idea?"

We listened to Gladys's theory with incredulity at first. Rob said it was ridiculous and I found it simply bewildering.

"I don't see *why,*" I said. "Mortimer's the one with the good reasons for getting rid of Rafe."

"Reasons he might have but when it comes to actually *doin'* things, it's another matter," said Gladys, which gave me pause. I remembered doubting whether Mortimer would ever actually have tried to use his forged letters.

Brockley, frowning, said: "It's possible . . ."

"I think about it and I don't see him stabbin' the boy," Gladys said. "Not *doin'* it, not even if he wanted to and who's to say he wanted to anyhow? Never even thought of it, likely as not. Look at what he did with you! He could have had you done in and carted out in sacks, and dumped somewhere but no, you're taken to the mountains and locked up instead and not a finger laid on you. All that was his notion, mark my words."

Rob said thoughtfully: "There was something that my wife said to me. It was the reason why she was so anxious to get Meg out of the castle. Yes, it could add up. Mattie said . . ."

I was frowning as deeply as Brockley. Something was astir in my mind; a fugitive memory which kept slipping away before I could grasp it. Rob, while he was recounting what Mattie had told him, was also watching me. "What is it?" he asked.

"I'm not sure. I don't know. I just—somehow—think Gladys may be right. I can't . . ." I put my hands to my temples, and felt them throb ominously with the strain of trying to remember. "There is something I ought to remember but it won't come. I just think—that, yes, it could be. It's as though it *feels* right. Yes . . ." The fugitive memory wouldn't surface but one or two other things now did so. I spoke of them. Brockley, his brow clearing, bore me out.

"But what can we do about it now?" I said. "It's a matter of questioning, I suppose."

"Ye . . . es." Rob sounded doubtful. "Hard questioning can achieve results but it has drawbacks. In the last few years, Cecil has sometimes employed me as an interrogator, and I've learned that people can be forced into confessing to things they didn't do. I want to get this right and know for sure I've got it right. I would like to get my hands on some solid evidence, I must say. So far, all we have are hints and pointers. What I would like," said Rob wistfully, "is blood on someone's hands or an eyewitness or an unforced confession. Ursula, Brockley, think hard. Is there anything more that you noticed or heard that might show us a way forward or help us to find one?"

For a moment, we were all silent. Then my mind, searching for inspiration, flickered over the events of the last few days and showed me a picture, of myself standing at night in Sir Philip's study, with the incriminating letters in my hand, telling Brockley that we must get out of the castle quickly, and warning him on no account even to breathe on the lute he was carrying. "Brockley," I said, "that lute we bought on the way back to Vetch—do you still have it with you or did you leave it in the Feathers?"

"I still have it," he said, puzzled. "I suppose so, at least. I never took it out of my shoulder pack so I suppose it came back here with me. But . . ."

"I have an idea," I said.

It was not a kindly idea. Brockley was doubtful. "What if we're wrong, madam?"

"Then we're wrong," I said briefly. "But we could at least try."

"But what if we just wait all night and no one comes?"

"That won't happen. I'll make it an order," said Rob decisively. "I wish we had more time to lay our plans, though."

"I think," I said, "that the foundations have been laid already. Quite unintentionally, Gladys did that for us. Maybe we could build on that, so to speak."

* * *

The May night was warm and there was no fire in the blue parlor. I had opened one of the windows a little. The room was well lit, however, for Rob, ruthlessly giving orders as though Vetch were his castle instead of Mortimer's, had seen to it that there were four triple candlesticks, all provided with new candles. The ornamental clock said it was the hour of midnight. Outside, the sky was clear and pricked with stars, but there was no moon. The castle walls, the battlements and towers around the courtyard, were solid masses of blackness, barely discernible, and yet I could feel them there, looming over us, encircling us, watching what we did. As on the night when I had made my first attempt to get at the strongbox, I was acutely aware of the castle's age and its past. The darkness seemed full of the shades of those who had lived and died at Vetch.

We waited, watching the door to the tower parlor, four of us. Rob and I were the principals, and each of us had a supporter, Brockley for me, and Geoffrey Barker for Rob. Barker was interested by the scheme if not very sanguine about its outcome.

"I've got my doubts, like Brockley here," he said in a low voice, as we waited. "Orders must be obeyed, yes, but if games with that lute fool anyone, my name isn't Barker."

"You haven't lived all your life at Vetch," I said, and then caught my breath. As well as watching the door, we had all been listening for footsteps. We hadn't heard any. But the door was opening. My heart lurched. If Gladys was right, then Rafe's murderer was about to come through it. I could see the glow of a candle, carried in the hand that in all probability had wielded the dagger. Then, quietly, her slippered feet making no sound, Lady Thomasine stepped forward into the brightly lit room.

"Well, Master Henderson, Mistress Blanchard, I am here, as you see, and alone, as I was bidden." She was perfectly self-possessed.

"My maid could not have come, in any case," she remarked. "Nan is a foolish woman, I fear, and lately she has not been doing her work well. First she was distracted like all the rest because of Rafe's death and then, a few days ago, there was a great stir because some of the servants swore they had seen a face at a window in the haunted tower. Nan was one of them.

"She was almost prostrate with shock that day, and this afternoon, believe it or not, it all happened again! She and Olwen and a couple of the menservants were gossiping in the courtyard and Olwen cried out that someone was looking out of the tower and then, of course, all the others imagined they could see it too. Nan came running to me in hysterics. I had to give her a soothing draft and put her to bed and then I had to wake her up to help me dress for this meeting—her hands were still so shaky that I needed to do half the work myself. Anyone would think she was the mistress and I the maid!"

Despite Nan's shaky hands, Lady Thomasine was as elegant as I had ever seen her. Although she lived on the borders of Wales and rarely left home as far as I knew, she still kept up with the latest fashions. She was wearing the newest kind of ruff, a little bigger than its predecessors and edged with lace, and her rose-colored overgown, embroidered with golden flowers, adorned with high shoulder puffs, and worn over a pale blue kirtle and undersleeves also sewn with golden flowers, could have appeared at any court function.

She was wearing the slippers with the cerise roses, and she also wore a great deal of the pearl jewelry which Elizabeth had made so popular. Her hair, crimped in front of a pearl-edged cap, was noticeably faded at the temples, as though recent events had aged her. But her face was smoothly powdered and her lips carmined. She was dressed for battle, I thought, as a medieval knight might put on armor.

"I hope Nan will be better tomorrow," said Rob gravely. "But I think that in a moment, you will agree that it is best that you came alone. I apologize for keeping you from your sleep and for summoning you from your chamber. As a matter of delicacy, I did not wish to intrude on your private quarters; and by holding this interview at this late hour, we can avoid letting the rest of the household know that you have been questioned."

Lady Thomasine's fine brows rose. "I have no need to fear your questions. It is a matter of indifference to me whether the household knows or not. You have come here with armed men and virtually taken charge of this castle. You have taken it upon yourself to give orders. I thought it best to comply with grace, that is all."

"Barker," said Rob, taking no notice of this, "will you go into the tower parlor and make sure that no one comes through it? And, Brockley, will you guard the door into the courtyard, please? Go and stand just outside it."

They went out. I heard the courtyard door click as Brockley passed through. Rob invited Lady Thomasine to sit down.

"Is it necessary," she asked, as she arranged herself gracefully on a settle, ringed hands clasped in her lap, "for Mistress Blanchard to be here as well? I have not made public my accusation against her. She is a member of my family after all and I have been concerned from the start with my family honor. But why must I be troubled by her presence now?"

"I am innocent of the charge, as well you know," I said coldly.

"I know nothing of the kind. Well, Master Henderson. You have questions for me, it seems. You may ask them. I am listening."

There was a short silence. The candle flames wavered in a draft from the open window. Lady Thomasine looked at us inquiringly, and as the silence lengthened, we saw her become nervous.

Then, in a perfectly ordinary voice, as though he were merely wondering whether it would rain again soon, Rob said: "When you stabbed Rafe, was it in here or in the study where he was found?"

Surprise tactics sometimes work but these failed dismally. "When I did what?" said Lady Thomasine disdainfully.

"We know you killed Rafe," I said. "Why else did you want Brockley and me to disappear and die in that hut in the mountains? If we had come to trial, too much might have emerged. Master Henderson and his wife would certainly have attended the trial and Mistress Henderson knew that you and Rafe were lovers—or had been, till he turned away from you to a young girl."

"You are mad," said Lady Thomasine coolly, and so convincingly that for one unpleasant moment, I almost wondered if we were wrong.

Then I heard Gladys's voice in my head, justifying her remarkable theory.

"Told you, didn't I, up at the hermitage, that she'd had Pugh and Evans in her time? Past taking lovers now, she is, I said to you, and I believed it then. I thought Rafe just flattered her and played music to her. Hardly more than a boy, he was, and she nigh to sixty. Didn't think it could go further. You think I'm just an old woman with a mind as grimy as me shawl"—Rob at this point had turned an embarrassed crimson—"but I got my sense of decency. All the same, thinkin' about it: she's vain. A cock pigeon spreading his tail isn't any vainer than Thomasine. She got rid of me from the castle because I was old age on feet and she'd look at me and think: Gladys today is Thomasine tomorrow. She couldn't stand it, so she threw me out. If it did go further, between her and Rafe, how d'you think she'd feel when she found out he'd fallen for Alice?"

Then, as we sat there talking it over among the supper things, and I tried to drag into the light a haunting memory that wouldn't come (and still wouldn't, although I was conscious of its shadow even now), I had recalled other things. I had remembered how very funereal Lady Thomasine's mien had been the day that Rafe declared his love for Alice. Her mood hadn't lightened, even though Owen Lewis was in a fair way to ousting Rafe from Alice's affections, almost at once. And I had also recalled that Lady Thomasine had been surprisingly close at hand that night. "She and Mortimer came into the study together," I had said, remembering. "Yes. If Mortimer did it, why was Lady Thomasine involved at all? What was she doing out of bed at such an hour?"

"She was in a loose wrapper," Brockley added thoughtfully. "As though she'd been fetched from her chamber. But would Mortimer really have done that? Deliberately fetched his mother and made her his accomplice? She came into the study with him and later on, lighted our way across the courtyard. She was so much a part of it. Too much, if Mortimer did it. But if she killed Rafe herself, she might well have gone to Mortimer for help."

Now, in the candlelit parlor, Rob said to Lady Thomasine: "We have noticed a number of things which point to you as Rafe's killer. A lovers' quarrel, was it? As Mistress Blanchard has said, my wife knew of the affair between you. She told me about it shortly after we took Meg away from here. It seems that one afternoon—it was before Mistress Blanchard came to the castle—she wanted to see you, and not finding you anywhere else, she went up to your room and knocked. There was no answer but the door wasn't latched and swung open to her tap. You and Rafe were on the window seat, clasped together, she said, and when I said, well, maybe it was just a brief friendly hug, she said no. She said she knew the difference, and she'd already seen the two of you exchange looks, and noticed the way Rafe sometimes sang love songs to you. She said it was improper and it created an atmosphere and that the atmosphere had been very strong when she looked into your room. She said it was feverish and unhealthy and she'd been glad to get Meg out of it."

"I thought," said Lady Thomasine now, "that you and your wife had taken Meg to London to buy clothes. Though I remember wondering at the time why Hereford wasn't good enough. Merchants from everywhere sail up the Severn to Hereford."

"Hereford would have been good enough," Rob agreed. "We just wanted Meg away from here. We waited in Tewkesbury, to be near Mistress Blanchard, should she need us."

"As she apparently did. Did she bring you here to back up these insane allegations against me?"

"You have a certain reputation, my lady," Rob said. "Your butler, Pugh, and the falconer Evans—in the past they have been more to you than just good servants, have they not?"

"They are still devoted," I said grimly. "They had no hesitation in helping me to my death, and my own two loyal servants with me."

As I said, Lady Thomasine would have made a brilliant jouster. She showed no signs of disquiet, but remained sitting regally motionless, and if the candlelight flickered on the gold and pearl rings which adorned her clasped hands, it was only because the flames were moving in the breath from the window. The hands themselves were still.

"All this," she said, "is an utter tarradiddle. Rafe was my son's ward, my adopted grandson, and sometimes my minstrel. He was a good boy who respected his elders. I do not understand what Mistress Blanchard means by her talk of dying in a hut in the mountains; still less do I know why she chooses to blacken the names of two honest men whose only crime is to serve me well."

She moved at last, but only to get up. "If that was all you wanted to say . . ."

"Sit down," said Rob, so strongly that she actually did so.

"It is not all," said Rob. "Mistress Blanchard and Roger Brockley both recall that when Rafe died, deep in the night, you were close by and broad awake when most folk are fast asleep, abed. Also, you helped eagerly with their arrest and imprisonment and oversaw their departure for the mountains. You were so *very* much involved. Did your son fetch his mother to help him hide his crime—is he really so dependent on you, or so sure of you!—or did a frightened woman, with blood on her hands, call on her son for help?" He stepped across the room and stood over her, bending his face close to hers. "What *did* happen, Lady Thomasine? Did you have a tryst with Rafe downstairs? Or did you follow him and accost him as he set out for a meeting with Alice, or left one? Did you quarrel about Alice?"

He was hectoring her and using his physical nearness like a bludgeon. Yet Lady Thomasine was hardly listening. Her face had changed. She edged sideways, away from him, looking toward the open window. Rob turned his head, letting his voice die away, and in the quiet that followed, we could all hear what Lady Thomasine had heard before us.

It was so soft, so faint, no more than a ripple of music on the edge of sound. As we listened, it faded away and then waveringly resumed. "So someone is practicing music in their room," said Rob dismissively. "What of it? Lady Thomasine . . ."

The music came again, a little louder now, just enough to make the melody recognizable. Drifting through the darkness, softly, hauntingly, making the gooseflesh prickle on my skin and disturbing the hairs at the back of my neck, was the tune which Rafe had made, to which he had sung the ballad of the knight who found a shining sword in a foul and dirty cave.

"No." Lady Thomasine whispered it. "No." I glanced at her and saw with satisfaction that her clasped hands were trembling at last. Her eyes glinted bright in the candlelight. Too bright; only tears caught the light with that diamond glitter. But still she did not break. Still her head was high and her body was held rigid.

I looked at Rob, wondering what to do next. Then, beyond the door to the tower parlor, there was a sudden disturbance. I heard Barker exclaim, and a woman's voice protesting. "That's Nan!" Lady Thomasine was roused at last. She came to her feet. "Let her come to me! Nan! Nan!"

"Let her in, Barker!" Rob shouted. The door was at once flung open, and Nan rushed through it. She was dressed in cap and wrapper, but her feet were bare and her face frantic. She ran to her mistress.

"Oh, my lady, my lady! I heard the music from the window! It's them! It's the ghosts! They've come out of their tower and something terrible's going to happen!" She had thrown herself on her knees before Lady Thomasine and clutched her mistress's hand like a terrified child. Outside in the courtyard, Brockley, hidden in the shadow of the wellhead, went on playing his lute, changing the melody to something older, a traditional country tune. There were uncertainties in the playing, with false notes now and then, but Nan was far too distracted to notice. "There it is again! Oh, my lady, my lady! Oh, God protect us!"

"Get up, Nan. Get up." Lady Thomasine's voice shook, but she still had herself in hand. "As Master Henderson has just said, someone is practicing music. That's all it is. In any case, what harm can come to us even if the ghosts are out and about and wandering? We are all here together, safe in a well-lit room. There is no need for these vapors."

We were going to fail. Silently, I cursed. We had known that Lady Thomasine was strong-minded but she was far stronger than we had guessed, and she wasn't going to admit her guilt. She was going to defend both herself and Mortimer by holding to the story that I was responsible. Short of somehow producing the phantom of Rafe himself, in a shining white shroud with spatters of blood on it, we were not going to jolt her into a confession.

There were more sounds of disturbance, this time outside, voices and distant shrieks of alarm. Looking across to the servants' quarters, I saw that lights were being kindled. A door opened and candlelight streamed onto the cobbles and there came a confused medley of voices. The music ceased abruptly.

Nan, however, still on her knees, continued to gulp and shudder, and Lady Thomasine grew impatient. She shot out a daintily slippered foot, applied the sole of it to Nan's shoulder and shoved the unfortunate lady's maid backward so hard that she keeled over at my feet. I stooped to help her up and found myself, as I had been in the dungeon, nose to toe with Lady Thomasine's slipper, still petulantly swinging.

And then I saw it, and with that, from the depths of my mind, the fugitive memory surfaced, a Leviathan of proof.

I had seen it first in the dungeon but then, confused and frightened, I hadn't understood. I had only taken in that the slippers were dirty. Yet my eyes had made a faithful report and somewhere in my mind, the honest clerk of memory had written down what they told him.

I hauled Nan up, sat her sobbing on a stool, and then stooped again and seized Lady Thomasine's ankle. Ignoring her cry of protest, I held her foot so that I could look closely at the slipper. There was no doubt. I wrenched the slipper off. "Rob!"

He came to me at once and I pushed the slipper under his nose, my finger pointing to one of the cerise roses. "Look, look at that!"

"What's the matter? What are you doing?" demanded Lady Thomasine.

"Studying an embroidered rose," I told her. "Only, it isn't quite the right shape, and half of it is darker than the rest—nearer brown than cerise. Some of it isn't embroidery at all. It's a stain, a dark brown stain, like old blood. But when I saw it in the dungeon, it was nearly fresh, still red. It almost matched the embroidery then, and I didn't take in what I was seeing—but even so, some part of me remembered it. I've dreamed of your slippers repeatedly since then."

I looked at her grimly. "Rafe bled a little, not much, but still, a little. When you came into the study with Sir Philip, you knelt beside Rafe's body, but not where his blood could have touched your feet, or any part of you. You kept away from it, so carefully, so fastidiously, that I noticed. But you might have got his blood on your shoes when you actually stabbed him and not realized it. The stain is not so very easy to see, and neither you nor Nan did see it. You would have washed or brushed the slippers otherwise, I suppose, or made Nan do it."

"What is she talking about?" wailed Nan. "Ma'am, what does she mean?"

Lady Thomasine lunged out and snatched the slipper. She stared at it for a moment and then dropped it, shaking her head as though denying what she had seen. She began to twist her ringed hands together and her mouth worked as though she were trying out phrases before uttering them. There were a dozen excuses she could have made: a nosebleed; a cut finger that dripped. That she said none of these things was itself an indictment. But her wordlessness could not be called a confession. For a moment, it was still touch and go.

But Brockley had not finished. Outside in the darkness, the music began again. He was taking a risk, since men with lanterns were now out in the courtyard, but he was a resolute fellow and the shadow of the thatched wellhead, which we had chosen as his hiding place, concealed him well. He had changed the melody again, to another old traditional tune, a simpler one, easier to play, so that his lute now spoke with more assurance. I didn't recognize the music but it was a lament, full of sorrow and a dreadful longing as if for something deeply beloved and irrevocably lost. It moved my heart and Nan, terrified all over again, sat up, gasping with fright.

And Lady Thomasine's rigidity gave way at last. She turned her head this way and that, as though she wanted first to hear the music better and then as though she were trying not to hear it at all. She began to cry. She did not wipe the tears away but let them stream as though she had not noticed them. "Nan, you are a fool," she said. "If only you had done your work as you should and washed my slippers clean. But it doesn't matter. Oh, stop that, Nan!" The maid had begun to sob for forgiveness. "I am so tired," said Lady Thomasine.

We waited, watching her.

"Shut that window!" She almost screamed it. "Shut it, shut out that . . . that noise! I don't know what it is and I don't care. Maybe it's a ghost and maybe it isn't. I'm too weary to go on pretending. You'll badger me until I die of exhaustion or give in; I can see you will. So I'll give in now. I'll tell you the truth."

22

Grief for Times Past

Lady Thomasine was vain and she was ruthless. She had murdered Rafe and she had tried to murder me and the Brockleys and in a most unpleasant way at that.

And I ended up, in some weird, backhanded fashion, pitying her.

"First of all," she said, wiping her eyes at last and assembling her dignity around her, "I would ask mercy for my two good servants, Simon Evans and Harold Pugh. They love me and they obey me. They took you to the mountains because I ordered it. Does Queen Elizabeth not demand obedience from her servants? And after all, you did not die."

"I make no promises," said Rob coldly. He had sat down behind a table, giving himself a judicial air. I remained standing. Outside, Brockley's music had ceased. "Go on," said Rob to Lady Thomasine.

She turned to me. "You are young," she said. "Not in your first youth now, but young enough. You still have beauty. I see one or two faded strands in your hair but mostly it is still dark. The hazel of your eyes has not dulled and your complexion yet has bloom. Men smile when they look at you. But one day it will change. You will be talking to a man; buying something from a market stall, perhaps; speaking to a groom in an inn yard; exchanging gossip with a young gallant in a gallery at Whitehall. And suddenly, his attention will wander; his eyes will slide away from yours. You will turn to see why and find that a lovely young girl, all dew and roses, has walked by and his gaze is following her. Even if he goes on speaking civilly to you, his mind is not on you. You might be nothing but a piece of furniture. He is thinking only of that young girl.

"And you will go to your chamber and look in the mirror, and you will see that your hair is no longer glossy like hers; and that on your face are the first lines, time's footprints; the marks of adult knowledge. You may be grateful then if you have a faithful husband to whom you are still dear. I," said Lady Thomasine, "had not. Not long after the day when the mirror first told me that my looks were dwindling, I found Edward in the arms of a maid-servant. My son, I am sorry to say, has the same casual habits."

"As I well know," I agreed softly.

"All that is by the way, now," said Lady Thomasine. "Believe me, Ursula, a woman who is growing older and whose husband has turned away from her is glad of any faithful admirers in whose eyes she is still fair, as she was when first they were entranced by her. In those circumstances, you might find yourself, as I did, taking care with your dress, anointing and powdering your skin, striving with all your might to hold back the deadly years. Women have little power in this world. Even if we come to marriage with money and land, the husband takes control of it. Our only authority is vested in our looks, in being desirable. To lose that is to lose everything. Besides, we do have our longings. I was not ready," said Lady Thomasine, "to withdraw from the lists of love."

I had thought of her as a jouster. It seemed that she saw herself in that way too.

"My husband," she said, "ceased to be my lover after the day I caught him with someone else. We hardly spoke to each other in private from then on, though in public we kept up appearances. I learned to live with it. We kept the pretense up until he died. Meanwhile, I tended such looks as I still had and for a time, at least, I still had Pugh and Evans! But in the end"—her voice grew bitter—"I knew I must let go of them too, and I knew I was right when I heard the note of relief behind their protestations that they still wanted me.

"I set them free of me and so I kept their loyalty. No woman ever had better servants. Pugh has never married though he has had his affairs among the maids. Evans was married for a while but lost his wife in an outbreak of plague. But my own need for affection, for the satisfaction of the body, refused to die. I starved. I suffered. Then Rafe came into the house and like a young maiden, I fell in love."

She paused and the room was quiet, although we could still hear people moving about outside. I glanced out again and saw that the search of the courtyard had become more organized. A chain of men with torches and lanterns was working its way across. To my relief, the outer door clicked just then and Brockley glanced in. I gave him a nod, and he replied with a smile, as he withdrew.

"Who was that?" demanded Lady Thomasine.

"Just my manservant, who has been watching the courtyard door," I told her. "He looked in to see if he was needed."

"Please continue, Lady Thomasine," said Rob.

"You have guessed most of it, no doubt." She let out a heavy sigh. "I will tell you something else you may not know, Ursula. One's taste in men does not necessarily change with time. I mean that an older woman does not necessarily fall in love with older men. Why should she? Do not older men retain their eye for pretty young girls? I retained my eye for a virile young man. Rafe, with his smooth skin and his hard muscles and his vitality, was a wonder and a glory.

"And he was willing. That was the marvel of it. He was willing to lend that young strength to me, to let me rejoice in the touch and smell and vigor of him. And to me, it was all as though it had never happened before. My love for Rafe was sharp-edged and bright, like a new-forged blade."

She was almost talking to herself now. She had brushed away her first tears, but once more, the candles picked up their glitter in her eyes.

"I was grateful to him," she said. "I showed it. I showered him with gifts of jewelry and money." I shivered, seeing the pathos of it, but Lady Thomasine seemed unaware of any pathos. "I was so happy," she said. "And then—then came Alice. Last Christmas. From that time on, Rafe was lost to me. He still played his lute for me and showed me pretty attentions in public, but he no longer came tapping on my chamber door at night or whispered to me to meet him here in the parlor after dark. He refused the gifts I offered him. And I . . . could not live without him." She met our eyes defiantly. "I could not live without him. I had drunk too deeply of him. Like anyone who drinks strong wine too deeply and too often, I was caught.

"Again and again, I pleaded with him. Sometimes he would spare me an embrace. Mattie saw us once. But that was all. I would waylay him, beg him to come to my bed, to make trysts with me, but he said it was over, that he had given his heart to Alice . . ."

"His body," I said under my breath. I did not think that Rafe had had much heart to give to anyone. Lacking Alice, he had certainly been prepared to offer himself to me. Rafe, in fact, was the kind who took whatever chances came his way.

"On the night he died," said Lady Thomasine, "I went to his chamber. It's—it was—on the floor below mine. But he . . . he . . ." Her voice faltered. I saw torment in her face, the shadow of a rejection too painful to put into words. I helped her out with a question.

"You both came down here that night. Why was that?"

In a low voice, she said: "He had just begun to undress when I went into his room. He had taken his doublet off. He told me to go away so that he could finish undressing in private—he said that to me, who had disrobed him with my own hands, so many times! I . . . I said as much to him and he ran out of the room in his shirt and hose and rushed away down the tower stairs. I ran after him and caught him up in the tower parlor. I confronted him again. I . . ."

"We have no need of the details," said Rob, I think as much out of embarrassment as out of pity. But Lady Thomasine shook her head impatiently.

"No. You must know why I did what I did. I want you to understand. If you have ever known love, then remember it now. Ask yourself how you would feel if the object of your love let you abase yourself and then cast you off with despising words. Don't think that it hurt me less because I am nearer sixty than fifty, and he was only twenty. It hurt me more. I was being put away for something that was only on the outside of me. Inside, I was—I am—still only twenty. I said that to him too! I implored him to listen. I . . . knelt! Knelt before him! I pleaded! But he put me from him and he ran from me again, and came in here."

She straightened her back and drew a long, tremulous breath. "Again I followed; again, here in this room where we are now, I confronted him. He told me to go back to my chamber. I begged him to come with me. We quarreled, but all in whispers because there were people sleeping overhead. Alice was up there. He was afraid she would hear. At last, because he could not be rid of me, he said, come into the study; we won't be heard so easily there. He took the key from its place and let us in. There was still a fire in the hearth here. He lit a candle at it and took it into the study. He closed the door. Then I learned why he was so anxious for us to be secluded, for he meant to be cruel, to break our bond finally by breaking my heart and he feared that I would cry aloud."

"Did he laugh at you?" asked Rob quietly.

She nodded. "He said it had amused him for a while, to be my lover. He had been flattered by my interest and he had liked the gifts I bought him, he said. That was a lie, for we were lovers before I ever gave him his first present. Oh, what does it matter now? He said it was all over, that his services were no longer for sale, and yes, he laughed. I suppose he did it to make me go away. He told me to . . . to look in the mirror and compare myself with Alice. I became angry, so angry. He hurt me so much and he didn't care. He laughed at my pain. I . . . I tried to swallow my anger. Tried to swallow my pride. I made one last appeal. I tried to put my arms round him. He was a cleanly boy," said Lady Thomasine. "He washed himself all over twice a week. I used to help him, sometimes. He used a perfumed soap. He got it in Hereford. I told you: they have everything under the sun in Hereford. Merchants bring goods up the Severn from Bristol; there is nothing you can buy in London that you can't buy in Hereford. I don't know what the perfume was—it was spicy, not sweet; a man's smell. I always loved it. To stand near him and breathe the scent of him would make my senses reel. I breathed it then and it melted my whole being with longing. Do you understand?"

I said: "Yes," with feeling. Owen Lewis had done just that to me, although he'd never known it and never would. Gerald and Matthew had done it, too. They had known it perfectly well, of course, and thank God neither of them had ever thrown me off with cruel words or laughed at me.

"Rafe pushed me off," she said. "As though I repelled him. He said he was going back to his room and would bolt the door against me. He said he hoped I wouldn't shame myself by hammering on it and shouting and rousing the whole castle. I was weeping, and he said my tears made me even uglier than age had made me. I couldn't bear it. I was beside myself. When he'd said his say, he made for the door again. By the light of the candle, I saw the dagger gleaming on my son's desk. I picked it up and . . .

"I didn't know what I was doing," said Lady Thomasine bleakly. "I wanted to hurt him as he had hurt me. I wanted to . . . to . . . stop him from leaving me. I wanted to reach him, to make him aware of me. To make him *respect* me, to know that I wasn't a nothing, a toy that he could throw away if he pleased, with impunity. I struck! He staggered forward and fell. I stooped over him and said *oh, my God* . . . or something like that. I tried to get the dagger out of his back but it wouldn't come. Some blood came, though. I suppose that's when it got onto my slipper. He moaned and turned his head and stared up at me and then . . . then his eyes . . . changed and I knew I had killed him."

She fell silent. "Oh, ma'am!" said Nan, inadequately. "I didn't know. Was that why you wanted me to stop sleeping in your room and made me take the little room above? So that he could come to you? And not because I snored?"

"Quite," said Lady Thomasine. "You don't snore, if it's any comfort to you. I didn't expect you to understand how it was with me and Rafe. I took trouble to keep it from you. I sent you to sleep alone so that Rafe could visit me at will." She turned to Rob. "I went to my son. Who else when I needed help? He was still up, reading in his room. I clutched at him and told him what had happened. He . . ."

"Did he already know about you and Rafe?" Rob asked.

"We had never told him but I thought he must know, or guess, and I was right. He had seen things, once or twice, as your wife did. When I went to him that night, he told me so. I said to him: 'Whatever you think of me, please help me now,' and he said: 'But I thought no ill of you. You are a great lady. Why should you not please yourself? The boy was willing, I suppose, and a young man can learn much from a woman with knowledge of life. I let it be.' He is a good son, my Philip. He said he would help."

"I think we did once wonder if he had killed Rafe for being too close to you," I said. Lady Thomasine shook her head.

"I can do no wrong in my son's eyes." It was not a boast but a statement of fact, something she took so much for granted that she had never questioned it. "He is loyal unto death, my Philip. He said he would come down to the study to look; that perhaps I was wrong and Rafe wasn't dead. So down we came and found you there, you and your manservant, standing by the body! Philip was clever. He thinks quickly. He pretended I had brought him there because I had thought someone was creeping about in his study. We both pretended to be taken by surprise when we saw Rafe lying there. It was as though we were thinking with one mind. Then I accused you, and Philip understood at once and followed where I led."

"How much did Pugh and Evans know?" I asked.

"They believed what we told them; that you had killed Rafe. They thought that in getting rid of you and arranging for Rafe to be found at the foot of the Mortimer Tower, I was protecting my family's good name, that it was all because you and I are related through the Blanchards."

"Sir Philip knew what you had done with us," I said as a statement, not as a question, and she nodded.

"I was afraid of you," she said. "An inquiry by the sheriff of Hereford could be so dangerous. You are a former lady of the court, a friend of the Cecils'. You would be listened to. I knew that Mistress Henderson probably guessed about me and Rafe. I saw her that time she looked into my room when we were embracing. I said we must get rid of you, but Philip shrank from murder."

"Yes, that was what Gladys thought," I said.

Lady Thomasine looked at me as though I were a little insane. "What has Gladys to do with it? I shrank from outright killing too. One was enough. One was too many! I am not a murderess by nature. Rafe . . . oh, poor Rafe! Then I thought of shutting you in the hut."

"That was kinder than stabbing us?" I inquired. "Or was the idea to give us a sporting chance?"

"It wasn't like bloodletting!" said Lady Thomasine hysterically. "Philip said very well, but he did not want to know any more. I should do as I wished and he would not interfere. Perhaps it *was* giving you a chance in a way but I didn't think you could escape. I don't know what I was thinking! I just hoped never to hear of you or see you again! I wanted you not to exist! Why did I ever bring you here? Why did you have to go to the study just *then,* and find Rafe? I wanted it all not to be! We thought we could pretend that Rafe had killed himself and be believed. Then there began to be whispers—but we caught Gladys and thought she could be blamed." Lady Thomasine showed no sign of remorse concerning Gladys. Her voice was tinged with savagery as she said: "Then, yesterday, you came back! You were supposed to be dead but there you were, prepared to shout from the housetops that Rafe had been stabbed. To go back to what we said at the beginning, to saying that you'd killed him yourself, was all I could think of to stop you, to protect myself and my son. I was desperate."

She was visibly exhausted but her anger gave her strength. "What else could I do? I brought you to Vetch to protect Philip, Mistress Blanchard. Are you now going to throw him to the gallows? Don't, please don't! He didn't kill Rafe and he only let me send you to the Black Mountains; he didn't plan it or take part. I did all that. I planned everything and Pugh and Evans did the . . . the physical tasks. Oh God. I could not bear to look on what the fall from the tower had done to Rafe. I crept away from his wake, to cry alone. My son only kept my counsel and what son wouldn't?"

The porch door opened again and Gladys peered in. Her unlovely face was ineffably smug. On impulse, I beckoned to her.

"Nan," I said, "meet the face at the window. It was Gladys that people saw looking out of the haunted tower, both a few days ago, and this afternoon just gone. You did well, Gladys. Most of the castle thought the ghosts were at large, before Brockley twanged a single note on his lute. Oh yes. It was Brockley out there, pretending to be the ghost of Rhodri."

Gladys bobbed an ironical curtsy to Lady Thomasine, who stared at her with astonishment and loathing. Nan gave a shriek. "You mean it was all a trap, a snare to take my lady? Oh, you wicked thing, you cruel, wicked . . ."

"It was both wicked and cruel to take Mistress Blanchard and her servants to a cottage in the hills and lock them in to die," said Rob acidly.

"So there were no ghosts," Lady Thomasine said wearily. "Just a man with a lute and an old woman peering from a window. I should have known. But it's so late at night and I'm so very, very tired." She turned once more to Rob. "What now? You have said nothing about Philip. What will you do? Is it the dungeon for both of us or only for me? Will you drag my son from his bed? Or can he sleep at least till day, and can I begin my captivity by passing the rest of tonight locked in my own chamber?"

"I will permit that," Rob said, "although I shall place a guard at your door. In the morning, I will take a final decision on what shall be done with the two of you. Barker will be your guard."

We took Lady Thomasine to her chamber quietly, without disturbing anyone else. The search in the courtyard had reached its unsuccessful end, and the menservants had gone back to their quarters. There were still a few lights over there, and no doubt a good many of the servants were still huddling together, half terrified and half excited, chattering about ghostly minstrels. But none of them came over to Aragon or the Mortimer Tower and Lady Thomasine was locked into her room in discreet fashion.

She refused to have Nan with her, although we would have allowed it. Nan cried bitterly over that, but Lady Thomasine said coldly that she was not impressed by the tears of a maid as careless as Nan had been, and that she wished to spend the rest of the night in prayer, alone. "You shall come to me in the morning, Nan," she said, "and I hope you will be mistress of yourself by then and mistress also of your neglected trade!"

"In the morning," said Rob, when we were downstairs again, "we will take Mortimer in charge, and those two men, Pugh and Evans. As they haven't been alarmed, they presumably won't run for it and we'll collect them at breakfast. Just now, I feel more inclined to go to bed for what's left of the night."

We all agreed with him. Once in bed, I fell instantly asleep. It seemed only a moment before I woke to find Gladys shaking me and saying: "Wake up, mistress! Wake up! Master Henderson wants to see you. Something's happened—terrible it is, terrible—get up, do."

I scrambled out of bed, got myself into a wrapper, and rushed out of my room. Rob, fully dressed and pale of face, was just coming to fetch me. "It's Lady Thomasine," he said. "She's lying in the courtyard, below the Mortimer Tower. She's dead."

"I never expected this," Rob said to me as we stood side by side, looking down on Lady Thomasine. She had not changed her clothes, and lay on the cobbles in last night's finery. One twisted, shattered leg protruded from her disordered skirts, and its slipper had come off. The other leg was decorously hidden except for the foot, which still wore the slipper stained with Rafe's blood. The pearl-edged cap had tumbled awry so that her hair flowed loosely about her head.

Beneath it was something at which I did not want to look closely; a dreadful hint of blood and brains and splintered bone. But her face was unharmed and perfectly quiet, as though the shock of death had been so swift that she had felt no pain. I hoped this was so.

"So many of the windows in the towers are arrow slits," Rob said. "But not in her room. I've just been up there and the casement is modern. There are mullions, and the windows in between can be opened and they're wide enough for someone to get through who isn't fat. Lady Thomasine was quite slender. She must have been very quiet about it. Barker was outside her door but he heard nothing."

"I think her father modernized the windows," I said. "I—am not as surprised by this as you are. I wondered, even last night."

"Did you, indeed? Typical of you not to say anything. I know," said Rob, "of a previous occasion when you helped a condemned man evade the gallows. Cecil told me."

A footfall made us turn. Mortimer was there, with two servants, who were carrying a tabletop between them. A dark cloth lay on it. "We want to move her," Mortimer said. "She is to be taken into the chapel and laid out decently."

I moved aside for him, and his almond-shaped, greenish eyes met mine with bitterness. "Why didn't you leave Rafe's death alone?" he said. "Nothing now will bring him back. I blame you for my mother's death. Master Henderson has told me all that passed last night. All else apart, I gather that I am myself under house arrest as an accessory. As though I would not have done anything—anything—to protect her."

He stared down at her and I heard the gasp of a muffled sob. "Look at her. Look at her. She was the best of mothers to me. She couldn't bear to grow old, that was all. She couldn't bear the loss of her beauty. You never knew her when she was young. She was the most exquisite being you ever beheld. And to see her now like this . . . I adored her when I was a boy and I still do, whatever she has done."

"I am sorry," I said, though I wasn't quite sure what it was I was sorry for—his bereavement, Lady Thomasine's grief for her lost youth, or the hopeless disaster in which they and Rafe had become enmeshed.

"No doubt. Oh, I'm sure you thought you were doing right. That's what busybodies always say." He raised his eyes to me again, his face more bitter than ever. "Well, it is better this way, perhaps. The inquest will be bad enough but perhaps, Mistress Blanchard, you would not enjoy thinking of Lady Thomasine with a rope round her neck. Any more than I."

23

Lioness Rampant

The following morning, Rob Henderson ordered Pugh and Evans to be locked into their respective rooms, and then took two men with him to Mortimer's chamber and questioned Sir Philip for an hour. Then he returned to the guest keep, his face grim.

"We have to ride for the court without delay," he said. "Before we go, I must send a messenger to St. Catherine's Well. When I come back, I want to find William Haggard here. He will have to be questioned as well. And just what am I to do meanwhile with Mortimer and those two delightful henchmen of Lady Thomasine's—Pugh and Evans? Last night, I decided to arrest all three of them and be done with it. But now—I find myself uncertain. I don't want to make a mistake. Once in a while," said Rob with regret, "I do make mistakes."

I didn't comment. Matthew was alive and free because Rob had once forgotten to place a guard at the back of a house. I recalled the occasion with thankfulness but I knew that Rob didn't.

"From the start," he said now, "the queen and Cecil said that discretion was important. And the more I look at these horrible forgeries, the more I agree with that! I long to bundle Mortimer into his own dungeon on a charge of treason and being an accessory to murder. I long to drag him to the Tower. I'd dearly love to put him in the charge of the sheriff of Herefordshire. But I can't be sure if the queen would have me do so—and there's another difficulty."

"What difficulty?" I asked.

"When I was questioning Mortimer, he said something highly disquieting." Rob's good-looking face was grimmer than ever. "Damn the man. Damn him!" He took to pulling at his flaxen beard in indecision.

I said: "Brockley and I have been to the stables. Our horses are not there, nor is our saddlery. Before we leave, will you ask Pugh and Evans what was done with them?"

Rob looked at me as though he thought me incurably frivolous but he did as I asked. Under his bullying, Pugh and Evans admitted that before they collected me and my servants at dawn to take us to the Black Mountains, they had led Bay Star and Speckle quietly from their stable and turned them out in a secluded pasture near the castle. "And after they returned from locking you in that hut," Rob said, "they went back to the horses and took them off to turn them loose on the Malvern Hills. God knows where they are now. Your saddlery's all right—pushed under a heap of oddments in a storeroom. Too good to throw in the moat, I fancy! They seem to be provident folk at Vetch! I've retrieved it. It's in Barker's quarters for the time being."

"We might find the horses yet," I said.

"We've no time to worry about them now," said Rob shortly. "What *am* I to do with Mortimer and those two cretinous oafs who so devotedly served his mother?'

Eventually, he decided to leave the three of them confined to their rooms, except that Mortimer was to be allowed, under escort, to attend his mother's funeral. Geoffrey Barker and two other men were to guard them. Mortimer's men were warned of dire consequences if they attempted to interfere. Rob's remaining two men came with us. We were carrying the deadly letters and felt the need for guards of our own.

We took Gladys with us as far as Ledbury. Since half the people in Vetch still seemed to think she was a witch, she wouldn't be safe in either the castle or the village and she had now decided not to go back to the hermitage after all. She had, in fact, attached herself to me and was demanding to go where I did. "Well, you can wait for me at the Feathers," I told her.

When we reached Ledbury, we found Dale still ailing. The

cold had turned into a bad cough and she had become feverish again. I left Brockley there with her, but Rob would not let me stay there myself. He even made us ride straight past Tewkesbury without calling in on Mattie and Meg, so great was his haste to reach the court at Richmond.

I understood the urgency. I also dreaded having to watch Elizabeth's face when she read those letters. We made our first report to Cecil, and he took us to an audience with Elizabeth in a private room shut away beyond an antechamber. It was here that the letters were put into her hands. I can only say that if I hadn't already been sure that Elizabeth was a true daughter of King Henry, I would have become sure of it then. I shrank back out of her way as she strode up and down, a lioness rampant, satin skirts swishing, golden-brown eyes hot with rage. It was the authentic Tudor fury, the kind for which King Henry was famed. Anger like this had sent men and women to the Tower, to the block. In Elizabeth at that moment, her father lived again.

"I want Mortimer dead!" she shouted at us, brandishing the offending letters in Cecil's face as she passed him. "I want him dismembered before my eyes!"

Cecil had had leave to sit in the royal presence because his gout was troubling him. His left foot was propped on a stool and his face was lined with pain. "Ma'am," he said patiently, "the less said about this in public, the better, even though the letters are not genuine, which is beyond question, thank God. Mortimer has confessed to forging them. It wasn't his first foray into forgery! It seems, from what Mistress Ursula says, that when he left the court ten years ago, it was because of a forgery scandal."

Elizabeth had interrupted our report when she lost her temper and we hadn't finished it. She slowed her furious pacing at the mention of a forgery scandal, and Rob now set about telling her the rest.

"Before we left Vetch, I spent an hour questioning Mortimer. It wasn't difficult. A graphic description of the death awaiting traitors, from someone with authority to set him on the road to it, had him almost pissing blood," said Rob dispassionately. "And it unlocked his tongue like magic. I got everything out of him. He admitted forging the letters but assured me, on his knees, in tears, that he never, never meant to publish them—and didn't really mean ever to threaten such a thing. It was all just a dream in his mind, he says. He swore he was innocent of everything but foolish imaginings. He got the idea from something that really was found in a piece of furniture, but it wasn't the letters."

"I'm relieved to hear it," observed Elizabeth.

"It seems," Rob said, "that Sir Philip's father, Edward Mortimer, once bought a piece of furniture, some kind of desk, which had formerly belonged to Mark Smeaton, the minstrel. The name . . . will be known to you, I expect."

"Yes, what of it?" barked Elizabeth.

"When I first began to question Mortimer," Rob said, "he blustered and tried to pretend that the letters really were discovered in the desk, but once I'd got him past that, he told me that what Edward Mortimer found was nothing more than a harmless ballad about springtime and cuckoos, signed by Smeaton. But there was a note at the foot in a different handwriting. The note says: "A pretty song. Thank you, Mark." It is signed with an *A*. Edward told his son about the ballad, and Sir Philip found it among his father's things when Edward died, about eight years ago. He found it and gave it to me and I have it here. It would seem that he assumed the note signed *A* to be the writing of Queen Anne Boleyn. He imitated it for the purpose of the forgeries. He was so terrified of me by that time that I am sure he spoke the truth."

"Are you trying to convince *me* the damned things are forgeries?" Elizabeth spat. "What else can they be?" She brandished the letters again. "Show me this note!"

Rob had it ready and handed it to her. She went to the window and stood in the light, comparing it with the letters. Watching her, I realized that although Rob and I were both sure that Mortimer's confession was true, Elizabeth herself, for all her protestations, had secret doubts. I actually saw the moment when those doubts were dispelled, saw the relaxation of her muscles. I heard her faint sigh.

Elizabeth never spoke of her mother. Well, almost never. I did once hear her break that private rule but she did not break it now. What she did do was go to the anteroom door and shout. A lady-in-waiting hurried to her and curtsied. "Fetch my oaken box from my bedchamber! Quickly!" Elizabeth snapped.

She went back to the window and stood staring out of it, with her back to us, until the box was brought. I took it at the door and carried it to her. She put it down on the broad windowsill, took a couple of sheets of paper from it, and beckoned us to look. We gathered around her, Cecil included, leaning on a stick.

"This is a list of clothes and toilet things to be packed for some journey or other," she said, pointing. "And this, an old letter to my aunt Mary when she was still Mary Boleyn. Her daughter, Lady Katherine Knollys, gave it to me as . . . as a keepsake. A note that says: 'A pretty song. Thank you, Mark,' does not contain all the letters of the alphabet. Our clever Mortimer imitated the letters in the note well enough but he had to guess what the rest ought to look like, and he guessed wrong. There is no letter *j* in the note found in Smeaton's desk, but here it is in one of these vile concoctions where it says 'my heart's joy' and here it is in this list where it says 'a jar of elderflower ointment.' Behold the difference."

We understood, without being told, that Anne Boleyn had written the list and the letter to her sister Mary.

We understood too that we had been vouchsafed a glimpse into an unmentionable sorrow and a searing conflict. Elizabeth remembered her father well and often said that as a child she had admired him and sought his affection. Her throne depended on her claim to be his legitimate daughter. Yet he had had her mother beheaded and she might well have some faint recollection of Anne Boleyn: a presence, a scent, a voice. A memory of love.

Surely she had, for though she never spoke of Anne, she had kept these little bits of her mother's writing; these souvenirs.

If she would not speak openly of Anne Boleyn, then we must not presume to do so. We must not offer sympathy. Our loyalty would have to do instead.

Elizabeth swept on triumphantly: "There is no *q* in the note either, but here in the forgery are the words 'queen of the realm' and in the letter to my aunt Mary is the word 'question' and also many words such as 'liking' and 'lovely' with the letter *l* in them, and see how different it is from the way it is written in these abominable letters, in the words 'wholly' and 'revels.'"

"He was clever," Cecil said. "He has used parchment already old and somehow faded the ink."

"In sunlight, perhaps," I said.

"Yes, very likely. A cunning knave."

Rob said: "There's more. We haven't yet told you about Rafe and Lady Thomasine."

We shared the telling as we recounted the sorry tale of murder and attempted murder, of suicide pretended and real. Elizabeth listened with a cold countenance. At the end, she said: "Well, this Mortimer has played into our hands, it seems. Not content with plotting treason, he has soiled his soul with murder. We understand that it may be best if he is not brought to trial on a charge of forging these letters. But we could perhaps charge him with murdering Rafe. It would appear that Rafe took advantage of Sir Philip's mother. That is right, is it not? Most juries would think he had a good motive. It is a stronger charge than that of simply concealing the murder to help his mother. It would be," said Elizabeth, her lioness's claws unsheathed and glinting, "a surer way of stretching his neck. Lady Thomasine cannot now protest and if Mortimer did not actually stab his ward, he concealed the murder and connived at trying to kill Mistress Blanchard and her servants."

There was a silence.

"He has deserved the gallows," said Elizabeth. "Does it matter what the charge is?"

"Ma'am," said Rob, "how I would like to agree with you. Believe me, I would!" His tone was heartfelt. Blithe, insouciant Rob Henderson, who had occasional cracks in his efficiency, also had a very ruthless streak. He was shaking his head now but with infinite regret.

"What is the objection?" inquired Elizabeth, her thin eyebrows raised.

Rob sighed. "When I questioned Mortimer before we left the castle, I deliberately set out to frighten him. But I may have overdone it. He is not a fool, even when terrified. He well understands the harm those letters could do—obviously he does! That potential harm was the foundation of his plot. He harbors the hope that he will not be tried for forging them for that very reason. Without making promises, I encouraged that hope in order to encourage him to talk. But when he had talked enough, I pointed out that there was still the matter of Rafe's death. He might well hang for that, I told him. I even hinted that perhaps he might be charged with the murder outright. That occurred to me too. His answer was to look at me in a knowing fashion and say that if he were brought to trial for that, it would only be because we were afraid to charge him with forging the letters. 'What if I say as much in open court?' he asked me."

Cecil, who had made his way back to his seat and put his painful foot up again with obvious relief, said testily: "The man must be mad! He would be risking the knife instead of the rope!"

"I told him that! But I think," said Rob glumly, "that to quite an extent, he actually is mad. He says he will fight for his life by claiming that any charge connected with Rafe's death was trumped up because we fear to accuse him of something else. He said to me that he would throw himself on the mercy of the court and declare the existence of the letters and swear that he believed them to be genuine and also that he never meant to show them to anyone."

"He would never get away with it. He must know that! He'd never take such a wild chance!" I spoke with conviction and a sound knowledge of the way Mortimer's mind worked. "Any more than he would ever, I think, have really used the letters. Or stabbed Rafe, or killed us outright, either."

"I told him that I knew he'd never do it," said Rob. "I laughed at him. I left him thinking that I was not impressed. But can we be quite sure?"

"What does all this matter?" Elizabeth demanded. "Let him twist and turn and say what he likes! Bring him to trial for murdering his ward! We have proved that the letters are forgeries. We have no need of his confession. There is no doubt."

There was a silence. It went on for a long time. "Well?" Elizabeth demanded at last. "What is it? What are you all afraid to say to me?"

"Ma'am," said Cecil at last, looking intently toward her, "mud sticks."

They had a curious, complementary partnership, those two.

Cecil, the middle-aged family man; Elizabeth, still comparatively young, who had never really been part of a family. His levelheadedness; her stormy, mercurial Tudor temper. Cecil's core of warmth; Elizabeth's core of ice.

But both were logical, both knew the value of caution; they understood each other. She knew when to listen to him. The lioness now paused and with narrowed eyes considered the adhesive properties of mud.

"If we conceal the fact of the letters," she said slowly, "but try Mortimer for something else, he may blurt their existence out. And then the world will think Elizabeth was so afraid of them that perhaps there is truth in them. Is that it? We must arrest him now for forging them, or else not arrest him at all, for anything?'

"Exactly," Cecil said. "I think I understand now. It would seem that no one can be sure what a man like Mortimer is capable of doing, especially under the fear of death! My advice is that the best means of avoiding scandal is total silence. Let Mortimer—and his brother-in-law William Haggard—be terrified into lifelong discretion. Let them know that they will both find themselves in the depths of the Tower if ever they whisper one word of those letters, but let them be reassured that silence means safety. Let all events at Vetch be lost in oblivion; that is safest for us and above all for you. Rafe's murderess is dead; there is no point in raking the muck heap. Let the lad Rafe lie in his suicide's grave. He merits nothing better, after all. Let Lady Thomasine's inquest declare that she killed herself out of grief for the sudden death of her son's ward. Let it be said that she thought of him as an adopted grandson. Let it be said that as sometimes happens to women in later years, her mind was disturbed. Can you arrange that, Master Henderson?"

Rob raged all the way back to Ledbury. "'Can you arrange that, Master Henderson?' Just stand on this beach like bloody Canute and tell the tide to go back! Just point at the sun and tell it to stop at noon! Just do a bloody miracle! How many people in the castle already know too much? I wonder."

"Probably not that many," I said soothingly. "Not about the

letters, anyway. I'm sure we can frighten Mortimer and Haggard into keeping quiet. As for Rafe's murder, I think Pugh and Evans are the only ones in the castle who know, apart from Mortimer and ourselves. I don't think they'll have talked. Lady Thomasine wanted Rafe's death to look like suicide and those two always accepted her orders. I have reason to know it."

"So all I have to do is make sure they go on not talking, and say whatever they're told to say at the inquest. What I've got to do is conceal two completely different crimes. And paint Vetch Castle pure white from turrets to dungeons, while I'm about it, I suppose! Well, there's one good thing. The letters no longer exist."

Elizabeth had burnt them. We had ourselves been witnesses as she cut them up, and ordered a brazier to be brought, and threw the pieces into it. I think I was as glad to see them vanish as Elizabeth was.

On the way back, we did stop in Tewkesbury, but the Woodwards told us that Mattie had gone to Ledbury, taking Meg with her. There had been an urgent message from the Feathers, they said. We took some food with the Woodwards, but then rode on in haste to arrive at the Feathers late in the evening. Mattie and Meg were there to greet us, but even as I joyfully hugged my daughter, Mattie told me why they were there, instead of in Tewkesbury.

"It's Dale. She took a bad turn just after you left and Brockley sent for me. He needed help. Joan and Bridget are with us and we've been looking after her as best we can. Joan's with her now and Bridget's asleep. I'm thankful you're here. Ursula, she's very ill indeed."

I refused to go on to Vetch Castle. "I must stay here with Dale," I said. "You don't need me at the inquest anyway. I can't leave Dale and I won't."

Rob was huffy, but Mattie backed me up. "I know you must go to Vetch," she said to him, "but Ursula's duty is here now."

"Very well," said Rob at last. "I'll go and produce this . . . this masque on my own! Wish me luck!"

He went. I forgot him before he was out of sight. Indeed, throughout the next few days, I never gave events at Vetch Castle a single thought. I concerned myself only with the fight for Dale's life, and so did Brockley.

The hardships of our adventure had nearly destroyed her. She had endured rain and cold, long weary hours in the saddle, the terror of the shepherd's hut, the squalor of the hermitage, and the bare, chilly misery of Isabel's Tower and it had all been far too much. Her cold had gone to her lungs and at any moment, her fight for breath might cease.

We all took turns, Gladys included. Mattie had made her clean herself up and borrowed some more of Joan's spare clothes for her, turning her into a moderately respectable, if homely, woman servant. Meg helped too, running errands.

We sent for a physician, but he could suggest only that we go on with the things we were already doing. It was day and night work, an endless business of clean sheets, damp cloths to wipe Dale's sweating forehead, drinks of water, hot milk, warmed wine, herbal possets—the landlord's wife had some recipes she swore by—inhalations of steam, reassurance, and desperate prayer. Two of us at least were always on duty at Dale's bedside.

On the fourth night, I found myself keeping watch with Brockley. Dale lay propped up to help her breathe better. She was unconscious—in the candlelight a thin glint of eyeball was visible, below half-closed lids. Her mouth was open and her waxen cheeks had fallen in. Except for the rasp and bubble of those difficult breaths, she might have been already dead.

Earlier, we had been busy. We had had to clean her, while she groaned and murmured, only dimly aware of what we were doing; and then support her so that she could inhale steam, before somehow coaxing a posset into her. Now she was quiet, and it was deep in the night, when the sick are most at risk. I sat on one side of her, and Brockley on the other. I noticed that several times he looked at me across the bed and seemed about to speak but then appeared to change his mind. At last, he spoke my name. "Mistress Blanchard . . ."

"Brockley?"

"She's weaker." He spoke very softly, perhaps afraid that Dale might hear him and understand. "She can't go on much longer like this. What will I do if I don't have Fran?"

I had no answer. I moved the candle, which was on a table near me, so that I could look at her more closely. He was right. Her breathing was harsher now and when I took her hand, it almost burned me. Brockley had taken her other hand but it lay flaccid in his, although when he first arrived at the inn, she had known him, and been able to grip his fingers and smile at him.

Someone tapped on the door. I called a low "Come in," and Gladys entered, with a brimming goblet of something that steamed.

"What's this?" I asked tiredly. "Another of our hostess's possets? She means well but none of them seem to do any good."

"Not hers. This is a potion of mine, indeed." Gladys's Welsh voice was soft and persuasive. "Give it a try for her. Been out all evening, I have, looking for what's to go in it, and up all night since, brewing it. See if it does any good."

"But what is in it?" I demanded. I took the goblet, sniffed at it and recoiled. It both looked and smelled horrible.

Gladys gave one of her dreadful cackles. "You don't want to know. But try it. What have you got to lose?"

"Dale's life," I said frankly. "She's too weak already."

But Brockley had come to my side. "Let me look. Dear God, it reeks of Lord knows what. Of course Fran can't touch that. Except that . . ." His voice was harsh with worry. He took the goblet and gingerly sipped it himself. "Gladys, promise me that whatever is in this, it isn't poisonous."

"It ain't poisonous. What do you take me for? It'll do no harm if it does no good, but it might do good. I've known it work for others. I'm not a witch, whatever those fools of villagers think, and I don't poison folk, neither!"

"We've tried everything else," Brockley said to me. "Can you think of anything we haven't tried?" He straightened his shoulders. "I'd ask her if she were conscious but since she isn't and can't speak for herself, I have to speak for her. I'm her husband. All right. We'll see. Come and help me."

I was hesitant, but he and Gladys supported Dale between them and Brockley poured the concoction down her throat. She choked and retched as well she might but she swallowed most of it. Then they laid her down again.

"Let her be, now," I said. I meant, let her rest in peace. There comes a point when it seems no longer decent to harry the dying, even with cures, not unless there is some hope that they may actually work.

Gladys gave me a hurt look. "I said, it'll do no harm even if it don't save her. I'm for my bed now. If she gets better or worse, you just call me."

She went away. Brockley sat down again and stared miserably at his wife. "It was a last hope," he said. "I don't really expect it to work. I think we're losing her."

Unable to bear the wretchedness in his face, I rose and went to him. I patted him awkwardly on the shoulder. Abruptly, he let go of Dale and turned to me, putting his arms around me and burying his face against me, like a child in need of comfort. I stroked his hair, but it was not a sensual thing. He might have been Meg, with a grazed knee.

After a moment, he drew back his head and looked up at me as I stood beside him. "This reminds me of that dungeon," he said in a quiet voice. "But it isn't the same, is it?"

"No," I said. "It isn't. I am glad you were wise then." I paused and then said: "I am not very wise but I have some common sense, I hope. I would not cling where I have no right."

"You are blessedly unlike Lady Thomasine, madam," Brockley said. "May you never change."

"I am luckier than she was," I said. "I have Matthew. But I hope that I never come to resemble Thomasine." Drawing myself gently away from him, I went back to my stool on the other side of the bed. I gazed sadly at Dale, and to ease the strain of anxiety, went on talking about myself and Lady Thomasine.

"I think," I said, "that I should take up some kind of study. Lady Thomasine disapproved of education for girls but she might have been happier if she had had things of the mind to turn to. The queen likes to read history and study languages. I learned Latin as a girl. I might study that. I might even start Greek. Then, one day, I can amuse myself by doing translations. Or reading poetry in Latin and Greek. Anything to have an occupation so that when I grow older, I won't pine for my lost youth as Lady Thomasine did."

"You may not call that wisdom," he said. "But I do."

Silence fell, except for the sound of Dale's difficult breathing. We sat there beside her, waiting, waiting, until at length a trace of dawn appeared at the window. Then Brockley said, "Her breathing's fainter."

I nodded sadly. It was true. Even as the light strengthened, the harsh sounds from the bed were fading away.

"My poor Fran," Brockley said. He reached out and took her hand again. "My poor, poor love. I . . ."

He stopped. His eyes turned to me, widening. "What is it?" I said. "Brockley? She hasn't . . . oh no, please . . ."

"No. Her pulse is still beating . . . and she's cooler."

Dale sighed. She stirred, turning to press her face against Brockley's hand. She sighed again and for one heart-stopping moment, I thought it was a last gesture of farewell. I could no longer hear her breathing. Then I understood that this was not because the breathing had stopped but because the roughness had almost gone. Her eyes had closed properly. She seemed to be in a natural sleep.

"Told you so," said Gladys, coming into the room and crossing it to stand by the bed and look down at Dale with an air of triumph. "Pity you think that because I'm old and ugly I must be daft as well. I knew that draft 'ud loosen the knot, if anything could."

I rested during the morning on a truckle bed in the same room and woke at midday to find that Dale had been conscious for a while and had taken some meat broth. She was now sleeping again, with Mattie and Joan sitting by her. "If she's carefully nursed," Mattie whispered, "she should pull through."

Joan and I went on with the vigil, to give Mattie a rest. Dale woke once and smiled at us, and I fetched her a little more broth. Presently, however, Mattie called me. Rob had returned, and wanted to talk to us both, and at once. "You go. I can manage alone now," Joan said, and I hurried off to the Hendersons' chamber with Mattie, to find Meg there, sewing with Bridget, and Rob slumped on a settle, his chin unshaven and his face drawn with tiredness.

"Have you come from Vetch?" I asked.

"I have indeed. The inquest is over. What a farce! I'm worn-out. I've told the landlord to send up some wine." He glanced at Bridget. "Best take Meg out of the room. Here." He got out his purse and handed some money to Bridget. "Take her out into Ledbury and buy her some material for a new gown or something like that. I need to talk to my wife and to Mistress Blanchard in private."

Bridget removed my daughter and Rob turned to me again. "My God," he said with feeling. "The lies I've made people tell—and on oath, at that!" He rolled his eyes toward heaven. "I ought to take to writing plays. I never want to live through another few days like the last few. And I wish the landlord would hurry up with that wine."

24

The Raddled Face of Truth

The wine arrived at that moment. While the maidservant was pouring it, Mattie helped Rob off with his riding boots. Then the maidservant went away and finally, with his feet at ease and a full goblet in his hand, Rob told us what he had achieved at Vetch.

"And *achieved* is the right word. I never thought I'd manage it," he said. "So much to be concealed, not only now but for all time."

"The castle is painted white?" I said.

"The castle is as snowy as the robe of an angel. The raddled face of truth has been creamed and powdered to the likeness of innocent maidenhood. I'm sure Lady Thomasine would have been full of admiration. Those who work for Elizabeth and Cecil," said Rob, "need to be resourceful!"

I remarked that I knew that. He gave me a shrewd look.

"I daresay you do. But this! You wish to know how I did it?"

"Yes." Mattie and I said it simultaneously.

Rob took a heartening gulp of wine. "When I got back to Vetch," he said, "I found that William Haggard had arrived in answer to my summons. He'd demanded to see Mortimer and since I didn't leave any orders to the contrary, he'd been allowed to. The two of them were up there in Mortimer's chamber, having the great-grandfather of all quarrels. When I walked in on them, they were on the point of blows. I gathered that Mortimer had told Haggard everything—I do mean everything: all about Rafe and Lady Thomasine and how they really met their ends—

and William was so furious, he was gibbering. He was shouting that he'd not only been dragged into treason, he'd been half-drowned in a cesspool as well, and what if his daughter had been contaminated . . . ?"

"Er . . ." I said.

"Well, Mortimer didn't tell him *quite* everything because Mortimer himself doesn't know it all. Neither he nor William Haggard know you found Alice and Rafe in each other's arms in front of the study hearth. They have no idea the two younglings were meeting clandestinely after dark. I saw no need to inform them, either! I broke in on the dispute, ordered it to stop, and then had Mortimer and Haggard marched down to the dungeon. I decided that the sight of stone walls and dirty straw would be good for them. I had Pugh and Evans brought down and put in another cell too. Then I talked to both pairs separately.

"I didn't waste time asking Mortimer and Haggard any more questions. I just told them that I now had official orders for them, issued by Elizabeth herself, and reminded them that they were in no position to argue. At the inquest they would say what I told them to say and they would never, never speak either of the letters or of Rafe's murder, all their lives long, or . . . well, I described a few things that might happen to them in the Tower if they didn't cooperate. Mortimer had heard most of it before, of course. Down in the dungeon, it was even more effective! Then I left them shaking and went to deal with the other two."

"That was surely easier," Mattie said sympathetically. "After all, Pugh and Evans don't know about the letters—do they?"

Mattie herself knew because when we first arrived back from court, Rob had told her. They had no secrets from each other. But bubbly Mattie was actually as discreet as a tomb.

"No," Rob agreed. "They don't, and never will. What they did know, of course, was that Rafe was stabbed, and it appears that they genuinely believed that Mistress Blanchard and Brockley had done it. It took me a long time to convince them that you hadn't."

"So pleasant to know that one has made a good impression," I murmured.

"They told me most earnestly that Lady Thomasine didn't want you arrested because you're a family connection of hers. They believed what she told them about protecting the honor of her family. She told them that she meant to conceal the fact that Rafe was murdered, but that you were not going to get away with it, all the same. She ordered them to take you to the shack in the mountains and leave you there and they did as they were bidden."

"Had they no sense at all of what a serious crime they were committing?" Mattie asked. Rob shook his head.

"Do you know, I don't think so. You don't understand them, and nor does Ursula, I fancy. They have lived all their lives at Vetch Castle; they look on its owners as their authority, their law. They know the sheriff of Herefordshire exists but he is not real to them. They know that Queen Elizabeth exists but she isn't real to them either. Vetch, its castle and lands, makes up their world and Lady Thomasine was their queen. They took her orders. If she wished to protect her family's good name from ruin and in the interests of that, told them to do away with a disgraceful relative—that's you, Ursula—and her entourage—which means Dale and Brockley—then they took her orders. Their horizons may be somewhat broader now. I told them the truth—about Rafe, I mean, not about the letters. I informed them that their beloved Lady Thomasine had killed Rafe, and why. They wouldn't believe me at first but I told them that it didn't matter what they believed. I had orders, from a royal level, that since Rafe's murderer was now dead, the matter was never again to be mentioned."

"How on earth," I asked him, "did you explain why the queen should wish to hush up Rafe's murder? After all, it was hardly a matter of state!"

"I didn't," said Rob candidly. "I couldn't think of a convincing explanation so I told them that her reasons *were* matters of state, which I was not obliged to explain to such common persons as themselves. They had obeyed Lady Thomasine as though she were the queen, I said; now they must obey the real queen. And I made my description of the consequences if they didn't, *very* graphic. I convinced them of Lady Thomasine's guilt in the end. After all, they'd both been her lovers in the past. Perhaps they'd had a glimpse of the strength of her passions. I think they accept the truth now.

"To be fair," Rob said, after pausing for another heartening draft of wine, "all concerned wanted to protect Lady Thomasine's good name. Even Haggard did—after all, she was Bess's mother. They came to the inquest like lambs and said exactly what they were told. Oh, my God, that inquest!" Rob said, and actually moaned faintly like a woman coming around from a swoon. "Have you ever tried to fix an inquest? Have you the faintest idea what it means?"

"Bribing the coroner and packing the jury?" I offered, intrigued, because now that Dale was mending, I really did feel interested.

"Impossible," Rob said. "The coroner was a yeoman farmer from near Hereford, barely literate, accent broad as the Severn pastures, and so respectable that if he found a single penny lying in the street, he'd take it to the local constable and ask him to look for the owner. Offer him a bribe and he'd take *you* to the constable. The jury was mostly the same type: farmers and a couple of merchants from Ledbury and Hereford. None of them knew much about Vetch except for one—and that was the foreman of the jury. He was Hugh Cooper! Still, even he doesn't know more than most of the others in the castle—that Rafe and Lady Thomasine were both found lying at the foot of the Mortimer Tower, and that you and I burst in unexpectedly, took over the castle in an aggressive manner and stopped Gladys from being charged with murdering Rafe by witchcraft.

"I," said Rob, counting on his fingers, "had three things to explain. It wasn't originally supposed to be an inquest on Rafe—after all, there's been one—but the whole locality knows now that the possibility of murder has come up, thanks to Mortimer's wretched dramatic performance when he had Gladys dragged in front of him in his hall. I gathered from the coroner beforehand that because the word *murder* had been mentioned in connection with Rafe, he had had instructions from the sheriff of Herefordshire to include Rafe's death in his inquiries. There was no avoiding our confounded little lust-crazed minstrel! I wanted him to be just the cause of Lady Thomasine's grief, but no, instead he had to be one of the central characters!"

"In death as in life," I said thoughtfully. "He was like that."

"Evidently! So there it was. First, I had to reinforce the verdict of the original inquest on Rafe and quell all whispers about murder. Second, I had to explain why you and I returned to the castle and burst into it as we did. And third, I had to explain the suicide of Lady Thomasine."

He leaned back, still grasping his goblet, and closed his eyes. "When the proceedings started, the coroner wanted to deal first of all with you, me, and Gladys, to clear us out of the way, as it were. So I stood up there before them all, in my widest ruff and my best blue doublet slashed with silver, the picture of a courtier, and declared that I was in the employment of Sir William Cecil, Secretary of State—well, that part was true!—and had recently accompanied you on a family visit to Vetch, and then returned later on a confidential court errand concerning the Mortimer family; nothing at all to do with Rafe. I said that you had come back with me because you were Lady Thomasine's kinswoman and thought she might be glad of your company. I regretted that my position required discretion and said I was not able to give details . . .

"And then," said Rob gloomily, "I found myself in trouble. The coroner said that this here was a special case and the dignity of a crowner's—that's how he pronounced *coroner's*—court was the equal of any in the land, and he'd got to ask me to enlarge. So I appeared to yield, and said that out of respect for the dignity of the occasion, I would go so far as to explain that it concerned the genuineness of Sir Philip's claim to be a legitimately descended member of the Mortimer family." At this point, Rob opened his eyes and briefly grinned. "I gave Mortimer a sympathetic look, as much as to say that alas, his legitimate descent hadn't been proved, and he looked at me as though he'd like to kill me, which I daresay he would, and the whole court sniggered and I'm thankful to say that the coroner seemed satisfied.

"Then I said that you and I were shocked to find Gladys being charged with witchcraft because we had some acquaintance with her—and then I had to rephrase that because the coroner had never heard of the word *acquaintance* and wanted to know what it meant. I said that I meant we had got to know her on our first visit to Vetch. I told him that we couldn't believe that she was a witch. I said we had then taken it upon ourselves to question Mortimer and Lady Thomasine and others in the castle and that it soon became perfectly obvious that the first verdict was the true one and that Rafe could most certainly have had reasons for killing himself, and no need of witchcraft to help him to it."

"I wish I could have been there," I said.

"I wished myself at the ends of the earth," Rob said grimly. "After I'd testified, it was Mortimer's turn. He said that he had arrested Gladys in good faith after rumors began that Rafe had been murdered, but now agreed with my view of the matter and marveled that the rumors had ever arisen. He explained about Rafe falling in love with Alice, and gave some colorful detail about Rafe moping in his chamber after Owen Lewis appeared and more or less snatched Alice's affections away from him. He also said that he now knew he'd been too harsh with the boy—he implied that he'd beaten him. He was convincing, I must say. A born liar!"

Rob took another deep gulp of his wine. "Dear God, I'm exhausted. I was on edge throughout, afraid someone would say the wrong thing or ask the wrong questions and there were some bad moments. The coroner wanted to call some of the castle servants and settled on the Raghorns because they had served in the guest keep—served you and me, that is—and he was very persistent in some of his questions. He got rather too much out of them. Jack Raghorn said that the rumors had started because Rafe hadn't bled enough, and Susanna Raghorn repeated the gossip about you having killed him."

"Oh, no!" I said.

"It's all right. Hugh Cooper himself got up at that point, and said roundly that all that was just silly talk and you'd hardly have come back to the castle and rescued Gladys if you were guilty. As for Rafe not bleeding, he'd no doubt been killed instantly and the dead don't bleed. It was all daft servants' chatter that meant nothing. I could have kissed him but I thought it might be overdoing things, so I just nodded to him in recognition of his good sense. The coroner seems to think it was good sense, as well, thank God.

"Well, to get back to Mortimer. When he testified, he also told the court that his mother had been very fond of Rafe, looking on him as a grandson, and that she had been strange in her manner in recent months, as though there was something amiss with her mind. I did make one bad mistake," said Rob, rather pathetically. "The maid Nan had to testify. I'd forgotten her completely until an hour before the inquest started! But mercifully, she'd been prostrate on her bed since Lady Thomasine died and hadn't talked to anyone, and when Mortimer said, quite casually, that she might be called, and I rushed to find her, I found her as willing as anyone to protect her lady's reputation. A verdict of suicide would be bad enough but—let the whole world know that Lady Thomasine was in love with a boy of twenty? Never! She was only too anxious to hide that! I told her what to say and she said it. In fact, she wept most persuasively as well. She told the jury that Thomasine had been muddled in her mind of late and apt to brood over even little things.

"I think we've got away with it. William Haggard and the butler, Pugh, both testified and they backed up everything Mortimer had said. Rafe died because he was crossed in love and frightened of his guardian; Thomasine wasn't in her right mind, as often happens with women in later life, poor things, and was overset by grief for her son's ward, whom she looked on as a grandson. The verdict of an unbalanced mind means she can be buried in consecrated ground. You and I are court representatives and have nothing to do with any of these sad events. No one mentioned daggers in the back or forged letters. Those letters! The more I think about it, the more dangerous they seem! Lady Lennox would value them above rubies and so would Mary Stuart. I doubt if William Haggard will ever speak to Mortimer again. It seems that you made him understand how near he came to the gallows, and when I had him down in that cell, I made him understand still better!"

"What is happening about Alice and Owen Lewis?" I asked. "Did you chance to find out?"

"Oh yes." Rob nodded. "Lady Thomasine has been buried now, and William Haggard is on his way home to St. Catherine's for his daughter's marriage. It's going ahead at once. Lady Thomasine's death won't delay it. It seems that Alice has agreed and Lewis, it seems, really wants to marry her. He's not asking for any dowry in money though he's taking the land. Lewis, Bess and Alice, by the way, will know only the official version of what happened at Vetch: the one given out at the inquest. William Haggard made no trouble about that. He does not confide in his wife, it seems, let alone his daughter."

"No," I said. "He doesn't."

"I think all the leaks have been stopped," Rob said. "And just as well. Mortimer and Haggard, pale and sweating, assured me over and over that they would never really have sent those letters to any interested party, and I know that you think that, Ursula, but I do wonder. Foolish men with foolish dreams often do very stupid things, and the Lennoxes would have paid them well. You've been in France, and there are things you may not know. Lady Lennox is dangerous. It's not only likely that she has a list of Catholic exiles in the Low Countries who are ill-disposed to Elizabeth, but one of our agents in Edinburgh has actually found a list, in Mary Stuart's possession, of Catholic families in England who have promised to back her up in any claim. Just imagine what they might do with a rumor that Elizabeth isn't King Henry's daughter at all!"

"Hush!" said Mattie warningly.

"I shall never mention it again," Rob said reassuringly. He gave me a sharp look. "Your Matthew," he said, "may well have had a hand in getting that list of English supporters compiled and sent to Lady Lennox."

I said nothing. It was very likely true and I didn't want to think about it.

"Yet you are a faithful servant of the queen. At Vetch, you have proved it," Rob said. Tired or not, he looked into my eyes with his own full of challenge. "How do you reconcile the two sides of your life, Ursula?"

"I would like to reconcile them," I said with emphasis, "by going back to France and staying there, out of it all."

"With that man, you will never be out of it all," Mattie said suddenly. I turned to her indignantly, but she shook her head at me.

"It's no use being angry, Ursula. I love you, as I love Meg, but I am speaking the truth and you know it."

"Well, you've spoken it," I said. "But I would rather you didn't do so again. Matthew and I are man and wife, and what is between us is our own business."

"Ah. I'm sorry. Fatigue has made me forgetful," Rob said. "I have brought two things back from Vetch for you, Ursula. I've brought your saddlery, though not your horses, which I suppose are still wandering on the Malverns, and I've brought you a letter from your husband. It arrived at Vetch while I was there. Here."

He took it out of his doublet and handed it over. Seizing it eagerly, I took it to the window to open it. It was a single sheet, covered with Matthew's dear, familiar writing. Once, in the past, I had been fooled by a forgery of Matthew's hand but this I knew was honest, for it began: *"My dearest Ursula, my Saltspoon . . ."*

No one but Matthew ever used that nickname; no one beyond us two knew of its existence. It was a private code between us now, a means of proving that a letter was real.

It went on: *". . . you have not been gone so very long, but I miss you very much and I was glad to receive a letter from you, to know that you had reached England safely and that Meg too is safe. I look forward to the day when you bring her here and we can become a family. God willing, we will add children of our own one day. You will be better in health when you have your daughter with you.*

"Saltspoon, I shall miss you all the time, and I shall worry in case over there in England, you begin to forget me. Please don't let that happen.

"Above all, don't give your devotion too deeply to the queen you serve, whatever gifts she may give you. But don't misunderstand me. You ask in your letter if you should accept Withysham. You need not have asked; do you think me so ungenerous? Life is never certain. I know you, my Saltspoon. If I should die, you will want to go home to England. You would need somewhere to live. You have my permission to accept the queen's gift—yes, even Withysham. I admit that I do not wish to see the place again, but when I was in England, I bought it and I still regard it as mine. Your queen is, therefore, only restoring my rightful property. I bestow it on you. The revenues from it, you shall treat as your own.

"But alas, my Saltspoon, you and Meg must not come back to Blanchepierre yet. Plague has broken out in the village here. It is early in the year for it; usually plague does not start until the summer is well under way. But there have been deaths already and I would not have you or your

daughter in peril. For your own safety and hers, Saltspoon, stay in England until summer is past, and come home in the autumn. The plague always dies out when the weather cools. Have no fear for me. I am keeping at home and have forbidden any of the household to go to the village. Any servant who shows signs of infection will be isolated at once.

"In the autumn, we will be together, you and I and Meg. I shall count every day until then. Your true and loving husband, Matthew."

I read the letter through twice, in a muddle of emotions: joy at the love which rose from every word on the page; dread in case Matthew caught the plague; gratitude because I could have Withysham; and dreadful grief because instead of going home to him within weeks, I must wait for months. Here in England, doing my strange and unwomanly work, I had been healed of the malaise which had attacked my mind after that disastrous childbed. It annoyed me to think Rob and Brockley had been right in supposing that my task at Vetch would do me good, but it was true. Only I had looked forward to returning to Matthew in health, and to taking Meg with me and now . . .

Such a welter of conflicting thoughts was anguish. Tears came into my eyes. But what was between Matthew and me was private, as I had said. I brushed the tears fiercely away and turned to Mattie and Rob.

"Well," I said, as brightly as I could, "it seems that I can't go back to France yet because there's plague at home. And Matthew has agreed that I should take Withysham. I'll have to pass the time by setting it in order."

It was hard to maintain the brightness and I was relieved when a knock at the door interrupted us. Mattie opened it, and in came Brockley. He looked worn, as well he might, after the time we had had with Dale, but his normally expressionless face was beaming. "Such news, madam!"

"What is it, Brockley? I could do with some cheerful news, I must say," I told him.

"I've been out," Brockley said. "I slept awhile this morning, but I couldn't sleep long. I came to see Fran—you were fast asleep and never stirred—and Fran knew me and spoke to me. I believe she'll be all right now, given time. Then I felt I needed the open air, so I exercised one of the ponies and rode toward Tewkesbury. The floods have completely gone and there are some animals out on the pastures again. Madam, I've found Bay Star and Speckle."

"What? Where?" I sat up straight, excited. With so many weighty matters on our minds, we had had no opportunity to pursue the matter of my horses any further, nor indeed the matter of any of the belongings we had left in the castle when we were taken away. Rob had retrieved our saddlery but that was all. I had made a cursory search for my personal things and found them gone, and assumed that they were at the bottom of the moat. As for the horses, out on the Malverns, they could have strayed for miles. I had meant to arrange a search but first there had been the ride to Richmond and then Dale's illness. This was like a gift from heaven.

"They were on the Severn pastures," Brockley said. "They must have wandered down from the hills. They were grazing with a couple of donkeys. I found the donkeys' owner. He said he'd been ill and he was slow going out to bring his animals to safety when the river came over its banks. He was only just in time. There were no other animals on the pastures by then except for his donkeys, and two strange horses grazing with them. No one seemed to be bothering with the horses, so he brought them in with the donkeys. When it was safe again, he turned them all out together. He supposed the horses' owner would turn up eventually—and so she has, madam, with me as your representative."

"Have you brought them back?' I asked eagerly.

"I have indeed. I paid the donkeys' owner for the fodder he gave them while they were in his stable and I fetched them back here. They've lost condition but not too badly."

Our personal items were probably gone for good, but what of it? Clothes and toilet things could be replaced and I could buy another copy of Sir Thomas Wyatt's poems. The horses were dearer to me than any of them. "Thank you, Brockley," I said. "It's wonderful news. I'll go to the stable and see them, at once."

25

Unwise Questions

I was interested by the news that Alice Haggard and Owen Lewis were to be married so quickly, despite the deaths of both Lady Thomasine, who was Alice's grandmother, and Rafe, who had been her lover. Owen Lewis had been winning Alice over, but I had myself seen her wearing black for Rafe. But when Dale was strong enough, we left the Welsh Marches and over twenty years went by before I heard of Alice again.

Then, a young man came to Elizabeth's court, as a mixture of secretary and musician in the employ of the Earl of Leicester, who had once been Robin Dudley, the queen's Master of Horse. I saw him at a party at the earl's house and something about him seemed familiar. I asked his name and Leicester said: "Oh, that's William Lewis. He's recently come to court from South Wales. Just turned twenty and plays the lute like an angel. We'll hear him later on."

I looked at William Lewis again and this time I knew what I had recognized. I had seen that combination of thick brown hair and long greenish-blue eyes with a slightly asymmetrical setting in someone else long ago. Of course. He must be a son of Alice and Owen. He was the image of Alice. There was nothing of his father in him.

Then he turned to speak to someone and I saw his profile, the sharp nose and the chin just a little too long for beauty.

I was wrong. He did have some of his father's features, after all. I remembered Rafe, kneeling by Lady Thomasine's chair at that first, pretentious dinner I had attended at Vetch Castle. I recalled Rafe's profile very well.

I spoke to young William casually later. I made believe to be an arch and somewhat foolish woman with an interest in astrology and hazarded the guess that he was born under the sign of Aquarius. He was impressed. He was indeed an Aquarian, he said. In fact, he was born on the seventh day of February 1565.

He could well have been conceived on the night I found Alice and Rafe asleep in each other's arms. Alice had been married—I cast my mind back—about three weeks later, perhaps a few days more than that. She couldn't have been sure so soon that she was with child—though some women do guess very quickly—but she might have begun to fear it. Perhaps then she had been thankful to find Owen urging the wedding forward. I wondered if her parents, for the sake of propriety after Lady Thomasine's death, had hesitated and if she had admitted to them that she had lain with Rafe, so that they would agree.

How much, I wondered, had Owen known or guessed? Had he thought the child was his, perhaps born early? Carefully pumping William Lewis, I learned that Alice and Owen were still alive; that he had brothers and sisters and, apparently, a happy home. Whatever secrets lay hidden within the marriage, it had prospered.

When we finally set off for Thamesbank, Gladys came too. Gladys was determined to remain in my service somehow. When I tried to persuade her to go home, she pleaded, cried, said it was because she was ugly and was that her fault? and then took to sulking and scowling and threatening to put a curse on me. But her misery at the idea of going back to the hermitage was obvious, and besides, but for her we might well have lost Dale.

For these reasons, and not for fear of her curses, I finally did as she asked and sent word to her family in the Black Mountains to say that she was not returning. Since I was to become the mistress of Withysham, the problem of what I was to do with her was solved. I had already decided that when I went back to

France, Brockley should stay at Withysham as my steward, with Dale to help him. Gladys could go there as well, to give general help in house and kitchen, as far as her age allowed. Brockley would look after her. That way she and the Brockleys could remain in my employ but need not come to France with me.

I would spend the summer at Withysham. Meg could stay with me. My heart lifted, thinking of that. I would hire a tutor who would instruct us both, for here was my chance to begin the serious study of Latin and Greek. Whether or not I lived to be old was in God's hands, not mine. But if I survived the business of producing a son for Matthew (I was afraid of childbirth now and ashamed of being afraid), I would build myself a life of the mind, so that in the years to come, I would not need to hide wrinkles and gray hairs; nor would I need to pretend to be a witch to gain some respect from my fellow creatures.

A little more learning might even be useful while I was still young. Lack of authority had often been a nuisance to me. Lady Thomasine's remarks on that subject had hit home. But my looks had never helped me to the kind of authority I needed. I would see what using my brains could do.

Making these plans helped to keep me in good spirits as I contemplated the months ahead. I wrote affectionately to Matthew, and the act of writing to him seemed to bring him nearer.

At Thamesbank I found a message that I was to attend court as soon as possible. Arriving at Richmond, I learned that I had been summoned to be officially presented with Withysham. I was called to the queen's private apartments and the presentation was made in one of the smaller rooms there, with Sir William Cecil and his wife, Lady Mildred, and a few other ladies as witnesses. When it was over, and I had curtsied my thanks, and the deeds of Withysham had been placed in my hands, Elizabeth took my arm and led me aside into a deep bay window. The others stood back, recognizing that she wished for a few minutes of private conversation.

"So, Ursula, you are a woman of property now, and I hear that you will not be leaving England until the summer ends. I take it you intend to visit Withysham?"

"Yes, ma'am. Well, naturally."

"Naturally," Elizabeth echoed. "But it is only June. You will perhaps be in England until October. You have some months still to spend here. Will you spend them all in Sussex? Or could we interest you in visiting another part of England?"

"Another part of England?" Had she found me something further to investigate? I wouldn't have been surprised at it. But she was smiling.

"We are going on Progress to Cambridge in August. It may be a more peaceful journey than if Mortimer had been allowed to intrude on it. We are grateful to you, Ursula. If you would like to join the Progress as one of our suite, you would be more than welcome."

With Elizabeth, kindly invitations and royal orders were indistinguishable and I knew I must say yes. But the idea was attractive. I had no wish to object.

"I shall be happy to come to Cambridge, ma'am. And no one is more relieved than I am that Mortimer has been stopped."

"Just in time," Elizabeth said calmly. "We only wish we could stop the Lennox ambitions too. You have heard the rumor that Lady Lennox would like to marry her son to Mary of Scotland?"

"I had heard something about it, yes, ma'am."

"A most objectionable idea," said Elizabeth. "Darnley and Mary would be a diabolical combination, with two links to our royal house. Well, Mortimer will not help her, not now. Perhaps he will help us instead. He has some curious skills which we may be able to use and he is hardly in a position to refuse us. However, I didn't take you aside to discuss the Lennoxes or Mortimer or Mary Stuart's marriage plans. I wanted to talk to you about your marriage."

"*My* marriage?"

"Yes. I have taken further advice. You were certainly married to Matthew de la Roche under duress. It should be possible, I think, to get the marriage set aside if you would agree. We would so much like to keep you in England."

There was a dreadful moment when dishonorable and faithless words took shape in my head. *Stay in England, and be safe. Stay single and avoid death in childbed.*

Stay in England and be free. Beneath my fear of childbirth

was another fear—of the stifling formality of Blanchepierre and of Matthew's loving protectiveness, which I ought to appreciate but couldn't, because its roots lay in a belief that women were lovable things but in constant need of guidance because they were unable to think for themselves. Ever since Matthew's letter came, telling me not to return to Blanchepierre yet, I had been expecting to suffer one of my sick headaches, out of disappointment, but I had not done so. Why? Because England meant freedom and safety?

There, at that moment, in Elizabeth's presence, I felt my spirits unaccountably lift, and I was shocked at myself. Matthew loved me so, and I had missed his desirable body and kindly heart so much. Generous Matthew, who did not mind that I should own Withysham, which had once been his.

No. I would not listen to the treacherous whispers in my mind. I was Matthew's wife and I longed only for the autumn, and my return home.

"Ma'am, I would be so sorry to displease you. But . . ."

It was never easy, with Elizabeth, to talk about love between men and women. Her father had had her mother beheaded, and later, he had done the same thing to her young stepmother Katherine Howard. The first man to court her, Admiral Seymour, had died for his presumption. To Elizabeth, love and violent death were two faces of one coin.

This time, however, she spoke of it herself. "You would say you love him?" she asked. "And yet I hear that shortly before you came to England, you were quarreling with him."

"Who . . . ?"

"Your servants are discreet but I have eyes and ears in many places. At Blanchepierre, the whole village knows that just before you left for England, you were throwing things at your husband."

She was obviously amused. "We did have one dispute at table, ma'am," I said stiffly. "I threw a candlestick at him, yes. I was . . . not myself at the time."

"Did it hit him?" Elizabeth inquired with interest.

"No, ma'am. And, ma'am, it meant nothing, not . . . not fundamentally. Couples do—quarrel sometimes. It doesn't mean . . . well, it doesn't always mean . . ."

"I know," said Elizabeth, taking pity on me. "It is like being two people in one body. One burning hot, the other icy cold. Don't think I don't understand, because I do."

She understood, I think, far more than either of us had put into words. Years later, she did find words for it. *"I am and am not, freeze and yet I burn; since from myself my other self I turn."* When I heard that, I remembered that talk in the window bay at Richmond. I thought too of the strange relationship between her and Robin Dudley.

Time and again, she had refused him, and once, she had even offered his hand to Mary Stuart though no one ever believed she meant it and neither he nor Mary showed any enthusiasm for the notion. I have sometimes wondered why he didn't pursue the chance of being king of Scotland. If he still had hopes of melting Elizabeth's core of ice, I could have told him that he was wasting his time. And yet, for all that, I was certain that she loved him.

Elizabeth, meanwhile, was signaling that our little audience was over. "Let it be," she said. "We will not pursue the matter, nor mention it again. Come to us if you change your mind. And come with us to Cambridge, if you will."

"Certainly I will, ma'am," I said.

I was dismissed. Carrying the precious scroll which contained the deeds of Withysham, I rejoined Dale and Brockley, who were waiting for me, and we set off upstream to Thamesbank in a hired ferry.

Now that I had the deeds in my hands, I could reveal my plans for the stewardship of Withysham, and as we sat in the ferry, I did so. Dale and Brockley were not sure how to respond.

"I've got to admit," Dale said, "that I didn't like France. But I can hardly abide the thought of not being with you all the time, ma'am."

"I'll be sorry too, Dale, but I think attending on me has worn you out. You'll be happier, staying in England."

"It's a grand opportunity and we have to thank you, madam," Brockley said. "Though I hope you'll get along all right, without me to look after you."

"My husband will look after me," I told him. The ferry splashed on, carried on the last of the Thames tide before its influence faded away inland. "Brockley," I said, "I don't think I ever congratulated you on that wonderful lament you played on the lute at Vetch Castle—that third melody, I mean. I meant to, but what with all the drama over Lady Thomasine, and Dale being so ill, somehow I never have. I'm sorry. Let me do so now. You probably don't realize it, but it was that lament that broke Lady Thomasine and got her to confess. Where did you learn it? You played it beautifully. It wasn't familiar to me but it sounded like a very ancient tune."

Brockley regarded me with surprise. "What is it?" I asked.

"Madam, I played only two melodies, and neither was a lament. I played Rafe's song, which was a straightforward tune that I could pick out quite easily—I did a little quiet practice beforehand in our quarters—and then I played an old folk song I learned as a boy. I was somewhat fumble-fingered with both, but perhaps not too badly. After that, I stopped. It would have been unsafe to go on. People were coming out into the courtyard with lanterns, playing hunt the minstrel."

"But, Brockley, I heard you. We all did! You played a third tune, a very sad and plaintive one, and as I said, that was what finally broke Lady Thomasine."

"No, madam," Brockley said in definite tones. "I finished the folk song and then I slipped away before the lanterns came any nearer, for fear I should be caught. I kept in the shadows and got back to the porch of the Aragon Wing. I meant to wait there but when I realized how thoroughly the courtyard was being searched, I didn't feel too safe even inside the porch, so I took the liberty of coming right into Aragon."

"But we heard it! We all heard it!" I was bewildered. "After you had finished playing the first two tunes, there was a pause and then you began again and played that lament! It was such a very sad, yearning air. Lady Thomasine . . ."

"No, madam," said Brockley, very firmly.

It is usually cold on the river, even in summer. I had a cloak to keep off the breeze. But the cold which fingered my bones then came from another source.

Dale felt it too. Her face had whitened. "It's all right, Dale," I said quickly. "We're here on the Thames. Vetch Castle is miles away and so are any ghosts that happen to be haunting it."

"I did see footprints in Isabel's Tower, ma'am," Dale said in a low voice. "They were faint but they were there; footprints in the dust. You said I was imagining them, but I wasn't, truly. Some bigger than others; like a man's and a woman's. I saw them."

"I heard no other lute, after I stopped playing mine," Brockley said. He put a hand over Dale's. "Perhaps we would do well not to talk about this any more. It's all over now. Madam, can you tell us whether . . . ?"

He asked a question about Withysham. I let him change the subject. So did Dale.

Do I really believe in ghosts, or not? I am not sure. I found that I didn't want to think about it. What I wanted then was normality, an ordinary life, a life of reason. I wanted to get my hands on a Latin grammar. Latin is such a clear-cut, logical language. And I wanted to take Meg home to Blanchepierre, and to be with Matthew.